THE KILLER

AT THE LAKE

A ROBERT VANCE THRILLER

RICK VAN ETTEN

PROUD POINT
-PRESS-

DES MOINES, IOWA

The Killer at the Lake
Copyright © 2023 by Rick R. Van Etten

ISBN: 978-1-7348269-1-3

Published by
Proud Point Press
Des Moines, Iowa

Cover design by Eric Labacz
www.labaczdesign.com

DEDICATION

For Linda, Karen, Tracy (in absentia), Susan, Katie, Tom, Bob and Barb, Drew, Terry and all the other Maffitt Reservoir regulars.

And in memory of Mike Stephenson, 1952-2022
We miss you, guy.

VANCE'S RULES FOR CONTRACT KILLINGS

1. No personal involvement…i.e., there must be no personal feelings whatsoever attached. This would cloud judgment.
2. No collateral damage. Absolutely unacceptable; must remain true to purpose—righting a wrong, stopping a bully, etc. Eliminating bystanders/witnesses not permitted. Ditto letting an innocent person take the fall.
3. Never keep a handgun after it's been used.
4. No politicians (regardless of how much they might deserve it); too well protected; too much public scrutiny and investigation.
5. No organized crime members. Flat-out too dangerous, and too much risk of touching off a gangland war that might result in innocents being killed.

PROLOGUE

EVENING AT THE LAKE, and the predator was watching. Watching and waiting.

The predator was sitting in his parked vehicle at a gravel turnout on a high grassy point above a cove on the west side of the lake. He was facing toward the dam at the north end of the water, and from his position he could look across the cove and see a small portion of the road that began at the west entrance and wound around to the turnout where he was parked.

He was watching for a specific vehicle, a dark blue Ford Explorer driven by a woman named Hannah Wilkinson.

It was a few minutes past seven on a Wednesday evening in late July, warm and humid. The predator had the front windows of his vehicle rolled down and he sat with his left elbow cocked on the open window frame. He kept his gaze focused on that small section of road across the cove, imagining himself a keen-eyed raptor riding the thermals and watching for signs of prey below.

No, he decided after a moment, not riding the thermals. Because he was stationary, he revised his thinking and imagined himself perched atop a high vantage point, ready to launch into action. A red-tailed hawk at the top of a tall dead tree, maybe. Or a golden eagle on a rocky crag. Ready to launch with deadly talons extended.

The predator liked to think of himself as being able to change form at will in the manner of Native American shape-shifters. Sometimes he imagined himself a coyote trotting silently along a deer trail through the woods, or a bobcat crouching motionless in ambush on a fallen log in a dense thicket. Maybe, if he was in a more whimsical mood, a raccoon prowling the lakeshore, looking for something edible at the water's edge. The predator chose these images carefully, based on where he was and what he was doing. But he was always a predator, never prey.

He knew the lake and its surrounding woods intimately. He also knew most of the people who came to the lake regularly: the kayakers and canoers, the fishermen, the hikers and bicyclists, the dog walkers. He knew most of their names, or first names, anyway, and most of them knew his. He was fine with that, because—he smiled at the thought—none of them really knew him. They saw only his public face. The non-predatory one.

That was the face Hannah Wilkinson saw, and that was the person she thought she knew.

Won't she be surprised to learn differently, he thought. He smiled at the realization that soon, very soon, her belief, certainty even, that he was a nice guy, a friendly acquaintance and nothing more, would come to an abrupt end.

End being the operative word.

HANNAH WILKINSON WAS RUNNING LATE. Earlier in the day she'd agreed via text to meet a friend at the lake for an evening walk. They were supposed to meet at seven o'clock at one of the gravel turnouts on the west side of the lake, where they would leave their vehicles. Then, Hannah guessed they would probably follow the roadway around to the metal gate at the head of the main hiking trail.

Hannah wasn't sure whether they would slip past the gate and continue on the main trail or turn and walk back to their vehicles. It was a warm night and she wanted to be sure her golden retriever, Maisie, didn't become overheated. Maisie always accompanied Hannah on her walks at the lake and ensuring Maisie's safety and well-being was a top priority of Hannah's.

Like most golden retrievers, Maisie was friendly and greeted everyone with a wagging tail and—Hannah was sure of this—a smiling face. Maisie and Hannah were both well-liked by the other lake "regulars," including the friend she was supposed to meet at seven. *We're two of a kind, Maisie and me*, Hannah sometimes thought. *We like people, and they like us.*

Her home life, unfortunately, was not quite so idyllic. Hannah was an attractive forty-four-year-old blonde, and she was trying to come to grips with the end of her twenty-one-year marriage. Her husband Craig was an attorney in one of the city's better known law firms and they had been separated since the first of the year. Craig had moved into an apartment downtown near the firm's office, leaving Hannah alone, except for Maisie, in the huge executive home they owned in the River Oaks development west of the lake. Their nineteen-year-old daughter Jessica was a junior at the University of Northern Iowa in Cedar Falls, where she was attending summer classes this year.

Craig had recently broached the subject of divorce, which hadn't totally surprised Hannah but left her reeling emotionally, nonetheless. The finality of her marriage ending was something she was struggling to accept, and she had begun confiding in several of her friends, including the one she was meeting this evening.

She suspected, but had no real proof, that there was another woman involved, that Craig's growing detachment from their marriage was due to his having begun a relationship with someone else, and that his subsequent mention of divorce was triggered by his desire to pursue this new relationship. *Trading me in for a newer model*, Hannah sometimes thought, although she had never seen the other woman, if in fact she existed. Hannah couldn't bring herself to hire a private investigator to confirm her suspicions.

Now, hurrying out of the house to her Ford Explorer—she'd been delayed by a surprise after-dinner phone call from Jessica, for whom she would *always* make time—she opened the rear hatch and told Maisie to jump in. Maisie obliged, Hannah closed the hatch, went around the side of the vehicle and climbed into the driver's seat. She started the Explorer, backed down the long driveway, and they were on their way.

It was just a few minutes past seven and the lake was no more than five minutes away. Hannah was confident that the friend she was meeting would forgive her tardiness. He was, after all, understanding about such things and not the sort to give her a hard time.

A nice guy, Hannah thought. *A very nice guy.*

THE PREDATOR DIDN'T WEAR a wristwatch but after turning off the engine of his vehicle when he'd parked, he'd returned the ignition switch to the on position so the radio would continue to play. He glanced at the lighted display on the radio and saw that the time was 7:10 p.m. The predator was listening to a classic rock station and the Eagles were singing "One of These Nights."

Patience, he told himself. *You must have the patience of the wild.* He knew that phrase, "the patience of the wild," was from his favorite Jack London novel, *The Call of the Wild.* He loved the book and had reread it many times. It was the story of a magnificent dog named Buck, stolen from his home in California and transported to the Yukon during the Alaskan gold rush to work as a sled dog before ultimately reverting to the wild and becoming the leader of a wolf pack. The predator envied Buck's transformation.

The predator suddenly sat up a little straighter. Hannah Wilkinson's dark blue Ford Explorer had just crossed the section of road he could see across the cove. She was heading his way and in another minute or so she would join him at the turnout.

The predator smiled. The patience of the wild had been rewarded.

HANNAH WILKINSON PULLED HER EXPLORER onto the gravel turnout and parked alongside her friend's vehicle. She turned off the ignition and stepped out onto the gravel and moved around to the rear of the Explorer. She opened the hatch and Maisie jumped out.

While she was doing this, Hannah's friend powered up the windows of his vehicle and turned off the ignition. He climbed out and joined her. He was greeted by Maisie, who immediately jumped up to be petted. "Maisie, down!" Hannah commanded. "No jumping!"

Maisie ignored the command and Hannah's friend

laughed. "She's okay," he said, rumpling the golden's ears. After a moment Maisie dropped back down to all four legs and Hannah smiled apologetically.

"She knows she's not supposed to do that," Hannah said. "She's just…irrepressible. And happy to see you."

"Not a problem," her friend said. "I'm happy to see her too…well, both of you. Shall we walk back to the gate?"

"Sure. And by the way, I'm sorry we're late. Jessica called just as we were leaving."

"No worries. Is everything okay with Jessica?"

"Yes, she just wanted to tell me she was planning to come home this weekend." Hannah laughed. "She said she needed a break from her two roommates."

They followed the roadway around a curve and passed the canoe launch. Two vehicles, an SUV and a Toyota pickup, were parked at the side of the sloping launch, and although Hannah didn't see it, her friend frowned. He realized what he'd done and quickly said, "I'm sure you'll have a good time with her."

"Oh yeah, a mom-daughter weekend is always fun," Hannah said, then added a bit ruefully, "It'll be nice to have some company in the house."

"Anything new on the Craig front?" Hannah had been confiding in him for some time now so he felt safe asking this.

"Not really. We've talked a couple times on the phone, mostly just stuff about the house and that kind of thing. I told him I needed to call a repairman because the dishwasher was making a funny noise and leaking some water, and he said I should go ahead and do it and he'd take care of the bill."

Her friend laughed. "That's nice of him."

"Yeah, really." There was no missing her sarcasm.

They walked on in silence for a couple minutes with Maisie trotting ahead of them, her plumed tail high. She carried a stick she had picked up alongside the roadway. When they reached the double metal gate at the head of the hiking trail—chained and padlocked to prevent vehicles from entering and driving on the trail—Hannah's friend asked, "Shall we go back on the trail a little ways?"

Hannah hesitated, then said, "Sure, why not."

THE PREDATOR SLIPPED PAST THE CORNER POST of the gate and Hannah followed. Maisie was already twenty yards ahead on the trail, and she paused to look back and make sure they were coming. She was still carrying her stick.

"It's pretty warm tonight, how far are we going to go?" Hannah asked.

"Oh, maybe as far as the pine grove and the big rock," the predator replied. He knew Hannah would recognize the place he was referring to, as they had walked back to the same spot several times previously. It was about a half mile from the gate.

"OK, but I have to be careful with Maisie. I don't want her to get overheated."

"When we get to the rock she can go for a swim," the predator said, smiling. "It's a nice night for it."

"You're right, it is."

They continued on the trail, first walking east toward the lake, then after a sharp bend, back toward the west. At the second bend they headed south and in another couple minutes reached the side trail that led down through a grove of towering pines.

Maisie led the way down the side trail, thickly carpeted with rust-colored pine needles that made for silent walking. A slight breeze stirred the pines and Maisie quickened her pace, eager to reach the water.

Hannah and her friend got to the big rock on the shoreline and saw Maisie already swimming about twenty yards out. She'd dropped her stick and was gulping at the water as she swam, relieving Hannah's worries about her becoming overheated.

The big rock, a pinkish-tan granite boulder about the size of an overstuffed easy chair, made a natural and inviting place to stop and sit. Hannah stepped down off the low bank onto the sandy shoreline and sat down on the boulder. The predator followed, thinking, *this is almost going to be too easy.*

He scanned the cove in front of them, looking out across

the water for any signs of other people. Remembering the two vehicles parked at the canoe launch, he was relieved to see neither a canoe nor kayak in the cove. Apparently he and Hannah had this part of the lake to themselves. All good.

"Maisie is making the water look awfully inviting," he said, smiling again.

"Yes, she is," Hannah agreed. "Too bad we aren't wearing swimsuits!"

"Actually, we could probably get away with taking a quick dip," he said. Swimming was prohibited at the lake but it was a restriction that was frequently violated. "As warm as it is, we'd be dry by the time we walked back to our vehicles." He hoped he sounded confident without being pushy. "Are you game?"

Hannah was surprised at the suggestion. She wasn't a risk-taker by nature and she hadn't intended her swimsuit comment to be taken seriously. But her friend was right; it was a warm night and she knew that people did occasionally swim in the lake. There was no one in sight and with dusk coming on, there was little chance of them being seen and reported.

"Sure," she said impulsively, surprising herself. She was wearing tan shorts and a pale yellow t-shirt; she wondered how transparent the shirt would be when it was wet but figured she wouldn't reveal too much, as she was wearing a bra. And, she thought recklessly, so what if her friend got a peek at her boobs? Maybe it was time for her husband to receive a little payback.

Hannah bent over to untie the laces of her athletic shoes, light gray Nikes with bright green trim and laces. She stood up and toed them off and saw her friend doing the same. He glanced over at her and smiled. "Sexy toes!" he said, noting her bright red toenails.

She laughed. "Oh, thanks!" she said, thinking, *I'm glad somebody appreciates them.* Hannah pulled her cell phone and her keys from the pockets of her shorts and placed them on the boulder. She'd left her wallet in the console of the locked Explorer.

The sandy shoreline felt warm beneath her bare feet. She

smiled impishly. "Ready?" she asked as her friend added his wallet, phone and keys to hers atop the boulder. Like her, he was wearing shorts and a t-shirt. She turned and waded out a few steps then made a shallow dive into the clear water.

The predator followed her into the water with a dive of his own. He surfaced and saw Hannah standing a few feet away; the water was only waist-deep this close to shore, with no steep drop off. She was using both hands to comb her wet hair back from her face and she was laughing.

"Wow!" she said. "This is great. I can't believe we're doing this!"

"It does feel great," he replied. "Maisie definitely had the right idea." As he said this, he saw the dog swim toward them. He also couldn't help notice Hannah's breasts beneath her wet t-shirt. He laughed and said, "I'm gonna make a scientific wild-ass guess that you're wearing a pink bra."

Hannah laughed and said, "Actually it's peach, but you're close!" She leaned backward into the water and began back-floating away from him. As her feet came up in a flutter kick he reached out and grabbed her left ankle. He ran his fingertips down her sole, tickling her, and she laughed again.

"Hey!" she said. "Stop that!"

But he didn't stop, and he didn't relinquish his grip. As her right foot came up he grabbed that ankle also and lifted both of her feet out of the water.

"Hey!" Hannah said again, this time with a trace of alarm. She flailed at the water with both arms, trying to keep her head above the water. "Let go!"

Holding both of her ankles, the predator pushed Hannah farther out into deeper water. He lifted her feet higher, which had the effect of driving her head and torso downward. She flailed harder with her arms but couldn't get any leverage to keep her head above the water. She managed to get out one more strangled "Let go!" before her head went under again.

The predator lifted both of Hannah's feet to his shoulders. Keeping a firm grip on both ankles, he continued walking into deeper water, pushing her before him. She continued to flail with her arms but now the angle was too extreme and she couldn't raise her head above the surface. She tried to thrash her legs as well—walking Maisie regularly had kept her in good shape—but his grip on her ankles was too tight for her to break.

In a little less than a minute, Hannah ceased struggling.

The predator stood in chest-deep water, still gripping Hannah's ankles with her heels at his shoulders. The water was clear and he could see her blonde hair waving gently around her face. Her eyes seemed to be staring up at him but he knew she wasn't seeing him.

"If only you'd thought of me as something besides a friend," he murmured. It was a thought he'd had previously on more than one occasion, and with other women besides Hannah. "If only you had." He loosened his hold on her ankles and eased her legs down to the water. Released from his grip and the angle at which he'd held her, Hannah's body slowly sank and settled on the bottom, several feet below the surface.

The predator stood looking down at her for a moment longer, then turned and waded back to the shoreline. As he did so he noted that Maisie had already left the water and was standing expectantly on the bank above the big boulder, her thick coat dripping.

The predator paused next to the boulder. He considered throwing Hannah's cell phone and keys far out into the lake but decided against it. He didn't know if her death would be ruled a suicide but he hoped it might be. He reasoned that she would have had no reason to dispose of her phone and keys if she had decided to take her own life but might have deliberately left them there to help in identifying her body.

He sat on the boulder to put on his shoes. Then he scooped up his keys, wallet and phone and climbed up onto the bank. He regarded Maisie for a moment, wondering if she would attempt to follow him back to his vehicle. He hoped she wouldn't.

"You stay here," he said, stretching his hand toward her with the fingers upraised and the palm outward, the universal signal for the "Stay!" command. Maisie stood uncertainly but made no move to follow him as he walked back up through the pine grove to the main trail.

Once on the trail, the predator picked up his pace. Full dusk was coming on and he knew that the entrance gates to the park would be closed and locked at a little after nine o'clock. He also knew that a security officer would drive through the park to verify all vehicles had left before the gates were locked.

The predator wanted to be long gone before the security officer made his rounds. Hannah's vehicle would still be where she'd parked it, of course, but he hoped this wouldn't concern the security officer unduly. He doubted that the officer would call in an alarm but would probably assume the vehicle had been left there by someone who was either sleeping somewhere in the park (not legal but it occasionally happened) or had gone home with a friend and planned to return for the vehicle the following morning.

Rather than returning by the same route he and Hannah had taken to the pine grove, the predator veered off the main trail onto a little known shortcut through the woods. It was a deer trail he'd discovered several years earlier, and now he imagined himself a wolf slipping silently through the twilight. The deer trail cut several minutes off his return trip to the gravel turnout where they had parked.

Reaching his vehicle, the predator quickly unlocked it and climbed in, cranked the ignition and shifted into reverse. He backed away from the gravel turnout onto the roadway and shifted into drive. He followed the roadway around to the entrance gate, stopped briefly, then pulled out onto the highway and headed for home. A three-quarter moon was rising in the eastern sky, its reflection shining across the water of the lake. On the radio the Rolling Stones were singing "Satisfaction."

MAISIE WATCHED THE MAN WALK up through the pine trees to the trail. She'd been told to stay and she knew Hannah was still nearby, but Maisie sensed something was amiss. She turned back toward the lake, but Hannah was no longer visible.

Maisie whined and looked back toward the trail once more. The man was gone. She was here alone and Hannah had somehow disappeared. Maisie barked once, sharply, but Hannah did not reappear. Maisie whined again, then stepped down off the bank onto the shore. She hesitated a moment, then began wading out toward where she had last seen Hannah.

She was soon beyond her depth and had to swim. When she reached the spot above Hannah's body she could smell Hannah's scent faintly but she could not see her. Like many retrievers she would occasionally submerge her head to pick up an object that was underwater, and she did so now. But Hannah's body was several feet below the surface and the water, clouded by the sediment stirred by Maisie's swimming, prevented the dog from seeing her.

Maisie swam past the spot several more times, then she turned and swam back to the shore and stood next to the boulder. She shook herself then lowered her head to sniff at Hannah's Nikes. She looked out at the water again and whined, still hoping to see Hannah. She sniffed at Hannah's keys and cell phone atop the boulder, whining once more. Hannah still did not appear.

With a little whimper Maisie curled up beside Hannah's shoes to wait for her return.

PART ONE: SECRET LIVES

Everyone has three lives—a public one, a private one and a secret one.

Gabriel Garcia Marquez

CHAPTER 1

MY LAST ASSIGNMENT HAD gone badly, and I was starting to think it might be time to retire from my second job.

For quite a few years now, nearly thirty, in fact, I've had a second job as a contract killer…a hit man, in the parlance. But calling it a second job is actually a little misleading. I don't kill people because I need the income, nor because I especially enjoy killing.

I do it to make things right.

There are quite a few people in this world who have made the lives of others miserable, even unbearable. They relish inflicting pain and many times their victims are without recourse, at least within the framework of our criminal justice system. All too frequently that system fails to administer justice and the offenders remain unchecked and unpunished, the ultimate cruel irony.

Of course, some of those offenders don't limit themselves to damaging lives. For them, nothing short of total destruction, i.e., killing their victims, will suffice.

When this happens, I'm sometimes sought by those who feel they have no other place to turn. Whether it's the brutalized victim, or someone seeking retribution for a murdered loved one, they contact me to balance the scales. And over the years, I've become very good at this.

But don't get the wrong idea. I'm not some kind of crusading white knight. Not even close. I'm a pretty average guy actually, size and appearance-wise. I'm not ex-military or ex-CIA, not some invincible combat veteran or former spook who's well-schooled in the martial arts and who still has access to a lot of high-tech weaponry and friends in powerful and/or clandestine places.

No, I don't have that kind of background or support. What I do have going for me is an abiding hatred of bullies and injustice. That's what drives me to occasionally step in and eliminate those individuals who, as the old expression goes, just need killing.

That is, until recently. More specifically, until my last assignment left me beginning to doubt, or at least question, my abilities.

Something else was contributing to those uncertainties.

I began qualifying for senior citizen discounts a couple years ago and lately I've noticed more and more people—much younger people, especially—are calling me "sir." I guess that's preferable to being called a lot of other things ("old geezer" or "old fart" immediately come to mind) but I can't deny I sometimes cringe a bit when I hear it. Sure, I realize it's a term of respect and they mean well—giving them the benefit of the doubt here—but still…

It's not just the killing that I'm thinking of quitting. I'm beginning to think seriously about retiring from my day job as well. I'm the editor of an outdoor sporting magazine, a "hook and bullet rag," and I've held that job for twenty years. After editing thousands of articles and stories and writing dozens of features and editorial columns myself, I'll admit I'm starting to feel a little jaded.

Aw, hell. I'll just come right out and say it. I'm starting to feel old.

Much as I hate to use the O-word to describe myself, there's no denying that I'm no longer as quick or strong or limber as I used to be. I'm an upland bird hunter by avocation, which fits hand-in-glove with my job as the editor of *American Wingshot* magazine. I occasionally tell folks that hunting is part of my job description, and they usually think I'm joking. I'm not.

But my days of being able to follow a bird dog or two through the uplands for six or eight hours are pretty much over.

Luckily, Preacher, my seven-year-old German wirehaired pointer (she's named for Clint Eastwood's character in the movie *Pale Rider*; she has a beard similar to Clint's in that film) has begun to slow down a bit as well. She's middle-aged herself so her pace and mine are pretty well matched.

A good two- or two-and-a-half-hour hunt is fine with both of us, then we're ready to call it a day. We return home and while I clean the birds we've taken (assuming we weren't skunked) and wipe down my shotgun, Preacher snoozes the afternoon away, usually on the living room sofa. Meanwhile, I pop some ibuprofen to head off the inevitable aches and pains.

Now, speaking of aches and pains, something about that last assignment that left me troubled. I live in Iowa, and the assignment had taken place about eight months earlier in neighboring Illinois during the state's firearm deer season. The assignment came off without a hitch, or so I initially thought. But things went to hell in a hurry when a well-meaning citizen discovered the body of my target and wound up being charged with the death.

I have five self-imposed inviolate rules for my contract killing, the second of which states that no collateral damage is allowed. Eliminating bystanders or witnesses is not permitted, nor is letting an innocent person take the fall. So I couldn't avoid getting involved and risk seeing someone else convicted and imprisoned for something I'd done.

It took some real scrambling on my part, and no small amount of luck, but I'd managed to make things right. Still, it was a rather messy ending to what had initially seemed like a fairly straight-forward assignment, and that messy ending was due to a serious (and presumptuous) miscalculation on my part. Some eight months later I was still troubled by that miscalculation.

So troubled, in fact, that I hadn't taken any more assignments. I'd had a few nibbles, people responding by email to my innocuous online ad that hints at what I do. But for various reasons—their waffling and my own general lack of interest—nothing had come of any of those initial queries.

And that was just as well, I thought. When I do take an assignment, I'm meticulous in my planning. I try to make sure all the i's are dotted and the t's are crossed, so very little is left to chance. At the same time, I try to avoid making things overly complicated…I'm a firm believer in the rule of KISS.

But above all, I don't allow myself to become careless or sloppy. While I'm always convinced that my targets deserve the fate I deliver—I never take an assignment *unless* I'm convinced—I realize that various law enforcement agencies would—ahem—take a different view of my actions. In simplest terms, I don't want to spend my remaining years in a prison cell because I failed to do a good enough job of covering my tracks.

Which brings up yet another concern. I'm not quite a Luddite (although some friends and colleagues might disagree) but I'd be the first to admit I'm not especially tech-savvy, either. Not only has my editorial job become a lot more complicated over the years, requiring me to learn quite a few editing and design software programs to stay current, but so too have the methods employed by law enforcement.

When I first began taking assignments, DNA analysis was in its infancy. Now it's the method by which many, perhaps most, violent crimes are solved. Or to put it another way, it's damned hard to commit a crime these days without leaving some telltale trace of yourself behind. If you do leave such a trace, and if your DNA is on file somewhere— something everyone might want to think hard about before paying money to one of those genealogy-tracing outfits— you're going to be caught. It's just that simple.

Even further complicating matters is the fact that the technology has now advanced to the point that a *relative's* DNA can be used to catch you. That's right—if you leave your DNA behind, and a relative—a parent, a sibling, a cousin, whatever—has submitted theirs to one of those outfits, there's a very good chance law enforcement will be able to link theirs to yours and ultimately apprehend you. Damned if you do; damned if you don't.

Then there's the matter of cameras.

Nowadays they're everywhere. Surveillance cameras record nearly every move—*every move*—made by an unsuspecting public. Combine these recordings with sophisticated face-recognition software, and once again it's almost a slam-dunk for law enforcement.

And of course, there's also the matter of cell phones. Everyone has one, and everyone uses them almost constantly to snap photos and shoot video—smile, you're on *Candid Camera*. (Sorry about the hoary reference.) Again, unless you commit your crime in the absolute dead of night and in an extremely remote location, there's a very good chance you're going to be seen and, quite possibly, recorded.

All of which is to say, my second job has gotten a lot tougher. That, combined with the fact that I had seriously miscalculated on my last assignment, was leaving me thinking it might well be time to withdraw from the field.

There's a great line in one of Ian Fleming's James Bond novels. Bond is reflecting on the killing he occasionally has to do in the course of his job, and that there is no room for feeling any regret about those killings. Regret, he notes, is the deathwatch beetle in one's soul.

I could substitute doubt for regret in that equation. I was feeling like I might be starting to hear that deathwatch beetle.

CHAPTER 2

A SINGLE SHARP BARK stirred me from my gloomy reflections.

It was Preacher, barking on the back yard deck. I recognized the sound as a summons, a "C'mon, let's get going!" call to action. When you live with a dog 24/7—that is, when your dog shares your home with you and isn't relegated to a kennel in the back yard—you learn to recognize her various barks just as readily as she recognizes your commands. And ideally, both of you respond accordingly.

I was sitting at my kitchen table nursing my second cup of coffee. I'd been trying to read James Lee Burke's new Dave Robicheaux novel but wasn't having much luck. This was no fault of Burke's; he's a superb stylist and when he writes about his beloved Louisiana you can feel the humidity in the air, smell the smoke from the barbecue pits and almost taste the ham and onion sandwiches that Dave favors. But this morning my mind kept wandering.

I was, as the saying goes, sunk in a funk.

I glanced at the clock on the wall and saw that it was 7:10 a.m. The day was already warm and humid and would get much warmer. The television was on in the living room and a few minutes earlier I'd heard the Channel 13 meteorologist say that the temp was already nudging 80 degrees and would top out in the mid-90s. She'd commented that we were experiencing what Iowans call "state fair weather" although the state fair was still three weeks away.

It was going to be a scorcher, so I needed to get Preacher out to the lake for our morning ramble before the heat became unbearable. We'd stay close to the water and I'd toss a retrieving dummy for her to shag a few times. As a versatile sporting dog, she is an enthusiastic swimmer and retriever, although (it pains me to admit this) probably not quite as proficient in the water as a Labrador or Chesapeake.

I sighed and stood up. I headed back to the bedroom and donned a pair of khaki cargo shorts and a favorite old t-shirt emblazoned with the slogan, "Get off my lawn!" The t-shirt was a gag gift from a very good friend, a woman named Rachel James. Pulling it on over my head, I couldn't help thinking that the words matched my current mood pretty well.

Maybe, I thought, as I shuffled my bare feet into a pair of worn canvas boat shoes, a trip to the lake would give my spirits the boost they so sorely needed. Or at the very least, something would happen to shake me out of my funk.

I'd have done well to remember the old adage that warns us to be careful what we wish for.

THE LAKE IS OFFICIALLY known as Dale L. Maffitt Reservoir, and it's the backup water source for the city of Des Moines. The reservoir is about ten miles southwest of the city and is managed by the Des Moines Water Works. It was constructed in the 1940s and was named for the fellow who was general manager of the Water Works at that time.

The lake itself is approximately 200 acres and includes numerous coves and inlets. The surrounding property is about 1,500 acres comprised of woods and open fields seeded to native prairie grasses and wildflowers. The bulk of the property is located in Polk County but it extends into neighboring Warren, Madison and Dallas counties as well. The property is laced with hiking trails, including a winding main trail that runs completely around the southern end of the lake for some three and a half miles.

A half-mile long dam at the north end of the lake separates the two entrances to the property. The entrance on the east side of the dam leads to a wooded park and picnic area filled with magnificent centuries-old oak trees, a tiny cemetery and a couple of small fishing docks. The entrance on the west side leads to a few smaller picnic spots and a canoe and kayak launch. Motorized boat traffic is prohibited.

It is popular with hikers, fishermen, bird watchers, photographers and dog walkers like myself. I'd been taking my dogs to the lake for the twenty-plus years I'd lived in Des

Moines, and both Preacher and I were well known to most of the other folks whose days, like ours, began with an early morning ramble at Maffitt. While I knew the last names of very few of these people, nor did most of them know mine, we all recognized each other and our dogs and always exchanged greetings.

Starting the day at Maffitt not only provided Preacher and me with an opportunity to stretch our legs; our outings also served as an excellent head-clearing exercise for me, helping to banish the mental cobwebs that had accumulated overnight.

I hoped that would once again be the case this morning.

RETURNING TO THE KITCHEN after dressing, I retrieved my coffee mug from the table and refilled it at the coffee maker on the side counter. I turned off the coffee maker, grabbed the milk from the fridge and added a dash to the coffee, then scooped up my keys from the corner shelf at the end of the cupboard above the counter. I pulled a khaki bill cap off a hook by the back door, put it on and stepped outside. I pulled the door shut and gave the knob a couple of quick tugs to confirm it was latched and locked.

Preacher was waiting on the deck; she quickly turned, trotted down the three steps to the driveway apron and crossed it to the garage. I followed with my full coffee mug in one hand and my keys in the other.

I unlocked the small side door to the garage and stepped inside with Preacher following. I opened the driver's door of my SUV, a pewter-gray Chevy Equinox, and leaned inside to place my coffee mug in the cup holder on the console. Then I opened the back seat door on the same side and pulled out the folding ramp that I now use to help Preacher get into the vehicle.

This was something we'd begun doing toward the end of the previous hunting season when I'd noticed Preacher favoring her left hind leg after we'd hunted for more than an hour or so. I'd taken her to the vet for an examination and X-rays confirmed she had some arthritis in the hock joint of that leg. The vet, Dr. Bryan, had also warned me of the danger of

Preacher blowing out an anterior cruciate ligament.

This was a risk with which I was already familiar. ACL ruptures are, unfortunately, fairly common among sporting dogs, especially the larger, heavier breeds, and we'd run several articles on the injury in my magazine. A dog that suffers an ACL rupture will require surgery and a lengthy rehab period, both of which are extremely trying for the dog and the owner. Avoiding an ACL rupture is the best course, and with that in mind, Dr. Bryan had advised me to stop letting Preacher jump into and out of the SUV. So I'd ordered a lightweight ramp.

The ramp folded in the middle and I stowed it on the back seat of the Equinox in a long, flat, plastic box, the kind some folks use to store extra clothing under their bed. It only took Preacher two or three practice runs in the driveway to accustom her to going up and down the ramp to enter and exit the vehicle, and using it quickly became part of our daily routine.

Now, I unfolded the ramp and hit the button on my key fob to raise the rear hatch cover of the Equinox. I put the ramp in place and said, "Climb in." Preacher trotted up the ramp and settled herself on her thick dog pillow in the cargo space. I removed the ramp, touched the button again to lower the hatch cover, folded the ramp and replaced it in its box on the rear seat.

I hit the switch to open the main garage door, got into the Equinox and cranked the ignition. I shifted into reverse and as I was backing out of the garage, I recalled the scene in *Trouble with the Curve* in which Clint Eastwood scrapes the side of his vintage Mustang while backing out of his garage. He growls something about the garage being designed by goddamn midgets, and the recollection put a smile on my face.

Had I known what awaited us at the lake, I wouldn't have been smiling. In fact, I probably would have chosen to forego the outing altogether and spend the day at home.

CHAPTER 3

PREACHER WAS ABOUT TWENTY yards out in the water, swimming for the orange knobby retrieving dummy I'd just tossed, when another dog I recognized came running up. It was a female golden retriever named Maisie who belonged to a woman named Hannah Wilkinson.

I knew Hannah and Maisie from encounters at the lake; Preacher and I had walked with them quite a few times, either on the roadway through the park or on one of the hiking trails, and Hannah and I had shared conversations on a variety of subjects. She was an attractive blonde in her early forties and had recently confided that she was going through a divorce.

When Preacher and I arrived at the lake that morning I'd parked next to Hannah's dark blue Ford Explorer at one of the gravel turnouts on the west side, so I knew she and Maisie were somewhere nearby and I wondered if we might run into them. After parking, Preacher and I walked on down the roadway a short distance to the canoe launch, a graveled slope with a circular turnout where canoers and kayakers left their vehicles. The slope provided easy access to the water, making it an ideal spot to toss a dummy for Preacher's water retrieves.

Given the warm morning I was surprised there were no vehicles parked at the launch; I would have guessed at least a few people would be out on the water. But because it was Thursday, a workday, maybe most folks were otherwise occupied. I was also surprised to see Maisie approaching without Hannah, and as she came closer I could see that she was carrying something. She stopped before me and dropped the object at my feet.

It was a woman's athletic shoe, a gray Nike with green trim and laces. I remembered seeing Hannah wearing the same shoe, and its mate, when we'd walked together in the park a few days earlier. Why Maisie was now carrying one of

Hannah's shoes, and why she was unaccompanied by Hannah, was a mystery.

Preacher had returned from the water with the dummy and now stood next to me, waiting for me to take it and throw it again. Maisie wagged her tail and touched noses with Preacher in a canine greeting. Preacher growled and quickly turned her head to the side, protecting the dummy in case Maisie made a grab for it.

"Take it easy," I said by way of admonishment. "That's your friend you're growling at." Preacher and Maisie were ordinarily on good terms but I knew that Preacher, like most German wirehairs, was super-protective of anything she retrieved, dummy or gamebird, and wouldn't tolerate any attempts by another dog to take it from her.

I reached down and took the dummy from her to head off any problems, then I addressed Maisie. "Where's your partner?" I asked. "And what are you doing with one of her shoes?" Even as I spoke I realized my questions sounded similar to, and just about as silly as, that old cliché, "What's the matter, Lassie? Did Timmy fall down the well again?" It wasn't like Maisie was going to answer me.

But Maisie responded by picking up the shoe and starting back in the direction from which she'd come, along the roadway that led to the double metal gate at the head of the hiking trail. After running maybe twenty yards in that direction, she turned and looked back at Preacher and me.

Okay, so maybe she *was* answering me, after all.

"C'mon," I said to Preacher. We started down the roadway after Maisie. Seeing that we were following, she turned and continued toward the gate, still carrying Hannah's shoe.

I hurried to keep up with her, Preacher pacing alongside. After every ten or fifteen yards, Maisie stopped to look back at us, apparently to make sure we were still following. I wondered if this was some sort of game Maisie was playing; if perhaps Hannah had picked up a piece of gravel in her shoe and, when she'd taken it off to remove the gravel, Maisie had grabbed the shoe and run off with it.

That wasn't a likely scenario but given the playful nature of most golden retrievers, it wasn't entirely impossible, either. Then again, if Maisie had grabbed the shoe to initiate play, it was more likely she would have remained close to Hannah, teasing her with the shoe in a canine version of keep-away.

Regardless, I figured Hannah was probably somewhere along the roadway just ahead, either walking back in our direction or waiting for Maisie to return with her shoe. If so, I thought we'd probably hear Hannah calling for Maisie.

But we made it all the way to the double gate at the head of the hiking trail with still no sign of Hannah. That Maisie would have run this far without her, even in play, seemed more and more unlikely. Equally puzzling was Hannah's absence along the roadway.

I felt the first stirrings of unease.

Maisie reached the double gate and paused only momentarily before ducking under it and heading up the hiking trail. I slipped past the near corner of the gate and Preacher followed. About forty yards past the gate the main trail made a sharp left turn to the east but Maisie continued straight ahead, following a smaller trail up a hillside.

This trail, I knew, topped out at the crest of the hill, where hikers could turn to the west and walk through a huge grassy field that abutted a neighboring equestrian center. Riders from the center occasionally used the trails on the lake property, but given the heat, I doubted any would be out this morning.

We followed Maisie to the top of the hill, where a small break in the brushy fence line separating the two properties afforded me a look at several horses grazing in the center's paddocks. One of these was a handsome black and white paint that reminded me of the horse ridden by Michael Landon in the old *Bonanza* TV series.

I stood for a moment, admiring the horse and catching my breath after toiling up the hill. My t-shirt was stuck to my skin with perspiration, and I lifted my cap for a few seconds to cool my scalp. Then I turned my attention back to Maisie.

Rather than swinging west toward the big field, she was crossing the top of the hill toward a small trail that led down through the woods to reconnect with the main trail where it wound back around from the east. The small trail was a shortcut I'd used myself on many occasions, and I knew that it rejoined the main trail near a grove of tall pine trees, below which was a large granite boulder at the lake's edge.

Maisie started down this small trail, still carrying Hannah's shoe.

I hustled to keep her in sight. At the height of summer, the undergrowth was lush and the trail was overgrown. Mindful of the fact that I was wearing only a t-shirt, cargo shorts and boat shoes—not exactly proper attire for serious bushwhacking—I kept an eye out for poison ivy and used Preacher's retrieving dummy to fend off the overhanging branches as I followed Maisie down the small trail. Preacher ranged ahead of me, her wiry coat impervious to the undergrowth.

We soon emerged from the woods onto the main trail where Maisie stood waiting. As soon as she saw us she turned back to the east and the large pine grove.

My unease lessened. Now I figured we'd probably find Hannah at the big boulder below the pines, maybe sitting on the boulder dangling her feet in the water—that would explain Maisie's appropriation of her shoe. It wouldn't explain why Maisie had run so far to find us or lead us back here, however. But if Hannah were musing on the boulder, that would account for our not seeing her on the roadway or the trail.

We started down through the pines, walking silently on a thick carpet of fallen pine needles. The scent of the pine trees was strong in the warm, humid air. This was one of my favorite places on the lake property, and Preacher and I visited it often throughout the year; in fact, we had walked down to the big boulder quite a few times with Hannah and Maisie.

By the time Preacher and I reached the low bank above the shoreline and the boulder, Maisie had already waded out into the lake and was standing belly deep in the water. She'd dropped Hannah's shoe next to its mate beside the boulder and was staring at something floating just a few yards offshore.

Hannah Wilkinson's body.

CHAPTER 4

MY FIRST THOUGHT WAS an irrational one.

Maybe because I didn't want to believe that Hannah was dead and I was looking at her body, or maybe because my mind simply refused to accept the finality of what I was seeing, my first thought was that Hannah was simply floating on her back, enjoying the water on this warm July morning. That she had impulsively decided to take a dip to cool off. My reaction was the kind that causes people to cry "No!" when they're informed of the unexpected death of a loved one.

All of this in a fraction of a second.

Her body was perfectly still in the calm water. There was no movement of her arms or legs to maintain her floating position. She was maybe ten yards from shore and appeared to be staring up at the sky, her blond hair waving gently around her face.

I called Hannah's name, hoping for a response.

Then reality bit.

I dropped Preacher's retrieving dummy and stepped down off the bank onto the hard-packed sandy shoreline. Preacher jumped down beside me and started wading out toward Maisie. I glanced at the big granite boulder and saw Hannah's keys and cell phone sitting on top of it. For some reason the sight of her personal effects placed there so carefully struck me as ominous, and I felt a chill. But the sight also stirred me to action.

I pulled my own cell phone, keys and wallet from my pockets and dropped them next to Hannah's. Then I started wading toward her.

The water was a little over waist deep when I reached her. She was wearing a pair of khaki shorts and a yellow t-shirt made nearly transparent by the water. I reached out to touch her left leg, the one closest to me. Her skin felt cool.

I glanced back toward the shore and saw both dogs still standing in the water and watching intently. Then I moved alongside Hannah, and stooping slightly, slid my arms under her shoulders and knees. I tried to avoid looking down into her sightless eyes as I straightened up, intending to carry her to shore. Her head lolled against my shoulder and I drew a deep breath, suppressing a shudder.

With the water helping to support Hannah's body, the first few steps were easy. But when the water level dropped below my waist and her full weight rested in my arms, the going got tougher. Hannah wasn't overweight but like a lot of guys my age, I've suffered a few bouts of sciatica over the years, which has made me wary of doing too much heavy lifting. I knew I might pay a painful price later for carrying her ashore.

But I couldn't just leave her floating in the lake.

I realized that Hannah must have drowned at least several hours earlier, probably sometime during the night or maybe the previous evening. I'm no forensics expert but I knew—or thought I knew, anyway—that a drowned person initially sinks when the lungs fill with water. It's not until some time has passed that gases within the body cause it to rise to the surface and float.

Even as I thought this, I berated myself. Hannah was a friend and I felt she deserved more from me than such an analytical observation. Then again, maybe I was just trying to process the reality of the situation, employing the same sort of detachment used by cops when they investigate violent crimes.

By the time I reached the shoreline I was almost staggering. I caught my balance and continued for a few more steps to the low grassy bank that rose a foot above the sandy shore. As gently as possible, I eased Hannah's body down onto the bank.

Preacher and Maisie had moved aside as I came ashore but now they both crowded closer, sniffing Hannah's body. "Get back!" I told them, with little effect.

Maisie let out an anxious whine.

I blew out a sharp breath and shook my head, realizing I wasn't thinking too clearly about any of this. I was now soaked myself but the water was doing little to cool me off. I glanced at my watch, an old waterproof Expedition model, and saw that it was just past 8:30. When Preacher and I had left home an hour earlier it was already warm, and it was even warmer now. I pushed my cap back from my forehead.

Gazing down at Hannah, I shook my head again, feeling a sense of despair. I couldn't help murmuring, "Oh, Hannah, what did you do?" From our recent conversations I'd known she was upset about her pending divorce but I never would have thought her to be suicidal.

It was only then that it occurred to me that I might have just disturbed a crime scene.

A DEPUTY FROM THE Dallas County Sheriff's Police was the first to arrive.

After laying Hannah's body on the bank and taking a minute to catch my breath, I retrieved my cell phone, wallet and keys from the top of the boulder, but I left her phone and keys where they were. I punched in 911 on my phone and when the emergency operator answered I identified myself and told her what I had found. I described the location, gave directions on how to find us and said that I would wait there until the police arrived. I wasn't going to leave Hannah's body unattended.

Then I sat down on the bank a few feet from Hannah's body. I thought of covering her face but had nothing but my own wet t-shirt or cap to use, so I dismissed the idea. I turned and gazed out across the lake at the lush green woods on the opposite shore, a quarter mile away. Heat waves danced above the water.

Both dogs prowled along the shoreline. I hadn't carried a lead when Preacher and I had left our vehicle earlier so I had no way to tether either dog. I could have attempted to make them lie down and stay in place, but I doubted I could keep them in that position for any length of time. The "down" command was one I'd never enforced too stringently with

Preacher and I didn't know if Maisie had been trained to respond to it at all. For want of a better solution or any way to restrain them, I let them roam.

Nearly half an hour passed before the deputy walked down through the pines to where I was sitting on the bank. While I was waiting, I ran various scenarios through my mind—how could I not?—in an attempt to understand what had happened. I was having a hard time believing that Hannah had, in fact, purposely drowned herself. But no other explanation readily presented itself. Unless…

I wondered if, on the previous evening, she had impulsively decided to go for a swim to cool off. If so, perhaps she had swum too far and had been unable to get back to shore. Then, after drowning, her body had drifted in closer to where I had found it.

Much as I wanted to believe this—because it would mean Hannah's death was accidental, not deliberate—it didn't seem likely, partly because there was no wind and the water was glassy smooth and unmoving. But if she and Maisie had walked down to the boulder on the previous evening and Hannah had become overheated, that might explain why she'd entered the water after placing her keys and phone atop the boulder and leaving her shoes next to it.

I tried to recall if there'd been a breeze last evening. I didn't think so, but I wasn't certain. Also, for her body to have moved closer to this shore on the west side of the lake, any breeze would have had to come from the east, which was relatively rare in the Midwest.

Once again I wondered if I'd stumbled onto a crime scene.

I shifted my attention from the opposite shoreline to the sand right in front of me, just below the bank I was sitting on. The sand was sun baked and hard-packed and hadn't registered any footprints, either human or canine. At the height of summer the shore was nearly as dry and hard as a concrete sidewalk.

There was nothing in the sand to indicate Hannah had been accompanied by anyone other than Maisie when she'd come down to this place. Or at least, nothing that I could see.

Crime techs might find something, of course. I wondered if the police would send out a team to scour the shoreline or if they would simply chalk this up to a suicide by a woman made distraught by the ending of her marriage. With no obvious signs of a struggle or wrongdoing, I was inclined to believe the latter. Then again, a medical examiner would undoubtedly perform an autopsy on Hannah's body, and if the ME found signs of wrongdoing, that would pretty much eliminate the suicide-by-drowning scenario.

The dogs returned from their wandering and jumped up onto the bank beside me. Maisie sniffed at Hannah's body and then lay down beside her. Preacher came over to sit next to me. I sighed and returned my gaze to the woods on the opposite shore, wondering what was taking the police so long.

A minute or two later Preacher turned her head to look back up toward the main trail. She growled softly and I turned and saw a khaki-clad officer making his way down toward us through the pines.

CHAPTER 5

I STOOD UP AND LAID a restraining hand on Preacher's collar. Seeing the approaching officer, Maisie jumped up and bounded toward him, tail wagging. Despite the circumstances I couldn't help thinking, *once a golden retriever, always a golden retriever.* Goldens typically believe everyone loves them and will be happy to see them, and more often than not they're right.

The officer reached down to pet Maisie just as I called, "Maisie, get back here." To his credit, the officer didn't seem at all put off by having a large wet dog jumping at him, asking for attention. Maisie ignored my call but stopped jumping and followed the officer down to where I stood holding Preacher.

"Mr. Vance?" he asked, and I nodded.

"I'm Deputy Sheriff Robinson," he said. He was a young man, probably in his mid-thirties, with short-cropped sandy hair and fair skin. A few freckles across his cheeks and nose added to his boyish appearance. His khaki uniform was sharply pressed, and his short-sleeved shirt was open at the neck, with a white t-shirt showing underneath. His badge was pinned to his left breast pocket and a nametag was pinned above the right. The tag confirmed his name was Robinson.

He wasn't wearing a hat or cap and I wondered if that was due to the morning's heat, or if it simply wasn't a uniform requirement. His shoes were highly polished black oxfords but dusty from walking the trail to reach us. A gleaming black service belt and holstered semi-automatic completed his attire.

"I'm Robert Vance," I said. I gestured toward Hannah's body. "This is Hannah Wilkinson. I found her floating just offshore about a half hour ago. I waded out and carried her in and laid her there, then called 911." For some reason I felt foolish reciting this, like I was babbling or belaboring the obvious.

Or volunteering too much information.

Officer Robinson nodded. "Okay," he said. "A team and an ambulance are on the way. I was closest when your call came in; that's why I'm here." He hesitated, then said almost apologetically, "While we're waiting, I'd like to ask you a few questions."

I'd expected as much.

"Sure," I said.

Officer Robinson stepped closer to Hannah's body. He knelt next to her and studied her for a moment but made no effort to touch her. Then he stood up and removed the radio from his service belt. He keyed it and a voice said, "Go ahead, 618."

"I'm on the scene with Mr. Vance," Robinson said. "As reported, we have an apparent drowning victim, white female, middle-aged…" as he said this he gave me a questioning look and I nodded. "No obvious signs of trauma or violence."

"Okay, 618," the voice said from the radio. "Ambo and detectives are on the way; they should be there very shortly."

"Copy that," Robinson said. He returned the radio to its holster on his belt.

Now, I thought sarcastically, the fun begins.

Time for a disclaimer.

Generally speaking, I have nothing against cops.

That probably sounds a little strange coming from a guy who occasionally moonlights as a hit man—a hit man who naturally has no desire to be apprehended—but it's true. Unlike many folks, I don't harbor a deep-seated resentment toward cops, nor do I automatically define them as bullies with badges.

Most police officers are fine people who are doing—especially in today's political climate—a thankless job, often without adequate funding or resources, and with very little public cooperation or support. I don't believe they're always looking for an opportunity to harass citizens, bust heads or otherwise strut their authority. That stereotype—and it most definitely is a stereotype—is largely undeserved.

That said, I also can't deny that any encounter with a

police officer immediately puts me on my guard. I usually try to avoid such encounters altogether. For obvious reasons I'm a firm believer in staying below radar whenever possible, but if I do have to talk to an officer, I try to remember that simple old adage: less is more.

Many people, especially if they're nervous about talking to the police anyway, believe that the more they say, the more favorably a cop will regard them for trying to be helpful. But they're wrong about this. When talking to a police officer, you should provide basic, unadorned answers to the questions you're asked, and you should not succumb to the temptation to become chatty.

Or to put it another way, the more you say, the more likely you are to say something incriminating. Talking to cops is one of those times you should definitely practice the rule of KISS.

I realized I might already have violated this rule.

"You said her name was Hannah Wilkinson?" Robinson asked.

I nodded. "That's right." I'd released my hold on Preacher's collar and she and Maisie had begun poking around under the pine trees the way dogs will, checking for anything that smells interesting. I half expected Robinson to ask me to restrain them but he didn't do so. Maybe he'd already concluded that Hannah's death was a suicide and he wasn't concerned about the dogs spoiling any evidence of a possible crime. Or maybe, given his age, he was still a little green in his investigation skills.

"How well did you know her?"

"We were casual friends," I said. "We knew each other from here at the lake. We'd occasionally run into each other and walk our dogs together." Once again, I felt like I might be babbling. *Shut the hell up*, I told myself.

"How long had you known her?"

I gave it some quick thought. "Six or seven years, I think." I almost volunteered that I'd met her shortly after she and her family had moved here from Chicago, but I managed to stop myself.

"Can you tell me any more about her? Does she have family?"

There it was, an open invitation to spill my guts. I almost sighed but didn't. I realized I wasn't going to be able to play this nearly as close to the vest as I'd hoped. And while I wanted to keep my answers short, I also knew that lying to Robinson—even if it was lying by omission—was risky. It wouldn't be smart to pretend not to know things about Hannah that the cops might eventually discover I *did* know.

It also occurred to me that, despite his boyish appearance and rather laid-back demeanor, Deputy Sheriff Robinson might be a much sharper investigator than I'd thought.

"Yes, she has…er, had…family," I said. "Her husband is an attorney and they have a daughter in college. UNI, I think." I hesitated then gestured toward Maisie. "This was her dog."

Robinson nodded. "Do you know her husband's name? First name, I mean?"

"Craig."

"And the daughter?"

"Jessica." Again, there seemed no reason to pretend I didn't know this.

Robinson smiled. "Sounds like you knew them pretty well."

I shook my head. "Not really. I knew Hannah, like I said, from our walks here at the lake. She talked about her daughter quite a bit; her husband not so much. She told me recently that they were getting a divorce."

"Really," Robinson said. "That's interesting. Did she seem especially upset about that?" I thought the question sounded a little naïve—who isn't upset when they're going through a divorce?—but I guessed he was looking for any additional confirmation that this was a suicide.

I tried not to sound sarcastic. "She was upset, yes. Most people are when they're going through a divorce. But I didn't get the impression she was depressed or despondent if that's what you mean." I hesitated, then added, "She was angry about it; I know that much."

"Oh? How do you know that?"

"From the occasional nasty remark she'd make about her husband."

Robinson smiled and studied me for a moment before responding. I wondered if he was beginning to think my relationship with Hannah had been more than casual. I resisted the urge to say anything further.

"Okay," he said finally. "You said you found her floating offshore. How did you happen to find her this morning…did you know she was going to be here?"

"I knew she was somewhere out here, yes. I parked next to her vehicle, the blue Ford Explorer back at the gravel turnout on the point. My vehicle is the gray Chevy Equinox…you would have passed them if you drove all the way into the gate at the head of the trail."

He nodded. "I saw both vehicles." He said nothing more and I assumed he wanted me to continue.

Now I did sigh. I realized I wasn't going to be able to explain how I'd found Hannah's body without going into some detail, despite my conviction that I needed to keep my answers brief. I'd have to be careful but I saw no other way to account for my actions.

"Let me back up a bit," I said. "I'll start at the beginning."

CHAPTER 6

"THIS MAY SOUND A LITTLE farfetched," I said, and immediately regretted my choice of words.

I was thinking of how Maisie had shown up unexpectedly, carrying Hannah's shoe, and had then led us back to the pine grove and the big boulder, where I'd found Hannah's body just offshore. Maisie's actions were a variation of the whole Timmy-falling-down-the-well joke that had crossed my mind earlier, although I doubted Deputy Sheriff Robinson was old enough to recognize that reference. Lassie's storied heroism was probably well before his time.

Nevertheless, I realized that I should not have begun my account by suggesting it wasn't believable—why plant that seed in a cop's mind? I really needed to up my game and start thinking a little more clearly and choosing my words more carefully.

Apparently finding Hannah's body had left me more rattled than I'd realized.

Robinson smiled and said, "Just tell me what happened." I didn't know if he was trying to be encouraging, reassuring, or just wanted me to get the hell on with it. Maybe a little of all three.

"Okay," I said. "Preacher, that's my dog here, and I got out to the lake at a little before eight this morning. I parked next to Hannah's vehicle and we walked down to the canoe launch so I could toss this dummy for her to retrieve from the water." I gestured downward and toed the orange dummy where I'd dropped it on the bank. Robinson glanced at the dummy and then back up at me.

"Okay, go on," he said.

"I'd tossed it three or four times when Maisie came running up to us, carrying one of Hannah's shoes." I pointed to the pair of gray Nikes next to the boulder. "One of those shoes there."

"The dog was carrying one of those shoes?"

"That's right," I said, feeling like my story was already starting to unravel. Hell, I'd have found it hard to believe myself if it hadn't happened to me. "She dropped it in front of me, then picked it up again and started running back down the road with it. We followed her and she led us down here."

Robinson arched his eyebrows. "She led you down here, carrying the shoe?"

"I told you it was going to sound farfetched. But yes, that's what happened. When we got down here I saw Hannah's body, maybe ten yards out. I called to her but she didn't answer and that's when I started wading out to her. But I think I must have already realized she was dead. There was no movement."

"So you waded out to her, and…?"

"And I picked her up and carried her here and laid her on the bank. I'll admit I maybe wasn't thinking too clearly. But I didn't want to leave her in the water. So I carried her in. Then I called 911."

He nodded. "Okay. Anything else you can think of…any more details?"

I thought for a moment. "Before I waded out to her, I noticed her keys and cell phone on top of the boulder." I pointed to them. "I took my own phone and keys and wallet out of my pockets and dropped them next to hers. Then after I carried her in, I picked my stuff up. I left hers there." I almost added that it was at that point I'd realized maybe this was a crime scene. But I didn't say so. I'd let Robinson come up with that on his own. Or not. I wasn't going to suggest it to him.

Robinson stood looking out across the lake for a moment, like he was trying to assimilate everything I'd just said. Then he turned back to me and said, "Do you think she killed herself?"

The question caught me by surprise. I wasn't sure if he really wanted my opinion or if he was just trying to get a better grasp on the situation. I didn't feel comfortable speculating about Hannah's actions or state of mind, but I wasn't prepared to flat out deny the possibility, either.

"It looks that way," I said, for want of a better answer. "But I can't really say whether she would have done that. Like I said before, the last time I saw her she didn't seem depressed."

"The last time you saw her was when?"

"Monday morning. We ran into her and Maisie in the park on the other side of the lake. We walked the roadway through the park together. She seemed okay then."

"You say you ran into her. You hadn't planned to meet her that morning?"

Warning bells started clanging. I didn't like what Robinson was implying—or what I thought he was implying—namely, that Hannah and I had been something more than casual friends. That we might have been engaging in an illicit rendezvous at the lake.

"No," I said, trying to keep any trace of anger out of my voice. "Like I said before, we just knew each other from out here. We didn't have any contact otherwise." As I said this I couldn't help wondering if Robinson thought I was lying. Even though I wasn't.

He gave me another long look. "Okay," he finally said. "I think we'll be reporting this as a probable suicide, but I will need your contact information in case we have any more questions."

"Sure," I said.

A COUPLE OF MINUTES LATER a circus descended on the pine grove.

Bad word choice, I suppose. But with the arrival of the ambulance, the EMTs, two Des Moines Police Department detectives and another Dallas County deputy sheriff, things got hectic. Or at least a lot busier.

Someone—probably a Water Works employee—must have unlocked the padlock on the double gate at the head of the hiking trail. Unlike Deputy Robinson, all of these people had driven their vehicles back to the pines. The trail was wide enough for vehicular traffic and it was kept mowed in the summer but I knew there were several places with deep ruts. It must have been a bumpy ride.

The EMTs went immediately to Hannah's body and I tried not to watch as they began their examination. The DMPD detectives introduced themselves as Jarrett and Madison. Jarrett was a middle-aged white guy with a pot belly straining his white dress shirt. He wore a tie, loosened at his unbuttoned collar, but had apparently left his suit jacket in his vehicle. Given the heat, I couldn't blame him.

Detective Madison was a tall, attractive, black woman wearing dark gray slacks and a lighter gray blouse of a silky material. A fine sheen of perspiration showed on her forehead but otherwise she appeared much cooler than her partner. For some reason she made me feel self-conscious in my t-shirt, old cargo shorts and run-over boat shoes. Topped with a sweat-stained khaki bill cap and two days' worth of beard stubble, I realized I probably looked like a burnt out, saltwater fishing guide.

"You found the body?" she asked me.

"Yes."

"How long ago was that?"

I glanced at my wristwatch. "About 45 minutes ago, give or take a couple minutes."

She nodded. "And you knew the victim?" Jarrett wasn't saying anything, but he stood staring at me as Madison asked the questions. Although she appeared younger than Jarrett, I wondered if she was the senior partner of the two.

"Yes. Her name was Hannah Wilkinson. We'd occasionally walk our dogs together."

"These are your dogs?"

"The wiry one is. The golden retriever belongs… belonged…to Hannah. Her name is Maisie."

Madison gave me a long look, much like Deputy Robinson had done a couple times. Finally she said, "Why don't you tell us what happened." Something in her tone made me think she was hinting at a confession. Or maybe that was just my paranoia getting the best of me.

"Okay," I said. I nodded toward Robinson, who was

standing a few yards away, talking to the other Dallas County officer. "I've already told him. But long story short, I came out with my dog for some exercise this morning and Maisie found us and led us back here. I saw Hannah's body floating a few yards out in the water. I waded out, picked her up and carried her back to shore. Then I called 911." This time around I was sparing with the details.

"You say her dog led you back here?"

"That's right."

Detective Madison smiled. "Can you tell us how she did that?"

Well, hell. So much for keeping my answers brief.

AFTER RUNNING THROUGH THE WHOLE story again, describing how Maisie, carrying Hannah's shoe, had come up on Preacher and me, and how we'd then followed her back to the pine grove, I was starting to feel irritable, or at least impatient. I knew my account probably sounded implausible—I'd glanced at Detective Jarrett a time or two and caught him smirking—but I figured to hell with it. They could believe me or not. I'd done nothing wrong and had no reason to feel guilty about anything. Nor did they have any evidence that my story wasn't true.

But of course, as the old saying goes, no good deed goes unpunished. I should have known I wouldn't just be able to report finding Hannah's body and then be free to leave the scene and drive home. That this was, in fact, a workday for me and I should have been at home in my office by now, logged onto the company computer and editing magazine copy, was of little concern to the investigating officers.

The temperature had continued to climb as well, and the heat added to my irritability and impatience. Though it was shaded under the pines, everyone on the scene was now perspiring, and both dogs had returned to the lake several times, wading out into the water and lapping at it. I almost felt like doing the same.

The EMTs finished their examination of Hannah's body and I turned away as I saw one of them unroll and unzip a body bag. I didn't want to watch this part of the process.

As a hit man I've certainly seen my share of bodies over the years, and I'm ordinarily not squeamish.

But it's different when it's the body of a friend.

CHAPTER 7

PROBABLY BECAUSE OF THE LOW-HEELED pumps Detective Madison was wearing, or maybe because Detective Jarrett *was* the junior member of the team, he was the one who clambered down off the low bank onto the sandy shoreline to retrieve Hannah Wilkinson's keys and cell phone from atop the boulder and her gray Nikes from beside it.

There was nothing graceful about his actions. He stepped down awkwardly with arms flailing to maintain his balance. Watching him, I guessed his natural turf was pavement.

I tried not to laugh. When I glanced at Detective Madison, I saw her biting her lower lip, suppressing a smile. I quickly looked back toward Jarrett.

An EMT had supplied him with a pair of latex gloves and several Ziplock bags that I assumed were used for evidence. Stepping up to the boulder, Jarrett snapped on the gloves, opened one of the bags and gingerly picked up the phone. He dropped it into the bag, zipped it shut, and repeated the process for the keys.

He placed both bags on top of the boulder, opened a larger bag and bent to pick up the shoes. He dropped them into the bag and zipped it shut. Then he gathered up all three bags and managed to scramble back up onto the bank. By the time he reached Detective Madison and me under the pines, he was sweating profusely and his face was red. *That's more exercise than you've had in a week,* I thought.

Detective Madison turned from Jarrett and startled me with her next question.

"When we check the phone, are we going to find any calls or text messages from you?" she asked.

I bristled at the implication but made a conscious effort not to let my anger show. "No, you won't," I said. I was tempted to elaborate, to explain again that Hannah and I were casual friends who had known each other only from walking our dogs together. But I remembered an old axiom, he who excuses, accuses, and kept my mouth shut.

Detective Madison nodded. "Okay," she said. "Is there anything else you want to tell us before we wrap this up?"

"Nothing I can think of," I said. I hesitated then asked, "What about her dog?"

"One of the Dallas County officers will take her and impound her until she can be claimed by a family member. That is, unless…" She gave me a questioning look.

I blew out a breath and nodded. "I can take her and keep her at my place," I said. "You can tell the family to contact me and they can pick her up at my house." Even as I said this, I wondered what the hell I was letting myself in for. This didn't exactly jibe with my plan to keep my involvement to a minimum.

But I didn't like the idea of Maisie being impounded, even if only for a few hours.

"Thank you," Detective Madison said. "We appreciate that, and I'm sure the family will too. Now, I need your contact information." She produced a small notepad and pen from the pocket of her dress slacks. Detective Jarrett stood nearby, holding the evidence bags and sweating.

"Sure," I said, and gave her the information, including my address and phone numbers. "Tell them they can stop by whenever, but they might want to call me first to make sure I'm home. I work out of my home so I'm usually there during the day, but I do go out occasionally to run errands."

"You say you work out of your home? What is it you do?"

"I'm a magazine editor," I said, knowing what the inevitable next question was going to be.

"Oh? What magazine?" Bingo.

"*American Wingshot*," I replied. "It's a magazine about bird hunting and sporting dogs."

Detective Madison smiled. "So you really do know something about dogs," she said. Was there a trace of sarcasm in her comment, implying again that my story of Maisie leading us to Hannah's body wasn't believable?

"Well, I'd like to think so, anyway," I said dismissively.

I wasn't in the mood to elaborate. I could have tried to impress her with my creds; could have told her that I was a lifelong dog lover and as a kid I'd read every dog book I could get my hands on by Albert Payson Terhune, Jim Kjelgaard, Fred Gipson, Jack London, James Oliver Curwood and others; that I'd begun studying sporting dogs, especially, when I was still in high school and had begun pheasant hunting with my dad, all of which had eventually led to my current job. I could have told her those things but what I really wanted to do was end our conversation.

Detective Madison wasn't quite ready to let me go, however.

"And you said you work out of your home?"

"That's right. We do everything electronically. Most of the actual production work is done at one of our offices in Illinois. That's where my associate editor and art director are located." So much for not elaborating.

"Interesting," Detective Madison said, although I doubted that she really thought so. "That must be nice, being able to work out of your home. Your schedule must be pretty flexible." Another implication, perhaps, that I could pretty much come and go as I pleased?

"Not as flexible as you might suppose," I said. "Someone has to stay in the office and make sure the magazine gets to the printer on time."

"Oh, sure," she said. "Deadlines. I understand. How often do you publish?

"We're bimonthly."

"So you do six issues a year?"

"That's right."

"I see." She nodded and I wondered if she was trying to estimate how much time I'd be required to spend in my office overseeing a magazine that was only published six times a year.

I glanced over at Detective Jarrett, who was still red-faced and sweating. I didn't want to appear like I was in a hurry to leave—although I was—but neither did I want to get into a detailed discussion of our publishing process, which was where Detective Madison appeared to be heading with her questions.

"It's getting awfully warm out here and I need to get these dogs home," I said. I checked my watch. "And I should have been logged onto my company computer over an hour ago. I probably have a couple dozen messages waiting for me, plus copy to edit. You have all my information, so…" I let the sentence hang, hoping Detective Madison would agree to wrap things up.

She glanced at her partner also, and maybe his appearance reminded her of how good it was going to feel to climb into a vehicle with air conditioning. Or maybe she was worried that he might have a heart attack before they left the pines.

She looked back at me and said nothing for a moment. Then she smiled slightly and said, "You've been very helpful, Mr. Vance. I think we're probably looking at a suicide here, but we'll know more after the autopsy. In the meantime, we'll inform her family and let them know that you have her dog. I'm sure they'll be contacting you. Thank you for agreeing to take care of the dog until then."

"No problem," I replied. "Just have them give me a call. And let me know if you need anything further." I had no doubt she'd do so, even without my offer.

"We'll do that," she said.

WHILE WE WERE TALKING the EMTs had carried Hannah's body up the slope through the pines to the ambulance parked on the trail. It would have been nearly impossible to roll a gurney down the slope through the brush and over the thick carpet of pine needles, and even more difficult to roll it back uphill with the added weight of a body. Carrying her was the only option.

I called Maisie back when she tried to follow them.

I heard the ambulance doors slam and then the engine catch. I listened as the ambulance pulled away and tried not think about the autopsy that would be performed on Hannah.

Detectives Madison and Jarrett took their leave, walking side by side back up the slope. Jarrett still carried the evidence bags. I watched them for a moment and then turned to face the two Dallas County deputies.

"I'm Deputy Lewis," said the officer I'd not yet met. Like Deputy Robinson, he was a youngish guy, dressed in an identical uniform. His dark hair was cut in a military buzz.

I nodded. "Robert Vance," I said, and he nodded in return.

"I guess we're done here," he said, then surprised me by asking, "Can we give you a lift back to your vehicle?"

"I'd appreciate that," I said. "You're okay with the dogs riding inside?"

"Yeah, shouldn't be a problem."

I called both dogs and we all started up the slope.

I knew I'd never feel the same about this pine grove again.

DETECTIVE JARRETT SAID, "SO what do you think of that guy's story?" He was driving and the first thing he'd done after starting the ignition was turn the vehicle's air conditioning to high. By the time they left the lake property, the blower was blasting out frigid air and Detective Madison reached over and turned the fan down a couple notches.

"About the dog leading him to the body?" she asked.

"Right."

She laughed. "I'm not sure. It sounds a little corny but maybe it's just crazy enough to be true." She pondered a moment. "Yeah, I think he was probably telling the truth," she added. "I don't think he was lying about that."

"Really?"

"That's my impression. But I'll admit he seemed a little…wary."

Detective Jarrett nodded. "I thought so too." He laughed. "'Show me the man and I'll show you the crime,'" he quoted.

Detective Madison smiled. "Maybe," she said.

CHAPTER 8

Getting both unconfined dogs home in the Equinox proved to be less of a challenge than I anticipated.

After the Dallas County deputies dropped us at the turnout where I'd parked next to Hannah's Explorer, I spent a moment trying to figure out the logistics of what I was about to attempt. I never crated Preacher during our trips; I'd trained her years earlier to stay on her thick dog pillow in the cargo space under the hatch. I'd done this by attaching a short tether to one of the hooks in the cargo space and clipping the other end to her collar.

The tether was just long enough for her to turn around and lie down but not long enough to let her climb over the back seat. She'd quickly adjusted to lying on her pillow for the duration of our trips, and after a few weeks I no longer had to bother with the tether.

Now, I considered putting both dogs in the cargo space and tethering Maisie to ensure she wouldn't try to climb over the seat. I decided against this, fearing it might be a little too crowded in the cargo space for both large dogs. Preacher knew that area was hers, and like most German wirehairs, she had a strong protective streak. I didn't want to risk triggering a dog fight, even though Preacher and Maisie generally got along well with each other.

I opted for spreading a large old bath towel—I always carry a couple in my vehicle for just such emergencies—on the passenger seat and inviting Preacher to ride shotgun. This was something I occasionally did on longer trips—say, when we were traveling to hunt somewhere out-of-state—so Preacher wasn't totally unfamiliar with the practice. In fact, it was something of a treat for her to be allowed to ride up front.

Then I opened the hatch and Maisie immediately jumped in without my having to tell her to do so. I wasn't certain she would remain in the cargo space, so I snapped Preacher's old tether to her collar. Maisie settled herself on Preacher's pillow and I stepped back and closed the hatch.

I walked around to the driver's door, climbed in and fired the ignition. After the morning's events I was definitely ready to put Maffitt Reservoir in the rearview mirror. More than ready.

But the morning had one more ironic jab to inflict. I always listen to an oldies radio station in the Equinox and the first song I heard as we pulled out was one I recognized immediately—the piano notes were unmistakable—although I hadn't heard it for many years. "Moody River," sung by Pat Boone.

The lyrics weren't an exact match for what I'd just experienced, but they were close enough.

Christ, I thought. *Gimme a break, already.*

ON THE DRIVE HOME I DID what I almost always do after having lengthy conversations with people, in this case, Detective Madison and Deputy Robinson. I tried to replay both conversations in my mind and analyze what was said and what was implied but—this is always the tricky part—not let myself fall into playing the old "Here's what I *should* have said" game. The latter, tempting though it may be, is an exercise in futility because of course I'd never have the chance to go back and use those remarks, no matter how pithy.

My conversation with Deputy Robinson had been brief, and while he'd hinted a time or two that I might have been better acquainted with Hannah than I admitted, he hadn't pressured me on the point. Detective Madison had made similar insinuations, but she too had been relatively low-key about the matter, not pursuing it with any real energy. When I told her she wouldn't find any record of contact between Hannah and myself on Hannah's phone, she seemed satisfied that I was what I claimed to be, a casual friend and nothing more.

Of course, both officers could have been dissembling in an attempt to put me off stride or get me to lower my guard. But both Deputy Robinson and Detective Madison had indicated they believed Hannah's death was probably a suicide and seemed willing, depending on the autopsy results, to let it go at that. If the ME confirmed this, the matter would most likely be closed without further investigation.

Whether Hannah's family would accept such a conclusion remained to be seen, however. I wondered how rigorously they might pursue matters if they couldn't accept Hannah's death as a suicide.

I had a sudden disquieting thought. My previous assignment, the one that was still haunting me, had come about because a young man named James Collins had refused to believe his sister Mandi's death was a suicide, despite the official ruling as such. He had done a fair amount of investigating on his own and eventually determined she had been killed by her boss, an attorney with whom she'd been having an affair. With evidence in hand, Collins had sought me out to see justice done.

If Hannah's family refused to believe she had deliberately drowned herself and they thought someone had actually killed her…

I shook my head, trying like hell to dispel the notion that history might be about to repeat itself.

CHAPTER 9

The predator was worried.

Driving home from Maffitt Reservoir on Wednesday evening after killing Hannah Wilkinson, the predator had felt almost exuberant. He had recalled another passage from *The Call of the Wild,* a passage from the final pages that included the lines, "…he was aware of a great pride in himself—a pride greater than any he had yet experienced. He had killed man, the noblest game of all…"

The predator wasn't troubled by the fact that Buck's victims were men while his own victim was a woman. He shared Buck's sense of pride in what he had done, and he felt his actions were justified. The predator had killed a woman who had wronged him by taking his friendship for granted, and he had killed her in a way that made it unlikely he would ever be found out. It wasn't the first time a woman had failed to recognize him as a potential sexual partner, but it was the first time he had avenged himself, and he felt an almost fierce satisfaction in having done so.

By the following morning however, his pride in his actions and his confidence in his success were waning.

The predator worked as a parking lot attendant at the Des Moines International Airport and his job afforded him plenty of time to think. On this Thursday morning he was assigned to one of the kiosks just outside the long-term parking garage opposite the terminal, collecting money from those individuals who chose to pay their parking fees with cash. Because most people nowadays paid with a credit card or debit card and could do so at one of the automatic kiosks, he wasn't very busy. Had he bothered to keep track, he'd have discovered he averaged only one customer every fifteen minutes.

But the predator wasn't keeping track or thinking of such things. Ordinarily he didn't mind being assigned to a kiosk because it gave him the opportunity, albeit, infrequently, to catch a glimpse from his elevated position of some attractive woman's boobs if she happened to be wearing a low-cut blouse, or her thighs if she was wearing a skirt, as she stopped her vehicle next to the kiosk window to pay her fee.

He was always careful not to make his ogling too obvious, and he was confident that the women were none the wiser. They usually seemed preoccupied, perhaps eager to get home after being away for several days, and he'd learned they weren't interested in chitchat. Any attempts at banter, no matter how innocuous, were usually dismissed quickly or ignored altogether, which might earn them a muttered "Bitch!" from the predator as they pulled away from the kiosk. Still, their snubs notwithstanding, he appreciated the view they sometimes provided.

Now, however, he was thinking of other matters.

There had been no mention on the early morning news of Hannah Wilkinson's body being discovered, so the predator didn't know yet if anyone had found her. He planned to watch the noon news on the tiny black and white television one of his co-workers had installed in the kiosk but until then all he could do was wonder and continue to hope that her death would be ruled a suicide. But he had realized, belatedly, that he might have seriously fucked up by not disposing of her cell phone.

He guessed that when her body was found and reported, the police would collect her phone and keys from where Hannah had left them atop the boulder. That is, unless someone—maybe the person or persons who found her—stole the phone and keys for their own use or profit.

Was that likely? The predator knew there was a black market for stolen cell phones but he had no idea if anyone in Des Moines trafficked in them, or if whoever found Hannah would think of selling the phone for cash. The odds of someone finding Hannah and also being of such a mercenary mindset were slim, he thought.

Ditto her vehicle. It was possible that if Hannah's body was discovered by, say, some teenagers, *and* they took her keys and phone from atop the boulder *and* they made the connection between the keys and Hannah's Ford Explorer parked at the turnout, they might elect to take the vehicle for a joyride. But that seemed very unlikely also. Even teenagers would probably report finding Hannah's body rather than leaving her floating in the lake and grabbing up her phone and keys for their own amusement.

Then there was the matter of Hannah's dog.

The predator had told Maisie to stay when he'd left the pine grove, and to the best of his knowledge, she'd done so. She hadn't tried to follow him back to his vehicle, so he assumed she'd remained in the pines, close to where she'd last seen Hannah. He wondered if she had stayed there all night, waiting for Hannah to return. He hoped so. He didn't want to think about her wandering around aimlessly, perhaps returning to the road and being hit by a vehicle.

The predator's thoughts were interrupted by a customer pulling up to the kiosk. A quick glance confirmed the driver wasn't an attractive woman but a middle-aged man. When the predator opened the window of the kiosk—thankfully, the kiosk was air conditioned—the man looked up and smiled as he handed the predator his ticket from the parking garage. "Warm morning," the man said.

"Yes, it is that," the predator said. He wasn't in the mood for idle conversation. He took the ticket and ran it through the machine to calculate the fee. "That'll be $24.80," he said.

The man handed him two twenties and the predator made change and handed the man his receipt. "You have a good day," he said, hitting the button to raise the bar across the exit lane. The man thanked him and pulled through as the predator closed the window to the kiosk.

He resumed his thinking.

The biggest problem was the cell phone, the predator now realized. He dismissed the idea that someone might have found it and sold it. Almost certainly, whoever found Hannah's body would report it to the police, and when they came out to investigate, they'd take the cell phone into evidence. The predator knew they would be able to trace

Hannah's recent calls and texts, and that would point them directly to him. They'd undoubtedly find the texts he and Hannah had exchanged yesterday when they'd agreed to meet at the lake at 7 p.m. for a walk.

Fuck. Why hadn't he thought of this last night?

He could have thrown the phone out into the lake or taken it with him and disposed of it on the way home—a quick toss from a bridge into the Raccoon River, maybe. By leaving it on the boulder where it would be found, he'd screwed up, big time.

Okay. The predator told himself, this was a mistake but it wasn't insurmountable. If forewarned was forearmed, then he should just assume the phone would be found and the police would be questioning him. So he needed to have his story ready.

He pulled out his own phone and keyed the message icon. He still had the text exchange with Hannah and he read through the messages. There was nothing there of a suspicious nature, he decided; it was merely an exchange between two friends agreeing to meet for a walk.

The predator thought back over the previous evening's events. There had been two vehicles parked at the canoe launch when he and Hannah had walked past on their way to the gate at the head of the hiking trail, but they hadn't seen anyone. When they'd reached the big boulder below the pine grove there was no sign of anyone on the water; they'd had that part of the lake to themselves. The predator remembered checking this before suggesting they go for a swim.

So, he was confident no one had seen them or witnessed what he had done…well, except for Maisie. That meant that while the police would know, based on the text exchange, that he'd agreed to meet Hannah for a walk, they wouldn't know anything more.

The predator considered telling the police that he hadn't seen Hannah; that they'd missed connections and he hadn't walked with her as planned. He thought about telling them he got to the lake a few minutes late and Hannah had apparently begun her walk without him; that he'd looked for her but she must have walked farther along the trail than he did and he eventually gave up trying to find her.

He quickly realized this wouldn't fly.

The police would ask why he hadn't called or texted Hannah to find out where she was so he could join her. That was what most people would do in that situation, and he couldn't think of any convincing reason for not having done so. That meant claiming he hadn't seen her was out.

Which also meant he was going to have to admit he'd walked with her. All right, so what? They met as they'd planned and walked together. He could say that they'd walked as far as the pines, gone down to the boulder and sat for a few minutes, then Hannah had tactfully asked him to give her some time to herself, saying she needed to be alone with her thoughts.

The predator mulled this over and thought it might work. He remembered someone's observation that the best lies were those that contained elements of the truth. Well, this fit the bill. He could admit he'd seen Hannah and walked with her, but then play up the aspect of her wanting some privacy; he could even mention that she seemed a bit moody or depressed. He would cast himself as the concerned but obliging friend, never suspecting she was contemplating suicide when he took his leave of her at the pines.

The more the predator considered this, the better he liked it. He'd have to be careful not to overplay his hand, but if he kept it simple, he should be okay. He'd admit to walking back to the pines with Hannah but stand firm on the fact that she'd still been alive when he last saw her. With any luck, they wouldn't be able to prove otherwise.

The predator smiled as another car pulled up to the kiosk. As he opened the window, he saw that this time the driver was a woman who appeared to be in her early thirties, smartly dressed in a lightweight summer business suit. She had dark hair and big wraparound sunglasses so he couldn't see her eyes, but she smiled up at him in return.

"Good morning," he said as she handed him her ticket. "It's a beautiful day, isn't it?"

CHAPTER 10

It was a few minutes past ten when I got home from the lake with both dogs. I typically feed Preacher a small meal when we return from the lake every morning. To reduce the risk of gastric torsion, I feed her twice a day, rather than a single large meal, and I did so again. Of course, with Maisie on hand, I felt obliged to feed her as well. I had no idea how often or how much she was fed, but she didn't hesitate when I put a bowl of Preacher's kibble down in front of her.

That task taken care of, I headed back to the bedroom and stripped off the clothes I'd worn to the lake. They had dried in the morning's heat but I wasn't of a mind to sit around in them all day after wading out into the lake and carrying Hannah's body to shore. I'd worked up a pretty good sweat doing so, and I needed a quick shower. I crossed the hallway to the bathroom and as I pushed open the sliding glass shower doors and stepped into the tub, it occurred to me that a psychologist would probably say I was trying to wash away the morning's events. I wouldn't deny it.

After showering and putting on a clean t-shirt and another pair of cargo shorts, I checked on the dogs and saw them sprawled at opposite ends of the sofa in the living room. Maisie had made herself right at home and I was relieved to see that Preacher apparently didn't resent her presence. I wondered if Preacher sensed something was seriously amiss with the morning and if that was contributing to her tolerance.

I pondered this for a moment, thinking I might be getting a little carried away with my anthropomorphism. Then I remembered how Maisie had shown up earlier and led us to Hannah's body, and I decided that maybe crediting Preacher with assessing the situation wasn't so unlikely, after all. Canine behaviorists tell us that dogs are much more attuned to our feelings and possess far more insight than we usually give them credit for, and that wasn't something I was prepared to argue; in fact, I was inclined to agree.

Well, whatever. For the moment both dogs seemed content, so I headed into my office to log onto the company computer. I did so with some trepidation, hoping I wasn't going to be swamped with messages requiring my attention.

I got lucky. Just as I'd predicted when I'd talked to Detective Madison, my email inbox was filled with messages but the majority didn't appear to be urgent. I scrolled through them quickly, deleting unopened the obvious spam and promotional stuff and noting the ones from senders I recognized, or based on their subject lines, those that appeared to be from readers. There were no messages from Bill McKenzie, the publisher of the magazine and my boss, so I was in the clear in that respect, at least.

Before I began reading and replying to those messages requiring a response, I glanced up at the production schedule thumbtacked to the bulletin board above the computer. As this was the third week in July, we were working on the October/November issue, due to go to the printer the second week of August and begin mailing to subscribers in early September. I still had a few features and columns to edit before sending them on to the associate editor and the art director, and I was planning to spend the afternoon trying to get through at least two or three of these. I hoped to have the initial edit on all of the stories completed by the end of the day tomorrow or Monday at the latest.

Fat chance.

The old landline phone, the one I use for business, rang. The lighted caller ID window said the call was coming from Brookings, South Dakota, but the caller's name wasn't shown. Given the location I guessed the call was probably from a reader so, somewhat reluctantly, I answered rather than letting it go to voice mail.

"Rob Vance," I said.

"Hello?" The voice was raspy and masculine and there was static and a lot of background noise, like the caller was talking on a cell phone while driving. "I'm trying to reach the editor of *American Wingshot* magazine." Something about the guy's tone sounded confrontational.

"That's me," I said, already sensing this wasn't going to be a pleasant conversation. "What can I do for you?"

"Well, for starters, you can answer a question for me." Here it comes, I thought. "When did you guys decide to start running articles on mongrels?"

I bristled but kept my voice steady. "What article are you referring to?" I said, although I'd have bet big money I already knew the one he was talking about.

"The one in your last issue with the guy hunting with a silver Lab," the caller said. Yep, I'd guessed correctly. "You know those dogs aren't really Labs, don't you?"

"No, I don't know that," I said, still trying to stay calm. After the morning I'd just been through I wasn't in the mood to argue with this hothead but I've learned from past experience—a lot of past experience—that usually the best course in such matters was to let the person have his say and hope he eventually ran out of steam.

"Well, nowhere in the Lab standard does it say anything about silver being an acceptable color," the caller went on. "The only acceptable colors are black, yellow and chocolate; anything else is prohibited." *Tell me something I don't know*, I thought. "The only way you can have a silver Lab is if you outcross to another breed, like the Weimaraner," he continued. "I can't believe you're promoting that in your magazine."

"We're not promoting anything like that in the magazine," I said. I was well aware of the whole silver Labrador controversy, and I'd known when we ran the article that we'd probably draw some heat for it. But it was a solid story backed up with exceptional photos—the author used his dog almost exclusively for pheasants and some of his shots were almost breathtaking—so I'd decided to roll the dice. "The silver Lab folks will tell you that their dogs are actually a dilute form of the chocolate gene, and that's where the gray color comes from," I said, knowing very well the caller wouldn't buy it.

He didn't. "That's bullshit," he said. "They know damn well their dogs are carrying Weimaraner blood and the only reason they're breeding them is so they can charge big bucks for the puppies, claiming it's a rare color. I cannot believe you're helping to promote them."

"Well, again, we're not helping anyone promote anything," I said, knowing I wasn't going to convince him. "It was a good hunt story with great photos and that's why we ran it. I've heard both sides of the silver Lab argument and it's one of those deals that I doubt will ever be resolved. You're right that the only colors accepted by the standard are black, yellow or chocolate, but I'm not an expert on genetics…I can't say whether the silver color is due to an outcross or the result of that dilute gene."

"Well, I can damn sure tell you it's due to an outcross. They've done the DNA testing and can prove it," the caller said. He didn't, of course, identify the "they" who'd done the testing.

"I've seen the references to DNA testing on websites both pro and con," I replied. "Both sides claim they have the evidence, so it's a little tough to know who to believe."

"You should believe us," he said, and I thought, *on your say-so alone?* But I didn't say this.

Instead, I replied, "Well, like I said a minute ago, I doubt it will ever be completely resolved. We thought the writer had a good story to share and some excellent photos, so that's why we ran it." I realized I was repeating myself but I was ready to be done with this guy. I had neither the time nor the inclination to continue sparring with him.

"Well, whether you admit it or not, you're promoting breeders who are just looking to make a quick buck off an unaccepted color," he said. "I can't support your magazine if you're going to do that, so I'll be canceling my subscription."

"I'm sorry to hear that," I said, thinking, *oh gee, we'll just have to try to survive without your twenty-five bucks.* "We always hate to lose readers, but that's certainly your prerogative."

"Well, I'll be telling my friends to cancel their subscriptions also," he said, and I thought, *so that means we might lose one more sub, or two more, at the most. Be still my heart.*

"Well, again, I'm sorry to hear that, but thanks for sharing your concerns," I said. "You have a good day."

A moment of silence followed, then the caller said, "Well…okay. Thanks for listening." He hung up and I wondered if he would, in fact, cancel his subscription. He hadn't given me his name so I had no way of following up to see if he made good on his threat. But I knew that sometimes letting an irate reader vent was enough to rectify the situation and he might not follow through.

Whatever. By refusing to engage, I'd tried to take the high road. Whether it would pay off and he'd decide not to cancel his sub, I'd never know.

Have I mentioned that I'm beginning to feel like I'm getting too old for this shit?

CHAPTER 11

I SPENT THE NEXT HALF HOUR or so answering emails, then started editing a story about hunting ruffed grouse in Pennsylvania.

The emails were, thankfully, pretty innocuous; I didn't have to reply to anyone else upset about the silver Labrador story in the previous issue. In fact, one reader, a silver Lab owner herself, complimented us for running it. In my reply I thanked her for her comments and as I hit "send" I thought, *you win a few, you lose a few.* I also hoped that would be the end of the whole silver Lab matter for a while.

The grouse story was one I was especially pleased to be running. Pheasant hunting stories from the Midwest were almost a nickel a dozen, but we didn't get many submissions from grouse hunters and this one reminded me of some of the classic stories of Burton Spiller and George Bird Evans. The author, a fellow named Dan Eastlake, was a fine writer, descriptive without being gushy, and he had provided a nice selection of photos, including several striking shots of his handsome tricolored English setter on point. The dog's name was Jazz.

Good as the story was, though, I had a hard time staying focused. Fortunately, Eastlake's writing didn't require much editing; it was almost letter-perfect. But I still felt my attention wandering, a cardinal sin when you're editing copy for publication. Even though the associate editor would also be going over the story, I didn't want to send it on to him after nothing more than a cursory treatment.

Not surprisingly, my mind kept returning to the morning's earlier events. Just as I'd replayed the conversations with the police while I was driving home from the lake, now I kept replaying the whole sequence that had led up to those conversations, beginning with Maisie leading us to Hannah's body. There was an element of incredulity in these recollections, as if I still couldn't quite accept or believe what had happened, or my role in it. And I kept coming back to that one nagging question: Did Hannah really drown herself?

The police seemed to think so, but I wasn't so sure. While waiting for them to arrive I'd wondered if I'd blundered into a crime scene, and I still wasn't convinced I hadn't. On the other hand, neither the DMPD detectives nor the Dallas County Sheriff's deputies—once they'd apparently decided my story about finding Hannah's body was credible—appeared particularly interested in digging into the matter much deeper.

Then again, the detectives had bagged her phone and keys and shoes as evidence. But maybe that was just standard procedure.

I also wondered briefly about any politics or territorial issues that might be involved in the investigation. Why two detectives from the DMPD had shown up and taken charge, as opposed to, say, someone from the State Police, along with the Dallas County deputies, was something I couldn't explain. Maybe it was because the drowning had occurred on Water Works property, which possibly fell under the city's jurisdiction.

I had no way of knowing if this was the case, so I dismissed it as something not especially relevant, at least as far as my own involvement was concerned. But I was interested in what the autopsy of Hannah's body might show. I told myself that if the autopsy revealed nothing out of the ordinary, and if there was nothing suspicious on Hannah's phone, then her death was most likely what it appeared to be. I had a tough time believing this, but…

My uncertainty gave rise to a couple more questions. If Hannah's death wasn't suicide, then who had killed her? And why?

Friendly and outgoing, Hannah was well-liked by everyone at the lake, at least she was to the best of my knowledge. While we'd been no more than casual friends, I couldn't imagine her having any real enemies, certainly not anyone who disliked her enough to kill her. Nor could I imagine her having offended someone so seriously that they would retaliate in such extreme fashion.

So naturally, I wondered if her estranged husband might have had something to do with it.

Except for his name and profession—Hannah had mentioned a couple of times that he was a lawyer—I knew very little about him. She had told me recently that they were divorcing, and I'd made the requisite sympathetic noises, saying I was sorry to hear this. She'd thanked me but again, she hadn't really elaborated. So beyond the fact that their marriage had apparently failed, I didn't know much about the guy.

Of course, given the circumstances, the spouse or partner is frequently the initial primary suspect or "person of interest," in many homicides. Or at least, so say the many crime shows on television these days.

Was it conceivable that Hannah's husband had joined her and Maisie on their walk the previous evening, and that when they'd reached the big boulder he'd somehow lured her into the water and drowned her? Maybe he was upset by the terms of the divorce settlement (assuming they were that far into the process) and his anger drove him to do something impulsive?

No. This was rank speculation on my part, and I quickly recognized it as such. Ditto any thoughts about Hannah's husband hoping to collect a large life insurance settlement after her death. That was the stuff of old movies and hack mystery novels, and it made for neat solutions, but I doubted that Craig Wilkinson would have resorted to such actions. It was just too obvious, and surely as an attorney he'd be smart enough to know that. He'd know that any hint of foul play would be thoroughly investigated and wouldn't take the risk.

For the same reason, I doubted he'd hired anyone else to kill her. That would involve making a payment that quite possibly could be traced—although I knew firsthand how to at least partially circumvent this—and again, it was almost too neat, too obvious. I just couldn't apply Occam's razor to this scenario with any real conviction.

I shook my head and turned back to the grouse hunting

story, determined to give it my full attention. It was almost time for lunch and I wanted to finish editing the story so I'd have something constructive to show for my morning.

Speak of the Devil.

Craig Wilkinson called me at 2:30 to ask about stopping by to pick up Maisie. I'd finished editing the grouse hunting story and had sent it on to the associate editor, and I was wrapping up another feature, this one on using dogs to hunt fall turkeys, when the phone rang.

Wilkinson introduced himself and said, "I understand you were the person who found Hannah this morning." His voice sounded calm and measured, and I wondered if he was struggling to project that tone. Their pending divorce notwithstanding, learning of his wife's drowning had to have been upsetting for him.

Then again, if he was a litigator, he had undoubtedly had plenty of practice at speaking under pressure.

"That's right," I said. "I was out at the lake with my dog. Maisie found us and led us to Hannah." I almost started to explain how I'd carried her body ashore, but I stopped myself. "I called 911 and reported what we found." I hesitated, hoping that hadn't sounded awkward, then continued, "After I talked to the detectives, I told them I'd take Maisie to keep her from being impounded."

"We appreciate that," Wilkinson said, still sounding calm. "My daughter and I would like to come by and pick her up if this is a convenient time."

"Sure," I said. I told him my address and asked if he needed directions. Even as I said the latter, I realized I'd probably just dated myself, that he could probably find my house with the help of the navigation system on his phone or in his vehicle.

"No, I think we can find your place," he replied in the same calm tone. "We're at home right now so I'm guessing we can be there in about twenty minutes or so."

"That sounds about right," I said. "I'll see you shortly."

"We'll see you shortly," he echoed. "And…thanks again."

CHAPTER 12

I was in for another shock.

Craig and Jessica Wilkinson got to my house at a few minutes before 3 p.m. One of them rang the doorbell and Preacher and Maisie both started barking. I quickly saved and exited the turkey hunting story I was working on, then left my office and walked out to the living room. I said, "Quiet!" to the dogs and Preacher responded with a final whine. Maisie kept barking.

Both dogs were crowding the door and I kneed them aside. I opened the front door and as I reached down to unlatch the aluminum storm door, I glanced through the door's glass pane at Craig Wilkinson and his daughter.

My eyes widened when I saw Jessica Wilkinson, and I knew I was doing the classic double-take.

She was the image of her mother.

Tall and blonde, with a slender, athletic build, she was standing just behind her father and slightly to one side. She was wearing a gold UNI t-shirt with purple lettering, shorts and flip-flops. I realized I was staring at her and she was returning my look. I quickly shifted my gaze to her father.

Craig Wilkinson appeared to be about my height and he had the build of a runner; apparently athleticism ran in the family. He had short, neatly barbered dark hair and was wearing khakis and a light blue polo shirt. His cordovan loafers gleamed with polish, and I wondered if he was one of those trendy guys who wore them without socks. From my vantage point inside my front door I couldn't tell, but I suspected he might be.

I opened the door and asked them to step in. Maisie crowded past me, whining and wagging her tail furiously. Jessica immediately dropped to one knee and pulled Maisie in for a hug. Preacher had backed off a few steps and stood by watchfully, almost as if she didn't want to intrude on the reunion. Or maybe she was just displaying a German wirehair's customary wariness around strangers.

Craig Wilkinson extended his hand and we shook. His grip was firm. "Thank you for taking care of Maisie," he said. "And…for everything."

I stopped short of replying with the standard "No problem," which would have sounded rather lame under the circumstances. Instead, I said, "You're welcome. Maisie wasn't any trouble." I hesitated a moment, then added, "I'm very sorry for your loss."

"Thank you," Wilkinson said. "This has been a real shock for us, as you can imagine." He turned toward his daughter, who was now standing with one hand resting on Maisie's ruff. "I'm sorry...this is my daughter, Jessica. She just got back to Des Moines about a half hour ago. She's attending summer classes at UNI."

"Jessica," I said, and extended my hand. I didn't say "Nice to meet you," which again would have sounded inappropriate, I thought. She shook my hand, and like her father, she had a firm grip.

I turned and stepped further back into the living room. "Would you like to come in for a few minutes?" I asked. "Sit down, maybe have something to drink?"

"Thanks, but no," Wilkinson said. "We won't take up too much more of your time. But I wonder if I could have a word with you in private?"

"Sure," I said. I wasn't keen on being grilled by an attorney, even one who had just lost his wife under highly questionable circumstances, but I could hardly refuse the request. I had a pretty good idea what was coming, and I couldn't blame Wilkinson for wanting more details about what had happened that morning, and especially my role in the matter.

He turned to his daughter and said, "Jess, maybe you could take Maisie out to the car?" I'd already glanced past them and had seen that their vehicle was a white Cadillac Escalade. I guessed it was Wilkinson's, as Hannah always drove a dark blue Ford Explorer.

Jessica shook her head and said in a surprisingly firm voice, "No. I'd like to hear what Mr. Vance has to say also." She was looking her father in the eye as she said this and her look didn't waver.

Wow, I thought. This was one self-assured young woman. Clearly she did not care to be coddled, and just as clearly, she was not going to be dismissed. I guessed her age at about 19, and once again I couldn't help noticing that with the exception of Hannah's laugh lines, how much Jessica resembled her mother.

"Okay," Wilkinson said, turning back toward me with a somewhat sheepish smile meant to convey, I guessed, *what can you do?* To relieve the tension I gestured toward the sofa.

"Why don't we sit down?" I said. Jessica and her father followed me into the living room and took seats beside each other on the sofa. As a matter of course, Maisie jumped up and sat next to Jessica.

"Maisie!" Jessica said sharply. "Get down!" She grasped the golden by the collar and started to pull her off the sofa but I intervened.

"It's okay," I said. "She can stay right there." I smiled. "Dogs have furniture privileges in my house."

Jessica smiled at me in return. "Okay," she said. Maisie curled up beside her and Jessica rested a hand on her shoulders.

I took a seat in the easy chair that sat at an angle at one end of the sofa. After a moment, Preacher stalked over and settled herself beside me. She sighed and we all laughed a bit nervously, but it was the ice-breaker we needed.

"Well," Wilkinson said, "as I said, we won't take up much of your time, but I was hoping you could maybe tell us exactly what happened this morning. The police have already filled us in on most of the details, and they seem to think my wife committed suicide." He glanced at Jessica then continued. "We're both having a hard time believing that." Jessica nodded in agreement but said nothing.

I hesitated for a moment before responding. I didn't sense that Wilkinson was implying I had anything to do with

Hannah's death, but then again, as an attorney he was probably good at leading witnesses. While I had nothing to hide and no reason to feel guilty, I realized I should proceed with caution.

"Well," I said, "as the police told you, I'm the one who found Hannah…actually, Maisie found us and led us to where…led us to her." I inwardly cursed my awkwardness, but I was struggling to keep the details to a minimum, as I didn't want to describe Hannah's body floating in the lake. That was an image I felt they should both be spared, especially Jessica.

Luckily, Wilkinson interceded while I was still struggling to frame my next comment. "Maisie led you to Hannah?" he asked.

"Yes," I said, thinking, *here we go again*. I was beginning to feel like I was simply pushing the "play" button on a tape recorder. "We were at the canoe launch and she came running up to us carrying one of Hannah's shoes."

"Really!" Wilkinson said, his note of disbelief unmistakable. But I glanced at Jessica and saw her smile briefly; apparently she was less skeptical than her father and was willing to credit Maisie with the action I described.

"I know it sounds a little farfetched," I replied, "but that's what happened. After finding us she turned and led us back to where I found Hannah."

"And then?" Wilkinson prompted. No doubt about it; he was good at soliciting testimony.

I sighed. Apparently there was no way I was going to be able to recount this without going into the details I'd hoped to spare them. And I couldn't really blame Wilkinson for wanting those details; I realized if I were in his position I'd probably be pressing for the same.

So for the third time that day I went through the entire sequence of events. I took them through it from the beginning, explaining that after Maisie had found us we'd followed her back to the hiking trail and down through the pine grove to the big boulder on the shoreline, and that I'd acted impulsively when I saw Hannah's body and had waded out and carried her ashore, then called 911. I described my conversations with the Dallas County deputies and the DMPD detectives, and how I had offered to take Maisie.

I also mentioned the EMTs who had attended to Hannah's body, but I did manage to keep those details to a minimum. I didn't say anything about the body bag, only that after working over Hannah for several minutes, they had removed her to the ambulance.

"After the ambulance and the detectives left, the Dallas County guys gave the dogs and me a ride back to my vehicle," I concluded. "I got them loaded up and we came on home." I paused, then added, "We've been here since then."

Craig Wilkinson and Jessica both sat silently for a moment, then Craig placed both hands on his knees and said, "Well, thank you for that. And for everything you've done." Jessica nodded beside him.

"You're welcome," I said. "And again, I'm very sorry for your loss."

Wilkinson stood and after a moment, Jessica did also. She grasped Maisie's collar and gently pulled her off the sofa. I stood up as Wilkinson said, "We won't take up any more of your time." He turned and started toward the door.

Jessica turned also, still grasping Maisie's collar. She started toward the door and I followed. Wilkinson opened the storm door and stepped out onto the front step. He turned back to me and said, "Thanks again."

I nodded. With Maisie in tow, Jessica started to follow her father but she turned at the doorway to look back at me.

I met her gaze. As I did so she said in a quiet but firm voice, "My mother didn't kill herself."

CHAPTER 13

"THAT SOUNDS LIKE A FAMILY member's typical denial," Daryl Nelson said. "Or more specifically, a daughter's denial; something she doesn't want to believe—or can't bring herself to believe—about her mother."

I nodded. "I thought the same thing," I said. "But there was something about the way she said it. She was dead calm—sorry, that was a bad pun—and she said it with absolute conviction, almost like she knew things that would confirm what she was saying. Like she had evidence that would prove beyond any doubt that her mother didn't commit suicide."

Daryl smiled. "Are you sure you're not reading too much into it, maybe because you don't want to believe it yourself?"

"I don't know," I replied honestly. "I didn't know Hannah all that well; I just saw her occasionally out at the lake when we were walking our dogs. She'd mentioned recently that she was getting a divorce, but she didn't go into detail. She seemed to be in control of things, not at all the hysterical type. She was friendly and outgoing and as far as I know, everyone at the lake liked her. Whenever I saw her, she wasn't moody or depressed, or at least didn't appear to be."

This was the fourth time I'd gone through the morning's events, but it was the first time I was able to do so without feeling the need to guard my words. Daryl Nelson and I had been involved for about eight months now; coincidentally, our relationship had moved beyond casual right around the same time as my last assignment, and I valued her insight and input. Or to put it another way, I was relieved to be able to confide in someone I trusted.

We were sitting in one of the dark wood booths in the dining room of Johnny's Italian Steakhouse on Fleur Drive, about a half-mile south of the airport. Unless one of us was up against a tight deadline—Daryl is a reporter and op-ed writer for the *Des Moines Register*—we usually had dinner together on Thursday evenings. It was our way of getting a jump on the weekend.

Daryl had suggested Johnny's and she hadn't had to twist my arm. It's one of our favorite restaurants, along with Skip's, which is also on Fleur Drive but in the opposite direction, about a mile north of the airport. We're regulars at both places, and the bartenders and most of the servers greet us by name when we come in.

"You're lucky I'm not the jealous type," Daryl said with another smile. "Otherwise, I'd be a little concerned about you spending so much time with another woman on those morning walks of yours."

I laughed. With her dark hair, dark eyes and strong jawline, Daryl bore more than a passing resemblance to actress Marcia Gay Harden. She also possessed the same unmistakable self-assurance that Ms. Harden projected in many of her roles. I had no trouble believing she wasn't the jealous type, but I still thought a little damage control might be in order.

"Like I said, I only saw Hannah Wilkinson occasionally if we happened to run into each other. Sometimes several weeks would pass and I wouldn't see her at all." I realized I was on the verge of overplaying things. "But I can't deny that finding her body this morning left me feeling a little rattled."

"That's understandable," Daryl said.

"I also realize I'm probably overthinking this. The cops seemed pretty sure this was a suicide, or at least that's the impression I got from them. They're probably a lot better at assessing these things than I am; in fact, I'm sure they are." Even as I said this, I winced inwardly, recalling that I'd concluded my last assignment by staging things to look like the target had committed suicide—something Daryl knew nothing about.

"I know it's tough to do, given the circumstances, but you should probably try to let it go," Daryl advised. "There's really not anything more you can do, is there?"

"I can't imagine what it would be," I said. "I told the police everything I knew, and they seemed satisfied to let it go at that. I mean, I don't think I'm under suspicion, or anything like that. I doubt I'll be talking to them again."

Daryl reached across the table to squeeze my hand. "Let it go," she said softly.

EASIER SAID THAN DONE, of course. But I wasn't going to ruin an otherwise good dinner at a favorite restaurant by endlessly rehashing events I'd already been over several times. I also tried to remind myself that, my friendship with Hannah Wilkinson notwithstanding, it wasn't my place to make a determination on her cause of death. Let the cops and the ME make that call.

But her daughter's assertion still troubled me.

I couldn't help wondering if Hannah had left a note or some kind of message for her family. I might never know the answer, so add that to the list of things with which I shouldn't concern myself. Still, it was an unanswered question that was likely to nag at me, at least for a while.

Then again if Hannah's death wasn't suicide…

Enough, I told myself. *Take your lady friend's advice and let it go. There's nothing more you can do.*

DARYL HAD ORDERED ONE of her favorites at Johnny's, steak de burgo, and I'd opted for cedar plank salmon. This was something of a reversal for us in that I was the one who usually ordered red meat and Daryl was more likely to order fish or seafood, but never let it be said we couldn't be flexible. It's hard to go wrong with any of the entrees at Johnny's.

"Will you save a bite of your salmon for me to take home to Ivy?" Daryl asked. Ivy was her golden tabby, a cat with whom I, a confirmed dog person, was on at least tolerable terms.

"Only if you save a bite of your steak for me to take home to Preacher," I replied.

"Hard bargain!" Daryl said, laughing. "I'll do it, but only if you promise me you'll give the steak to Preacher and not eat it yourself."

"Well…okay," I said. "Deal. I'm actually trying to cut

down on my red meat consumption anyway."

Daryl snorted. "Oh, right," she said. "Just like you're trying to give up drinking beer."

"Hey," I said. I was still on my first tall Blue Moon of the evening, which I thought showed admirable restraint, given the day's events. "A dog has to have a few fleas or he forgets he's a dog."

Daryl laughed again. "Who said that?"

"I don't know," I said. "Maybe Mark Twain. But speaking of dogs, Preacher is doing a lot better since we started using that ramp. She isn't limping anymore after we go out for our runs."

"I'm glad to hear that," Daryl said. "How old is she again?"

"Seven."

"Oh, she's just middle-aged. She's got a lot of years left."

"Thanks," I said. "I hope you're right." My previous wirehair, another female named Bristol, had lived to be thirteen and I was hoping Preacher would do at least as well.

"Trust me on this," Daryl said. "I know a thing or two about aging females." She gave me another smile as she said this, and I couldn't help laughing.

"There's an admission I wish I had on tape," I said.

Daryl picked up a bite of focaccia bread from the edge of her plate and tossed it at me.

I suppose I deserved that.

CHAPTER 14

Because the next day, Friday, was a workday for both of us—making this, as Daryl called it, a "school night"—we opted to end the evening with a hug and a goodnight kiss in the parking lot at Johnny's, rather than retiring to either of our homes.

"Promise me you'll give that steak to Preacher," she said as she climbed into her Corolla.

I laughed. "I promise," I replied. "Be safe driving home."

"I will," she said. She closed her door and started the ignition. She gave me a smile and a quick wave and reversed out of her parking space. I returned her wave and walked over to the Equinox parked several spaces away. We'd met at the restaurant at 6:30 and it was now a few minutes past eight.

I climbed in and dropped the small carryout box with Daryl's steak on the passenger seat. The box also contained a couple of leftover pieces of focaccia bread, which Preacher would eat almost as readily as the steak, especially since I'd dredged the pieces through the remaining de burgo sauce on Daryl's plate before putting them in the box.

Obviously, I don't believe in spoiling my dog. Not one little bit.

When I got home I let Preacher out into the back yard, then put the steak and one of the pieces of bread in her food bowl. I saved the second piece of bread to give her the next morning. Then I stepped out on the deck myself, turning on my cell phone as I did so. Daryl usually called or texted to let me know she'd made it home safely.

The evening was still very warm and humid. I'd worn shorts and a polo shirt to Johnny's—thank goodness for casual dining—and Daryl had been wearing a sundress with a bright aqua floral design on a black background. Neither of us is a big fan of hot weather, but you quickly learn to adapt during the summer months if you live in Iowa, or else, like Dave Carson, one of my best writers, you relocate to a cooler clime. Dave was an Iowa native but he'd moved to Montana many years ago and now described himself as a bird-shootin' cowboy. I couldn't deny I was somewhat envious.

I watched Preacher cruise the back yard in the dusk. Something was troubling me about my dinner with Daryl but I couldn't quite put my finger on it. Curiously, it didn't seem specifically related to Hannah's death, or her daughter's certainty that Hannah hadn't deliberately drowned herself. This was something aside from that, something tangential or a comment one of us had made in passing, maybe.

I struggled to bring it to mind. Like always, I started replaying our conversation, hoping the offhand remark would bubble to the surface so I could pin down what was bugging me.

My cell phone chimed, signaling an incoming text. I thumbed the message icon and saw the text was from Daryl. It read, "Home safe. Ivy says thanks for the salmon. Hope Preacher enjoyed her steak!" This was followed by a kissing emoji.

I'm not a big fan of emojis but I was willing to make an exception in Daryl's case, and even occasionally used one myself. I smiled and quickly tapped in a reply. "Preacher's in the back yard and hasn't had her steak yet, but she says thanks in advance." I attached a smiling emoji and hit the send arrow.

Daryl's reply was almost instantaneous: "Remember, you promised!" I laughed and replied with a thumbs-up emoji.

I waited a minute to see if Daryl would reply again, but she didn't. I cleared the open message app on my phone and then turned it off. My gaze returned to Preacher, who was sniffing along the chain-link fence at the back of the property. Something, probably a rabbit, had left a trail that Preacher found interesting.

I watched Preacher and let my mind resume replaying my dinner conversation with Daryl. I recalled my comment about the cops seeming pretty well convinced that Hannah had committed suicide, and that they were probably better at assessing such situations than I was. And with that recollection, I realized what was troubling me.

When I'd made that comment to Daryl, I'd felt a momentary guilty twinge related to the conclusion of my previous assignment. The guilt wasn't due to what I had done—I still believed the target deserved the fate I had delivered—but rather, the fact that Daryl knew nothing about it. It was a lie of omission, of sorts.

Or to nail it down more precisely, after being seriously involved—okay, intimately involved—with Daryl for the past eight months, she still had no idea that I was a contract killer. Even though I hadn't taken another assignment in the interim, my online ad was still running and I was still getting the occasional query. I'd not pursued any of these, but practically speaking, I was still in business.

Call me the ultimate hypocrite here, but I prize honesty in a relationship. I'm also a firm believer in the old axiom that says if you're doing something you wouldn't be comfortable telling your partner, you probably shouldn't be doing it.

In a nutshell, I was feeling guilty about having kept Daryl in the dark all this time.

She was a straight shooter, pure and simple. She pulled no punches in her op-ed pieces for the *Register* and that, in fact, was one of the reasons I was initially attracted to her. Our subsequent relationship had borne out this characteristic. With Daryl, I always knew where I stood. She wasn't into evasive answers or head games. My trust in her was based, at least in part, on her honesty with me.

I was struck by a sudden ironic thought. A little over twelve hours earlier I'd been sitting at my kitchen table contemplating retirement, both from my day job as a magazine editor and from my moonlighting gig as a hit man.

Maybe tonight's attack of conscience was a sign that it was truly time to get serious about retiring.

Ordinarily I don't put a lot of stock in that sort of thing—signs from "above," or whatever. But I couldn't deny that this realization—the fact that I was keeping something critically important from a woman about whom I cared deeply and who had, to the best of my knowledge, been completely above-board with me—was mighty disturbing.

I shook my head and gave Preacher a quick whistle to call her in. We stepped into the kitchen and I confirmed there was still about an inch of coffee in the carafe, left over from this morning, enough to fill a mug and nuke it, then garnish with one of the mini-bottles of Baileys Irish Cream I kept in the fridge.

I needed something a little stronger than another beer as a nightcap.

CHAPTER 15

The predator was pleased with himself. He'd stuck to his guns—well, his story, anyway—and he was confident he'd outwitted the cops. Or kept them at bay, at least.

When his shift in the parking garage at the airport ended at 3 p.m., he drove straight home. He lived less than ten minutes from the airport on the far south side of Des Moines in an area known as Greenfield Township. Because the township was just south of County Line Road, the predator lived in Warren County. He still had a Des Moines address, however, even though the city proper was located in Polk County.

This anomaly had the predator wondering which police department—DMPD, one of the county sheriffs' offices, or even the State Police—would come calling. He'd watched the noon news on the tiny television in the kiosk and had seen the brief report on the discovery of Hannah Wilkinson's body at Maffitt Reservoir earlier that morning. She had been found by an unidentified dog walker.

The female newscaster noted that Dallas County Sheriff's Police and the Des Moines Police Department had both responded to the call from the dog walker. The predator wondered if this was anyone he knew, and he guessed it probably was. The newscaster also said that Hannah's death was being considered a probable suicide. No foul play was initially suspected, the newscaster concluded, pending the results of an autopsy.

The predator had no idea how such jurisdictional matters were determined, especially since Hannah's death had occurred outside the city, but he was certain the police would eventually seek him out. He knew it was only a matter of time before they discovered the text exchange between Hannah and himself the previous evening, and that they would follow up accordingly. They'd want to know if he'd seen Hannah and if so, what had transpired.

He got his answer about fifteen minutes after he arrived home. After bringing in the mail from his curbside mailbox and dropping it unopened on the kitchen table, he'd snagged a Miller Lite from the fridge and gone out to the living room and turned on the television to watch *Jeopardy!* The game show aired at 3:30 p.m. on Channel 13 and the predator was a big fan. He always tried to play along, although he seldom knew many of the answers. He'd gotten lucky once, though, when an entire category was devoted to the works of Jack London. The predator had kicked butt on that one.

He'd just settled himself on the sofa opposite the television and cracked his beer when he heard the knock at the door. The predator rarely had visitors so he was fairly certain this would be the police. *Didn't take them long to find me*, the predator thought.

He set his beer on the end table next to the sofa and walked over to the front door. He opened it and saw a tall black woman and a shorter, beefy guy standing on the front step. The woman's badge was suspended on a chain lanyard around her neck and the guy's was on a holder clipped to his belt. An unmarked, midsize, dark gray sedan was parked behind them in his driveway. The predator hoped he looked puzzled as he opened the aluminum storm door and said, "Yes?"

The woman said his name but phrased it as a question. He replied, "Yes," and hesitated, still hoping to appear puzzled, then added, "Can I help you?"

"I'm Detective Madison and this is my partner, Detective Jarrett. We're with the Des Moines Police Department and we'd like to ask you a few questions. May we come in?"

The predator shrugged, trying for indifference, and said, "Sure." *Keep your cool*, he reminded himself, opening the storm door wider as Detective Madison stepped past him into his living room. Detective Jarrett caught the edge of the door and followed her inside.

"What's this about?" the predator asked.

Detective Madison faced him squarely and asked, "Do

you know a woman named Hannah Wilkinson?"

"Yes," the predator replied. "Why?" He almost asked if something had happened to her but caught himself.

"She was found at Maffitt Reservoir this morning, drowned. Her car keys and cell phone were found at the site. We checked her phone and found some texts from you. Apparently you were meeting her for a walk at the reservoir last evening?"

The predator shook his head and looked at the floor, feigning disbelief and confusion. Instead of answering the question, he said, "Oh, my God. She drowned?"

"That's right. Did you meet her last evening?" Detective Madison was not going to be put off her line of questioning.

"Yes, I did." *Keep it short*, he told himself.

"What time was that?"

"A little after seven o'clock." The predator hesitated. "About 7:15, I think." *So far so good.*

"Where did you meet her?"

"At one of the parking turnouts on the west side of the lake. I got there before she did and she parked next to me."

"And then the two of you walked together?"

"Yes, for a little while. Her dog was with her. We walked back on the trail to some pines. There's a big boulder down by the water and that's where we went." *Careful…don't overdo it!*

"Was that something you did with her regularly?"

"We got together and walked occasionally, but not always to the same place. Sometimes we walked in the park on the other side of the lake."

"How often did you meet and walk with her?"

"Oh, maybe once a week or so. It varied. Sometimes two or three weeks would go by and we wouldn't see each other. Last night was the first time we got together in almost two weeks."

"Okay, so last night you walked as far as the boulder by the pines; then what happened?"

"We sat on the boulder for a few minutes and then Hannah asked me if I would mind leaving her by herself for a while. She said she was sorry, but she needed some time to think about some things and she hoped I wouldn't mind."

"And did you?" This was Detective Jarrett, the first time he'd spoken.

"Did I leave her alone?"

"Yes."

"Yes, I did. I asked her if she was okay and she said she was, that she just had a lot on her mind and needed to sort a few things out. She said she'd be okay by herself with Maisie—that's her dog—there to protect her."

"Oh?" Detective Madison again. "Why do you think she felt like she needed protection?"

"I don't think she meant it seriously. She kinda laughed when she said it. I think she was just…I guess in a hurry to have me leave and was trying to convince me she'd be okay."

"So what did you do then?"

"I said something like, well, okay, good luck getting things sorted out, and she thanked me. Then I left. I walked back to my vehicle and drove home."

"And that was the last time you had any contact with her?"

"Yes."

"Aside from her asking you to leave her alone, did she seem upset about anything?"

"No, not really." The predator hesitated then added, "When we were walking she mentioned talking to her husband about getting the dishwasher repaired because it was leaking water. Awhile back she'd told me they were getting a divorce, so I knew she was dealing with that, but she didn't seem more upset than usual…well, maybe a little moody."

"A little moody?"

The predator shrugged again. "I guess. I mean, it's hard to say. I was a little surprised when she asked me to leave, but I didn't think that much about it. I just took her at her word, that she wanted some time to herself."

Detective Madison nodded. "So you left her sitting on the rock and returned to your vehicle, is that correct?"

"That's right."

"Did you see anyone else while you were out there? Talk to anyone?"

"No. When we started walking we followed the roadway around to the gate and there were a couple of vehicles parked by the canoe launch, but we didn't see anyone."

"And you never saw anyone after you left her?"

"No."

"What about the vehicles parked at the canoe launch? Were they still there?"

The predator thought for a moment. "I think one of them was gone," he said. "But I wasn't paying that much attention." He shook his head again. "I can't believe…I mean, she basically seemed okay. Do you think…" He hoped he wasn't laying it on too thick.

"At this point we're still investigating and waiting for the results of the autopsy. But it appears to be a suicide. Are you sure she didn't say anything, or give you any indication, of what she might have been planning to do?"

"No, she didn't. We just made small talk while we were walking." The predator almost added that Hannah had told him about her daughter coming home for the weekend, but he realized that was probably better left out of the equation. He figured he'd already said as much as he should.

"Okay, we'll let you get back to *Jeopardy!*," Detective Madison said, nodding toward the television. "Thank you for your time." She fished a business card out of her pocket and handed it to him. "If you think of anything else that might be helpful, please give me a call."

The predator took the card and looked at it, then said, "I will." He wondered if he should say anything more. He shook his head and added, "I still can't believe she would do something like that. But…thanks for letting me know." He hoped he sounded sincere.

"Thanks again," Detective Madison said, and she and Detective Jarrett stepped out through the front door and returned to their vehicle.

The predator closed the heavy front door behind them and blew out a long breath. *Well played,* he told himself.

"WHAT DO YOU THINK?" Detective Jarrett had the air conditioning running full blast again and Detective Madison had to raise her voice to be heard above the blower.

"I think we need to wait for the autopsy results," she said.

CHAPTER 16

ON THE TUESDAY AFTERNOON following Hannah Wilkinson's death, I attended her funeral.

It was held at 2 p.m. at a large funeral home on Hickman Road on the north side of Des Moines. The funeral home is a large tan brick structure with a circular driveway in front to accommodate hearses and funeral processions, and over the years I've attended several memorial services there. One of those was for the founder and original publisher and editor of my magazine.

On the Saturday before the funeral Craig Wilkinson had called and asked me to serve as a pallbearer. That's not the kind of request you can refuse, and it's something I've done several times previously, usually for friends or family members. But this was the first time I'd been a pallbearer for a person whose body I'd discovered.

Two of the other pallbearers were men I recognized from the lake. One was a fellow named Tim Sullivan, a retired short-order cook who was a few years older than me. Tim was well known to everyone at the lake; so well-known, in fact, that we regulars had nicknamed him the Mayor of Maffitt. A slim man with a wiry build, he walked at the lake every day no matter what the weather was like.

He also had made himself something of an unofficial caretaker of the place, picking up litter and tidying up the parking areas, removing fallen branches from the trails, even repainting the white posts surrounding the little cemetery at the entrance to the park. Everyone liked Tim and he in turn always had a cheery word for anyone he encountered…more than a word actually, as he was always willing to stop for a few minutes and "visit," as he called it.

I didn't know the other man from the lake nearly as well. I knew his first name was Greg because we'd run into each other and spoken briefly a few times, but not until I saw his name in the funeral program, along with mine and those of the other pallbearers, did I learn his last name was Fletcher. We nodded at each other, and I guessed Craig Wilkinson had probably also contacted him because he'd been another friend of Hannah's.

The other three pallbearers were men I didn't know, and I assumed they were either relatives or friends of the family. I was relieved to see I wasn't the only one not wearing a suit or sport coat; the temperature was in the 90s again and I'd opted for a pair of khakis and a light blue, short-sleeved oxford shirt. I was wearing a tie and so were the others, but none of us wore jackets.

Most of the other men in attendance were dressed similarly, although Craig Wilkinson was wearing a lightweight navy suit that I guessed was probably some of his lawyer garb. Most of the women were in slacks and blouses or sundresses. Jessica Wilkinson wore a pale blue sundress with white sandals and was accompanied by Maisie. I smiled when I saw the golden, who looked like she'd just come from the groomer, pacing sedately on leash at Jessica's side, and when I looked around I saw others smiling also. No one seemed bothered or surprised to see Maisie with Jessica.

I also couldn't help noticing—again—how much Jessica resembled her mother.

Hannah's death had been ruled a suicide. Except for some slight bruising around one ankle, which was thought to have perhaps been caused by the ankle weights she sometimes wore when walking—her daughter had supplied this information to the police—the autopsy had revealed nothing out of the ordinary. Hannah had not been physically or sexually assaulted and there was no evidence of foul play.

I knew this because, despite Daryl Nelson's recommendation that I let the matter go, my curiosity had gotten the best of me, and on Monday I had called Detective Madison. I identified myself and she had been surprisingly forthcoming, maybe because the investigation had already been concluded, based on the autopsy results. As there was no evidence of a crime, there was apparently no reason not to share the findings.

Still, after talking with Detective Madison I wondered briefly if I might have implicated myself in any way by continuing to show interest in the case. But I decided I hadn't because, again, the investigation was not ongoing, and the detective gave no indication that anything further would be done. Also, as the person who had discovered and reported Hannah's body, it seemed only natural that I might be curious regarding the outcome of the investigation. Or at least, that's what I told myself.

The funeral was an open casket service, and the minister did a nice job of skirting the whole issue of Hannah's suicide. During the eulogy he made one or two references to a troubled soul but otherwise managed to avoid mentioning anything specifically related to her death. Of course, there were also a couple "taken from us too soon" remarks but for once these didn't strike me as particularly cliché; the Hannah Wilkinson I'd known, if only casually, had been a vibrant person who, one supposed, still had many years to live.

I did have one bad moment, however.

After the final prayer at the end of the service, Jessica and her father and other family members remained seated at the front of the room while the rest of the mourners filed out. I gathered with the other pallbearers at the back of the room, waiting for the family to go forward to Hannah's casket to pay their last respects and say goodbye. After the family did so and left to go outside to their waiting vehicles, the funeral director would close Hannah's casket and we would then carry it to the hearse.

I watched as Jessica went forward to her mother's casket. She still held Maisie's lead and as they reached the casket, Maisie reared on her hind legs and placed her forepaws on the edge of the casket. Jessica made no effort to force her back down, and even from the back of the room I could hear Maisie's whine. Then she lowered her head and gently rested it on the edge of the casket, between her forepaws.

I had to look away.

Maisie's action had reminded me of the well-known

painting by Sir Edwin Landseer titled *The Old Shepherd's Chief Mourner*. Completed in 1837 and now hanging in the Victoria and Albert Museum in London, the painting shows an old-type black and tan farm collie sitting next to a plain wooden coffin over which is draped a white blanket or robe. No one else is in the room, and the shepherd's tam-o-shanter and crook are lying on the floor near the casket, with a Bible on the small table just above them. A folded pair of eyeglasses lie atop the Bible.

The dog is sitting as close as possible to the coffin, even leaning on it, and the dog's muzzle is resting on the coffin's edge. There is, at least to my eye, such an expression of loss and loneliness on the dog's face that looking at the painting never fails to put a lump in my throat. Call that anthropomorphic if you will, but I can't help empathizing deeply with the dog's sense of loss—and the painting's suggestion that the old shepherd was apparently mourned by few others.

Although I'd never seen the original painting—that was an item still to be checked off my bucket list—I'd seen reprints of it many times in various dog books and online, and it never failed to move me. Seeing Maisie adopt a similar pose at Hannah's casket just now was a too-poignant reminder of the loss and the grief she and Hannah's family must now be feeling.

As were her friends.

WHILE WAITING FOR THE FAMILY to leave, I glanced around at my fellow pallbearers and noticed that two of them had loosened their ties and unbuttoned their collars. I was tempted to do the same—even though the funeral home was air conditioned, the open front doors were letting in the sweltering heat from outside—but I decided I'd wait until we'd carried Hannah's casket to the hearse and I had returned to my own vehicle. Burial would be at Sunset Memorial Gardens on the south side of Des Moines, which meant we would be making a long, cross-town procession. I estimated it would take at least a half hour to reach the cemetery and I figured I would be running the AC in the Equinox on high for most of the way.

The family was now coming back up the aisle toward us. Jessica walked with her right arm linked through her father's and she held Maisie's leash with her left hand. Maisie continued to pace quietly at Jessica's side, reflecting the solemnity of the occasion.

As the group came abreast of us, Jessica glanced my way and her eyes met mine. She gave me a brief, wan smile and then, looking past me, her smile momentarily turned into a frown. She quickly averted her eyes and focused straight ahead, but there was no mistaking that she'd frowned at someone among the group of pallbearers.

I resisted the urge to turn and try to determine who it was. But I was certain of what I'd seen and my first thought was, *what the hell?*

CHAPTER 17

I SPENT MOST OF THE 40-MINUTE cross-town procession to the cemetery wondering what, or rather, who, had caused Jessica Wilkinson to frown so suddenly and unexpectedly as she and her family were leaving the funeral home.

There was no doubt in my mind that someone had triggered that reaction. Jessica had smiled at me so I didn't think I was the cause. But her frown had occurred so spontaneously, followed instantly by her eye-shift away from us pallbearers, that there was no doubt in my mind she was reacting viscerally to one of us. There was no mistaking her expression, fleeting though it had been. A frown, coupled with more than a touch of animosity.

Again, I thought, *what the hell?*

The procession to Sunset Memorial Gardens was led by two DMPD squad cars, and they kept the pace slowed to about ten miles below the speed limit. I'd loosened my tie and unbuttoned my collar as soon as I climbed into the Equinox, and I was running the AC on high, just as I'd planned. The ungracious thought crossed my mind that Craig Wilkinson could have chosen a cemetery closer to the funeral home, or vice versa, but maybe that hadn't been an option. I guessed that given the unexpected nature of Hannah's death, arrangements had probably, of necessity, been made hastily.

I was still pondering the cause of Jessica's frown when we arrived at the entrance to Sunset Memorial Gardens, marked by a granite and bronze crypt with a large cross on top and a sculpture of an open Bible inscribed with the Lord's Prayer, on the front side facing Fleur Drive. But as we turned into the cemetery, I put those thoughts aside and concentrated on not rear-ending the slow moving vehicle ahead of me.

The squad cars had pulled aside at the entrance and now, led by the hearse, the procession followed the roadway through the cemetery and down a slight hillside to where a small open-sided tent was set up next to the new grave. Under the tent were three rows of folding chairs for family members and close friends.

I parked along the roadside and took a moment to button my collar and snug up my tie before I turned off the Equinox's ignition. I waited another moment, savoring the coolness of the vehicle, before opening the door and stepping out into the blistering afternoon heat. I hoped, again somewhat ungraciously, that the minister would keep his graveside remarks brief.

THE PREDATOR WAS SWEATING.

He told himself it was primarily due to the afternoon's oppressive heat, but with the air conditioner in his vehicle running full blast, he knew there was another reason.

He'd seen Hannah's daughter, Jessica, frown at him as she and her family had left the funeral home. It was only for an instant, but he knew—*knew*—in his gut that her frown had been directed at him.

She'd quickly looked away. But even as she did so, he'd instinctively taken a half-step back so his face was partially hidden by the man standing in front of him, a guy he knew from the lake.

They'd spoken a few times out there and the predator knew the guy's name was Rob. He appeared to be in his sixties and he always walked with a big wiry-coated dog. The dog's name was Preacher—a stupid name for a dog, the predator thought—and he'd seen in the funeral program that the guy's last name was Vance.

The predator guessed Vance had been another friend of Hannah's, although he didn't remember ever seeing the two of them together. Another one of the pallbearers was an older guy named Tim Sullivan, and the predator knew he was a friend of Hannah's also…everyone at the lake was a friend of Tim's so it didn't surprise the predator to see him serving as a pallbearer.

He replayed the scene in the funeral home several times during the drive to the cemetery. He regretted stepping back when Jessica had frowned at him, fearing she might have construed his action as an admission of guilt. But he told himself there was no possible way Jessica could have known what had happened at the lake on the previous Wednesday evening.

He knew Hannah's death had been ruled a suicide, and he was confident the story he had told the police, that at her request he had left her alone at the big boulder below the pines, had held up. The cops hadn't contacted him again, so he believed he was in the clear. And as such, there was no reason for Jessica to suspect him of any wrongdoing.

Still, her frown had caught him off guard and he'd reacted involuntarily. He should have been more alert and better prepared, but he was already feeling unnerved—Jessica's resemblance to her mother was so uncanny that he'd been almost startled when he first saw her at the funeral home. Luckily she'd not noticed him as she entered the building with Maisie and her father, and he'd studied her surreptitiously throughout the service.

The funeral procession was now coming up on the entrance to the cemetery and the predator told himself to get a grip, that in just a short while he'd be done with all of this. He only had to help carry Hannah's casket from the back of the hearse to the grave, then stand by while the minister made a few closing remarks.

The predator hoped those remarks would be brief.

I GOT MY WISH.

I didn't think to glance at my watch after we positioned Hannah's casket on the frame above the open grave, but I'd guess the minister's remarks and final prayer took no more than ten minutes. Even so, I'll admit my mind wandered during those few minutes, chasing one random thought after another, and I registered very little of what he said.

Along with the other pallbearers, I stood at the back of the tent behind the rows of seated mourners. While it was still unbearably hot, we were at least in the shade, which made it slightly more tolerable. The minister had to know that everyone was wilting in the heat, and he kept things mercifully brief.

The family was seated in the first row of chairs, with Maisie lying quietly at Jessica's feet. She was panting but otherwise appeared at ease, and I couldn't help thinking again that she somehow appreciated the gravity of the occasion. I also wondered how she was going to adjust to her new circumstances now that Hannah would no longer be taking her for a daily walk at the lake. As a large, active sporting dog, she required a fair amount of exercise, and I hoped Craig and Jessica would be able to provide it.

I glanced around at my fellow pallbearers, still wondering which one of them had triggered Jessica's frown. I was beginning to realize now that I might be making too much of the whole matter; it was possible that Jessica had just had a sudden unhappy thought—not at all unlikely given the circumstances—and her frown hadn't really been directed at anyone. Maybe after smiling at me, she'd remembered that I was the one who'd found her mother's body, and that had brought a troubling image to mind. Maybe.

I suppressed a sigh and tried to think of something else. A comment made several years earlier by Scott Parsons, a friend and former grade school classmate, popped into my mind. Scott and I had both been pallbearers at the funeral of another classmate's father, and immediately after we'd performed our duties he'd said to me quietly, "Is it my imagination or do those caskets get heavier every year?"

I'd had to stifle a laugh then, and I tried not to smile now. I drew in a deep breath of warm, humid air and looked toward the minister just as he said, "Amen."

The predator didn't linger.

When the minister concluded the final prayer the predator took a quick look around. The other pallbearers were standing on either side of him and as the family members rose from their chairs, some going forward to place a flower on top of the casket, the pallbearers broke ranks and headed back to their vehicles. The predator felt it was safe to do the same but he was careful not to move too quickly.

The two pallbearers he'd recognized from the lake, Tim Sullivan and Rob Vance, were walking side by side a few paces ahead of him and talking quietly but the predator hung back so he wouldn't have to join them. He didn't want to talk to anyone just then.

What he wanted most of all was to get the hell away from the cemetery and this whole business. Earlier he'd been pleased, even amused, by the irony of being asked to be a pallbearer for the woman he'd killed, but that feeling had been replaced by one of…what? Dread, he admitted to himself. Attending and participating in Hannah's funeral had turned out to be a major mind-fuck, something he had never anticipated.

He knew much of this was due to Jessica's resemblance to her mother, and to the frown she'd directed at him at the funeral home. Both had left him shaken, and he struggled now to clear his mind and put his unease to rest.

He hoped he wouldn't see Jessica again anytime soon. Or for that matter, ever again.

CHAPTER 18

TWO DAYS AFTER HANNAH'S funeral, I learned that Jessica Wilkinson still refused to accept that her mother had committed suicide.

I hadn't had a chance to say more than a few words to Jessica at the funeral and none at the brief graveside service afterwards, but two days later, and exactly one week after I had discovered Hannah's body, I ran into Jessica walking Maisie through the park on the east side of the lake.

Once again I was momentarily surprised when I first saw her, still somewhat amazed by how much she resembled her mother. But after greeting each other and sharing a laugh as Preacher and Maisie began a frolic punctuated with lots of mock growls, we ended up walking together.

I told her to call me Rob instead of Mr. Vance and although she was initially somewhat reticent, she eventually opened up about a number of things. I wondered if perhaps she had been looking for an opportunity to confide in someone besides her father.

She told me that she was dropping out of her summer classes at UNI so she could stay at home and care for Maisie and also help her dad settle her mother's estate. She said he had tried to talk her out of dropping her classes but she had insisted, saying she wouldn't have been able to concentrate on her studies until she knew everything was taken care of at home.

Knowing her parents had been in the process of divorcing, I didn't probe for details, but I wondered if Craig Wilkinson was going to give up his downtown apartment and move back into the big house in River Oaks. Jessica didn't say and I didn't ask, figuring it best to tread lightly.

We followed the roadway as it wound through the park under the massive oaks. The morning was overcast; it had rained about an hour earlier, which had cooled things down and freshened the air. Jessica was wearing shorts, Nikes and a lightweight gray hoody, and she had her blonde hair pulled back in a ponytail. The dogs ranged ahead of us investigating interesting scents and watching for any squirrels on the ground that were asking to be chased.

We'd been walking in silence for a couple minutes, and I was reflecting on the irony of how I'd walked this same route with Hannah only a week and half earlier, when Jessica suddenly said, "Mr. Vance…Rob…I know my mother didn't kill herself." There was a catch in her voice as she said this and I winced slightly, wondering how I should respond. I didn't want to dispute Jessica's assertion but neither did I want to engage in a lot of fruitless speculation.

"Why do you think that?" I replied, the best I could do off the cuff. I hoped I didn't sound too doubtful or patronizing.

"Because I talked to her last Wednesday evening just before she went to the lake," Jessica said. "I called her to tell her I was coming home for the weekend. She was excited about us getting together." She hesitated, then added, "I know she's been lonely in that big house since Dad moved out."

"You talked to her just before she left for the lake?" I wondered if the police knew this.

"Yes, and like I said, she was excited about me coming home. She didn't sound depressed or anything."

"Did you tell the police this?"

"Yes, but they didn't seem to think it meant anything. The one detective, Jarrett, said something about depressed people doing things impulsively, that it wasn't always possible to predict what someone was going to do if they were suicidal."

The prick, I thought. Detective Jarrett hadn't impressed me when I'd met him at the lake. His partner, Detective Madison, had definitely seemed like the brains of that team, so it didn't surprise me that he would make an insensitive remark to the daughter of a woman who'd just drowned. I shook my head. "Sheesh," I said, for want of anything better.

"I think it's him," Jessica said, confusing me. She sounded like she was making an accusation but aside from acknowledging that he was a jerk, I couldn't imagine why she would be pointing the finger at Jarrett.

"Who?" I asked. "Detective Jarrett? What is it that you think he did?"

"No," Jessica said, shaking her head and sounding a bit impatient. "I think it's that guy Mom walked with Wednesday evening. Greg Fletcher. I think he killed her."

"Whoa," I said. "You're getting way ahead of me. I don't know anything about that. Your mom walking with someone that night, I mean."

"The police checked out her phone. They found texts from this Greg guy. He and Mom were supposed to meet at the lake at seven to walk. The police questioned him about it and he said he'd met Mom and they walked back to the big rock by the pine grove." She hesitated, then added, "The place where you found her. He said she asked him to leave her then, that she needed some time to herself. He says he left her there and went home. But I think he's lying. I think he killed her."

I couldn't help thinking Jessica was grasping at straws, but I couldn't tell her that or I'd risk sounding as insensitive as Detective Jarrett. I wanted to be supportive but I didn't want to feed an unfounded theory. Still, I couldn't deny that I'd also initially thought Hannah might have been murdered. I remembered that after I found her and carried her ashore, I'd wondered if I had compromised a crime scene.

I also realized that I knew the Greg she was talking about, although not well. We'd met a few times at the lake and exchanged greetings, but we'd never talked at length. He'd seemed like a decent sort, a little on the shy or unassuming side, and he'd petted Preacher a time or two, so he obviously liked dogs, or at least wasn't put off by them. He appeared to be in his early forties but beyond that, there was nothing really distinctive about him.

I also suddenly remembered that he'd served as one of Hannah's pallbearers. But I hadn't known anything at the time about him meeting Hannah at the lake and walking with her on the night she had died.

I realized Jessica was waiting for me to say something. "I think I know who you're talking about," I said. "This

Greg…he was one of your mother's pallbearers, right?" As I said this I also realized that I now knew who Jessica had frowned at as she and her family had left the funeral home.

"That's right, Greg Fletcher," Jessica said. "And I wasn't happy about him being a pallbearer. Dad said he wanted some of her friends from the lake to be included in the service because he knew how well-liked Mom was. I was already starting to suspect Greg so I said I didn't want him to be a pallbearer, but when Dad asked me why, I didn't tell him what I was thinking…I mean, I don't have any proof—not yet, anyway—so I just said okay, he could be one of the pallbearers. We were kinda scrambling to make the arrangements and I didn't want to give Dad a hard time or make things more difficult for him."

I smiled. "That was considerate of you."

"Yeah, well, I really didn't like the idea of Mom being carried to her final rest by the guy who killed her, but like I said, I don't have any real proof yet, besides the fact that he was the last person to see her alive. And the cops apparently don't think that's worth exploring."

I hesitated before asking the obvious 64,000-dollar question. But Jessica said nothing further so after a moment I said, "If you're convinced he killed your mother and the police aren't going to look into that, what are you thinking of doing about it?" I was afraid of what her answer was going to be.

Jessica confirmed my fear. "I'm going to find a way to prove it," she said. "Even if I have to get close to him to do it."

CHAPTER 19

I hesitated a moment, trying to think of how to respond. Again, I didn't want to sound patronizing—or encouraging—but I felt like I had to acknowledge Jessica's assertion. So I asked the obvious question: "How are you planning to do that?"

"Well, for starters, I'm hoping to run into him out here," she said, replying so immediately that I knew she'd already given this plenty of thought. "I know he walks out here quite a bit. Mom mentioned him to me a time or two, that they'd walked together, and like I said, I'm dropping my classes to stay home and help Dad get everything settled. I'll be walking Maisie out here every day, probably in the morning and again in the evening, so I'm guessing I'll see him sooner or later."

"And then what are you going to do?"

"I'll try to strike up a conversation. With any luck maybe we'll start walking together, like he did with Mom, and that will give me a chance to get him talking. I'm hoping he'll let something slip, maybe something I could take back to the police."

This sounded a little naïve to me, and not likely to be a successful strategy, but I didn't doubt her determination. I myself had originally thought Hannah might have been killed, so I could hardly fault Jessica for wanting to pursue this. Especially since she was convinced her mother hadn't committed suicide.

"That could be risky," I said. "I mean, if he did do what you think, his guard will be up. He's probably going to be extra careful about what he says to anyone, especially you." I realized even as I said this that it sounded like I'd already bought into her theory, or at least thought it was plausible.

"I know that. And I'm planning to be careful. But I'm afraid I may have already blown it."

"How so?"

"Well, I told you I didn't want him to be a pallbearer. But as we were leaving the funeral home I saw him standing with the rest of you and before I could stop myself I gave him kind of a dirty look…frowned at him, anyway. I looked away right away but I'm sure he saw me."

So did I, I thought. "You're sure of that…that he saw you?" I asked.

"Yes, because he took a half-step back like he didn't want to be seen…he was kinda hiding behind you, in fact."

I nodded. "Okay, so you think you may have tipped your hand?"

"That's what I'm afraid of."

"Well, like I said, trying to get close to him could be risky. Especially if he's already onto the fact that you think he killed your mother. He'll probably go out of his way to avoid any contact with you, would be my guess."

"I know that, but I can't come up with any other ideas. And I can't just let this go; can't just tell myself that Mom killed herself and I should accept that. Not when I know she didn't."

We were headed into a very sensitive area here and I knew I had to be careful. "I know you're convinced of that," I said, "but the police and the medical examiner couldn't find any evidence of wrongdoing. Is it possible…" *God help me here*, I thought, "that you're wrong?"

"No. I'm not wrong. Like I said, I'd just talked to her and she was excited about seeing me that weekend. And I don't care what that a-hole detective said, my mom wasn't the impulsive type. Or suicidal. She just…wasn't."

I sighed. "I'll admit, she didn't strike me as that type, either," I said, once again realizing I probably sounded a little more supportive than I intended. But what the hell; I also couldn't help wanting to give Jessica the benefit of the doubt. "I didn't know her all that well, only from walking with her occasionally out here, but I don't recall her ever seeming moody or depressed. She was always pretty upbeat and outgoing, actually."

"That was Mom. Which is why I know she didn't do what they said."

We made the loop at the far end of the roadway and started back toward our vehicles, both parked by the wooden restroom building just inside the park entrance. Preacher was still ranging ahead of us but Maisie had dropped back and was walking alongside Jessica.

"Besides the fact that he was apparently the last person to see your mom alive, is there anything else that makes you think this Greg guy is guilty?"

"You mean, besides the fact that he's a creep?"

Her answer triggered a quick laugh. "Why do you say that?" I asked.

"He kept looking at me during the funeral. He didn't think I noticed, but I did. I caught him at it several times. And even when I wasn't looking at him, I could feel his eyes on me." She shuddered slightly. "He's one of those guys…I think he's an incel."

"An incel? Really?"

"It stands for involuntary celibate," Jessica said. "It's a guy who wants to have sex with women—actually, incels feel like they're *entitled* to have sex—but they can't find a partner. For one reason or another, incels always strike out with women and that builds resentment. They can't connect and it becomes a vicious cycle. The frustration builds, and that sometimes leads to violence."

I knew what an incel was—I'd heard or read the term a few times—but I wasn't aware that a person so afflicted might resort to violence. That seemed awfully extreme. I figured something like an addiction to online porn was more likely. But then again, I'd never really given it much thought one way or the other. And given the thousands of rapes that occur every year, maybe I was naïve not to suppose incels were capable of violence.

"How often does that happen?" I asked. "I mean, that an incel might become violent?"

"Not often, thank goodness. Most incels tend to be on the shy side, as you might expect. They generally lack confidence around women, which of course is a big part of their problem. So the majority of them aren't likely to do anything violent or rash."

"What about rape?"

"Not very often. Again, the lack of confidence seems to hold them back. In fact, some of them even fantasize about *being* raped."

"What?!" That made no sense to me.

"It's true. Their lack of confidence can lead to them becoming submissive. In other words, because they're not confident, they fantasize about being dominated by a woman who will force them to have sex. That sort of absolves them of having to take the initiative but still might lead to them being…fulfilled."

"Good Lord. Talk about convoluted thinking."

"You got that right. A lot of incels are misogynists as well. They don't really like women; they tend to blame them for their problems, think they're manipulative, and so on. But they still have that sense of entitlement, believing they deserve the sex they're being denied."

"Let me guess," I said. "They have mommy issues."

She laughed briefly. "Yes, some of them do. But that's not always the case. Some of them may just be…unattractive. Overweight, or whatever. If they think they're unattractive—bad self-image, in other words--that leads them to think others feel that way about them also, and again, it shoots down their confidence." She hesitated a moment then added, "There are degrees of involuntary celibacy."

"Degrees?"

"Sure, like any other kind of emotional problem. Some incels may just be shy introverts, the kind who stay at home and watch a lot of TV or videos and fantasize about actresses, say. They're pretty harmless. But others may be really hardcore—sorry about the bad pun—and more prone to the extreme."

"What do you mean by extreme?"

"Oh, stuff like joining online forums and sharing their stories with other incels. They tend to egg each other on, and reinforce each other's negative feelings toward women, that sense of entitlement, and so on. They might even encourage someone to take action, and that's when things could get dangerous or violent, if that person decides to act on their suggestion. It doesn't happen very often, but it does happen. Maybe more than we know."

"You seem to know a lot about this subject," I said. I was still trying to process everything Jessica had just told me. She'd painted a picture of a rather dark world.

She glanced at me and smiled. "I should," she said. "I'm a psych major."

"Really," I said. "How did you happen to choose that?"

She hesitated and she stopped smiling. "It's because of something that happened a few years ago, when I was in high school," she finally said.

I sensed her reluctance to continue, but I went ahead and asked, "What happened?"

"It was when I was a sophomore. One of my classmates, a girl named Jenny Roberts, was the victim of bullying. Cyber-bullying, especially. We weren't really friends, but I knew her; we'd had some classes together. And I knew what was going on. I didn't take part in the bullying, but I didn't do anything to stop it, either."

Oh boy, I thought. *I know this story all too well.*

"And what happened?" I asked quietly. I was pretty sure I already knew the answer.

"She killed herself."

I knew that's what she was going to say. And yes, it was a story I knew all too well.

CHAPTER 20

His name alone—Milton Mulberry—was enough to guarantee he'd be targeted by bullies.

Why any parents with the last name Mulberry, or parents with any other last name, for that matter, would choose to name their son Milton was one of those mysteries that would forever defy explanation. Maybe Milton was a family name, handed down through the generations, and his parents had felt compelled to continue the tradition.

Or maybe—even more unlikely—they both held PhDs in English lit and wanted to honor the author of *Paradise Lost.* Even so, wonky academic credentials notwithstanding, you'd think they would have to have known they were setting their son up for torment.

I first met Milton in eighth grade.

We lived in one of Chicago's northwest suburbs at the time. It was the late 1960s and what is now called middle school was then called junior high. The school I attended was named for a Native American tribe, as were most of the other schools in that district. Political correctness had yet to rear its head, at least in our conservative town, and no one gave a second thought to the school names.

There were ten or twelve homeroom classes in the school's eighth grade, and Milton was in mine. Quite honestly, I never paid much attention to him, one way or the other. He was on the quiet side, and while most of us guys were into James Bond and *The Man from U.N.C.L.E.* and the Rolling Stones and the Yardbirds and after-school pickup games of football and basketball, Milton was a devoted fan of the *Batman* TV show, starring Adam West. He didn't seem to realize the show was high camp and not intended to be taken seriously, and he invited further harassment and ridicule by decorating his notebooks with bat stickers.

Whether Milton fantasized about being a superhero with

a secret identity, I couldn't say. If so, it would have been quite a stretch, but then, aren't most fantasies? Milton wasn't particularly effeminate, but he was overweight and not the least bit athletic. He was always the last kid to be chosen for a team because neither side wanted him dragging them down. In fact, he usually wasn't chosen at all, but just taken by whichever team had the misfortune to have last pick. They got stuck with him.

Despite his lack of athleticism, Milton might have been able to sail along under radar relatively unscathed if it weren't for his name, and the fact that our homeroom class had not one but three bullies. It's one of those cruel universal truths that bullies are always on the lookout for a target, and they quickly homed in on Milton and made his life hell.

Their names were Dick Sorensen, Russell Wheeler and Bill Olson. Sorensen was the leader of the trio and usually initiated things, but Wheeler and Olson were quick to follow up and contribute their share of torment.

The torment took a variety of forms. One of the most frequent was dumping Milton's books as we moved from one classroom to another. When doing so, most of us carried our books in one hand, propped against our hip. Everyone got their books dumped occasionally; it was considered a fairly harmless prank if a teacher didn't catch you, but it happened to Milton almost daily. It was an easy matter for Sorensen, Wheeler or Olson—they took turns—to come up behind him, grab the top of his books and yank sharply downward.

Unless Milton was quick enough to tighten his grip and prevent the spill—and he usually wasn't—the books hit the floor. Sorensen was especially adept at performing a drop kick on the books just as they landed, sending them flying in all directions. If Milton was carrying a notebook along with his textbooks, the kick was sometimes enough to pop open the notebook and scatter his papers, including any homework assignments, all over the hallway.

Milton would have to scramble to pick up his books and his papers and oftentimes that made him late to class. The teachers would censure him and sometimes assign him to detention but Milton never made an excuse for his tardiness and never ratted out the perpetrators. Maybe this was because he feared further reprisal, or maybe it was because it just wasn't in his nature to be a tattletale. Possibly it was a combination of both, but whatever the reason, Milton kept his mouth shut.

This might have worked in his favor, earning him a reputation as a stand-up guy, but there were too many other factors, including his name, conspiring against him. Not surprisingly, he tried to go by the nickname Milt, but when we learned in biology class that the fertilizing agent secreted by male fish was called milt, that was enough to earn him the nickname Fish Sperm, abbreviated FS and soon pronounced "Effs." The nickname stayed with him for the remainder of the year.

I saw a lot less of Milton when we got to high school. Our class had more than 800 students and the entire student body numbered a little over 3,000, so unless you were one of the elites—called rah-rahs by those of us in the middle of the pack—it was relatively easy to maintain a low profile and get lost in the crowd. By the time we were sophomores Milton had grown several inches taller, so he wasn't quite the same hapless, pudgy kid he'd been in eighth grade. But he still attracted the attention of bullies, and now there were more of them.

Besides Dick Sorensen, Russell Wheeler and Bill Olson, our class had a couple of "bad boys" named Art Merino and Dennis Maitland, both of whom had been held back a grade. And when we were juniors, it was Milton's supreme misfortune to wind up in second hour P.E. class with four of those five guys—Sorensen, Olson, Merino and Maitland. Only Wheeler was missing.

I was also in that class.

The bullying began almost immediately that fall. Sorensen and Olson quickly resurrected Milton's eighth grade nickname and in a very few days almost everyone in the class was calling him Effs. Even the instructor, Coach Morton, picked up on this and called him Effs, although the coach had no clue as to the name's origin.

This was long before the days of cyber-bullying; the internet and social media were still decades in the future, and Milton might have survived the name-calling…in fact, he more or less went along with it, smiling in a half-hearted way when he heard it, perhaps hoping to deflect anything further by pretending to be a good sport.

But then things took a more physical—read, violent—turn.

Egging each other on, the quartet of Sorensen, Olson, Merino and Maitland soon began using Milton as a punching bag in the locker room. As he was changing from street clothes into gym shorts and a reversible t-shirt bearing the school's logo, they would surround him and start pounding away. They were careful to confine their blows to Milton's shoulders and abdomen and never struck his face—they didn't hit him anywhere that would leave an incriminating mark that would be noticed by teachers or the coach and lead to questions.

Milton would attempt to fend them off as best he could; occasionally he'd go so far as to angrily tell them to leave him the hell alone, which usually just provoked them further. But he never actually struck back at them. Maybe he realized it would be futile and might goad them to even more punishment. And, just as in eighth grade, he never reported their actions to anyone on the faculty.

The rest of us kept our distance while this was going on and pretended not to notice what was happening, thankful we weren't on the receiving end of the beatings, especially those meted out by Maitland and Merino, who were bigger and stronger than Sorensen and Olson. Luckily for Milton, the slugfest usually lasted no more than a minute or two until the coach's whistle summoned us out into the gymnasium for calisthenics.

After a few weeks of this, Milton's tormenters tired of the game. They began to ease up on the beating, maybe just giving him a shot or two on the arm in passing on their way out of the locker room. They still called him Effs—by that point, we all did—but otherwise they left him more or less alone, and

Milton relaxed his guard.

Big mistake.

The torment began again when Maitland and Merino started snapping their towels at the rest of us as we were exiting the showers at the end of class. One of them had discovered that getting a corner of the towel soaking wet made it pop even harder, and they soon became adept at snapping their towels with the proficiency of bullwhips.

Sorensen and Olson were quick to join in. At first they weren't selective about their targets, and all of us got our asses snapped a time or two. They were able to get away with this because the coach seldom monitored the activity in the locker room, and most of us soon learned how to dodge the towels or, if we were feeling especially bold and were fast enough, to grab the towel as it was coming our way. Because everyone was generally hurrying to get dressed and make it to the next class on time, catching the towel or dodging it was usually enough to prevent any follow-up or retaliation from the four. They simply laughed and chose another target.

Then they began zeroing in on Milton.

The first few times they simply surrounded him in the shower. One snap apiece, a lot of laughter from the four, then they let Milton leave the shower and go to his locker and get dressed.

But it quickly escalated. One snap apiece quickly became two or more as Sorensen, Olson, Maitland and Merino fell into a pattern of rotation, taking turns so that Milton was continually being snapped by one or two of them as the others were readying their towels for another snap. They'd corner him and keep it up until Milton's thighs and buttocks were a mass of red welts.

Once again, Milton managed to get through these assaults without an outcry. He'd wince at the pain and maybe grunt a time or two, but he generally stuck it out for the few minutes it lasted until the four of them quit to go to their lockers and dress. At that point, Milton would pull himself together, hurry to his own locker and get dressed. He usually made it to his next class in time, but often just barely.

Then came the day that Milton caught Maitland's towel in mid-snap and gave it a sharp yank.

The move caught Maitland, and all of us watching, totally by surprise. No one expected Milton to do anything other than cower and put up with the snapping, as he'd always done previously. But for whatever reason he'd finally reached the breaking point. Milton retaliated.

Having caught the towel, Milton yanked it, hard. And because Maitland was standing barefoot (and naked) on the shower room's slick tile floor, Milton's action caused Maitland to lose his balance and fall. In fact, it was more than a fall, a cartwheeling crash actually.

We were all too surprised to do anything except stand there and stare as Maitland, after lying stunned for a few seconds, struggled to get back to his feet. Knowing him for the badass he was, none of us dared to laugh at his spectacular pratfall.

And Milton? He too stood there silently. Then, with something of a shrug and perhaps the ghost of a smile, he simply dropped Maitland's towel and turned away.

That was his biggest mistake.

Certainly none of us faulted him for finally standing up to one of his tormenters. In fact, we were silently cheering his actions. But by contemptuously turning his back on Maitland, Milton left himself wide open to a follow-up attack.

Which was almost immediate in coming.

Maitland finally managed to scramble to his feet on the slick tile floor. He howled with outrage—there's no other way to describe it—and launched himself at Milton's back. With his arms crossed in front of him, he clipped Milton right below the shoulder blades and sent him sprawling.

Then Maitland proceeded to beat the living shit out of him.

Milton managed to get to his hands and knees before Maitland began raining blows on him. He didn't limit himself to Milton's shoulders and arms but pounded on his head and back. He landed several blows on Milton's kidneys and Milton sank to the floor, gasping. Had it not been for the fact that

Maitland was barefoot—we were all naked in the shower—and trying to retain his balance on the slippery floor, I had no doubt he would have begun kicking Milton as well.

But he came up with something worse.

With a whoop, he grabbed his cock and stepped forward. Then he proceeded to piss all over Milton's back. And Milton, apparently beaten too badly to resist or even move, simply laid there. After a few seconds he turned his head toward the group of us who were still standing and watching but were too stunned or frightened to intervene. He looked up at us and for just a moment his eyes locked on mine.

I saw something in his look that was imploring, almost beseeching. But it was quickly replaced by bitter resignation, the realization that no one was going to help him.

To my everlasting shame, I did nothing.

After a few seconds Maitland finished urinating, and it was then that Sorensen and Merino stepped forward and caught him by the arms. "C'mon," Merino said. "That's enough." And Maitland, his rage apparently sated, backed away.

The rest of us quickly turned away as well. We grabbed towels and headed for our lockers, leaving Milton lying on the shower floor.

Two nights later Milton stepped in front of a rushing Chicago Northwestern commuter train and was killed instantly.

This happened on a Friday night. Milton's death made the weekend news in our suburb and on Monday morning a special assembly was held at our high school. The principal and one of the guidance counselors spoke about Milton's tragic death, although by then we all knew about it, and they said that any student who wished to attend his funeral, which was to be held on Wednesday afternoon, would be excused from class.

Only a handful of students attended his funeral. I did not, although I considered doing so. I convinced myself that because Milton and I had not really been friends, my attendance was not necessary.

But I knew the real reason I skipped the funeral was the guilt I was feeling. I kept seeing Milton on the shower room floor, and the look he gave me. I should have done something, I kept telling myself, and for weeks afterward I was haunted by this.

Eventually, of course, those feelings diminished, although they never completely left me. Years later, at our class's ten-year reunion party, I would learn that Dennis Maitland had been killed in Vietnam, and I suppose I felt that to some degree Milton had been vindicated.

But I never felt absolved myself. I could have done something that day in the locker room, but I hadn't.

CHAPTER 21

"ROB? MR. VANCE?"

We were coming up to our vehicles and I realized I'd fallen silent for a minute or so, thinking of Milton Mulberry. Jessica's comment about her classmate's suicide had reawakened some painful memories, which I now tried to shake off.

"Sorry," I said. "My mind wandered for a moment." I attempted a laugh. "Happens every so often when you get to be my age." I wasn't going to share Milton's story with Jessica. She had enough trauma in her life at the moment without my burdening her further with something from my distant past. "But I'm sorry about your classmate…you said her name was Jenny?" Maybe with a bit of damage control I could convince Jessica I wasn't a totally befuddled old geezer.

"That's right, Jenny Roberts. She died when we were sophomores. And like I said, that's what made me decide to major in psych. I want to work with teenagers and hopefully help them if they're dealing with the same issues."

I smiled at her. "Admirable choice," I said. "I'm sure you'll be good at it."

"Well, I hope so," she said as we stopped beside our vehicles. "In the meantime, thanks for walking with me and letting me unload on you about Greg Fletcher." She hesitated, giving me a long look. Then: "Do you think I'm crazy for pursuing this, trying to prove that he killed Mom?"

I smiled and shook my head. "Not crazy," I said. "But it's not going to be easy, and like I said earlier, I think you need to be very careful." I hesitated, then added, "I can't say I really approve of what you're doing, but I understand why you think you need to do it." Once again, I hoped she wouldn't mistake this last for an endorsement of her plan.

"Okay," she said. "Thanks. And…I'll probably see you out here again sometime."

"I look forward to it," I said.

She turned toward her mother's Explorer and thumbed her key fob to unlock it. She opened the passenger door. "C'mon, Maisie," she said, and the golden jumped up into the passenger seat. I remembered that Hannah had usually made Maisie ride in the cargo space under the hatch, but apparently Jessica accorded Maisie front seat privileges, as I sometimes did with Preacher.

Jessica closed the door and turned back to me. "Bye," she said, smiling again, and I nodded and said "Bye" in return.

I'd seen that same smile a number of times previously. It was Hannah Wilkinson's.

As I was driving home on Highway 5, the four-lane bypass that skirts the south side of Des Moines, my mind seemed to split and go off in two directions.

One part followed my usual practice of replaying the conversation I'd just had, weighing Jessica's comments and my responses. Despite my own uncertainties about Hannah's death, I still doubted that Jessica would be able to come up with any real proof that Greg Fletcher had killed her mother. I also couldn't help being concerned—okay, worried—about the risk Jessica might be taking by attempting to get close to Fletcher; especially if her suspicions about him were correct.

My second train of thought went back to Milton Mulberry. Having reawakened those memories—memories that were more than fifty years old, I realized—now I couldn't seem to push them back into their dusty file drawer. The image I kept returning to was that final scene in the locker room, the day Dennis Maitland lost all semblance of control and beat Milton so unmercifully, and Milton had sent me one fleeting, imploring look before lowering his head and suffering further humiliation when Maitland began urinating on him.

Remembering that image now, two additional random thoughts came to mind.

The first was something I'd learned in American history class a few months after Milton's death. In early April, on the fourth anniversary of the assassination of Martin Luther King,

Jr., our teacher, Mrs. Kovacs, devoted the hour to a discussion of King's life and his work in the civil rights movement. She gave us all copies of a handout with a number of quotations, including several key passages from his "I Have a Dream" speech. But the quotation that had the greatest impact on me that day wasn't from that speech. It was this:

"Never, never be afraid to do what's right, especially if the well-being of a person or an animal is at stake. Society's punishments are small compared to the wounds we inflict on our soul when we look the other way."

Sitting there in history class, I read those words and felt like they had been aimed directly at me. In Milton Mulberry's moment of extreme need I had indeed looked the other way. And yes, I'd already experienced the self-inflicted wounds to my own soul that King described. The hours I'd spent agonizing over what I might have done—*should* have done— were ample evidence of the spot-on accuracy of his words.

The second random thought, somewhat related, was something I'd seen several years later in a Clint Eastwood movie, *High Plains Drifter*. There has long been some dispute among Eastwood fans regarding who his character is, exactly; but most of us, myself included, believe—spoiler alert!—he is the avenging ghost of U.S. Marshal Jim Duncan, who had been bullwhipped to death one night by three outlaws while the townspeople watched from the shadows…and did nothing to intervene.

The scene is replayed several times throughout the movie in a series of flashbacks. In the last such scene, as Duncan lies dying in the street, he looks up at the townspeople and says through gritted teeth, "Damn you all to hell!" This after appealing to them to help him, to no avail.

Even though Milton had said nothing that day in the locker room, I couldn't help equating his look with that of Jim Duncan's just before he died. I had to wonder if Milton's thoughts at that moment might very well have been the same, damning us all to hell—and perhaps me specifically, for failing to help him.

It was a far-fetched comparison, admittedly, but it felt

valid, nevertheless. I considered it for a moment then shook my head to clear my thinking and focus on my driving. We were nearing our exit from the bypass so I eased up on the accelerator and flipped on the turn signal.

As I did so, a final curious thought intruded. Jessica Wilkinson had said she'd chosen to major in psychology because one of her classmates had been bullied into committing suicide, and Jessica wanted to be able to help other teens in similar straits.

A classmate's suicide causes some of us to become psych majors, I thought.

And some of us it turns into contract killers.

PART TWO: REFUSAL TO BEAR

Some things you must never stop refusing to bear. Injustice and outrage and dishonor and shame. No matter how young you are or how old you have got.

William Faulkner, *Intruder in the Dust*

CHAPTER 22

"You're not going to be able to let this go, are you?" Daryl was smiling as she said this, so I was pretty sure she was making an observation and not chiding me. Well, maybe a little of the latter.

I shifted in my seat—we were sitting at one of the small tables next to the bar in Skip's—and said, "I honestly don't know. I thought I'd be done with it after Hannah's funeral. After the police ruled her death a suicide, I guess I figured that was that. I was *ready* to put it behind me, but then when I talked to Jessica this morning…" I shrugged for want of a more definite answer.

Daryl reached across the table and squeezed my hand. She was wearing another one of her sundresses, this one pale yellow with large white flowers. Her dark hair gleamed in the subdued light of Skip's and her eyes flashed. Do I need to add that she looked lovely?

"I understand," she said. "But if you don't mind my asking, exactly what more do you think you can do at this point?"

"I don't know the answer to that, either. I tried not to sound like I was encouraging Jessica to pursue this theory she has about this Greg Fletcher guy, but I'm afraid she may have misunderstood me. I did warn her a couple of times to be careful."

Daryl nodded. "Well, that was a good thing to do."

"Right. But again, I'm not sure whether it really made an impression. She's determined to get something on him that will prove her mother's death wasn't suicide."

This time Daryl shook her head. "And if she does, then what?"

"I guess she plans to take it back to the cops and hope they'll re-open their investigation."

"That sounds like a real longshot."

"I told her the same thing."

We were interrupted by the arrival of Keri, our favorite server at Skip's, with our salads. "How are you two doing on drinks?" she asked.

"I'm fine for right now," Daryl said. Her glass of chardonnay was still half full.

"I'm ready for another," I said. I was drinking Blue Moon.

"I'll be right back with your Blue Moon, Rob," Keri said. She was a tall blonde and had been our server on our first dinner date some eight months ago. We'd since become regulars and whenever possible, we tried to sit at one of her tables.

As Keri left our table I smiled at Daryl and said, "Sorry. Didn't mean to slug that first one down so fast."

"No problem," she said. "But getting back to what we were saying…what are you going to do about Jessica?"

I shrugged. "Besides talking to her at the lake if I happen to run into her—maybe asking if she's having any luck—I don't know that there's much I can do." I laughed. "I'm not planning to play guardian angel, if that's what you're thinking."

Daryl laughed also. "No, I can't quite see you in that role," she said. "You're not exactly the angelic type."

I thought, *if you only knew.*

JUST AS KERI ARRIVED WITH OUR entrees—seared ahi tuna for Daryl, a medium rare ribeye for me—I glanced toward the doorway and saw a tall, handsome black woman enter, accompanied by another woman, shorter and blonde.

It took me a second to recognize Detective Madison. Although I'd talked to her on my one follow-up phone call, I'd not seen her again since the morning I discovered Hannah's body and she had questioned me at the lake. She was dressed in similar fashion to that morning, gray slacks and a silky blouse. The blonde was wearing khakis and a light blue oxford shirt with the cuffs rolled up a couple of turns. They were met at the door by one of the servers and after exchanging a few words, the server led them to the empty table next to ours.

Oh boy, I thought.

Daryl and I had already moved on from our discussion about Jessica Wilkinson's plan to get evidence against Greg Fletcher. Now, it looked like we might be revisiting the subject…that is, if Detective Madison recognized me and chose to bring up the matter of Hannah's death.

She recognized me, all right. As she and her friend were getting seated, she looked over and smiled. "Well, hello, Mr. Vance," she said.

I nodded and smiled in return. "Detective," I said. I was willing—hoping—to let it go at that. But no such luck.

"Good to see you again," she said. "This is my partner, Beth Palmer." I was a little surprised that she'd volunteered this information—that the woman was her partner, anyway—but apparently she was in a social mood, and not at all averse to letting it be known she was gay.

Beth Palmer wasn't quite so cordial, however. She was already studying her menu but she did glance over at us. She nodded curtly but didn't speak, and I recognized the look she gave me. It was one I'd seen several times before and it said, as plainly as if she'd spoken the words aloud, *you're a man, and that's reason enough for me to despise you.*

I wasn't going to engage. I gave her an innocent smile and said, "Nice to meet you. This is my friend, Daryl Nelson."

Daryl said, "Good evening," smiling also.

"Daryl Nelson?" Detective Madison said. "I read your columns in the *Register*. I always enjoy them."

"Thank you," Daryl said. Beth Palmer had already turned away from us and was again looking at her menu. She obviously had no intention of engaging in chitchat.

Detective Madison took her partner's hint. "Well, I should let you get to your dinner," she said. "Enjoy."

"Thanks," I said and turned toward Daryl, who gave me another smile.

"I told you that you weren't going to be able to let this go," she said impishly.

DARYL HAD NAILED IT. Hannah Wilkinson's death—or its after-effects—seemed to follow me wherever I went. From earlier conversations Daryl knew that Detective Madison was one of the investigators who had questioned me the morning I found Hannah's body. The coincidence of Madison—I still didn't know her first name—and her partner showing up at Skip's and being seated at the table next to ours was almost too ironic.

Yet despite sitting one table away from the detective who'd grilled me that morning, I didn't feel particularly anxious. I had no reason to, really. I reminded myself again that I had nothing to feel guilty about and, Jessica Wilkinson's theory about Greg Fletcher notwithstanding, I still considered the matter closed. Running into Detective Madison was nothing more than a coincidence, another example of that old saying, *Des Moines is just a large small town.*

But of course I couldn't dismiss the matter entirely.

We'd been eating silently for a minute or two when, apropos of nothing, I said quietly, "Let me ask you something."

Daryl looked up from her tuna with a slightly puzzled expression. "Okay," she said.

"Do you think I should say anything to the detective about Jessica Wilkinson? About her plan to try to get close to Greg Fletcher?"

Daryl's brow furrowed slightly and her expression changed from puzzled to thoughtful. She didn't speak for several seconds, then she shook her head and said, "No."

"No?"

"No." She glanced over at their table, then back at me. "There's no real evidence that Greg Fletcher did anything wrong, right?"

"Right."

"Okay, so you'd be pointing the finger at him for no real reason. Basically just repeating Jessica's suspicions, which are really nothing more than gut feelings at this point. You wouldn't quite be bearing false witness against him, but..."

She shrugged and smiled.

I shrugged in return. "I guess you're right. But I thought if I told the detective what Jessica has in mind, she could…I don't know…maybe warn Jessica off? Tell her not to pursue what she's planning to do?"

"Even if Detective Madison did that, and I doubt she would, do you think that would make Jessica stop?"

"No."

"Well, there you go. Like I said, you'd be casting suspicion on Greg Fletcher for no real reason, and it probably wouldn't accomplish anything anyway. Wouldn't make Jessica stop, I mean."

I sighed. "You're right. I'd just be meddling."

"That's right. Besides, didn't the detectives already talk to Greg Fletcher?"

"Yes. He was the last one to see Hannah the night she died. He told them he'd walked with her but she asked him to give her some time to herself, so he left her at the big boulder below the pines." I drew a breath. "Where I found her the next morning."

"And they believed him?"

"Apparently so. Or at least they couldn't prove otherwise."

"Okay, so unless Jessica comes up with something, they're not likely to pursue things any further."

"No, probably not."

"Let it go," Daryl said again. "You've done all you can do."

"You're right," I said. Wishing I could convince myself.

AFTER FINISHING DINNER WE PAUSED next to Detective Madison's table just long enough for me to say, "Good to see you again." Even as I said it I felt somewhat hypocritical. What could be good about seeing a detective whom you'd recently met only because she was investigating the death of one of your friends? But it was the same phrase she'd used earlier, so I figured it was as good a throwaway line as any.

Madison smiled up at us and said, "You too. Nice to meet

you, Daryl."

Daryl returned her smile and said, "Nice to meet you also."

Beth Palmer looked up at us but said nothing.

WHEN I GOT HOME—this being another Thursday night, Daryl and I had parted with our usual hug and kiss in the parking lot at Skip's—I had a phone message from a good friend named Mike Stevenson.

"Hey, Rob, it's Mike," said the recording. "Wondered if you and Preacher would be available to run some honoring drills with Rusty on Saturday morning. We'd need to go fairly early before it gets too hot, but I've got a line on an old strip mine lake where we can shoot over the dogs. Give me a call and let me know."

Talk about just what the doctor ordered. Rusty was Mike's young Labrador retriever and we'd begun working our dogs together in preparation for the upcoming hunting season.

It was just the distraction I needed to get my mind off the matter of Hannah Wilkinson's death.

CHAPTER 23

Greg Fletcher wasn't feeling like a predator.

In fact, he felt more like prey, like he was the one being hunted.

He hated the feeling, even as he recognized it as (probably) baseless paranoia. The story he'd told the cops, that he'd walked with Hannah Wilkinson on the evening of her death but left her alone at the boulder below the pines, had apparently held up. They hadn't contacted him again, and he knew her death had been ruled a suicide. To the best of his knowledge, he was in the clear.

But he couldn't shake the feeling that someone or something was stalking him.

He attributed this, at least in part, to the frown Jessica Wilkinson had directed at him at Hannah's funeral. Something about her expression signaled that she knew the truth.

But, he'd asked himself repeatedly, how could she?

She hadn't seen what had happened, how he'd talked her mother into walking back to the pines, then coaxed her into going for a swim, and…

No, there were no witnesses besides himself (well, except Hannah's dog) to what he had done, so there was no way Jessica could know exactly what had transpired that evening. At best, she could only speculate. And even if she did suspect the truth, he was confident there wasn't anything she could do to prove it.

Still, he couldn't rid himself of his fears.

He tried reminding himself of the passage from *The Call of the Wild* in which Buck feels great pride at having killed Man. But this time recalling that passage gave him no sense of pride or even satisfaction. If anything, it left him feeling more shaken.

Yes, he had killed Hannah, and yes, he'd felt justified in doing so. What he hadn't anticipated, however, were the lingering effects on his own psyche. He'd not expected to feel any guilt or misgivings. Or fear.

That fear was making him extra-cautious, and he tried telling himself that was actually a good thing. He had avoided Maffitt Reservoir for more than a week, partly due to that old saying about criminals always returning to the scene of their crime (he wasn't sure he believed this, but he wasn't taking any chances) and partly because, he admitted to himself, he was afraid of running into Jessica.

He didn't know she would be out there, but he suspected she might, if only to walk Maisie. He had no knowledge of her schedule or activities or whether she had returned to college after Hannah's funeral. He remembered Hannah telling him, on the night of her death, that Jessica was coming home for the weekend. He didn't know how Hannah's death might have altered Jessica's subsequent plans, and he had no way of finding out.

All of which led him to err on the side of caution. Instead of Maffitt Reservoir, he began walking at Ft. Des Moines Park on the southeast side of the city. The park was only a couple minutes from his home in Greenfield Plaza and he could reach it by walking up his street to County Line Road, crossing the road and cutting through the parking lot of Studebaker Elementary School. The back and one side of the school property abutted the park.

The park's actual entrance was located on Southeast Fifth Street but there was no need for Fletcher to drive to it when he lived nearby. Within the last few years the park had undergone a major renovation and now, in addition to a small lake encircled by a hiking trail, there were modern restroom buildings, shelter houses and fishing docks.

The park wasn't nearly as large as Maffitt but he told himself it would suffice for his exercise needs, at least in the short term. Eventually he would return to Maffitt but not until Hannah Wilkinson's death had ceased to be news or gossip fodder among the reservoir's other visitors.

In the meantime, he would go to work at the airport as usual, walk at Ft. Des Moines Park, and otherwise lie low.

He told himself there was no shame in this, and he even managed to find a passage in *The Call of the Wild* that supported his caution. (He preferred thinking of it as caution, not cowardice.) In the chapter titled "The Law of Club of Fang," he read this about Buck: "All his days, no matter what the odds, he had never run from a fight. But the club of the man in the red sweater had beaten into him a more fundamental and primitive code. Civilized, he could have died for a moral consideration, say the defense of Judge Miller's riding whip; but the completeness of his decivilization was now evidenced by his ability to flee from the defense of a moral consideration and so save his hide."

It was that last part, especially, about fleeing and saving his hide, that he found reassuring. There was no sense in putting himself in harm's way unnecessarily. Avoiding Maffitt Reservoir and Jessica Wilkinson and the other regulars just made good sense…it was cunning, even.

But he also knew that, as one of the regulars himself, staying away indefinitely might also attract attention and raise questions. He didn't want to become conspicuous by his absence.

He'd give it another few days, he decided, and then maybe he'd risk a quick trip out there. Just to reconnoiter and, as the expression goes, see which way the wind was blowing.

He knew that generally speaking, predators preferred to hunt into the wind.

CHAPTER 24

MIKE STEVENSON PICKED US UP at six o'clock on Saturday morning. We'd touched base on Friday and he told me that the abandoned strip mine lake he'd located, left over from the surface coal mining that had been done in southern Iowa several decades earlier, was about an hour south of Des Moines.

Mike's a diehard waterfowler and he'd found the lake a couple months earlier when doing some pre-season scouting, looking for more places, preferably off the beaten path, where he could build a blind and place decoys. As he'd said when he told me about the place, duck hunters could never have too many honey holes.

Mike is a few years younger than me and we've been hunting together for nearly twenty years, ever since we'd first run into each other while hunting pheasants at the Neal Smith National Wildlife Refuge near Prairie City, about a half-hour east of Des Moines. We'd struck up a conversation and admired each other's dogs; at the time I had a young female German wirehair named Bristol, Preacher's predecessor, and Mike was hunting with an older black Labrador named Trapper. We had agreed to finish the day's hunt together.

That decision proved fortuitous. We were working one of the refuge's huge switchgrass fields and although Bristol was a wider ranging pointing dog and Trapper a close-working flusher, they'd quickly settled into a nice complementary rhythm. We bagged three roosters in that field—Mike shot two and I got one—and that was enough to seal the deal. We exchanged contact information and we'd been hunting together ever since.

During that time, we'd also both lost the dogs we had on that first hunt.

Trapper died just a few years later, and Mike soon acquired a chocolate Lab puppy he named Beaver. When

Beaver was old enough, we began working him in the field with Bristol in the same manner we'd worked her with Trapper. Once again, the two dogs complemented each other's styles, and we'd used them for both pheasants and waterfowl, the latter being the Lab's strong suit.

Bristol died a few years later at the age of thirteen. After giving myself time to get past the loss—I've been through it more times than I care to remember, and it never gets any easier—I'd purchased another female wirehair, eight weeks old, and named her Preacher. By then Beaver was the middle-aged veteran of our team, and we'd repeated the process, working Preacher and Beaver together in what proved to be a highly effective partnership.

Then Mike lost Beaver at the age of eleven.

This had happened some eight months earlier, right around the time I was trying to conclude my previous assignment in Illinois. As something of a fringe benefit to that assignment—or more precisely, the *only* benefit—I'd rescued a young yellow Labrador named Dusty. He had belonged to my last target, an abusive son of a bitch whom I'd seen kick the dog on the town square.

After taking care of the target, I brought the Lab back home with me to Des Moines. I renamed him Rusty and presented him to Mike and his family and told Mike I'd acquired him through a rescue organization that had contacted me at the magazine. (Yeah, I know; that was a barefaced lie, but I don't make a habit of it, and there was no way I could tell Mike how I'd actually acquired the dog.) Still grieving over the loss of Beaver, they had immediately taken to Rusty, and Mike had begun training him for field work. This morning's outing was intended to further prepare both dogs for the upcoming hunting season.

Preacher and I were waiting when Mike pulled up in his truck, a black, late model Ford F-150 XLT crew cab. Compared to my Equinox, it's a real beast of a vehicle, with a 5.0 liter engine and a 10-speed transmission. Mike has added a topper, under which are dog boxes and built-in storage compartments for guns and gear. And of course, there's also a hitch beneath the rear bumper for trailering Mike's duck boat. It is, as you'd surmise, the consummate hunting rig.

"Howdy, howdy," Mike said as he stepped down from the cab onto my driveway. He's a stocky guy, maybe an inch or two shorter than me, with sandy hair and a neatly trimmed mustache and goatee. He was wearing lightweight brush pants, a Ducks Unlimited t-shirt and a camo bill cap.

"Are we really gonna go do this awful thing?" I asked. I'd been up for about an hour and drunk several cups of coffee, but it wasn't yet daylight.

Mike laughed. "We are indeed," he said. "You ready to roll?"

"We are," I said. Preacher was standing beside me.

"Let's hit it then," he said. "Preacher can ride up front with us."

I walked around to the passenger side of the truck. I opened the side door and motioned for Preacher to climb into the rear seat. Rusty greeted her with whines and a wagging tail. I closed the side door, opened the passenger door and climbed in.

Mike dropped the vehicle into reverse and backed out of my driveway. In the eastern sky, a faint glow was just beginning to show above the horizon.

THE SUN WAS STILL LOW in the sky, barely topping the horizon, when Mike pulled off the highway onto a gravel access road. We followed the road for a mile or so, with thick white clouds of gravel dust billowing up on both sides of the vehicle, before Mike slowed and turned into a narrow, overgrown lane. On both sides of the lane, lush green corn stood nearly waist high, well past the old "knee-high by the Fourth of July" measuring standard.

As we went bumping down the lane I asked, "How'd you find this place?"

"With onX," he said, referring to the GPS mapping app that not only shows topography but also identifies property owners. I don't use the app myself—further confirming my Luddite status—but thousands of sportsmen do, and we'd even run a feature on it in the magazine. "The farmer's name is Swanson," Mike added.

"And you said he's okay with us shooting out here?"

"Yes. I told him what we were doing, working our dogs to get them ready for duck season, and he said he was fine with that. But I actually didn't bring a gun today; I just brought my old dummy launcher. I figured that would be enough noise this time."

I nodded. We'd take turns firing the launcher, I knew. I was glad I'd remembered to stick a set of ear plugs in my pocket.

"What about hunting?" I asked.

"He didn't give me a definite answer one way or the other. 'Let's see how it goes,' he said. I said that was fine. I think he wants to make sure we won't trash his land, drive through his cornfields or shoot any livestock." Mike laughed. "We need to be on our best behavior today."

"Got it."

THE DRILL WE WERE RUNNING consisted of having one dog sit and honor—remain immobile, or "steady" in gun dog parlance—while the other dog was sent for a retrieve. It's a must when you're hunting with more than one dog in a duck blind, as Mike and I often did. Unless both dogs are under control and can be trusted not to break for a retrieve, chaos is apt to result if both dogs break simultaneously to fetch a downed bird.

Preacher and Beaver, Mike's previous Lab, had worked well together in this regard, both remaining steady, and we were hopeful that with some pre-season practice we could achieve the same reliability with Rusty. I knew Mike had been schooling him in obedience for the past few months and today we would be testing that obedience, tempting him to break when we sent Preacher for a retrieve.

We'd also be doing the opposite, expecting Preacher to remain steady while Rusty was retrieving. This was familiar stuff for my wirehair but running her through a refresher course prior to hunting season was never a bad idea. Plus, we hadn't hunted these two dogs together yet, and introducing a new dog to the scenario usually required some adjustment. Although he was a Lab like Beaver, Rusty would have his own style and personality and we'd have to adapt accordingly.

About a half mile in from the gravel road, the lane widened out into a grassy area surrounding the lake Mike had found with onX. The lake appeared to be about an acre in size, with cattails growing along the shore in several places that would offer concealment and a good place to build a duck blind if the farmer decided to allow us to hunt. It looked like a promising spot, made even more so by the pair of mallards and the string of half-grown ducklings we saw paddling along the opposite shore.

"Good looking spot," I said, and Mike nodded.

"Yeah, I drove in and checked it out last weekend after I talked to Swanson. He actually has two lakes out here, both left over from when this area was strip mined years ago. But he told me this one was the better one of the two for what we wanted to do; he said the other one is just a deep pit with steep banks around most of it. He told me he lost a cow in it last year. I guess it fell in and drowned; it couldn't get back up the bank."

"Good Lord," I said. "Did he get the cow out or did he have to leave it in there?"

"He got it out. He said they managed to snag it with a rope and pull it out with a tractor. He said he needs to fence that one off, or maybe bulldoze it in, because he doesn't want to lose any more livestock."

"Well, that's understandable."

"Yeah, no kidding."

We both exited the cab and opened the side doors to let the dogs out. They made a quick circuit through the grass to relieve themselves while Mike went around to the tailgate to rummage under the topper. He came out with his dummy launcher and a mesh bag full of retrieving dummies.

"Now for the fun part," he said, grinning.

"Yeah," I said, reaching into my pocket for the earplugs.

CHAPTER 25

MIKE'S OBEDIENCE TRAINING PAID OFF.

Like all young Labs, Rusty was eager and bursting with energy. But he also exhibited a high degree of self-control, showing almost remarkable restraint for a dog that was probably no more than eighteen or twenty months old.

Given the circumstances under which I'd acquired Rusty, we had no way of knowing his exact age, but Mike's vet had estimated he was about a year old, possibly a little younger, when Mike had first taken the dog in for an exam and vaccinations. This was just a couple days after I'd given Rusty to Mike, and the dog was still in the leggy, gangly adolescent stage.

Since then he'd filled out nicely and developed into a truly handsome animal. His coat was a medium golden yellow, paling to a light cream on his belly, and with darker russet ears. The latter had prompted the new name I'd bestowed upon him before giving him to Mike. I figured providing the dog with a new identity couldn't hurt; the less association with his origins, the better.

During that initial examination, the vet had also scanned Rusty for a microchip. I was hugely relieved when Mike told me later that Rusty hadn't been chipped. Apparently his previous owner, my last target, hadn't bothered. If he had, that could have led to serious complications if anyone had bothered to trace the microchip's registration, which would include the owner's name. But due to his negligence I got lucky, and Mike had Rusty microchipped and registered to him that same day at the clinic.

All good.

WE STARTED THE TRAINING SESSION with a few "happy dummies," as retriever trainers call those dummies they toss and let their dogs fetch without enforcing any discipline…the dogs aren't required to sit and remain steady until commanded to retrieve, but are allowed to break as soon as the dummy is thrown. It's a good way to build enthusiasm and it also helps to take the edge off a dog that is keyed up and raring to go, especially a young dog like Rusty.

It was about 7:30 when we got started, and the day was already warm and getting warmer, so we didn't bother with any retrieves on land but tossed the dummies into the water, and Preacher and Rusty were only too happy to go plunging in after them. We kept things unstructured and didn't alternate the retrieves but let both dogs shag their dummies simultaneously. Then after ten minutes or so, we called them in and got serious about training.

Mike and I took turns, with one of us having our dog sit and remain steady while the other guy sent his dog for the retrieve. Old—excuse me, middle-aged—pro that Preacher was, I was able to keep her steady and sitting at heel beside me with a voice command and a hand signal. Rusty, younger and more rambunctious, required more restraint initially, so for the first few times Mike used a belt cord, a light nylon rope about five feet long and attached at one end to his belt.

Mike slipped the free end of the rope through Rusty's collar and held it with one hand while he tossed the dummy with the other. If Rusty broke before being commanded to fetch, Mike gave the rope a quick pop to remind Rusty to stay put until he heard the command. Then when Mike told Rusty to fetch, he released the rope. As the Lab charged forward the rope slipped free of his collar and he hit the water to complete the retrieve.

Sitting beside me at heel while Rusty was retrieving, Preacher trembled and whined, eager for her turn.

Mike also used the belt cord to keep Rusty steady and in place while Preacher was making her retrieves. But after the first couple times, Rusty didn't break so Mike tried it without the cord, and although Rusty half-rose from his sitting position when I tossed Preacher's dummy and it hit the water, he remained in place when Mike cautioned him.

"He's really coming along," I said as Preacher swam out

to her dummy.

Mike grinned. "I hope so," he said. "We've been working on this for several weeks."

"No e-collar?" I asked. The belt cord Mike was using was somewhat old school. Many trainers nowadays would have opted to keep their dog steady with light "nicks" from an electronic collar.

"No, no e-collar," Mike replied. "At least not yet. Rusty's a soft dog, not as tough as old Beaver. I don't want to rush things with him."

"That's probably smart," I said, mentally giving Mike props for evaluating his dog's temperament and adjusting his training regimen accordingly. We both used e-collars—I became a convert many years earlier when I had to break a setter of her obsession with chasing deer—but neither of us regarded the collar as a magic button for all training situations.

"Let's try a few with the dummy launcher," Mike said. He picked up the launcher, a hand-held unit made by DT Systems, and one of its special dummies from where he had laid them in the grass. He opened the launcher and dropped in a .22 blank load, then snapped it shut and locked it.

"You're sure Rusty's ready for gunfire?" I asked.

"Well, pretty sure. I've shot some blanks with him when we were out in the field, and a few times when he was retrieving. Didn't faze him, so I think we're good," Mike said.

"Okay," I said. I reached up and pushed my earplugs in a little deeper, and I saw Mike do the same. The .22 blanks used in the dummy launcher make a rather nasty crack when the launcher is fired, and hearing protection is definitely recommended. "What loads are you using?" I asked.

"Green. The lightest. They'll put the dummy out there 50 yards or so, and that's plenty for what we're doing."

I nodded. I knew the heavier loads would send the dummy at least twice that distance, which would come later when Mike began training Rusty on longer marks and blind retrieves. But for now, the light loads would suffice.

Mike handed me the launcher. "Why don't you go first," he said. "I want to handle Rusty and make doubly sure he's okay with the shot."

I took the launcher and pointed it at a 45-degree angle out toward the water. You fire the launcher by pulling down the knob at the end of the handle. The knob is attached to a spring-loaded, point-tipped metal rod that, when released, snaps back up inside the handle. The rod's point acts as a firing pin, striking the primer of the blank load and launching the dummy.

Even with light loads, the launcher has a fairly heavy—read, unpleasant—kick or recoil. The trick to managing that recoil, or at least making it more bearable, is to hold the launcher with the heel of your hand upward, toward the dummy, rather than holding it in the more natural position with the top of your hand upward. Mike and I had both learned this the hard way.

"Ready?" I asked Mike. I noticed he'd run the belt cord through Rusty's collar again. The Lab was sitting at Mike's left side.

"Ready," he said with a nod.

I glanced down and saw that Preacher was sitting at my left side. It's customary for retriever trainers to command "Mark!" as they throw or launch a dummy, which basically means "Pay attention and mark the spot where this lands." But because I'd trained Preacher primarily for upland work, not waterfowl, I didn't use that command. Instead, I cautioned Preacher with "Whoa," the equivalent of "Stay" to a pointing dog. Then I fired the launcher, sending the dummy arcing out over the water.

It landed with a splash about fifty yards out. "Fetch!" I commanded, and Preacher sprang forward and hit the water. She began swimming strongly toward the dummy.

I turned toward Mike and Rusty. The Lab was trembling with eagerness and watching Preacher intently, but he hadn't moved from his position. I noticed that Mike had let the belt cord go slack, so Rusty was staying put on his own. And the sound of the dummy launcher hadn't bothered him.

In the few months he'd been working with the dog, Mike had obviously made some impressive strides.

As before, we took turns firing the launcher and sending our dogs for the retrieve. After four or five retrieves apiece, Mike said, "What do you think? I'd say that's enough for this morning."

"Agree," I said. The dogs were still more than willing, but it's always better to quit before they lose their enthusiasm. Or worse yet, become bored.

We gathered up the dummies scattered around us in the grass and returned them to the mesh bag. I glanced at my watch and saw it was almost 8:30. We'd been at this for about an hour. It was noticeably warmer than when we'd started, another reason to wrap things up.

I removed my earplugs as Mike stowed the bag of dummies and the launcher under the truck topper. "Let's check out that other lake," he said.

"Okay."

Both dogs had coats that dried quickly in the heat. They were still damp but not wringing wet when we loaded them into the back seat of the crew cab, where Mike had installed a waterproof seat cover. It would have been too hot for them to ride in the dog boxes under the topper.

Mike started the truck and pulled back onto the grassy lane. It continued on through the standing corn and I asked, "You know where this other lake is?"

"Swanson said it was about three quarters of a mile on past the first one. I'm just curious to see what it looks like."

The lane soon left the cornfield, which was fenced on both sides. We emerged into an open grassy field that was apparently sometimes used for pasture, although I didn't see any cows. We followed the tire ruts through the grass for another hundred yards or so until we came to the second lake.

We climbed out for a closer look but left the dogs in the cab. The lake was, as Mike had said earlier, steep-sided. The banks were nearly vertical and probably a good fifteen or twenty feet high, although at the far end there appeared to be a lower area that sloped more gradually to the water. From our vantage atop the high bank, it looked more like an abandoned quarry pit than a lake.

"You said this was left over from a strip mine?"

"That's what Swanson told me. He said it's really deep also, maybe thirty-five or forty feet. Why they didn't fill it in when they reclaimed the land he didn't say."

"I can see how a cow could drown in this if it couldn't make it to that low area at the far end."

"Yeah. Swanson said he's going to fill it or fence it off one of these days," Mike said, repeating what he'd mentioned earlier.

"I can see why," I said.

CHAPTER 26

THE FIRST PERSON GREG FLETCHER saw when he returned to Maffitt Reservoir was the Mayor of Maffitt himself, Tim Sullivan.

It was Saturday morning and Fletcher opted to walk through the park on the east side of the lake. He parked at the first turnout, next to a small grove of crabapple trees, and locked his vehicle, a dark gray Dodge Durango. Then on foot he followed the paved roadway, bordered on both sides by patches of woods and fields of tall switchgrass, as it wound around to the park. It was about 7:30 a.m. and just becoming fully light when he came to the white posts surrounding the cemetery at the park entrance.

He continued on into the park and had just passed the wooden restroom building when he saw Sullivan stumping toward him, the older man's gait immediately identifying him. *Oh, shit*, was Fletcher's first thought, knowing Sullivan's tendency toward garrulousness. Then, *might as well get this over with.*

"Good morning!" Sullivan called out when he was still several yards away. He was wearing a gold Hawkeye t-shirt, gym shorts and gray and white New Balance athletic shoes. He was hatless and Fletcher noted that the old man's skin was almost as tan as saddle leather, no doubt the result of the many hours he spent walking at the lake.

"Morning!" Fletcher replied, feigning a jocular friendliness he wasn't feeling. "Kinda warm!"

"Yeah, it is that. Thought I'd get my walk in before it gets any hotter."

"How far'd you go?" Fletcher asked. He hadn't seen Sullivan's vehicle, an old red Ford Ranger pickup, anywhere on his way into the park.

"It'll be about three and a half miles by the time I get back to my truck," Sullivan said. "I parked at the equipment shed and walked across the dam, then all the way through the park." The equipment shed was on the west side of the dam and the north side of the road, opposite the west entrance.

"That's a hike, all right," Fletcher said. "Especially when it's this hot."

The old man was sweating and he pulled up the tail of his t-shirt to wipe his face. "Yeah, but you know me," he said, grinning. "I like to get my miles in!"

Fletcher laughed. "I do know that about you." *Maybe this isn't going to be so bad after all.* "See any wildlife this morning?" One of the usual questions they asked when they ran into each other.

"It was still pretty dark when I started out, but I could see four deer feeding in that field below the dam when I walked across it," Sullivan replied. "Those are the first deer I've seen in a couple weeks. With it this hot, I think they must be staying back in the woods most of the time. Out of the sun."

"That could be," Fletcher agreed. He hadn't seen any deer recently, either, but he hadn't been out to the lake for nearly two weeks. He decided to push the envelope. "See any people?"

"Not this morning. Yesterday I ran into Hannah Wilkinson's daughter. She was walking Maisie, the golden retriever."

Fuck me. Fletcher struggled to keep his voice calm. "Really? I thought she was in summer school." Even as he said it he wondered if this was a safe remark. But if Sullivan questioned it, he could always say that Hannah had told him this awhile back.

But Sullivan didn't question it. "She was," he said, "but she told me she dropped out of her summer classes to stay home and help her dad get things settled." He hesitated, then shook his head and added, "That was terrible, what happened to Hannah."

What happened to Hannah. Not, *what Hannah did.* Did the old man suspect something? Had Hannah's daughter said something to him? Maybe told him she didn't believe her mother had committed suicide?

Fletcher wanted to probe, wanted to find out what the two of them had talked about. But he knew it would be safer not to betray too much interest. Again, he struggled to keep his voice calm. "Yes, it was," he agreed. He hoped he sounded suitably somber. "I guess we just never know what…what people are thinking, or what they might do."

"No, we never do," Sullivan said, gazing levelly at Fletcher. After a moment he shook his head again and said, "Well, I better get a move on. Still have to get back across the dam, and it's not getting any cooler."

"No, it's not," Fletcher said, forcing a smile. "Don't stay out in the sun too long."

"No longer than it takes me to get back to my truck," Sullivan said, raising a hand in farewell as he passed Fletcher and continued on out of the park.

WHAT THE FUCK!

Or more specifically, what did the old man know? Or suspect? What had he and Jessica Wilkinson talked about? Had she told him she believed he had killed her mother?

Take it easy, he told himself as he walked the roadway through the park. *Jessica Wilkinson doesn't know jack about what happened. At the most, she could only suspect you. The police have already cleared you, and there's no way she can prove otherwise.*

He shook his head and realized Sullivan had answered one of the questions he'd had. He now knew that Jessica Wilkinson hadn't returned to summer school, that she was still around and apparently would be for the rest of the summer.

Which meant he was going to have to be extra vigilant and watch out for her if he continued to come out to Maffitt. Maybe he should confine his walking to Ft. Des Moines Park and avoid the reservoir altogether.

Then again…

Maybe, he thought suddenly, instead of avoiding Jessica, it would be better to let her see him. Maybe even orchestrate a meeting. That way he could strike up a conversation and try to determine whether she suspected him of anything.

He mulled this over as he completed the loop of roadway through the park and headed back to his vehicle. *The best defense is an offense,* he told himself. Instead of hiding from Jessica Wilkinson, it might be time to go on the offense. Get a line on what, if anything, she knew or thought she knew.

He smiled as he unlocked the Durango and slid into the driver's seat. He'd have to be careful and not overplay his hand, but what the hell, he should be able to outsmart a college coed.

After all, he'd fooled her mother, hadn't he?

CHAPTER 27

IT WAS ABOUT A QUARTER PAST ten when Mike dropped us off at home. I climbed out of the truck and as I opened the back door of the crew cab to let Preacher out, Mike turned in his seat and caught Rusty's collar to prevent him from following Preacher. "Hey," he said, smiling a bit sheepishly. "Thanks again. I mean…for Rusty. And everything."

"Sure," I said, smiling also. "I'm happy to see him working out for you." And I was. I was happy for Rusty as well. Mike was the kind of owner every dog should have.

"Depending on the weather, maybe do this again next Saturday?"

"You bet," I said. "In the meantime, tell Janice I said hi."

"Will do."

I nodded and closed the door. Mike backed out of the driveway and Preacher and I headed inside.

I FED PREACHER HER MORNING meal then headed back to my office to check the answering machine for messages. I had one from Daryl.

"Hey," said her recorded voice. "I'm thinking because it's so hot, maybe just taco salad for dinner tonight. I only have one bottle of Blue Moon left so you'll need to bring beer. Let's plan to eat about 6:30…see ya."

I smiled and hit the button to delete the message. It was Daryl's turn to cook—we usually alternated Saturdays—and taco salad sounded fine for dinner. Besides beer I'd also pick up a bottle of Kendall Jackson, her favorite chardonnay.

In the meantime, I had the day to kill. I was caught up on yard work since I'd mowed the lawn on Thursday afternoon, and it was now too warm to do much outside anyway. For want of anything better, I sat down at my desk and logged onto my personal computer, not the one provided by the company for magazine work, to check my email.

I quickly deleted the usual spam, everything from life insurance and financial planning offers to solicitations from senior dating websites, and opened the three legitimate messages. The first was a political cartoon from a friend and former coworker named Marcia Thompson whose leanings matched my own. I smiled at the cartoon, replied to Marcia with "Love it!" and a laughing emoji, then deleted her message.

The second was from my cousin in Colorado, reporting on his aging springer's latest checkup at the vet. The news was positive; despite being nearly thirteen, the dog was in reasonably good health although suffering from some arthritis. The vet had prescribed a painkiller and Randy was hopeful that Hooch would make it to his thirteenth birthday, which they would celebrate with an ice cream cone at DQ. I replied that I was happy to hear Hooch was doing so well and I thought the ice cream cone sounded like a fine idea.

The third message was from Rachel James, asking if she could come by sometime and print a couple of insurance documents. She explained that she still hadn't gotten around to hooking up her new printer (her old one had shot craps a couple months earlier) as she needed her daughter's help to do so, not being any too tech savvy herself. Because Rachel's daughter was married with two kids of her own and lived in another town, they hadn't yet been able to agree on a time for the printer installation. Rachel apologized for the inconvenience but said she'd bring beer.

How can you turn down an offer like that?

"ANYTHING NEW ON THE DROWNING victim you found?"

Rachel and I were sitting on my deck, beers in hand, when she posed the question. She was drinking a Miller 64—I always have some in my fridge for her—and I was drinking one of the Blue Moons she'd brought for me. We had already printed the insurance forms she needed and then adjourned to the deck. It was a little after two o'clock and I'd positioned my chair so I was sitting in the shade offered by the overhang of the roof, but Rachel was sitting in the sun.

She was wearing a sleeveless red t-shirt, denim shorts, and a pair of red ballet flats. Actually, she was barefoot, as she'd kicked off the flats as soon as we sat down. She was also wearing dark sunglasses with black frames and large square lenses. With her long, wavy brown hair and wide smile Rachel often reminds me of Sofia Vergara, lacking only the actress's Latin accent. And yes, in case you're wondering, she's similarly endowed.

Rachel and I have known each other for more than twenty years; we met when I took the job as editor of *American Wingshot* and the magazine was still locally owned. Rachel was the company's circulation director at that time and our friendship was kindled by an offhand remark I'd made to her soon after taking the job.

I don't remember what triggered the remark, but I'd said that if I didn't work in publishing, my job of choice would be training guide dogs; that nothing warmed my heart like seeing a guide dog performing its duties. A consummate dog lover herself—she currently had a huge, handsome Saint Bernard named Alexander the Great—Rachel told me much later that she'd known at that moment we were going to be friends. Very good friends, as it turned out.

Before you get the wrong idea, however, I should also mention that Rachel is married, and her husband Al is a good friend as well. They live just a few blocks away from me in Greenfield Township, and besides Daryl, they are the only people with keys to my house; that's a measure of how much I trust them. And, as long as I'm spilling my guts here, I'll also note that Rachel is my source for the pharmaceuticals I sometimes need for my second line of work. She no longer works in publishing and I'm not going to divulge what she now does, but I will tell you that it's nothing healthcare-related. I have no idea how or where she gets the drugs I occasionally request, nor will I ever ask.

"Funny you should mention that," I replied. "Just a couple nights ago Daryl and I ran into one of the cops who came out to the lake and questioned me that morning. The female detective, Madison." Rachel didn't know I was trying to let this all go, as Daryl had suggested, so I couldn't fault her for broaching the subject. And, if I was honest with myself, I knew it was still very much on my mind. Not uppermost, necessarily, but still there.

"Really? Did she say anything more about that woman…what was her name? Hannah something?"

"Hannah Wilkinson. And no, Detective Madison didn't say anything about her. We were having dinner at Skip's and she came in with her partner…romantic partner, that is, not another detective. A woman named Beth Palmer. She introduced her to us and I gotta say, Beth Palmer was none too friendly." I laughed. "When she looked at me I could feel the man-hatred coming off her in waves."

Rachel laughed. "Are you sure you're not projecting a little bit?"

"I don't think so. Daryl and I talked about it later and she got the same vibe."

"So what did the detective say after she introduced her partner?"

"Not much, actually. She told us to enjoy our dinner and that was about it. Ironically, they had the table next to ours, but we didn't try to carry on a conversation back and forth. I'd guess the detective doesn't like to talk shop when she's off duty, and it was obvious her partner didn't want anything to do with us."

"Sitting that close to them must have been a little awkward."

I shrugged. "Oh, not really. Daryl and I carried on our own conversation and they did the same. It wasn't that bad."

Rachel laughed again and shook her head. She took a drink from her bottle of 64 and said, "What a small world we live in."

"Ain't that the truth. And get this, along those same lines, I saw Hannah's daughter, Jessica, out at the lake that same morning. She was walking Maisie, their golden retriever." Rachel knew that I took Preacher for a run at Maffitt Reservoir every day, and that I knew most of the other dog walkers out there.

"Really! What did *she* have to say?"

"She's convinced her mother didn't kill herself. She thinks her mom was killed by another guy who walks out there, a guy named Greg Fletcher."

Rachel frowned slightly. "Why does she think that?"

"He was with Hannah the night she died. Apparently they walked together, back to the boulder where I found her the next morning. He claims she asked him to leave her alone and he says he did, but her daughter thinks he killed her."

"Wow. The plot thickens. Does she have any proof?"

"Only that she'd called her mom earlier that evening to tell her she was coming home for the weekend, and her mom was excited about seeing her. Plus, Jessica says she knows her mom wasn't the type to kill herself."

"That could just be denial."

"Daryl said the same thing."

"So what's she going to do?"

"She said she's going to try to get close to Fletcher to get some proof. She's hoping he'll let something slip that she can take back to the police."

"That sounds risky. And probably not real likely to be successful."

"I said the same thing. In fact, I told her as much. I also warned her to be careful."

Rachel shook her head and drained the last of her 64. "This all sounds pretty crazy." She gave me a rueful smile. "I bet you're sorry you went out there that morning and found that woman."

"You got that right." I nodded toward her empty bottle. "Ready for another one?"

Rachel hesitated. "What time is it?" she asked.

I glanced at my watch. "A little before three. About ten 'til."

Rachel sighed. "I'd better not. I'd like to but Summer and the boys are coming over to spend the night. I need to go home and get ready for them." Summer was Rachel's daughter.

"Okay," I said. "Tell them I said hi."

"I will," Rachel said, then gave me one of her wide

smiles. "Maybe Summer and I can get my printer hooked up."

I snorted. "I'll believe that when I see it."

Rachel laughed as she popped me on the calf with her bare foot.

"Smartass!"

CHAPTER 28

WHATEVER YOU DO, *DO NOT* imagine an elephant with large tusks, ears flared and trunk curled high.

OKAY, BE HONEST. If only for a second or two, you pictured an elephant, didn't you?

A philosophy professor at the university I attended used this example to illustrate a universal truth to our class—namely, telling someone not to think of something guarantees he or she *will* think of that something, if only fleetingly. Also, by extension, the more you try not to think of something—especially if it's something troubling—the more likely you will find yourself returning to it. And—here's the kicker—even if you do eventually manage to suppress those thoughts, the universe will keep sending you little reminders.

So what do you do? The professor's suggestion was simply to go with the flow. Stop trying to suppress the thoughts and just acknowledge them. Let them play for a minute or so but not to the extent of dwelling on them. Eventually, he maintained, the thoughts would fade away of their own accord, and the universe would stop sending those reminders.

Right. If only it were that easy.

WHILE STANDING IN THE SHOWER before heading up to Daryl's for dinner, I thought about what I'd told Rachel regarding Hannah Wilkinson, encountering her daughter at the lake and seeing Detective Madison when Daryl and I were having dinner at Skip's.

I hadn't shared Jessica Wilkinson's theory about Greg Fletcher being an incel, mostly because I hadn't wanted to prolong our conversation with a lot of "is he or isn't he" speculation. Rachel probably would have found it interesting and probably also would have had an opinion on the matter but getting into a lengthy discussion didn't fit my attempts to let go of the situation. Maybe I'd have told her if she'd opted for another beer, but that hadn't happened.

Let it go, I told myself for the umpteenth time.

Except, just as the philosophy professor had told our class many years earlier, the admonition was counterproductive. Especially when, as he'd also warned, the universe would keep sending me reminders.

Which it seemed to be doing with almost alarming frequency.

I sighed and turned off the water, slid back the glass shower door and reached for a towel. I had a pleasant evening with Daryl ahead of me, and I didn't want to cart along my misgivings about Jessica Wilkinson's plan. Surely I could put those thoughts on hold for a few hours. And maybe the universe would relent.

Maybe.

DARYL LIVES IN A SMALL BRICK HOUSE in Beaverdale, one of several communities within the city of Des Moines. Beaverdale is north and west of the downtown area, and depending on traffic, it's about a twenty-minute drive from my place in Greenfield Township on the far south side.

En route I stopped at the HyVee on Fleur Drive to pick up a six-pack of Corona bottles—I opted for Mexican beer instead of Blue Moon to go with Daryl's taco salad—and her Kendall Jackson. The beer was in the large walk-in cooler and luckily there were several bottles of the chardonnay in the smaller cooler reserved for wine. With the AC in the Equinox running on high at a little after six—the outside temp was still in the upper eighties—I wasn't worried about the beer or the wine getting warm before I got to Daryl's place.

As I was paying I also snagged a lime from the basket next to the cash register because drinking Corona without a wedge of lime is one of those things you just don't do.

I pulled into Daryl's driveway and parked behind her blue Toyota Corolla. I smiled as I recalled a comment she'd once made about the Corolla, referring to it as the unsexiest car on the road. I'd laughed at the remark and, trying to be gallant, had said something about dependability. Then I'd kissed her for the first time in the parking lot at Skip's. That kiss marked the real beginning of our relationship.

Now, some eight months later, here I was, standing on her doorstep with wine and beer in hand and looking forward to dinner, conversation and maybe some intimacy. The one drawback was that I would not be spending the night; I'd need to leave at a halfway reasonable hour so I could get home and let Preacher out to pee before bedtime. Ah, the joys of being a responsible dog owner.

Earlier I'd briefly considered calling or texting Rachel and asking her to swing by my place around ten o'clock to let Preacher out for a few minutes. She'd done me this favor a couple times in the past, but I decided against it. I didn't want to intrude on her evening with her daughter and her grandsons, and I also didn't want to over-impose on our friendship.

Daryl answered the door just as I was reminding myself—again—not to say anything about Hannah Wilkinson or her daughter. She was wearing a pale green t-shirt that said "Cat Mama," white shorts and black flip-flops.

I laughed when I saw her shirt. "Did Ivy buy that for you?"

"She did!" Daryl said, smiling. "C'mon in."

I needn't have worried about avoiding the subject of Hannah Wilkinson's death. Turned out Daryl had a surprise or two of her own in store for me that would steer our conversation along different lines altogether.

In Iowa we have a phenomenon known as the walking taco. I don't know if it's exclusive to the Hawkeye State or if it's known elsewhere (and I'm not going to bother researching the subject) but it's definitely a favorite among Iowans. Thousands are sold every year at the state fair, farmer's markets, sporting events, outdoor concerts and the like.

Briefly, a walking taco consists of a small bag of tortilla chips—most vendors use the triangular, nacho-flavored ones—that is cut open along one side. Then the shredded lettuce, diced tomatoes, seasoned ground beef and grated cheese are added to the bag, along with salsa and, if the customer prefers, sour cream. (I always pass on the latter.) A plastic fork or spoon is also provided.

So, in case its name initially had you envisioning a fully loaded taco shell with little legs sauntering along the sidewalk, why is it called a walking taco?

For the simple reason that you can eat it while walking.

You carry the bag and eat the contents with the fork, easy-peasy, while you're strolling around. (Do I need to mention that dining al fresco is a favorite pastime among Iowans?) It's actually a neater way to eat a taco than the standard way, with your fingers. Not that I'm averse to that method either, of course.

Which brings us to Daryl's taco salad.

Daryl doesn't use the large taco shell bowls that you usually get if you order a taco salad in a Mexican restaurant. Instead, she also uses tortilla chips, and her taco salad is similar to a walking taco, except it's served on a plate instead of in a bag. Daryl always lets me build my own, and I usually have to be reminded whether the bottom layer is supposed to be lettuce or chips. I get it right (chips) about half the time, although I always stubbornly maintain it doesn't really matter.

We were sitting at her kitchen table and I was in the process of constructing my salad when Ivy, Daryl's golden tabby, strolled into the kitchen and announced with a loud meow that she deserved a spoonful or two of the taco meat.

"Oh, hush," Daryl said, and we both laughed. "This stuff's too spicy for you. But you can have a couple of treats." She rose from the table and grabbed a box of tuna-flavored cat treats from the counter. She dropped a few of the treats in Ivy's bowl and the cat sniffed at them, then began eating, apparently placated.

Daryl seated herself again and spread a layer of chips on her plate. "How did your training with Mike go today?" she asked.

"It went really well," I said. "He's been working with Rusty quite a bit and it shows. Rusty is really coming along.

Another session or two and he'll have the steadiness thing down. We should be ready for duck season."

"That's great." Daryl doesn't hunt but she's not of the anti-hunting mindset and in fact she enjoys the occasional wild game dinner I prepare for her. "How did Preacher do?"

"Oh, she was fine. She's an old hand at this stuff so this was just a refresher course for her."

Daryl laughed. "You'd better not let her hear you calling her old."

"Yeah, no kidding."

I WAS ON MY SECOND HELPING and second Corona when Daryl picked up her cell phone and said, "I want to show you something." As a rule we steer clear of our phones when we're eating, but after a quick scroll she handed me her phone and said, "What do you think?"

I looked at the phone's screen and saw a close-up of Kris Jenner, matriarch of the Kardashian family. No, I'm not a fan of their reality TV show; in fact, I've never seen it and I don't even know if it's still running, but I've seen enough photos of Kris Jenner to immediately recognize her. She was smiling at the camera.

"Kris Jenner?" I said. "What about her?"

Daryl smiled. "What do you think of her haircut?"

My mother only had one child, and she didn't raise him to be a fool. I knew there was only one correct answer to Daryl's question.

"It's cute," I said, trying to put as much sincerity as I could into my voice. "I like it." And in fact, I did like her short bob.

"Really?"

"Yes."

Daryl smiled. "I'm thinking of getting my hair cut like that," she said. "What do you think?"

Again, there was only one correct answer. I laughed and said, "Go for it."

Daryl reached over and took her phone back. "Let me show you something else," she said. She clicked and scrolled again, then handed the phone back to me.

This time the photo was of an older, bearded man, bald on top with his hair cropped close on the sides. He was handsome in a mature, craggy sort of way, and he looked vaguely familiar but I couldn't place him. Nevertheless, I had a feeling I knew where this going. In a weak attempt at deflection, I said, "What? You're also thinking of growing a beard?"

Daryl laughed. "No, of course not." She cocked her head and smiled impishly. "But...maybe you should."

"Oh, right," I said. "That's just what I need, something to make me look even older than I already do."

"Actually...it might make you look younger. Especially if you got your hair cut short like his."

I snorted. "This guy's bald! And who is he, anyway?"

"Corbin Bernsen. The actor. Remember him?"

I thought for a moment. "He was on *L.A. Law* quite a few years ago. He played a divorce attorney named Arnie Becker. He had blonde hair back then." I didn't add that *L.A. Law* had been one of my wife's favorite programs. Ex-wife, that is. And yes, I'd watched the show also.

"That's right," Daryl said. "This is what he looks like now." She laughed again. "You could rock that look."

I shook my head. "I don't think so. Not a big fan of beards, especially in hot weather. And like I said, he's bald."

Daryl arched her eyebrows and smiled. "Well...didn't you once tell me you never wanted to be guilty of a comb-over?"

I halfway remembered saying something like that, but I couldn't recall the occasion or what had prompted the remark. Probably seeing some guy with a comb-over who, as the old saying goes, was fooling no one but himself while everyone else laughed behind his back.

I sighed. "Really?" I said. "Is that what I'm doing these days? A comb-over?" I knew I was getting thin on top, but...

"Well...maybe not yet." Daryl looked down and toyed with her wine glass. "But...you might be getting close." Now she sounded apologetic. She gave me a wan smile.

"Really?" I repeated. I couldn't keep the exasperation out of my voice.

She sighed. "Don't be upset. It was just an idea. Food for thought, anyway."

I shook my head. "Thanks, but I don't think so." I couldn't picture myself bald with a beard. Or didn't *want* to picture myself that way. "That's not who I am."

CHAPTER 29

THAT'S NOT WHO I AM.

That line kept coming back to haunt me as I drove home at 11:30 that Saturday night.

Once we got past our somewhat testy exchange over the photo of Corbin Bernsen, the rest of the evening passed pleasantly. After dinner we'd watched an old DVD of *Enough Said*, a rom-com starring Julia Louis-Dreyfus and James Gandolfini. We'd both seen it previously but it's a nice little feel-good flick, perfect for when you're in the mood for something light with a happy ending.

It also made a nice prelude to intimacy.

Daryl was wearing a light terrycloth robe when she saw me to the door at the evening's end. As I turned toward her for a last kiss, she laid her palm on my chest and said, "Hey. Sorry about that business earlier with the haircut and beard. I didn't mean to upset you."

I smiled. "No worries. And I didn't mean to overreact. I was just a little…surprised, that's all. Not a big deal."

"Okay." She stood up on tiptoes to kiss me. "Be careful driving home."

"Will do."

"Love you."

"Love you too."

OKAY, I MIGHT HAVE LIED when I said it wasn't a big deal. Not because I was upset by her suggestion that I grow a beard and get my hair buzzed—I had no immediate intention of acting on that suggestion—but because of my choice of words when I'd dismissed the idea.

That's not who I am.

Those words kept nagging at me while we watched the movie, and I knew the reason. They'd reminded me, once again, that there was still a major part of my life that Daryl knew nothing about. Call it a Freudian slip if you will, and maybe it was. But I couldn't get around the fact that I was still keeping something from her that could seriously impact our relationship. Maybe even bring it to an end.

Those thoughts were still occupying my mind as I drove home. What would Daryl's reaction be if I came clean and told her I was a contract killer? Unquestionably she'd be surprised, even shocked. I couldn't help smiling as I wondered how I'd even broach the subject. Maybe just an offhand "Oh, and by the way, I occasionally kill people"?

Hardly.

I suddenly realized I'd never faced this dilemma before.

I'd begun taking assignments shortly after my divorce. That had been nearly thirty years ago, and back then, well before the days of the internet, it was a carefully worded newspaper ad in the personal columns of several major metropolitan newspapers that had brought me my clients.

Then, as now, they had been instructed to write to a P.O. box and include a phone number. I would review their message and decide whether to contact them. When I did—this was also before cell phones were commonplace—it was from a pay phone. I never called a client from the same pay phone twice.

As long as I'm rehashing this ancient history, maybe I should mention that my first assignment was also very nearly my last. I made mistakes and came close to being the one who wound up dead, rather than my intended target. But that's a story for another time.

Since that first assignment, I'd completed…well, the exact number doesn't matter here. I don't mean that to sound callous, but neither do I want to sound boastful. As I've already mentioned, I never take an assignment unless I'm convinced the target deserves the retribution I deliver, and because of that conviction, I don't suffer guilt afterwards.

I've never remarried, but over the years I've dated casually and have also been involved in several serious, long-term relationships. Those relationships all eventually ran their course and ended for one reason or another. Usually it was a growing matter of incompatibility, the "irreconcilable differences" that are cited as grounds in so many divorces.

But my current relationship with Daryl felt like something more, something that might go the distance. Ours was a relationship based not only on mutual attraction, but something with real substance, I believed—that is, except for what she didn't know about me and the effect finding out would probably have.

I wondered if following through on my plan to retire might be a way to circumvent this problem. Give up taking assignments and leave the past in the past. Move forward, concentrate on building a life with Daryl, never mention what had gone before, and never look back.

Would that be possible?

Is it ever?

I WAS STILL MULLING THIS over when I pulled into my driveway. I opened the garage door with the remote and pulled in. I turned off the engine, climbed out and closed the overhead garage door. I stepped out through the side door, locking it as I went.

Preacher was waiting at the back door when I unlocked and opened it. She trotted out, down the steps of the deck and out into the yard. I stood on the deck and watched as she took care of business and then made her customary circuit of the yard. The temperature had dropped into the seventies and a cooling breeze had sprung up. It was a clear night with stars overhead.

I thought about Daryl not knowing what I did, and about those few people who did know.

Rachel James knew, although I seldom shared many details with her about specific assignments. When I needed drugs, usually something to help me overpower a target, I told her only enough so she could determine what would work best for the situation at hand. Then she provided what I needed, and her judgment had always proven correct.

I suspected, but didn't know for certain, that her husband Al also knew what I did. We'd never talked about it, and I didn't know if Rachel had ever mentioned it to him, but I'd have been surprised if she hadn't at least hinted at it. If nothing else, he had to have wondered—and maybe asked—about all those times I'd told Rachel I needed a favor.

A pawnbroker named A.C.—his actual name was Gerald Matthews—on the south side of Des Moines also knew, or at least had an inkling. Over the years I've purchased quite a few untraceable handguns from him, and the fact that I'm a repeat customer must have suggested to him that I was disposing of those guns after using them. In fact, never keeping a handgun after it's been used is one of my inviolate rules. But he's never asked, and he never will.

Then, of course, there are my clients. But I never tell them my real name, and they make their checks payable to my innocuous-sounding LLC. Given the nature of our business, it's unlikely that they would ever try tracing the ownership of the LLC, but even if they did, they'd quickly run into a dead end. Pardon the bad pun.

That, to the best of my knowledge, was the sum of persons who knew I was a contract killer. A very small number indeed, and that of necessity.

I wondered if Daryl could be trusted with knowing.

Telling her, I realized, would put a tremendous burden on her. Or to put it another way, asking her to accept the fact that I killed people would be, as the expression goes, one hell of an ask. While I didn't necessarily think she would go running to the cops, I would be saddling her with something she would most likely find very difficult to live with. Plus, I'd be making her complicit in my actions.

So back to my earlier thoughts. Was it really necessary for her to know? Especially if I made good on my plans to retire? Couldn't the past remain buried?

I suddenly flashed on a scene from the movie *True Lies*, with Arnold Schwarzenegger and Jamie Lee Curtis. Upon learning that her husband is a spy, Jamie Lee asks Arnold, "Have you ever killed anyone?" and he replies with almost comic earnestness, "Yes, but they were all bad."

Well, I could say the same of my targets. But somehow I doubted that rationalization would suffice with Daryl.

CHAPTER 30

IT'S A TRUISM OF HUMAN NATURE that the problem you take to bed with you is the first thing that will pop into your mind when you wake up the next morning. In such circumstances, the notion of "sleeping on it" is all too accurate. You sleep on it—that is, if you're able to fall asleep—and it's right there waiting for you when you open your eyes the following morning.

I could attest to the accuracy of this observation.

At a few minutes after six Preacher came into my bedroom and whined, her signal that she needed to go outside. Fortunately I'm an early riser so this wasn't a big deal; I seldom "sleep in," even on Sundays, and in fact, I was already about half awake. My brain had already begun wrestling with the previous evening's dilemma—whether I should tell Daryl about my moonlighting gig as a hit man or just retire and hope the past remained buried.

I climbed out of bed and headed to the kitchen to let Preacher outside and to start a pot of coffee. While it was brewing, I leaned on the counter and continued my self-inflicted mind-fuck. Sorry for the crudity, but that's what I was doing to myself and there was no getting around it.

My coffee maker has an "interrupt" feature that allows you to pull the carafe out and pour a cup before the brewing cycle is completed. When there were a couple of inches in the bottom of the carafe I pulled it out and filled a mug, then put the carafe back on the warming plate. I grabbed the milk out of the fridge and added a little to the mug, then replaced the milk and carried the mug over to the kitchen table. I sat down.

It goes without saying, doesn't it, that as soon as I settled myself at the table, Preacher barked at the back door to be let back inside. I could have ignored her but this being early Sunday morning, and knowing that some of my neighbors probably did like to sleep in, I sighed, got up and let her in.

My neighbors are generally pretty tolerant and most of them own dogs also, but I didn't want to risk annoying them with Preacher's barking. Neighborhood feuds have started over less.

Preacher settled herself on an old rug in a corner of the kitchen and I sat down again at the table. I took a sip of coffee and tried to focus on the day ahead. In another half hour or so, as soon as it started getting light, I'd load up Preacher and we'd make our usual run out to Maffitt Reservoir.

Thinking on this, I realized that in at least one respect the previous evening had played out as I'd hoped. I'd gotten through the entire evening with Daryl with no mention of Hannah Wilkinson or any of my concerns about her daughter. I smiled at the thought that maybe, as my old philosophy professor had told our class, the universe was easing up on the reminders.

I'd find out soon enough that wasn't the case.

It was just past seven o'clock when I parked at the first turnout on the west side of the lake. I removed Preacher's ramp, unfolded it and put it in place against the rear bumper of the Equinox, then opened the hatch cover. After Preacher trotted down the ramp I folded it and stuck it in the cargo area on top of her dog pillow. I closed the hatch and locked the vehicle and we started down the roadway toward the gate at the head of the hiking trail.

It was another warm morning and I was carrying Preacher's retrieving dummy. My plan was to walk back to the canoe launch and toss the dummy for her for a few water retrieves. Then we would return to the vehicle and head home. The round trip to the canoe launch and back, plus the retrieves, would have to suffice for our morning outing, as I could already feel the heat beginning to build.

We hadn't made it to the first turn in the road when I saw someone walking toward us. Preacher was about thirty yards ahead of me and she trotted up to the person, wagging her tail. I recognized him as he stopped and patted Preacher on the head a couple times.

It was Greg Fletcher, my fellow pallbearer from Hannah's funeral.

I hadn't seen his vehicle when I'd driven in, so I guessed he had parked at one of the other turnouts, maybe the one on the point farther along the roadway. Or maybe, given the fact that he was approaching from the south, he'd left his vehicle in the park on the east side and had walked the hiking trail all the way around the south end of the lake, intending to make the complete circuit. I knew Tim Sullivan sometimes did this but I had no idea if Greg Fletcher was that ambitious.

We continued walking toward each other. Preacher, satisfied with the petting she'd received from Fletcher, angled off into the woods alongside the roadway. I didn't call her back but when I was within ten yards of Fletcher I nodded and said, "Good morning."

"Good morning," he said in return.

By then we'd come abreast of each other and we paused. Like me, he was wearing shorts, a t-shirt and a baseball cap. Unlike me in my old boat shoes, he was wearing a pair of expensive-looking Skecher cross-trainers. He smiled and said, "What's your dog's name again?"

"Preacher," I said. "For a character in a Clint Eastwood movie."

"Ah," Fletcher replied. He didn't ask which movie. "She's friendly."

"Yes, she is." We'd run into each other a number of times out here previously and covered the same ground, but maybe Fletcher was just trying to make polite conversation. Or maybe he was just forgetful. Regardless, this all struck me as rather pointless and more than a little awkward.

I hefted Preacher's retrieving dummy. "Gonna do a little water work," I said. "Need to get her some exercise before it gets much warmer."

Fletcher took the hint. "Good thinking," he said, smiling again and starting to move away. "Have a good morning."

"You too," I said to his back as he continued on down the roadway.

I PROBABLY DON'T HAVE TO tell you that after encountering Greg Fletcher I had a hard time focusing on Preacher's retrieving.

We continued around to the canoe launch as planned and I tossed her dummy a half dozen times. She dutifully swam out and retrieved it each time but I had the feeling her heart wasn't in it, either. Quite possibly she sensed my mind was elsewhere and she was just going through the motions accordingly.

As I stood there waiting for Preacher to complete her retrieves, I couldn't help wondering if I should have tried to engage Fletcher in a longer conversation. But to what end? Did I really think I could have tripped him up and maybe gotten him to reveal something about Hannah Wilkinson's death? The likelihood of that happening was awfully slim, I thought, Jessica's Wilkinson's conviction notwithstanding.

Which in turn led me to wonder if she'd encountered him herself by now and had any luck pursuing her theory.

I shook my head to clear it as Preacher came in and stopped in front of me, holding the dummy. "Good girl," I said as I took the dummy from her. I spun it by its throw rope a couple times and water droplets flew off in all directions. Preacher stood watching to see if I was going to throw it again. "That's enough for this morning," I said, and Preacher relaxed and gave herself a good shake. More water droplets flew.

"C'mon," I said, turning back toward the roadway. "Let's head back before it gets much warmer." We started up the gravel slope of the canoe launch, crossed the road and moved on up into a field of grass. My plan was to shortcut across the field rather than follow the roadway around as we'd done earlier. It would save us a few minutes getting back to our vehicle.

The field had been mowed recently so the walking was fairly easy. Preacher quartered ahead of me in the same pattern she used when we were hunting pheasants. I strolled along after her, swinging her retrieving dummy by its throw rope and still pondering whether I should have tried to keep Greg Fletcher talking. Once again, Daryl's admonition to let it go came to mind.

We reached the opposite side of the field and followed the road for the last hundred yards to the turnout where I'd parked the Equinox. As I pushed the button on my key fob to unlock it, another vehicle pulled in and parked beside us.

It was Jessica Wilkinson and Maisie in Hannah's dark blue Explorer.

CHAPTER 31

"HEY!" JESSICA CALLED OVER to me as she came around to the passenger side of the Explorer to let Maisie out. Jessica was smiling and seemed in good spirits. Maisie bounded down out of the Explorer and immediately came over to greet us as Jessica closed the door and thumbed her key fob to lock it.

"Hey yourself," I said, smiling in return. "How are you?"

"We're good. Just came out for our walk. Are you just getting here too?"

"No, we're just finishing up, actually. We walked back to the canoe launch and I tossed Preacher's dummy for her a few times so she could do a little swimming." I held up the dummy to confirm this and Jessica laughed and nodded.

"I'm sure Maisie will want me to throw a stick for her a few times," she said. She hesitated a moment, glanced around and then asked, "Have you seen anyone else out here this morning?"

I could have lied, but I didn't. "Well, as a matter of fact, I saw Greg Fletcher a little earlier," I said. Jessica immediately stiffened and the smile left her face. She drew a deep breath.

"Really?" she said. "How long ago?"

I glanced at my watch. "A little over half an hour or so," I said. "More like forty or forty-five minutes."

"Did you talk to him?"

"Just briefly. We said hi to each other and that was about it."

Jessica blew out a breath and shook her head. "I still haven't been able to connect with him. I seem to keep missing him, I guess. I've seen Tim Sullivan a couple times, but not Fletcher." She glanced around again and then asked, "Where was he when you saw him?"

I nodded down the roadway toward the south. "About down there at the first turn. He was walking this direction."

"Was he parked here?"

"No. I never saw his vehicle. I thought maybe he'd parked on around at the point, but it wasn't there, either. I wondered if maybe he'd parked on the other side of the lake, maybe in the park, and walked the trail all the way around."

"Yeah, maybe." She thought a moment. "If he did that, he'd have to have gotten out here awfully early, though. Before daylight, even."

"That's true; he would have. I hadn't thought of that."

"Or maybe he parked on that side and walked across the dam and back to the gate on this side, then turned and walked back."

I nodded. "That's probably more likely."

"If he parked on the other side, I wonder if I could catch him before he leaves."

I glanced at my watch again. "Like I said, it's probably been forty-five minutes or so since I saw him. He's probably gone by now." I was hoping to discourage her from taking off on a wild goose chase, especially since I thought I could hear some desperation in her voice. I still didn't like the idea of her confronting him.

Her shoulders slumped and she sighed. "You're probably right." She smiled ruefully and added, "I guess I need to start getting out here a little earlier."

I grinned. "Set your alarm clock."

"Set my…" she hesitated, then laughed. "My phone, you mean?"

Sheesh. Could I have dated myself any more obviously?

I laughed. "Sorry about that," I said. "Showing my age."

"That's okay," Jessica said. "I guess we'll just walk on this side. It's probably too late to catch Fletcher."

"You're probably right." I stopped myself from asking if she was still sure connecting with him was a smart idea. Her determination to talk to him obviously hadn't diminished since our previous conversation, so I knew she wasn't likely to be dissuaded. "Well, we need to be getting home," I said. "You two have a good walk."

"Thanks," Jessica replied. "Good to see you again!"

"Good to see you too."

She started down the roadway toward the canoe launch with Maisie trotting ahead of her. I watched them for a moment, then opened the hatch and removed Preacher's ramp. I unfolded it and put it in place, she trotted up it and settled herself on her pillow, and I folded the ramp and closed the hatch.

I stowed the ramp in its box on the rear seat, then climbed in and started the ignition. I sat there for a moment, looking out over the lake toward the park on the opposite side. I was looking into the sun and its reflection off the water was almost dazzlingly bright.

I sighed and dropped the transmission into reverse. I backed out of the parking area and drove out to the road. As we crossed the dam I thought about turning in at the east entrance and making a quick pass through the park to see if Greg Fletcher was, in fact, still there.

And what if he is, I asked myself. *What will you do then? Drive back to the west side and tell Jessica?*

Get a grip, guy, I told myself. *You really need to let this go.*

We passed the east entrance and headed home.

Sitting atop a picnic table, Greg Fletcher saw Jessica Wilkinson, driving her mother's dark blue Ford Explorer, pull in and park next to Vance's gray Chevy Equinox.

Fletcher had parked at one of the gravel turnouts in the park on the east side of the lake, facing the opposite shoreline. After talking to Vance earlier, he'd walked back across the dam and into the park, retracing his route and returning to where he'd left his Durango. He hadn't seen anyone else besides Vance and he was still hoping Jessica Wilkinson might show up with her dog.

He was in no hurry to get home so he had unlocked the Durango and removed the compact pair of Bushnell binoculars that he kept in the pocket on the driver's door. Then he had walked down to a picnic table sitting under an oak tree on the edge of the tall bank above the lake shore and settled himself on top of the table with his feet resting on the bench seat beneath him.

He removed the binoculars from their black nylon case and brought them up to his eyes, focusing on the opposite shoreline and propping his elbows on his knees to keep the binoculars steady. He wasn't worried about anyone seeing him and thinking he was some sort of voyeur; the lake attracted plenty of birdwatchers and should anyone ask, he could tell them he was watching the several families of Canada geese on the water.

He swept the shoreline from north to south and settled on the canoe launch, where he could see Vance and his dog. Vance was throwing the orange retrieving dummy out into the water for the dog to retrieve, just as he'd said. Fletcher watched them for several minutes until Vance turned away from the water and started up the slope of the canoe launch, twirling the dummy by its throw rope, the dog trotting ahead of him.

Fletcher guessed it would take ten minutes or so for Vance to return to where he'd parked. He decided to wait and see if his estimate was correct. He glanced at his cell phone to confirm the time.

It took Vance a little more than ten minutes—almost twelve, to be precise—to reach his vehicle. Fletcher saw him pause behind the Equinox and Fletcher guessed he was unlocking it and getting ready to load up his dog.

That's when he saw Jessica Wilkinson pull up in her mother's Explorer.

He saw Jessica climb out of the Explorer and go around to open the passenger door and let Maisie out. He saw Vance step out from behind his vehicle and saw his dog trot forward to greet the golden. Vance and Jessica began talking.

Son of a bitch.

Fletcher felt his anger mount. He'd hoped to see Jessica and now here she was, but on the opposite side of the lake and talking to someone else. Just his luck.

He continued watching them through the binoculars. He had no way of knowing what they were saying to each other and he wondered if Vance would mention seeing him. He clenched his jaw and wished there was some way to monitor their words.

After a couple minutes, he saw them part. Jessica and Maisie started down the roadway toward the south and Vance returned to the back of his vehicle. After a moment, Fletcher saw the hatch cover of the Equinox rise and he guessed Vance was loading up his dog.

Sure enough, a minute later he saw the hatch cover drop. Vance stepped around from behind the vehicle, carrying something. Fletcher couldn't make out exactly what it was, but it was large, flat and rectangular. Vance opened the side door of the Equinox and stuck the flat object inside. He closed that door, opened the driver's door, and climbed in.

Fletcher blew out a harsh breath. He continued watching.

Vance seemed to be taking his sweet time about starting his vehicle and leaving. The sun's reflection off Vance's windshield made it impossible for Fletcher to see what Vance was doing. He wondered if, like many people, Vance was checking his cell phone for messages.

Then, after another minute or so, he saw the Equinox back out of the parking area and head north toward the west-side entrance. He followed its progress as well as he could through the trees but it was soon lost to his view.

He assumed Vance was heading home.

He scanned the opposite shoreline again with his binoculars. While he did so, he considered the possibilities. He'd wanted to see Jessica Wilkinson, and now he knew she was somewhere along the roadway on the opposite side of the lake. He didn't know where she intended to walk, or how far. Given the morning's heat, he guessed she probably wouldn't go back on the main hiking trail but would probably opt for staying close to the water for Maisie's benefit.

He wondered if he should attempt to bump into her.

Was that plausible? What if Vance had mentioned seeing him earlier? Would that make Jessica suspicious, maybe cause her to wonder why he was still around?

Fuck it, he thought impulsively. *In for a penny, in for a pound. It might be a long damn time before I get another chance like this.*

CHAPTER 32

WHEN WE GOT HOME FROM the lake, I fed Preacher her morning meal then went back to my office and logged onto my computer to check for messages. I had a couple more political cartoons from Marcia Thompson that she'd emailed the previous evening, but nothing from Daryl.

That wasn't unusual as, unlike me, Daryl did like to sleep in on Sundays. On those occasions when she spent Saturday night at my place—approximately every other weekend—I would slip out of bed as quietly as possible on Sunday morning and take Preacher to the lake, and Daryl would usually just be waking up about the time we returned.

Sitting at the computer now, I wondered if she was awake. I glanced at my watch and saw it was just past 9:30. I considered calling her but decided not to risk waking her. I'd call later.

Thinking about Daryl resurrected the question of whether I should tell her about my contract killing. The outing to the lake with Preacher and bumping into both Greg Fletcher and Jessica Wilkinson had put the question out of my mind, or at least pushed it to the back burner. Now it returned in force.

I was no closer to having an answer.

Screw it, I thought. It wasn't something that had to be immediately resolved. I had no assignments pending, and if I did make good on my resolution to retire, that would remove any urgency about telling her. Maybe the matter could be put on hold until, say, we were both old and gray and long past the time when coming clean would have much of an impact on our relationship.

Almost immediately, I recognized the fallacy in this line of thinking. You don't build trust in a relationship by keeping things from the other person, and no matter how deeply buried a secret is, or how long that secret has been buried, when it surfaces, as it almost inevitably will, it *will* have an impact. Sometimes that impact will be devastating. In fact, the longer the secret remains hidden, especially a secret like the one I was keeping from Daryl, the more devastating its impact is likely to be. Call it damage with compound interest.

I shook my head and pushed away from the computer, still no closer to an answer. I stood up and headed back out to the kitchen.

Maybe some food would help.

My Sunday morning menu seldom changes, whether I'm cooking for Daryl and me or only for myself. Sometimes Daryl and I opt to go out for breakfast, but when I man the stove, it's scrambled eggs, toast, orange juice and coffee with Baileys.

I whipped four eggs with a fork in a small stainless steel bowl, added salt and pepper and a dash of milk, and whipped them again. Then I took five slices of Hormel dried beef from the jar in the fridge and diced them. While I was doing this a generous pat of margarine was melting in the skillet on the stove.

When the margarine was melted, I poured in the eggs, added the diced dried beef and popped two slices of English muffin toasting bread down in the toaster. I poured a mug full of coffee from what remained in the carafe, stuck the mug in the microwave above the stove and set it for a minute and twenty seconds. I pushed start, then stirred the eggs. They came up nice and fluffy.

The toast popped and I buttered it. The microwave beeped and I removed the coffee. I dished up some of the eggs onto a plate, carried everything to the table, then grabbed one of the mini bottles of Baileys from the fridge. I returned to the table and sat down. I glanced over at Preacher, who was watching me from her rug with laser-like intensity.

"Oh, don't worry," I told her. "I saved some eggs in the skillet for you."

She relaxed on her rug, relieved to have that matter settled. I dug in.

AFTER FINISHING BREAKFAST, feeding Preacher the remaining scrambled eggs and loading the dishwasher, I carried my mug of coffee and Baileys back to my office and sat down at the computer again. I checked my email but still had no message from Daryl. It was now a quarter past ten but I decided to wait a little longer before calling her.

I gave some thought to what I should do for the rest of the day. There was one project I could tackle that I'd been putting off for a while but it would require a quick trip to the Menards on Southeast 14th Street, about ten minutes away. The frame around the side door of the garage needed to be scraped and repainted, as the paint had begun to peel over the past few months. The whole project would probably take no more than hour, but I needed to buy the paint.

I decided I'd procrastinated long enough and should take advantage of the good weather while it lasted. The paint would dry quickly in the heat and I thought I remembered hearing something about thunderstorms being predicted for later in the week. I figured I might as well get the doorframe repainted before the storms moved in.

As I drove to Menards I mulled the project over and realized it would probably take longer than I'd initially thought. Because the paint on the doorframe had peeled down to the bare wood in several places, it would need to be primed first. Well, I could take care of that this afternoon, at least, and depending on how quickly the primer dried, either paint the frame this evening (if Daryl and I didn't get together) or sometime tomorrow.

I parked and headed inside to the paint department, located in a back corner of the store. I picked out a quart of white latex enamel and another quart of primer and, carrying a can in each hand, was on my way back to the checkouts at the front of the store when I heard a woman say, "Well, hello again."

I turned to see Detective Madison standing a few feet down the side aisle I'd just passed. I laughed and said, "Well, hi there."

Unlike the previous times I'd seen her, she was wearing

a pair of old faded blue jeans with several rips in the legs, black tennis shoes and an untucked blue denim shirt with the sleeves rolled up. I noticed several paint splotches on the shirt and guessed I wasn't the only one spending time on home improvement projects this Sunday. She had a shopping cart in front of her that held a gallon of paint, a roller and roller pan, and a couple of brushes.

I hefted my cans of paint. "Looks like we had a similar idea," I said.

She laughed. "Yes, Beth decided we needed to paint the bathroom today. She's getting things ready at home and I'm on purchase detail." She rolled her eyes. "Can you tell I'm thrilled?"

I laughed again. "I take it painting's not one of your favorite activities?"

"Oh, I don't really mind it. It's just all the mess, all the clean-up afterwards, that sort of thing. I'm not looking forward to that part, but it will look nice when we're finished."

I nodded. "Well, good luck," I said. I hesitated, then added, "Good to see you again, Detective."

"Oh, please," she said. "I'm off duty. It's Madeline."

"Madeline Madison?" I couldn't help smiling. "I should be able to remember that without any trouble."

She laughed. "I know, I get that a lot. What can I say; my mama loved alliteration."

"I have a friend like that," I said, thinking of Rachel James.

"Lucky you," she said.

"Right, lucky me." I hefted my cans of paint again. They weren't getting any lighter. "I need to get these paid for," I said. "My arms are gonna be six inches longer by the time I get them up to the register."

She patted the handle of her shopping cart. "That's why they have these," she said. "They're called shopping carts." There was no mistaking the mischief in her voice.

"I should know that, shouldn't I?"

"I highly recommend them. And by the way…" she hesitated, then continued, "I think I should probably apologize for my partner's behavior the other night when we saw you and your friend at Skip's. Beth isn't...the most sociable person, unfortunately."

I shook my head. "No problem," I said. "I didn't think anything of it." I hoped my lie wasn't too obvious.

The detective gave me a long look, then smiled again. "You take care, Mr. Vance," she said.

"It's Rob," I said. "You take care also."

"Always."

DRIVING HOME FROM MENARDS, I couldn't help reflecting on the way the ironic coincidences were piling up. *So much for putting Hannah Wilkinson's death behind me*, I thought. *It's obviously not going to go away anytime soon.*

Well, so be it.

I also replayed Detective Madison's apology for her partner's rudeness. I was a bit surprised by the apology, in fact, and I wondered if perhaps the detective had been embarrassed that I'd learned she was gay. She hadn't seemed so, but...

She needn't have been concerned. Generally speaking, as long as it doesn't involve children or animals or exploitation or violence—something practiced by consenting adults, in other words—I don't give a damn what people do sexually, or with whom they do it.

Thinking on that now, I was reminded once again of Jessica Wilkinson's theory concerning Greg Fletcher, that he was an incel whose frustration had led to him murdering her mother.

Damn it to hell, anyway.

The reminders just kept on coming.

CHAPTER 33

"You're limping."

Jessica Wilkinson forced herself to smile. "Got a piece of gravel in my shoe," she said, angling off the roadway to the picnic table where Greg Fletcher was seated. Maisie had already trotted over toward him but had stopped a few feet short, just far enough away to be out of his reach. The golden was standing perfectly still, not wagging her tail and not advancing any closer to be petted. Very unlike her, Jessica thought, as the dog continued to regard Fletcher warily.

"That can't feel good," Fletcher said. He patted the seat beside him. "Better sit down so you can remove it."

"That's my plan," Jessica said, thinking, *no way am I going to sit down next to you.* She walked around to the opposite side of the table and sat at the end of the bench seat. Maisie relaxed and moved over to her side. As Jessica bent over to untie her shoelaces Maisie lay down next to her in the grass. Fletcher swiveled to face them.

The picnic table was a few yards away from the turnout where Jessica had parked next to Robert Vance's vehicle a half hour earlier. Returning from walking Maisie to the canoe launch, she'd seen Fletcher's vehicle parked next to hers. At first glance she'd thought it was Vance's Equinox and that for some reason he hadn't left. Then she noted that the vehicle was a darker shade of gray and a Dodge Durango.

When she drew a few steps closer she recognized Fletcher. He was sitting at the picnic table with his back to the tabletop, leaning back on his elbows and facing the parking area. He smiled when he saw her and raised a hand in greeting. She felt a sudden chill, remembering what Vance had said about seeing Fletcher along this same stretch of roadway a little earlier. Now, for whatever reason, he was back. Her uneasiness increased but she forced herself to keep walking.

You wanted to talk to him, she thought. *Here's your*

chance. Just be cool. He's not going to do anything out here in broad daylight. As she took another step she felt a piece of gravel slip into her shoe, down along her instep. She winced. *Damn it anyway.* She kept walking and that was when Fletcher commented on her limping.

Now, facing her across the picnic table, he didn't seem put off by the fact that she'd chosen to sit on the opposite side. He smiled at her and said, "It's a beautiful morning."

"Yes, it is. Kinda warm, though." Her mind raced as she straightened up. She toed off her loosened Nike and picked it up. She shook out the piece of gravel. "That's better," she said. She stretched out her leg and wriggled her toes.

Watching her over the top of the table, Fletcher laughed. "Like mother, like daughter," he said.

What the hell? "What do you mean?" she asked.

"The color of your nail polish," he said, nodding toward her bare foot. "Your mother had that same bright red polish on her toes."

How could you know that? She laughed to cover her confusion. "Yes, that was her favorite color. Mom loved going for pedicures. That was something…we used to do together." She heard the catch in her voice. *Be cool!*

Fletcher shook his head. "I'm sorry if I brought up a painful memory," he said. "That was thoughtless of me."

Or stupid of you. "No, it's all right," she said. She wanted to keep him talking. "But I'm curious. How did you know the color of the nail polish on my mom's toes?"

He hesitated before answering. Was it her imagination or did he flinch slightly?

"Oh, she was wearing flip-flops out here one time when I saw her," he said. He hesitated again, then added, "That was a few weeks ago. Another hot morning, just like this one."

Liar! Jessica wanted to scream the accusation at him but she forced herself to remain calm. She nodded and smiled. "I see," she said. She shuffled her foot back into her shoe and bent over to retie it.

"Well, again, I'm sorry if I brought up a painful memory."

Jessica shook her head. "No, it's okay. And you're right.

She loved that bright red color."

"How are you and your dad getting along?"

Quick to change the subject, aren't we? Jessica smiled wanly. "We're doing okay. There's a lot to figure out. It's a good thing Dad's an attorney. He's handling all the legal stuff with Mom's estate and I'm helping him go through all of her things at the house." She sighed, hoping she wasn't sounding overly dramatic. "There's just a lot of stuff to take care of."

"I'm sure," Fletcher said. He stood up and said, "I'm very sorry for your loss. I really liked your mom."

"Everybody did," Jessica replied, standing up also. "I need to be getting Maisie home."

"I need to get home also," Fletcher said. He smiled again. "But it was good talking to you."

"Good talking with you also." She patted her thigh. "C'mon, Maisie."

The golden stood and followed her to the Explorer, keeping herself between Jessica and Fletcher and tightly pressed against Jessica's hip as they walked past him.

FLETCHER WATCHED JESSICA and Maisie climb into the Explorer, and he waited until they had backed out of the parking area and pulled away before starting for his vehicle. He saw Jessica glance his way as they drove past and he lifted a hand in farewell. She raised her hand from the steering wheel to acknowledge his wave and then the Explorer was gone, leaving a faint trail of gravel dust in its wake.

He climbed into the Durango and started the ignition, then sat looking out over the lake for a moment. Once again, he'd initially been surprised by how much Jessica resembled her mother—and not just because of their matching nail polish— but he was confident he'd concealed his surprise and had done nothing to raise any suspicion in Jessica's mind.

He was pleased with the way the conversation had gone, confident he'd shown just the right amount of concern, and he was especially proud of how he had fielded her question about knowing the color of the polish on Hannah's toes. Saying he'd seen her wearing flip-flops was nothing less than inspired, he thought, especially since he'd never actually seen her doing so. But didn't most women wear flip-flops in hot weather?

Bottom line, he hadn't gotten any sense that Jessica was upset with him or suspected him of any wrongdoing, and that was what he'd hoped to find out. *Mission accomplished*, he thought, and he smiled when he recalled how unnerved he'd been the afternoon of Hannah's funeral when he'd thought Jessica had frowned at him as she was leaving the funeral home, and all of the subsequent worrying he'd done since then.

He laughed aloud at the song that began playing on the radio. The Temptations, singing "Just My Imagination."

CHAPTER 34

AT 2:30 ON MONDAY AFTERNOON the phone rang.

I was sitting at the company computer editing an article on hunting chukar partridge in Idaho with a brace of pudelpointers. The writer was a fellow named Scott Henderson, a semi-regular contributor. His work seldom required much revision, and he always supplied a good selection of high-quality photos to back up his copy. He was especially good at catching his dogs in action or on point, and because pudelpointers are still a relatively rare breed in North America (although gaining in popularity), I was particularly happy to run Scott's feature and showcase his dogs.

I rolled my desk chair away from the company computer and over to the table on which sat my personal computer and the landline answering machine. I checked the caller ID and was surprised to see Jessica Wilkinson's name in the lighted display. I picked up the handset and said, "Hello."

"Hi, Mr. Vance…er, Rob," Jessica said, her voice coming out in a rush. "It's Jessica. I'm really sorry to bother you, but I need to talk to you about something."

"It's okay," I said. "Not a problem. What do you need to talk to me about?"

"Well, I was hoping we could get together so I could tell you in person. But I talked to Greg Fletcher yesterday after I talked to you, and I'd like to get your take on a few things."

"You talked to Fletcher?" I was remembering that I had assumed he'd left the lake after our encounter and before I'd talked to Jessica. Apparently I was wrong.

"Yes, he was sitting at the picnic table by where we parked when I got back there after walking Maisie." She hesitated then added, "It was almost like he was waiting there for me. Kinda creeped me out actually."

I didn't want to add to her alarm but I couldn't help saying, "That's understandable, I guess. What did you talk about?"

"That's what I wanted to talk to *you* about," she said. "He said something that I think proves he killed Mom. But I was hoping to get your take on it."

Here we go again. I was still reluctant to sound like I might be encouraging her in her quest. But I couldn't deny my curiosity was piqued by what Fletcher might have said to her, and by the fact that he had apparently orchestrated their meeting. Trying to sound as objective as possible I said, "If you really think you have evidence you should probably contact the police."

"I already did that. They don't think it's worth pursuing. But I *know* it is. That's why I was hoping to get your opinion."

"What about your father? Did you talk to him about this?"

"He wasn't convinced, either. In fact, I think he was kind of pissed—excuse me, upset—that I was still pursuing this. He wants me to let the whole thing go."

I'm not a father, but I could appreciate his concern and understand why he wouldn't want his daughter to continue digging into this. But I didn't want Jessica to think I was being dismissive. "Okay," I said, hoping she couldn't hear my sigh of resignation. "Why don't we meet out at the lake this evening after dinner. Say around 7:30, at the same place as yesterday?"

"That would be great. And…thank you so much."

AFTER HANGING UP, I SAT for a minute and stared at the blank screen on my personal computer, wondering what Fletcher might have said that had convinced Jessica he'd murdered her mother. The fact that neither the police nor her father had found her evidence—if it *was* evidence—compelling enough to warrant further investigation left me feeling rather skeptical as well. Once again I wondered if Jessica was desperately grasping at straws.

I glanced at my watch. In less than five hours I would listen to what she had to say and could judge for myself whether her claim had merit. In the meantime, I still had half a story to edit, plus several more waiting in the dock.

I sighed again and rolled my chair back over to the company computer and got to it.

IT WAS A FEW MINUTES past three when I finished editing Scott Henderson's story. I saved the document with the suffix ".rev," indicating it had been revised, then downloaded it to the file-sharing program we used. I also downloaded the folder of Henderson's photos. The associate editor would retrieve the story for proofing while the art director began screening the photos prior to laying out the feature. My part in the process was completed until the layout with copy and photos in place was returned to me for final proofing and approval.

I decided I needed a break before starting on another story, so I stood up and headed out to the kitchen. As I passed through the living room, Preacher, sprawled on the sofa, opened her eyes and thumped her tail a couple times. Like all German wirehairs, Preacher's tail is docked—the official breed standard stipulates two-fifths of its original length should remain—but she still has enough left to wag.

"Outside?" I asked, thinking she might need to pee. But she made no effort to get off the sofa and follow me. "Well, all right, then," I said. I walked on through the kitchen to the back door and went out to check on my painting project.

After returning from Menards the previous afternoon, I'd scraped the doorframe to get rid of all the peeling paint, then primed the bare wood and the rest of the frame. By the time I'd finished with the primer I'd worked up a pretty good sweat— the temp was still in the high eighties—and decided that was enough manual labor for one day. After rinsing out my paintbrush with the garden hose—you have to love water-based paint for its ease of clean-up—I'd gone inside and showered.

Daryl and I had met for pizza at Christopher's restaurant in Beaverdale that evening, and afterwards we'd returned to her place and sat on her patio, and as dusk fell, enjoyed a nightcap while we watched the lightning bugs and a couple of swooping bats. Daryl had joked about what a pair of old fogeys we'd become, and I'd laughed and agreed. Still, it was a pleasant way to wrap up the weekend. I was back home by a little after ten o'clock.

Now, looking at the primed doorframe, I could see that the areas of bare wood had sucked up the primer like the proverbial sponge, and I wondered if I should give those areas a second coat. I'd planned to paint the entire frame with the finish coat this evening after dinner, but that was going to be delayed now that I had agreed to meet Jessica at the lake. I decided a second coat of primer was probably a good idea, and I could take care of that right now. Because I'd already prepped the surface, it shouldn't take more than fifteen or twenty minutes.

Call it my afternoon coffee break, slightly extended.

JESSICA WAS ALREADY SITTING at the picnic table near the parking area where we had agreed to meet. It was a couple minutes past 7:30 when I pulled in and parked next to her Explorer. As I climbed out of the Equinox, Maisie trotted over to greet me, plumed tail high and waving. I reached down to ruffle her ears, then looked up and said, "Good evening."

Jessica smiled. "Good evening. Where's Preacher?"

"Snoozing on the sofa and soaking up the air conditioning," I said, and Jessica laughed. I crossed to the picnic table and sat down opposite her. She was wearing a powder blue t-shirt—I immediately noticed how it complemented her eyes—and a pair of white gym trunks. Instead of the athletic shoes I'd seen her in previously, she was wearing a pair of pink flip-flops and her toenails were painted bright red.

Maisie settled herself on the grass behind Jessica. I leaned forward on the tabletop and folded my hands. "So," I said. "You talked to Fletcher yesterday and he said something…?" I let the question hang without finishing it.

"Yes, and I hope you won't think I'm crazy when I tell you," she said. "And by the way, thanks again for coming out here and meeting me."

"No problem."

She drew a deep breath. "Okay, here's what happened." She smiled ruefully. "I hope I'm not making too much of this, but I really believe it's important."

CHAPTER 35

GREG FLETCHER WAS STILL FEELING pleased with himself on Monday evening. He'd worked his shift at the airport that day and had enjoyed the view on three occasions when attractive women stopped at his kiosk to pay their parking fees. Two of the women were wearing summer business suits but the third, a blonde who appeared to be in her early twenties, was wearing a tight pink t-shirt and white shorts. She was driving a Miata convertible with the top down, affording him an especially good look at her nice boobs and long legs.

When his shift ended he had come home and watched *Jeopardy!*, then he'd gone outside and mowed his lawn. After finishing that task, he went back inside and showered. He told himself it was too hot to cook, so he ordered a stuffed-crust Italian special pizza from the carryout Pizza Hut on Southeast 14th Street. He was in something of a celebratory mood.

After dinner he decided to go for another walk. He considered driving out to the reservoir but figured it would be smart not to push his luck. He thought the odds of running into Jessica Wilkinson a second time were pretty slim—he didn't know if she went back out there in the evenings—but he didn't want to risk it. He'd learned what he'd hoped to from their conversation yesterday morning, and that was enough.

He left his house through the back door, locking it as he went, and walked down his driveway to the street. He headed up the block toward Ft. Des Moines Park. Before leaving he'd glanced at his kitchen clock and had seen the time was just past seven o'clock. It was still warm and humid but he planned to take it easy and not push himself, maybe even spend a little time sitting in the hanging metal bench swing on the point overlooking a cove at the south end of the lake. He smiled at the thought that he'd already gotten enough exercise by mowing the lawn.

He crossed County Line Road and approached the park

from its back side, walking through the parking lot of Studebaker Elementary School. A graveled walkway forked beyond the parking lot, with one path leading almost straight north to the levee on the east side of the lake; the other angling northwest toward a parking area and shelter house. He chose the latter.

He passed the retention pond at the rear of the school property—a family of mallards was paddling along the cattails on the far side—and as he approached the shelter house he could see two vehicles parked just beyond, but no sign of other people. Most likely they were walking through the park and he might or might not run into them. No big deal either way, he thought.

Another walkway, this one concrete, led from the parking area down to the point with the hanging bench swing. Fletcher took this path down the slope through a grove of huge oaks, much like the ones in the park at Maffitt Reservoir. A fox squirrel raced down the path ahead of him carrying something in its mouth, but he couldn't see what it was. Probably an acorn, he guessed.

He ambled along until he arrived at the swing at the foot of the slope. After pausing for a moment to read the polished steel and black enamel plaque affixed to the back of the swing—it had been donated by Bob & Suzann Judge of Bob's Tools--he settled himself on the swing and gazed out across the water toward a wooden walkway on the opposite shore of the cove.

A family of five, two adults and three children, were standing on the walkway tossing pieces of bread to a flotilla of semi-tame ducks and Canada geese. He could hear the children's laughter and an occasional loud quack from the ducks and smiled again. His mind wandered and he rocked slightly in the swing.

Motion at the north end of the lake and the far end of the levee attracted his attention. A tall woman with long brown hair had just started walking southward along the top of the earthen levee that formed the east side of the lake. She was walking a large dog and Fletcher was certain, given its size and markings—auburn and white, with a black face mask—it was a Saint Bernard.

He was delighted.

He immediately recalled the first chapter of *The Call of the Wild* and the passage which noted that Buck's father was a huge Saint Bernard named Elmo. Fletcher was predisposed to liking Saint Bernards for just that reason.

He decided to act on that predisposition and, he admitted to himself, use the opportunity of a chance encounter to check out the woman. His mind shifted into predatory mode; he grinned at the thought and began calculating how to stage that encounter.

The levee was about a quarter mile long and the woman was walking briskly with the dog trotting ahead of her on its lead. He'd have to move quickly but he estimated that if she stayed on the walkway he could intercept her somewhere close to where the path forked behind the school. He stood up from the swing and strode quickly back up the wooded slope to the parking area and shelter house.

He didn't pause but started walking back toward the school, retracing his earlier path. He could no longer see the levee or the woman and her dog as they were screened by a stand of woods at the lake's south end. He broke into a jog, thinking, *so much for taking it easy.*

After covering about fifty yards he slowed to a walk again, not wanting the woman to see him jogging. He took a few deep breaths and continued on toward the fork in the walkway, and it was then that the woman and the Saint Bernard emerged from the woods.

He continued walking toward them, congratulating himself on the success of his strategy. When he was within about five yards of the approaching woman and her dog he smiled and said, "Good evening."

The woman smiled in return and said, "Good evening."

Fletcher wasn't especially good at estimating women's ages, but he guessed she was in her mid to late forties. She was wearing gray shorts and a black Kid Rock t-shirt. On her feet were black Chuck Taylor kicks with white shoelaces. She was also wearing black ankle and wrist weights and a pair of dark sunglasses with large square frames. Her long, wavy brown hair fell to below her shoulders, and although she was tall and slender, Fletcher saw that she had large breasts. *Nice tits*, he immediately thought.

The Saint Bernard pulled up short, maybe ten feet away, and stood regarding him warily. The woman stopped walking also and something in the dog's demeanor told Fletcher he'd be smart not to advance any closer. He said, "That's a beautiful dog."

"Thanks," the woman replied, and it was at that moment that the Saint Bernard let out a low rumbling growl. Fletcher involuntarily flinched and took a step backward just as the woman said, "Alexander! Stop that!" She grabbed the dog's lead with both hands and gave it a sharp jerk.

The dog continued growling.

"I'm sorry," the woman said. "You'd better give us some space. I don't know why he's growling; he's ordinarily very friendly."

"That's okay," Fletcher said, moving over to the side of the gravel path. To mask his fear—the huge Saint Bernard was definitely an intimidating animal—he laughed and said, "His name is Alexander?"

"That's right," the woman said. "Alexander the Great." She was still holding the lead with both hands but the dog appeared to relax somewhat.

Fletcher was tempted to say, "Not Cujo?" but realized the joke would likely fall flat. He wanted to keep things positive. He said, "That's a fitting name for such an impressive dog. He is a handsome fellow. How old is he?"

"He's four," the woman said, and Fletcher nodded. She looked at him expectantly, obviously wanting to end the conversation and continue her walk. He took the hint.

"Well, I'd better let you get on with your walk," he said. "But nice meeting you. My name's Greg. Greg Fletcher."

"Oh, Rachel James," the woman said. "Nice meeting you also."

Fletcher stepped off the path and the woman and her dog

moved past him toward the school parking lot. He watched them for a moment then turned away and started walking north toward the levee, as if he intended to follow the path around the lake in the opposite direction.

When he reached the woods at the south end of the levee he paused and looked back. The woman and the dog were nearing the far end of the parking lot where it opened onto County Line Road. *Interesting,* Fletcher thought. *She must live in my neighborhood.*

He continued watching until they were out of sight. He gave it another minute then reversed his course and started back toward the parking lot himself, intending to head home.

Despite the Saint Bernard's unfriendliness, he hoped he'd see the woman again. He might be able to win over the dog, and he thought another encounter was worth pursuing if for no other reason than to get another look at her impressive boobs.

Plus, he knew her name. At the very least, he should be able to find out where she lived.

CHAPTER 36

"IT'S ACTUALLY A COUPLE of things," Jessica said.

"Okay." I sensed her hesitation, perhaps fearing I was going to dismiss whatever she told me. I smiled to reassure her and said, "Just tell me."

She drew a deep breath. "All right," she said. "First, it was how Maisie acted when she saw him. You saw how she just acted with you, coming right over to be petted. She didn't do that with Fletcher."

"What did she do?"

"Well, I told you how he was just sitting here, like he was waiting for us. When Maisie saw him, she stopped and just stood there looking at him. She didn't go up to him to be petted like she ordinarily does with everyone. She didn't act afraid, exactly, just standoffish. It was more like she sensed something about him that was just…off, and she didn't want to get any closer."

I gave it a moment's consideration then said, "Hmmm," for want of a better response. I thought about it for another moment, then added, "That does sound a little unusual. Not like her, anyway. But I think you need to be careful not to read too much into it. Maybe she was just surprised to see him, and a little uncertain about whether he would appreciate her approaching him."

"I know what you're saying about not reading too much into it. But don't you see? She *always* goes right up to people. She never holds back. But it was almost like she associated him with Mom's death, and she didn't want anything to do with him."

I had to be honest with her. "Now I think you're reaching," I said. Much as I love and appreciate dogs, I don't believe they possess some sort of super power of intuition regarding a person's character. Sure, they like some people and dislike others, but I thought what Jessica had just suggested was too much of a stretch.

Then again, I reminded myself that I'd been surprised the morning Maisie had shown up carrying Hannah's shoe and had then led me to her body. I couldn't deny that dogs sometimes did things that surpassed what we humans thought them capable of doing.

Jessica sighed. "I know, I know. But even when I came over to the table and sat down, she still stayed away from him. She came over and laid down right next to me. I had the feeling she was being protective."

"Did she growl at him, or do anything like that?"

"No, but when we got up to leave, she stayed right beside me, between us. Between him and me, I mean. Again, it was almost like she was trying to protect me in case he tried anything."

"What did he do at that point?"

"He just stood there and watched us leave. And that reminds me of something else. Don't you think it was weird that he was waiting here for us when we got back from our walk? I mean, you said you'd seen him earlier but he wasn't parked over here. He must have driven over after you left. If he was parked on the other side, why didn't he just go home after you saw him?"

I shrugged. "That's hard to say. Maybe he just wanted to spend a little more time out here. It was a nice morning and maybe he just wasn't ready to go home." I hoped this didn't sound lame; even as I said it, I admitted to myself that yes, I thought it was a little weird that he'd been sitting here waiting for her. But I didn't want to alarm her.

She shook her head. "I think he came over here deliberately with the idea of seeing me."

"Why would he do that?"

"I don't know. Maybe because he feels guilty about what he did to Mom and wanted to find out how I'm feeling or what I'm thinking at this point?"

I sighed. "I have to tell you, Jessica, I still think you're reaching. Do you know that old saying about horses and zebras?"

She shook her head and looked puzzled. "No. Horses and zebras?"

"Right," I said. "It's a saying that doctors, medical doctors, sometimes use. It goes like this: When you find hoofprints in the sand, you should first think horses, not zebras."

She gave it a moment's thought then said, "Okaaay…"

"In other words, the simplest or most likely answer is probably the correct one. Don't immediately start assuming things and jumping to conclusions of a more exotic nature."

She smiled and said, "Like Occam's razor."

I smiled in return. "Right," I said, impressed that she was familiar with the theory. "I think you need to be careful and not read too much into things. What you've told me about Fletcher, even including Maisie's reaction to him, could just be coincidence."

"I guess so," she said. "But there's something else, and this is where I think he really gave himself away." Her voice kicked up a notch with excitement.

"Okay," I nodded. "Tell me."

"Well, the reason I came over here and sat down was because I had a rock, a piece of gravel, in my shoe." She pointed down the road toward the south. "I picked it up a little ways back down there, and I needed to sit down and take my shoe off to get rid of it."

"Okay," I said again, curious as to where this was going.

"When I did—take my shoe off, I mean—he looked over and said, 'Like mother, like daughter.'"

Still puzzled, I said, "Like mother, like daughter?"

"Yes!" she said. "I had the same reaction. I asked him what he meant, and he said that the nail polish on my toes was the same color as my mom's." Jessica lifted and stretched her right leg, flexing her foot so her flip-flop snapped against her sole. I glanced at her foot and saw the bright red polish again. "I asked him how he knew that and he said he'd seen her wearing flip-flops out here a few weeks earlier."

I still wasn't connecting the dots. "Sorry," I said. "Why was that suspicious?"

"Because," Jessica said, and there was no mistaking the triumph in her voice, "I know for a fact that Mom *never* wore flip-flops out here."

"Really," I said, "why was that?"

She smiled. "Mom loved going for pedicures; that was something we did a lot together. In fact, we were planning to do it that weekend I was coming home."

"All right," I said, "So she loved pedicures…"

"She loved pedicures, and she was always very careful in between so she wouldn't chip the nail polish. She said that for as much as you paid for a pedicure, you shouldn't turn around and do something that would spoil it."

"Oh? What does a pedicure cost?" I had no idea what women spent on such procedures.

"They aren't cheap if you go to a good salon. The place we went, a deluxe pedicure costs forty-five dollars. And of course, you're expected to tip the operator as well."

I laughed. "Of course," I said. I was tempted to ask what constituted a deluxe pedicure, as opposed to, say, the common garden variety, but I didn't. I was more interested in how this all related to Jessica's assertion about Greg Fletcher. "So your mom never wore flip-flops because she didn't want to risk spoiling her pedicure?"

"Oh, she wore flip-flops around the house, and sometimes to the store, places like that. But she never wore flip-flops out here because she was afraid she might walk through something or stub her toe on something and chip the polish."

"Are you sure about that? That she never made an exception? Maybe if she was in a hurry or just bringing Maisie out for a quick walk through the park?"

"I'm positive. We even talked about it. She always wore her Nikes, and she also wore ankle weights a lot of times when she walked out here. She was really conscious of staying in shape. I know she never would have worn flip-flops if she was walking Maisie."

I didn't say anything for a minute, taking time to assimilate everything Jessica had said. I remembered that I had, in fact, seen Hannah wearing ankle weights a few times when we'd walked together, and I was pretty sure I'd never seen her wearing flip-flops. Mention of the ankle weights triggered another memory. I hesitated to bring it up, but decided to go ahead.

"If I remember correctly, when they performed the autopsy"—I winced as I said this—"they found some bruising around one of your mom's ankles, and you said something to the police about her wearing the ankle weights."

Jessica frowned. "Yes, and I'm really sorry now that I told them that. I think Greg Fletcher caused that bruising. He must have grabbed her by the ankle when he was trying to drown her. In fact, I'd bet on it. If I hadn't told the cops about the ankle weights, they might have paid more attention to the bruising and used that to pin him down."

I shook my head. "Yeah, maybe," I said. "Then again…" I opened my hands and held them palms up, the universal symbol for "who knows?"

Jessica gave me a determined look. "So, now do you believe me? That Greg Fletcher killed my mom?"

I deflected. "Well, it sounds like you caught him in a lie, anyway. But you said you told the cops about this? And your father?"

"Yes, and they didn't think it was a big deal. I don't think the cops believed Mom never wore flip-flops out here, or at least, they didn't think it was worth checking out. I called that woman detective—Madison?—this morning and talked to her on the phone. I thought she might ask me to come in, but she didn't. She just asked me how she could help me, so I went ahead and told her what I just told you."

"You told her all that on the phone?"

"Yes. That the only way Fletcher could have known the color of Mom's nail polish was if he'd seen her take off her shoes, but she—the detective—didn't seem to buy it. She said that maybe Mom had taken off her shoes when they got down to that big boulder and she asked him to give her some time to herself, and that's how he knew the color of her nail polish."

"That wouldn't jibe with what he told you about seeing her in flip-flops." Now I sounded like I was the one pushing

Jessica's theory.

"That's exactly what I said! I told the detective that he hadn't said anything about seeing her take her shoes off, but she said maybe he'd just been confused and forgot to mention it."

Well, maybe. But it sounded to me like the cops were ignoring what appeared to be a rather critical inconsistency in Fletcher's account. I could have believed that of Detective Jarrett, but I was a little surprised by Detective Madison's apparent reluctance to follow up.

"What about your dad?" I asked.

Jessica shook her head. "Pretty much the same thing. He knew Mom wore flip-flops sometimes, so I think he just assumed I was wrong about her never wearing them out here. He said, 'Jess, you have to let this go.' He thinks it's unhealthy for me to keep pursuing this."

"I'm sure he's just trying to watch out for you."

"I understand that. But I'm not a child. And I *know* I'm right about this."

I hesitated to ask the obvious question, but I needed to know the answer. "So," I said, "what are you going to do about this? If the cops won't follow up, I mean?"

She made a huffing noise and shook her head. "I don't know. I haven't figured that out. But I know one thing for certain." She turned and looked out over the lake.

"What's that?"

"I want Greg Fletcher to pay for what he did." She took a deep breath and turned back and looked me in the eye. "Best case scenario, I want him to die just like my mom did."

CHAPTER 37

I CAN'T DENY THAT JESSICA'S words gave me a chill.

The dead-calm certainty with which she delivered them left little doubt in my mind that, given the opportunity, she would perform Greg Fletcher's execution herself, and do so without hesitation. This was, as I'd thought previously, one very determined young woman.

A moment later, I experienced an even bigger chill.

"That might be hard to pull off," I said, hoping to give Jessica a reality check and steer her away from her vindictive thinking.

"I know," she said, and there was no missing the bitterness in her voice. Then she laughed and said, "You wouldn't happen to know where I could hire a hit man, would you?"

God Almighty.

Like I said, an even bigger chill. I laughed to hide my discomfort. "Sorry," I said, shaking my head and telling myself that my answer was less a lie than an outright "no" would have been. I seemed to be splitting quite a few hairs lately.

Jessica sighed and Maisie stood up and rested her head on Jessica's knee. Jessica reached down to ruffle the golden's ears. After a moment she said, "I guess I don't know what to do next. If the cops don't believe what I told them about Fletcher lying when he said he'd seen Mom wearing flip-flops, I don't know where else to turn. I'm at a dead end." She shook her head. "Bad choice of words."

I gave it another moment's thought. "I don't know what to suggest either," I said finally. "I'm sorry the cops don't think it's worth looking into again." A thought occurred to me, but I hesitated to share it. Then I decided, oh, what the hell.

"What about your dad?" I said. "Is there any chance of convincing him? I know you said he wants you to drop it, but if you could convince him, do you think he could persuade the cops to take another look?" I was thinking that as a lawyer, he might have some clout with the law enforcement community. Then again, maybe not, given the opinion of lawyers held by many cops.

"I don't think so," Jessica said. "He's pretty determined to put this all behind us and move on. I doubt if I could change his mind." She paused, then looked up from petting Maisie and met my eyes again. "What about you?" she asked. "Do *you* believe me?"

Another 64,000-dollar question.

I chose my words carefully. "I certainly believe you caught Fletcher in a lie," I said. "And a pretty damning one, at that. If you're certain about your mom never wearing flip-flops out here—and I believe you are—then yes, I think he lied." I could see the disappointment in Jessica's face and I realized she thought I was just humoring her. But I wanted to complete my thought, regardless. "Whether that proves he killed your mother"—I shook my head again—"that I can't say."

"But why else would he lie?" she said, her exasperation plain. "If he wasn't trying to cover up what he did?"

"I don't know."

I could see her eyes filling with tears. "This is hopeless," she said. She stood up abruptly and wiped a hand across her eyes. She looked at me and forced a smile. "But anyway, thanks for coming out and listening."

I stood up also. "Jessica, I'm really sorry I couldn't be more help."

"It's okay. C'mon, Maisie." She turned and started for the Explorer, the golden trotting alongside her.

I watched them go. I couldn't remember ever feeling more useless.

As Jessica drove away she glanced over at me, leaning forward in her seat to see past Maisie sitting beside her in the passenger seat. Jessica gave me a quick, wan smile and a brief wave, then they were gone.

I remained standing for a moment, then sat back down at the picnic table. I glanced at my wristwatch and saw that it was a quarter past eight. Dusk was just beginning to fall but I could still clearly see the wooded shoreline on the opposite side of the lake. It wouldn't be fully dark for another forty-five minutes. I knew that at about nine o'clock a security officer would drive through, shooing out all of the late-stayers before locking the entrance gate for the night.

I stared out over the water, seeing one canoe and a couple of kayaks near the center of the lake. There was very little breeze and the surface was glassy smooth. A pair of Canada geese, wings set, came gliding down to settle with barely a ripple on the water in the cove.

I started thinking about everything Jessica had told me.

Her anger and frustration were obvious, and I hoped they wouldn't cause her to do anything rash. She was convinced Greg Fletcher had killed her mother, and she wanted to see justice done. My thoughts about her determination notwithstanding, I doubted she would try to take matters into her own hands. Then again, I couldn't be certain that she wouldn't.

Was her reasoning sound? I'd spoken the truth when I told her I believed she'd caught Fletcher in a damning lie. I was willing to accept Jessica's claim that her mother never wore flip-flops to walk Maisie at the lake, and as such, Fletcher's claim of having seen her do so must be false. But I wasn't certain that alone was enough to convict him, so to speak.

I also considered Detective Madison's apparent reluctance to further investigate the matter.

I had no idea how heavy the detective's caseload was. Des Moines is not a high crime city—at least, not compared to, say, Chicago or Detroit—but neither is it Petticoat Junction. I doubted that Detective Madison had much idle time on the job, and that might explain why she and her partner, Detective Jarrett, were not going to question Fletcher again. Trying to put myself in their shoes, I had to admit that knowing the color of nail polish on a drowned woman's toes hardly seemed like a significant clue.

But what if it was? What if Jessica had, in fact, come up with what had actually happened? She had said she believed the slight bruising on Hannah's ankle had been caused not by the ankle weights Hannah sometimes wore, but by Fletcher; that he must have grabbed her ankle when he drowned her.

I tried to imagine how that could have happened.

I remembered finding Hannah's shoes next to the big boulder at the water's edge, and her cell phone and keys atop the boulder. They appeared to have been placed there carefully. According to Jessica, when the police had questioned Fletcher, he told them he had walked back to the boulder with Hannah but she had then asked him to give her some time alone. He claimed to have respected her request, left her there and gone home.

But maybe he hadn't. Maybe, as Jessica supposed, he'd— what? Somehow talked her into entering the water, then overpowered her?

I tried again to visualize what I'd seen that morning when I found Hannah's body. I remembered that the sandy shoreline had been dry and hard and neither I nor the dogs had made tracks on it. There was no sign of a struggle in the sand.

Which further suggested that if Fletcher had killed Hannah, he'd done it in the water. In fact, that was the only way—or place—it could have happened.

I shook my head. I had to admit there was also the very real possibility that things had transpired as Fletcher said, that he'd left Hannah alone at the boulder and she had subsequently drowned herself. I didn't want to believe that, and it wouldn't account for Fletcher's lie about seeing Hannah wearing flip-flops, but it couldn't be entirely discounted, either. I remembered what I'd told Jessica about horses and zebras and reminded myself not to be jumping to unlikely conclusions.

I also realized that because Hannah had been a friend, and because her daughter had now become a friend as well, I might not be thinking about any of this as clearly as I should. I have five inviolate rules concerning contract killings, and one of these, the first, in fact, is that there must be no personal involvement. Almost by definition, personal involvement can cloud one's thinking and that in turn can lead to major, even fatal, errors in judgment.

Well. No one had hired me to avenge Hannah Wilkinson's death, so my inviolate rules didn't really apply here. But I knew I'd be wise to keep them in mind, just the same. Jessica Wilkinson was obviously convinced Greg Fletcher had killed her mother, and it was tempting to go along with her theory. But even assuming she was correct, I was not under any obligation to provide justice for her mother.

At least, that's what I kept telling myself as I drove home from the lake.

It was about 9:15 when I got home, and Preacher was waiting at the back door again when I unlocked it. I stood aside and she trotted out. I went inside and snagged a bottle of Blue Moon from the fridge. I uncapped it and glanced at the phone in the kitchen, one of several remote sets throughout the house that are networked to the landline answering machine in my office.

The red light on the handset was blinking, indicating I had a message.

I walked into my office and snapped on the desk light next to my personal computer. I punched the play button on the answering machine.

The message was from Rachel James, and she was atypically terse.

"Hey you," she said. "Call me."

CHAPTER 38

THE FIRST THING GREG FLETCHER did when he got home was grab a Miller Lite from the refrigerator. The second thing he did was sit down at his kitchen table, log onto his laptop and open a browser. He typed "rachel james des moines" into the search window—he never bothered with capital letters or punctuation when doing a search—and hit Enter. He was rewarded with several hits.

He chose one of the people-finder sites and clicked on it. Rachel James's profile popped up and he studied it carefully.

He learned that she was 52 years old—a few years older than he'd guessed—and she was married. As she'd struggled to hold back her unfriendly Saint Bernard, he'd noticed she wasn't wearing a wedding ring, but he knew that wasn't necessarily definitive. Part of her street address was blocked out, but the last part—"Pkwy"—was shown. He assumed that meant she lived on one of those east-west streets—Palomino, Marlou, Gepke or Greenfield—that was designated as a parkway in Greenfield Plaza. This confirmed she was one of his neighbors.

Her known relatives and associates were Allen James (probably her husband), John James (son?), Summer Gionelli (daughter?) and Ray Gionelli (son-in-law?) Several additional unrelated names were also shown, and Fletcher guessed these were friends or neighbors.

Her ethnicity was listed as Caucasian (*duh*, Fletcher thought), her religious views were Christian and her political affiliation was unknown. Her household net income was in six figures, which suggested that she and her husband both worked. He wondered what her job was.

He briefly considered paying the site's trial subscription fee to obtain the full "premium" report on Rachel James. The report would show her complete address, phone numbers, legal history, social media presence and other details, but he decided the information he'd already found would suffice for now; plus, he didn't want to pay the fee.

He scanned through the other hits. He saw that she was also listed on a career-linking website but he wasn't a member himself—he wasn't interested in employment-related networking—so he knew he couldn't access her page, having tried to do so previously to check out other women he'd met. He decided where she worked wasn't that important.

He returned to the top of the window and clicked on "Images." Apparently, there were quite a few women named Rachel James, including a British actress, because lots of thumbnail photos popped up. But after scrolling through two pages of the thumbnails, he couldn't find any that resembled even slightly the woman he'd just met in Ft. Des Moines Park. He clicked on the "back" arrow, then clicked it again to return to the browser's main page.

He sat for a moment, sipping at his beer, and reflecting on what he'd learned.

Rachel James was a neighbor in the Plaza, almost certainly. He'd never seen her before tonight, but if she regularly walked her dog at Ft. Des Moines Park, he thought he stood a very good chance of seeing her again, especially if he began walking in the park more frequently himself. The Saint Bernard might be a problem unless he could win it over, but he was reasonably confident he could do so. If not…well, he'd cross that bridge, etc.

That she was married was also somewhat troubling, but not overly so. In fact, he admitted to himself that as attractive as she was—once again, he thought of her big boobs—it would be unusual if she wasn't married, or at least involved in a relationship. This wouldn't be the first time he'd befriended a married woman. After all, he thought wryly, Hannah Wilkinson had been married. That hadn't stopped him from getting close to her.

He took another sip of beer, then typed "facebook" in the browser's search window. When the login screen for the social media site appeared he typed in his user name and password. When his page came up—he'd set it up with a fictitious name;

his profile photo was one he'd pulled off the internet of a wolf howling before a full moon—he again typed "rachel james des moines" in the Facebook search window and hit Enter.

A list of women named Rachel James came up with thumbnails of their profile photos shown next to their names. He scrolled down the list but saw no one who looked like the woman he was seeking. Apparently his Rachel James—he smiled as he realized he was thinking of her in possessive terms—either didn't have a Facebook page or, if she did, it was under a different name. *So she's careful about protecting her privacy*, he thought. *Well, so am I.*

He clicked the back arrow to return to his page, then logged out. He picked up his can of Miller Lite and took a final swallow. He stood up and returned to the refrigerator for another, tossing the empty can into the tall wastebasket in the corner along the way. He never recycled; it was too much bother.

Returning to the kitchen table, he sat down again and, after a moment, typed the name of another website into the browser's search window. The website came up and he logged in, then clicked on the site's forum tab. He hadn't checked the forum for several weeks—he'd thought it best to lie low after Hannah Wilkinson's death—but he wanted to catch up on recent messages and also post a comment or two of his own. Maybe even brag a bit.

He chose a thread titled "Punishment & Rewards" and clicked on it. He read the most recent comments, those posted within the last twenty-four hours, and he grinned when he read the latest message by someone with the username Mako. It had been posted only minutes earlier and Fletcher laughed aloud as he read Mako's account. It concluded with the line, "She won't try that again anytime soon," followed by a grinning emoji.

He clicked on "Reply" and typed, "LOL and congrats, Mako. Well played!" He added a double-thumbs-up emoji, then typed, "I have some news of my own to share."

He got an almost immediate reply. "Let's hear it! And btw, welcome back, Ghost Dog."

CHAPTER 39

The time stamp on Rachel's message was 8:50 p.m. I glanced at my watch and saw it was now 9:20, so I'd only missed her call by half an hour. That, plus the fact that I was pretty sure I'd heard some urgency in her voice, led me to decide it wasn't too late to call her back. I hoped the reason for her message was nothing critical.

She answered on the first ring. "Hey you," she said, our standard greeting to each other.

"Hey you," I replied. "Got your message. What's up?"

"If it's not too late for deck beers, I'd like to come over and talk to you about something."

"No, it's not too late," I said, my curiosity piqued. "What's this about? Is everything okay?"

"Everything's okay over here, but I wanted to tell you about an encounter I had this evening."

"Encounter?"

"I met Greg Fletcher."

I returned to the kitchen and while I waited for Rachel—she lived no more than five minutes away—I couldn't help thinking that the whole Hannah Wilkinson-Greg Fletcher situation was snowballing disproportionately. I also thought the ironic coincidences were piling up like vehicles in a mid-winter accident on I-80.

In the past day and a half, Rachel and Jessica Wilkinson had both had, as Rachel called it, an encounter with Greg Fletcher. I asked myself, *what were the odds*?

In Jessica's case, it was easier to explain. I still thought, as Jessica did, that Fletcher's apparent waiting for her at the parking area was a little unusual, but then again, he was a regular at the lake, so maybe it was nothing. Jessica didn't believe that, and I was skeptical myself, but I didn't want to read more into it than it deserved. Horses and zebras, I again reminded myself.

But Rachel's case really pushed the envelope as far as believability. That she should run into Greg Fletcher so soon after we'd just been talking about him two days earlier, on Saturday afternoon, and one day after Jessica had seen him…well, the odds seemed close to astronomical. That is, if it was the same Greg Fletcher.

My gut told me it was. Des Moines is just a large small town.

Preacher barked at the back door and I opened it to let her inside. As I stepped back into the kitchen, the headlights from Rachel's Camaro swept into my driveway. I went out to meet her.

"Good evening," I said as Rachel climbed out of her car. Her Camaro is a convertible and, not surprisingly, she had the top down. Her long hair was pinned up but a few strands had shaken loose. She was wearing a black Kid Rock t-shirt—I knew she was a longtime fan—shorts and black Chuck Taylors.

"Good evening," she replied. We headed into the house. Preacher greeted Rachel with a wagging tail and a subdued "woof."

"Hey, Preach," Rachel said as she reached down to ruffle Preacher's ears. I crossed to the fridge and pulled out a bottle of Miller 64 for Rachel. I still had about half of the Blue Moon I'd opened a few minutes earlier. I uncapped her beer and handed it to her.

"Outside?" I asked. My question was rhetorical; I knew Rachel would opt for sitting on the deck rather than inside in the air conditioning.

"Sure," she said, and we exited the kitchen and moved out onto the deck. Preacher accompanied us and trotted down the deck steps to make another patrol of the back yard. Rachel and I seated ourselves on the deck chairs, much as we had on Saturday afternoon.

"So," I said. "You ran into Greg Fletcher?"

"Yes, over at Ft. Des Moines Park." She took a pull from her bottle of 64 and I thought I saw her shudder slightly. "I was walking Alexander and he came up to us on the path behind the school. He said 'good evening' and something about Alexander being a beautiful dog. That's when Alexander started growling. I had to use both hands on the leash to hold him back."

"Interesting," I said, recalling what Jessica had told me about Maisie's reaction to seeing Fletcher at the lake. "What did he do then? Fletcher, I mean."

"I told him he'd better give us some space, and he stopped and didn't come any closer. Which was a good thing, because I wasn't sure I could hold Alexander."

I nodded. "That was smart of him."

"Right. Then he asked me about Alexander's name, and I told him it was short for Alexander the Great. He said he thought that was fitting and he asked me how old Alexander was. I told him four."

"Sounds like he was trying to chat you up by admiring your dog."

"That's exactly what I thought." She gave a little snort. "But I wasn't fooled. The whole time we were talking, he kept sneaking peeks at my boobs."

I laughed. "He was that obvious?"

Rachel laughed also. "Oh yeah, he was obvious." She took another drink of beer. "Trust me, a woman always knows when a guy is looking at her boobs."

"I'll have to remember that."

She laughed again and shook her head. "Men," she said.

I drained my Blue Moon and said, "How did you find out he was Greg Fletcher? Did he tell you his name?"

"Yes. After he asked me about Alexander he said something about letting us get on with our walk and then he said, almost like an afterthought, 'My name's Greg Fletcher.'" She gave another shudder. "And, like a dumbass, I told him my name too."

"Really? Your whole name?"

"Yes, damn it. I was still concentrating on trying to control Alexander and I just sort of blurted it out without thinking. I know; stupid of me."

I mentally agreed it was at least somewhat careless of her. It's hard enough these days—make that damned near impossible--to guard your privacy even without volunteering your name to strangers. But I wasn't going to chide Rachel for her slip.

"Oh, probably no big deal," I said. "But let's back up a bit, just to make sure we're talking about the same person. What did this guy look like?"

Rachel paused for a moment, gathering her thoughts. "Well, nothing special, really. He was about your height, maybe an inch shorter and not fat, not thin. Just pretty average. Brown hair. I'd guess he was maybe in his forties, age-wise. Like I said, nothing really distinctive."

"What was he wearing?"

"Shorts and a plain t-shirt, kind of a medium blue color with no logo or design." She paused, then added, "Well, I did notice he was wearing a pair of expensive-looking cross-trainers. Skechers, I think. I kinda got the impression he does a lot of walking."

I nodded. "It sounds like the same Greg Fletcher," I said. "I saw him out at the lake yesterday morning and he was wearing those Skechers." I thought about it for a moment. "Interesting that he was walking in Ft. Des Moines Park," I said. "I wonder if he lives around here."

"I don't know," Rachel said. "What I thought was interesting, or curious anyway, was the way Alexander reacted to him. He definitely didn't like the guy. Almost like Fletcher was giving off a bad vibe. Maybe even dangerous."

I couldn't help laughing. "That's the second time I've heard that this evening," I said.

Rachel looked surprised. "Really? Who else have you heard it from?"

"Well…" I said, "How's this for a coincidence? While you were having your encounter with Greg Fletcher this evening, I was out at Maffitt listening to Jessica Wilkinson tell me about *her* encounter with him yesterday morning."

"Really!" Rachel said. "Jessica Wilkinson…she's the daughter of the woman who drowned and you found her body?"

"That's right. I told you about how she doesn't believe her mother killed herself, and how she's convinced Greg Fletcher killed her. And that she was going to try to get close to him and get some proof. Well, when she saw him yesterday morning, she thinks she got that proof. That's what she told me about this evening out at the lake."

"Really!" Rachel said again. "What's the proof?"

I held up my empty Blue Moon bottle. "Are you ready for another?"

Rachel took a final swallow of Miller 64 and handed me her bottle. "You bet," she said. "This is getting interesting!"

CHAPTER 40

GHOST DOG: Her name was Helen. I met her walking her dog in the park. We started talking and walking together. That went on for a couple years. She started confiding in me, told me she was getting a divorce.

MAKO: Sounds like a match made in heaven. LOL

GHOST DOG: SMH. I thought so too. But it never got off the ground.

MAKO: Looks?

GHOST DOG: Tall, blonde. Long legs. Nice tits.

MAKO: Nice!

WINGMAN: Wow

GHOST DOG: Yeah.

MAKO: So what happened.

GHOST DOG: Not much. LOL. She just wanted a shoulder to cry on.

MAKO: Bummer. A bitch who needs something but gives you nothing back in return. Am I right?

GHOST DOG: Right.

MAKO: And?

GHOST DOG: I finally got tired of her telling me what a nice guy I was.

WINGMAN: Nice guys don't get laid.

MAKO: Thank you Wingman for sharing that universal truth. Now STFU and let Ghost Dog talk.

GHOST DOG: LOL

MAKO: So what happened. Do you still see her.

GHOST DOG: No. I don't see her. And she doesn't see anybody. ☺

WINGMAN: WTF???

MAKO: Meaning…

GHOST DOG: She doesn't tease cock anymore.

WINGMAN: LOL.

MAKO: Intrigued. Details?

GHOST DOG: Maybe later.

FLETCHER SAT BACK TO SEE if Mako or Wingman would reply again. He was expecting one of them, probably Wingman, whom he was pretty sure was much younger, to keep prying. But after a minute or so with no further responses, he logged out. Better to err on the side of caution, and he wondered if he'd already said too much.

He decided he hadn't. He hadn't used Hannah Wilkinson's real name (duh!) and he hadn't specifically stated that he'd killed her, only that she no longer teased cock. He also implied she was no longer seeing anyone but that could be taken a number of different ways—it didn't have to mean that she literally could no longer see. A lot of folks used the word "see" to indicate involvement, as in the ubiquitous dating question, "Are you currently seeing anyone?" Maybe it just meant that she had stopped getting chummy with guys she met in the park.

Fletcher was also confident that, even if someone did find his comments suspicious, they wouldn't be able to trace those comments back to him. The website was at least reasonably secure, he believed, and he doubted that law enforcement had the manpower or the resources to monitor the thousands, probably millions, of online comments posted in forums like the one he'd just visited. And even if they did, they wouldn't be able to investigate every posting of a faintly threatening or slightly incriminating nature. They might check out the more overt stuff, maybe, but nothing as vague as what he'd posted.

He smiled and had another swallow of Miller Lite. *Besides*, he told himself, *I've seen things on this site that are a lot worse than what I just said.*

Things that were much, much worse.

CHAPTER 41

WHEN I GOT BACK OUT TO THE DARK DECK with two more beers, Rachel was sitting forward in her chair, studying her cell phone. The light from the phone caused the frame of her reading glasses to cast black, sharply angled shadows up her forehead, resembling demonic eyebrows. I laughed as I sat down and saw this, and she looked up from her phone and said, "What?"

"Your phone is making you look Satanic," I said. "The light is making shadows from your glasses that look like eyebrows slanting up like this." I leaned forward and traced one of the shadows with a fingertip. "Makes you look demonic."

She laughed and said, "Demonic is good!"

I handed her her beer and leaned back in my chair. I nodded toward her phone. "Is everything okay?"

"Yes, everything's fine. I just got a text from Summer telling me about the boys' swimming lessons. They're both taking lessons at the Y this summer and she said they both passed into the advanced class this afternoon." Summer's sons were named Gabe and Sam—I'd seen them quite a few times over the past few years, and they were both good kids and excellent students—and Rachel was proud of them, as any grandmother would be.

"That's great," I said. "Please tell Summer I said congratulations."

"Will do." Rachel set her phone down on the small table next to our chairs. "So," she said, "let's hear about this proof Jessica Wilkinson got on Greg Fletcher." She took a pull at her Miller 64, then stretched out her legs and toed off her Chuck Taylors. She didn't bother untying the laces first.

"Okay," I said. "Let me start at the beginning. I saw Jessica myself out at the lake yesterday morning. She got there with Maisie, her dog, just as Preacher and I were getting ready to come home. We talked for a few minutes, and I told her that

I'd seen Greg Fletcher a little earlier. She said something about trying to catch him before he left, but then decided she probably couldn't, that he was probably already gone."

"Okay," Rachel said, sounding puzzled. "But you said she did see him."

"Right. She walked Maisie and when she got back to her vehicle a little while later, he was sitting at a picnic table waiting for her."

Rachel frowned. "That's creepy."

"Jessica thought so too. And she said Maisie refused to go near him, which is unusual for her. Usually she goes right up to people. But Jessica said she hung back, like she was trying to protect her. Trying to protect Jessica, I mean."

Rachel nodded. "Like Alexander's reaction to Fletcher over at the park this evening."

"Yeah, I guess so," I said. "Jessica said Maisie stayed close to her the whole time she was talking to Fletcher."

"So…is that her proof? She thinks Maisie's reaction to Fletcher shows that he's guilty?" I thought I detected a note of skepticism in her voice.

"No, there's more to it than that. Quite a bit more, in fact."

Rachel smiled and took another pull at her beer. "Do tell," she said.

So I did. I related the whole episode as Jessica had described it to me, beginning with her sitting down at the picnic table and taking off her shoe to remove a piece of gravel, followed by Fletcher noticing the color of polish on her toenails and commenting that it matched her mother's, and so on. I wrapped it up with Jessica's assertion that the only way Fletcher could have known the color of polish on Hannah's toes was if he'd seen her remove her shoes the evening she died; that she never wore flip-flops to the lake as Fletcher had claimed.

Rachel was silent for a moment, then she said, "Jessica is certain about that? About her mom never wearing flip-flops to the lake?"

"Yes. She said Hannah loved going for pedicures and because of what they cost, she didn't want to risk chipping the nail polish. She was positive Hannah never wore flip-flops out there. Around the house and to run errands, yes, but never to the lake."

"Well, Jessica would know that," Rachel said. She laughed and added, "Summer would know that about me, if it were the case."

"So…you're inclined to agree with her? That what Fletcher said is proof that he must have killed Hannah?"

"I'm not sure. It definitely proves that he's lying about something, but whether that means he killed her mother…I don't know."

I nodded. "I said the same thing. And I know I upset Jessica when I told her that. She's convinced, and she was hoping I would be too."

"Of course. She's looking for support. That's understandable. Has she told anyone else?"

"Yes. Her father and the cops."

"What did they say?"

"They pretty much dismissed it. Her dad told her she needed to drop the whole matter, that it wasn't healthy for her to keep pursuing it, and she needed to put it behind her. The cops apparently didn't think Fletcher knowing the color of Hannah's nail polish, or lying about the flip-flops, was worth checking out."

"So she's basically run into a brick wall."

"Yes."

We were both silent for a moment. Preacher finished her patrol of the back yard and trotted up the deck steps and sprawled beside our chairs, letting out a small groan as she did so. Rachel and I laughed.

"Let's go back to the dogs for a minute," she said. "I think it's interesting that both—Maisie?—and Alexander had the same reaction when they saw Fletcher. Like he was giving off some sort of danger vibe or something, and they sensed it."

"That's almost exactly what Jessica said when she told me about Maisie. Which reminds me of something else. She thinks Fletcher is an incel, and that's what led to him killing her mother."

"An incel?"

"Involuntary celibate. One of those guys who wants to have sex, or actually feels he's *entitled* to have sex with women, but for one reason or another can't seem to connect."

"Wow. This is getting weirder and weirder."

"Right. Jessica explained all this to me the first time we talked several days ago. She's a psych major at UNI and she seemed to know quite a bit about the subject."

Rachel nodded. "I told you about him staring at my boobs. He was definitely checking me out and I'll admit it was kinda creepy."

"That's all consistent with what Jessica told me about incels. She also told me that there are websites devoted to all this stuff. Apparently there's a worldwide online community of these guys and they post messages describing their encounters, supporting each other and egging each other on. She said it's all pretty misogynistic, as you would expect."

"Right." Rachel stretched one leg again and ran her bare foot along Preacher's back from her shoulders to the base of her tail. Preached sighed contentedly and we both laughed again.

"Our dogs really have it rough, don't they?" I said.

"They sure do. But hey, you said you saw Fletcher yesterday morning before Jessica did. What did Preacher do when she saw him?"

"She trotted right up to him and he petted her a time or two, then she went trotting off."

"So she didn't act suspicious or aggressive?"

"No." I laughed. "Maybe she's not as good a judge of character as Alexander or Maisie."

Rachel didn't laugh but looked thoughtful for a moment. Then she said, "No, I don't think that's it."

"What, then?"

"How about this? Preacher didn't act suspicious because she knew Fletcher didn't pose a threat to you. But if what you just said about Fletcher being an incel is true, then he probably gives off a threatening vibe when he meets a woman, or at least something that makes them uneasy, and that's what Alexander and Maisie picked up on."

I pondered this for a minute. It seemed like a stretch, but then again…

"I guess that's a possibility," I finally said. "If nothing else, it would explain the dogs' reaction to him. Or in Preacher's case, lack of reaction."

Rachel smiled. "C'mon!" she said. "You of all people should be able to believe that about our dogs. We both know they do things sometimes that surprise us, things we wouldn't think they can do, or that we can't explain."

"Well, you're right about that," I said, remembering once again how Maisie had shown up carrying Hannah's shoe that morning at the lake, and had then led me to her body. "I can't deny that it happens."

"Of course it does. And we'd be smart not to ignore it." Rachel took a final swallow of her beer and set the empty bottle on the table next to her phone.

I nodded toward the bottle and said, "One more?"

She sighed and said, "No, I'd better not. Have to work in the morning. But after what you just told me about Fletcher being an incel, I have to say, I think Jessica is probably on to something. I guess I'm inclined to agree that she's right, that he might very well have killed her mother. There are too many pieces of evidence that point to it, even if the cops don't think so."

"I guess I'm kinda leaning that way myself, but I'm still not sure. So then the big question is, what if she is correct? What then? It doesn't sound like the cops are going to do anything further. Which means that if everything Jessica suspects is true, Greg Fletcher is going to get away with murder."

"How do you feel about that?"

I knew Rachel wasn't just asking how I felt. She was giving me a very direct look and I knew what she was really asking was whether I might be thinking of taking any action against Fletcher. Specifically, whether I was considering avenging Hannah's death, and if I might need her help in doing so.

I sighed and answered her honestly. "I'm not sure," I said.

CHAPTER 42

We sat in silence for a minute or so, then Rachel said, "Well, I'd better get going. Thanks for the beers."

"You're welcome," I said. "Thanks for your input on this whole Greg Fletcher situation."

Rachel smiled. "No problem," she said. She stood up and reached down to pick up her cell phone and her empty beer bottle.

"Here, I'll take that," I said, reaching over for the bottle.

"Okay." She handed me the bottle then bent over and picked up her shoes. She walked barefoot down the steps of the deck to the driveway apron. "I'll just go out this way."

"I'll get the gate for you." I left our empty beer bottles on the deck table and walked down to open the gate onto the driveway.

Rachel stepped through and said, "Thanks." I walked through also and let the gate swing closed behind me but didn't bother latching it. I followed Rachel down the driveway to her Camaro. She tossed her shoes onto the passenger seat then leaned over the door and placed her phone on the console. She turned back toward me. She gave me another long look and then smiled again. "Let me know what you decide," she said.

I nodded. "I will." She climbed into her car and started the ignition. "Drive safely," I said.

"I will. Good night."

"Good night."

She shifted into reverse and backed down the driveway. I watched until she headed down the street, then I turned and walked back up the driveway. I opened the gate, stepped through and latched it.

I mounted the steps to the deck, where Preacher was still sprawled next to our chairs. I picked up the two empty beer bottles from the table and said, "Let's go inside." Preacher stood, stretched and followed me into the kitchen.

LET ME KNOW WHAT YOU DECIDE.

I knew, as I'd known a few minutes earlier, that Rachel was really asking me if I was going to take action against Greg Fletcher, and should I decide to do so, if I would need her help. I also knew, based on a years-long tacit understanding, that she would provide, without hesitation, any assistance I might require.

I rinsed out the bottles at the kitchen sink, then dropped them for recycling into a six-pack carton next to the tall wastebasket by the back door. As I did so, the thought crossed my mind that, even if I was still feeling uncertain myself, Rachel probably already knew the answer.

I SPENT ANOTHER RESTLESS NIGHT.

Whether it was the result of too many beers just before bed or the growing conviction that Greg Fletcher had, in fact, killed Hannah Wilkinson, or most likely a combination of both of those factors, I had a hell of a time getting to sleep. And when I did finally drop off, it was little more than a doze. My brain refused to disengage but continued to examine the problem from every conceivable angle. And, of course, failed to come up with a solution.

It was a feeling not unlike what I'd experienced when sitting in high school algebra class totally bewildered by the equations on the blackboard. The teacher assured us there were solutions to those equations, but I'd be damned if I could find them. Math was never my strong suit.

As usual, Preacher came into the bedroom at a few minutes before six the next morning and whined to let me know she needed to go outside. I got up and let her out, then started a pot of coffee. While it was brewing I ran through the facts, such as I knew them, for the umpteenth time.

Jessica Wilkinson was convinced Fletcher had killed her mother. Rachel James, whose opinion I respected and trusted, seemed to agree. Both women had had encounters with Fletcher that left them feeling uneasy, and Jessica had also caught Fletcher in what she believed was a rather incriminating lie.

On the other hand, neither Craig Wilkinson nor the investigating detectives apparently felt there was sufficient evidence against Fletcher to delve any further into the matter. So, stalemate? And if so, what more could—or should—I do?

I reminded myself once again of my first rule for contract killing, that there must be no personal involvement. I also reminded myself of Daryl's advice to let the matter go. The cops were convinced Hannah's death was a suicide, and aside from Fletcher's comment about her nail polish—nail polish!—there was very little to suggest otherwise.

Preacher whined at the back door and I let her inside. I thought about the reaction Maisie and Alexander had had to Fletcher and wondered whether that reaction was, as Jessica and Rachel believed, really an indication of something threatening, or at least unsavory, about his character.

Albert Payson Terhune, one of my childhood idols and one of the most popular and prolific writers of dog stories, especially those featuring his Sunnybank collies, repeatedly scoffed at the notion that dogs were trustworthy judges of character. He pointed out that some of history's worst scoundrels had been loved by their dogs, and that judging someone based primarily on a dog's reaction to that person bordered on the ridiculous.

And yet…

I sighed and poured myself a cup of coffee. I knew, Daryl's advice notwithstanding, I wasn't going to be able to let this go.

I WAS NO CLOSER TO A solution when Preacher and I returned from our morning ramble at Maffitt.

We hadn't seen anyone at the lake and I'd kept our outing rather short. It was another very warm morning and Preacher and I had stayed close to the water. I hadn't carried her retrieving dummy but we'd walked the shoreline and she'd splashed in and out of the water several times. After a half hour I called her in and we returned to the vehicle.

When we got home I fed Preacher her morning meal, then headed into the office to log onto the company computer. The art director had begun posting the layouts of the features and I was planning to spend the day giving them a final proofing and, barring any necessary corrections or revisions, approving them for release to the printer.

This was, in fact, one of my favorite steps in the whole production process. I always enjoyed seeing the designs the art director had come up with, and that, combined with the knowledge that we were getting close to completing another issue, made for a nice feeling of satisfaction. Most of the heavy lifting was done, so it was usually just a matter of a few minor last-minute tweaks and then we could call the issue a wrap.

I was especially grateful this morning for the moderate mental exercise the proofing would require, as it would help me get my mind off Greg Fletcher.

I opened the first feature, the grouse hunting story by Dan Eastlake. The lead photo was a full-page bleed of Jazz, Eastlake's English setter, locked up on a classic point in the autumn woods. The scene looked like something Robert Abbett might have painted and I mentally tipped my hat to the art director for his selection. Nothing like starting off the morning on a high note.

I started reading the copy. I was three paragraphs into the story when an idea occurred to me. It was triggered by Eastlake's somewhat sheepish description of missing the first bird Jazz pointed during their hunt, and the reproachful look she gave him as a result.

Preacher had given me that same look a number of times over the years when I'd whiffed on a shot. Anyone who has hunted extensively with gun dogs knows that look, a combination of disappointment and disgust at the gunner's failure to hold up his or her part of the bargain.

I remembered Preacher giving me that look during a hunt on a preserve in Illinois some eight months earlier...a hunt necessitated by my having to return to the area of my last assignment to correct a problem of my own making.

I pushed away from the company computer and rolled over to the file cabinet that stood next to the table on which sat my personal computer. I opened the bottom drawer of the cabinet and rummaged around until I came up with a piece of notepaper that bore a name and a phone number.

My next move was to open the package of a prepaid cell phone, a recently purchased burner, and one of several in that drawer. I powered it up and saw that it was charged and I had a clear signal.

I knew the person I was calling wouldn't recognize the number, but I hoped that wouldn't prevent him from answering. I didn't want to leave a message.

I was in luck. He answered after the second ring.

"James Collins," he said.

"James," I said. "This is the fellow you called Tom."

CHAPTER 43

There was a moment of hesitation, then he laughed. "Well, hello there," James Collins said.

I laughed also. "I know it's awfully belated, but I wanted to thank you for the Billy Joel tickets," I said. After I'd tied up the loose ends of my previous assignment, James Collins had sent me a pair of tickets to a Billy Joel concert at the Target Center in Minneapolis. He'd done this as a gesture of appreciation when I'd refused additional payment for handling those loose ends, and Daryl and I had driven up to Minneapolis from Des Moines and enjoyed the concert.

"Oh, you're welcome," he said. "I hope it was a good show."

"It was. My lady friend and I really enjoyed it. We made a weekend out of it, and it was a nice getaway for us."

"I'm happy to hear that." He laughed again. "But I'm guessing you're not calling all these months later just to give me a concert review."

I laughed also. "You're right. I'm calling to ask a favor."

I imagined him nodding. "Go ahead," he said.

"The last time we talked, you said something about being able to help if I ever needed some background on someone," I said. I deliberately didn't use the word "target" but I knew Collins would make that assumption. Given the nature of our previous business, he would assume I had a pending assignment and was seeking information I couldn't readily obtain myself.

"That's right," he said. "The offer still stands."

"I appreciate that," I said. "I'm hoping you can help me."

"Tell me what you need," he said, and I thought I could hear a note of excitement in his voice. Or eagerness, anyway.

"I need some background on a fellow here in Des Moines." When I said this I wasn't worried about Collins knowing my location; he'd mailed the check for the previous assignment, and the Billy Joel tickets, to one of my P.O. boxes here, so I had to assume he knew where I lived; approximately, that is.

"What's the fellow's name?"

"Greg Fletcher," I said, and Collins laughed.

"Couldn't you have come up with someone with a less common name?" he said. "Like John Smith?"

It was my turn to laugh. "Sorry," I said. "But I can give you a few more details about him. What little I know, anyway."

"Okay."

"For starters, I'm guessing his age is early to mid-forties. And I'm pretty sure he lives in an area known as Greenfield Township, or Greenfield Plaza. It's on the south side of Des Moines, just south of County Line Road. So he lives in Warren County, although the city proper is in Polk County. But he would still have a Des Moines address." I didn't add that I knew all of this because the same was true of me.

"Okay, that helps, assuming there's not more than one Greg Fletcher in that area. Anything else?"

"He drives a Dodge Durango SUV. I don't know the exact year but it appears to be fairly new, say less than five years old. It's dark gray, although I don't know if that matters. I don't know the license plate number but it would be registered in Warren County also."

"Okay, anything else?"

I thought for a moment. "No, not that I can think of offhand. I mean, I know that he walks out at Maffitt Reservoir, south of the city, pretty regularly, but that's probably not significant for you."

"Probably not. But you said you know that he walks out there…I'm guessing you've seen him out there yourself? That you know this guy?"

I hesitated. I always make it a point to play things close to the vest with clients, and not reveal much of what I have planned when it comes to completing an assignment for them. The old "loose lips sink ships" adage applies here, and generally speaking, the less a client knows of my specific actions, the better.

But James Collins was no longer a client; we'd concluded our business several months earlier. By calling him now and asking him to dig up some background on Fletcher, I was making him, for want of a better word, an accomplice. This made me a little nervous, but I also knew that we were bound to secrecy by the nature of our previous association. While I didn't expect we'd ever achieve the level of trust I enjoyed with, say, Rachel James, I did believe I could count on Collins to be discreet.

"Yes, I do know him, but not very well," I said. "I see him out at the lake—Maffitt Reservoir, I mean—occasionally, and we've talked a few times. That's how I know his approximate age and what he drives."

"Got it." Now Collins hesitated. Then he said, "Dare I ask why you're interested in this guy? Is he…um…"

"An assignment? No, at least not yet," I said. "But I have reason to think he might have been involved in the death of a friend of mine, someone else I knew from the lake. At this point I'm just trying to get a more complete picture; I'm hoping that will help me determine if he was in fact involved."

"I see," Collins said. "I don't mean to pry, but are there any other details you can tell me? Anything that might point me in a certain direction? That might be helpful; might give me an idea of what I should be looking for."

Once again, I hesitated. I was tempted to go ahead and tell him the details of Hannah Wilkinson's death, but if I did, he would probably research that as well. I couldn't remember if my name, as the person who had found her body, had ever appeared in any of the press coverage, but if it had and Collins dug into the matter, he would turn up my identity also. To the best of my knowledge, he still only knew me as a guy he called Tom, the name I'd given him when he had first hired me. For the moment, at least, I preferred to keep it that way.

"My friend, the one who died, was a woman," I said. "Without going into too many details, her daughter is convinced that this Fletcher killed her. She's talked to me about it and I have to admit I think she has a fairly strong case.

That's why I'm interested in finding out more about him." I paused, then added, "I guess I'm hoping there might be something that would convince me one way or the other."

"And if it turns out there is something?"

I laughed a bit nervously. "I'm not committing to anything just yet. I'm trying to keep an open mind and not jump to conclusions. In fact, that's why I called you."

"Fair enough," Collins said. "Are you okay with me asking Kevin and Mark for help on this?" Kevin and Mark were the two hacker buddies—or maybe they were coworkers—who had helped Collins do much of the backgrounding for my previous assignment. They'd done a deep dive on the target, an attorney named Frank Reynolds, and had come up with an almost astonishing amount of information, much of it obtained illegally, I knew. Although I'd never learned their last names, I felt I could trust them to be discreet as well.

"Sure," I said. "And that reminds me, I'll be happy to pay you for your time on this."

"No," Collins said. "Absolutely not. I appreciate the offer, but like I told you several months ago, I'll do this because of what you did to get some justice for Mandi."

His mention of Mandi reminded me of the circumstances of her death, and that triggered another thought. "Oh, there is one more thing," I said. "The daughter I mentioned? She's convinced Fletcher is an incel. She thinks that might be what motivated him to kill her mother, in fact."

"Interesting!" Collins said. "That gives us something to watch out for. I'll let you know if we turn up anything along those lines."

"Thanks, James. I really appreciate this."

"You're welcome. Let me get started on this and I'll try to get back to you in a couple days. Should I call you at this number?"

"Call or text, either one."

"Will do."

"Okay. Thanks again."

AFTER WE DISCONNECTED I sat for a moment and considered what I'd just done.

I hoped I hadn't made a mistake by bringing James Collins into this. But there was no question that he and his buddies, as he had reminded me himself months ago, could turn up more than I could ever hope to if I undertook the research myself. I'd learned firsthand just how proficient they were at breaching security systems and accessing the personal online correspondence of someone. Or several someones.

That realization gave rise to another sudden disquieting thought. I'd been smugly assuming that I had kept my identity a secret from Collins and his cohorts all these months, and that they still had no idea who I really was. But now I realized that, given their nature—call it natural inquisitiveness—they might very well have done a deep dive on me as well. I had never given them my real name, but I'd instructed Collins to make his check payable to my LLC, and now I wondered if they might have backtracked from that and figured out my identity.

I felt a sudden chill. Once in a while you instantly know, deep in your gut, that you've nailed it. Some folks might call it divine inspiration, but I tended to think more in terms of all the lock tumblers suddenly clicking into place.

I had that feeling now.

I blew out a hard breath. *Okay*, I asked myself, *so what's to be done about it? There's no way now to backpedal on this, so you might as well play it out and see what happens.*

I sighed and rolled my chair back over to the company computer where the rest of Dan Eastlake's grouse hunting story was waiting to be proofed and approved. I told myself to be thankful that I had this activity to keep me occupied for the next couple days.

Because now, having enlisted the help of James Collins, I would have to do something at which I'm not especially good.

I would have to wait.

PART THREE: CONVICTION

Always be sure you're right, then go ahead.

Motto of Col. David Crockett (1786-1836)
Frontiersman and raconteur,
Congressman and Alamo defender

CHAPTER 44

Detective Madeline Madison was troubled.

Two days after talking to Jessica Wilkinson, the detective couldn't shake the nagging feeling that she and her partner had taken the easy way out. Yes, the ME had ruled Hannah Wilkinson's death a suicide and yes, the case was officially closed. Craig Wilkinson, Hannah's husband, seemed satisfied with all of that and willing to let the ruling stand without challenge.

But Hannah's daughter was another matter.

Detective Madison had listened patiently as Jessica had laid out the details of her encounter with Greg Fletcher. She heard about Fletcher recognizing the color of nail polish on Jessica's toes and commenting that it was the same color her mother wore, and his claim that he knew this because he'd seen Hannah wearing flip-flops sometime earlier. Jessica said this was impossible because her mother never wore flip-flops to the lake, but the detective thought this might have been a stretch on Jessica's part.

It was easily enough explained, she told herself. Maybe Hannah had been in a hurry one morning and just hadn't bothered to put on her athletic shoes before taking the dog to the reservoir for a walk. Or maybe it had been especially warm and she had opted to wear flip-flops simply because they were cooler than shoes. Or maybe Fletcher had run into Hannah wearing flip-flops somewhere else, or any one of a dozen other reasons. Detective Madison wasn't convinced that Fletcher claiming to have seen Hannah wearing flip-flops at the lake was the telltale clue Jessica believed it to be.

And yet…

She couldn't deny that the afternoon she and Jarrett had talked to Fletcher, she'd thought he had seemed a little…what? Uneasy? Wary? Like he was trying to hide something?

Any of that, she realized, could have been a normal reaction to learning Hannah Wilkinson had drowned, and that he had been the last person to see her alive. Anyone being confronted with those facts would have been shaken, especially if they were a friend of the victim. Since Fletcher and Hannah had apparently been friends, his reaction was perfectly understandable.

Unless he had already known she was dead and he was only pretending to be surprised.

Sitting at her desk across from her partner, the detective sighed and shook her head. Her sigh was loud enough to cause Detective Jarrett to look up from some paperwork and say, "What?"

"Still thinking about that phone call from Jessica Wilkinson," Madison said. "She's totally convinced that Greg Fletcher killed her mother. I can't help wondering if we might have overlooked something."

"We didn't overlook anything. Fletcher admitted he'd seen the woman the night she died, and he said she asked him to give her some time alone. That's consistent with everything else. The ME didn't find any evidence of foul play and ruled her death a suicide. There's nothing that says otherwise."

"Except her daughter's certainty that Fletcher was lying about seeing her mother wearing flip-flops."

Jarrett shook his head and laughed. "That's awfully thin. I think it's more likely he *did* see her wearing flip-flops sometime, even if her daughter says she didn't. I mean, what woman doesn't wear flip-flops in Iowa in the summertime?"

"I know, I know. But it's just one of those discrepancies that keeps bugging me."

Jarrett threw down his pen and leaned back in his desk chair. "Meaning you want to take another run at Fletcher," he said. He knew his partner well.

Madison smiled. "I'll even drive," she said.

GREG FLETCHER WAS HALFWAY through *Jeopardy!* when he heard the knock at his front door. He considered ignoring it—he wanted to see the rest of the game show, as he thought the current champion, a woman named Megan Salazar, was a hottie—but when the knock was repeated he sighed, set his can of Miller Lite on the end table and got up from the sofa. He guessed it was most likely some kind of solicitor, and he could get rid of the person quickly enough.

He crossed the room to the front door. He opened it and was surprised to see the two detectives—the tall black woman and the chubby white guy—he'd talked to a few weeks earlier. The white guy was sweating and looked uncomfortable in the heat but the black woman appeared cool and collected.

His senses instantly went to high alert. Fletcher unlatched the storm door and opened it. He struggled to keep his voice calm as he said, "Detectives?" He was pretty sure he remembered the woman's name was Madison, but he couldn't recall the guy's name. He thought playing dumb, or at least puzzled, might be the way to go.

"Good afternoon, Mr. Fletcher. Could we come in for a moment?" The woman.

"Sure." *Be cool!* He held the door open but stepped aside so they could enter. "What can I do for you?"

"We just have a few questions. We're following up on Hannah Wilkinson's death, trying to tie up a couple of loose ends." The woman again.

"Okay." He tried to sound uncertain, like he couldn't imagine what remained to be settled. He frowned slightly. "I thought her death was ruled a suicide."

"That's right; it was," the detective said. "But we're just double-checking on a couple of the details before we write our final report. You said that when you saw Hannah that evening, you walked with her back to that big boulder below the pines, then she asked you to give her some time to herself. Is that correct?"

"Yes, that's correct." He wanted to buy a little time so he could try to determine where this was leading. He also doubted that they were still working on their final report; he guessed it had already been completed. He gestured toward the sofa. "Would you like to sit down?"

"No, that's all right," the woman said. "We won't be here

long."

"Okay," Fletcher said. "But excuse me for a second." He walked over to the end table, picked up the TV remote and muted the volume on *Jeopardy!* He set the remote back on the end table and turned back toward them with a smile. "That's better," he said.

The black woman smiled in return. "Thank you," she said. She paused, then added, "So, after she asked you to give her some time, did you leave immediately?"

Fletcher shrugged. "I think so," he said. "I may have asked her if everything was all right, because she seemed a little moody, but she said she was fine, that she just wanted a little time to think about some things."

"And her dog was with her?"

"That's right. Maisie, her golden retriever."

"Hmmm," the black woman said. Her partner still hadn't spoken.

Wait them out, Fletcher told himself. *Don't volunteer anything.* He put what he hoped was a questioning look on his face.

"Okay, we're still trying to get a complete picture here and nail down the timeline a little more specifically," the woman said. "So she told you she was fine and just wanted to think about things. What did you say then?"

"I said something like, 'Well, okay then. I'll leave you alone.'"

"And did you?"

"Leave her alone, you mean?"

"Yes."

"Yes. I told her goodnight and then I left and walked back to my vehicle."

"And what was she doing when you left?"

Be careful! "She was standing next to the boulder, kind of looking out across the lake. Maisie was standing next to her."

"Standing next to the boulder? Not sitting on it?"

"No, I'm pretty sure she was standing next to it." He tried to recall if this was what he'd said a few weeks earlier. He laughed slightly and said, "Does that matter?"

"Like I said, we're just trying to get all the details nailed down." Another pause. Then, "So she was standing next to the boulder, looking out across the water, when you left. Are there any other details you remember?"

Fletcher shook his head. "No, I don't think so."

The white guy spoke for the first time. "Do you remember what she was wearing?"

Fletcher laughed again. He couldn't help himself. "Shorts and a t-shirt," he replied. He knew cops sometimes did this, threw in a seeming non sequitur to keep a suspect off balance. What the hell difference could it make if he remembered what she was wearing?

"What about her shoes?" The white guy again. And Fletcher suddenly got it. This was a fishing expedition, and now he knew what they were fishing for. *Final report, my ass. You're hoping I'll say something about seeing Hannah remove her shoes, something about the color of her toenail polish. Her daughter put you up to this.* He'd have bet big money on it. And he thought he'd been so clever, telling Jessica he'd seen her mother wearing flip-flops.

He shrugged. "Athletic shoes. Nikes, I think."

"Is that what she usually wore? You walked with her quite a bit, didn't you?" The white guy was really bearing down.

"Yes, we walked together fairly often. And yes, she usually wore athletic shoes," Fletcher said, thinking, *Jesus, guy, could you be any more obvious*?

The black woman took a turn. "Did you ever see her wearing anything else?"

He shrugged again, hoping he wasn't overplaying it. "She wore flip-flops a time or two." That was consistent with what he'd told Jessica, at least.

"You're sure about that?" The white guy again.

"Yes, I'm sure about that." He shook his head again. "But what does that have to do with her death?"

"Probably nothing," the black woman said. "But again, we're just trying to nail down the details. We have to make sure we've dotted all the i's and crossed all the t's." She smiled and said, "We'll let you get back to *Jeopardy!* Thanks for your help with this."

"Sure," Fletcher said, smiling in return. "But I'm not sure how much help I've been."

"Oh, this should help us wrap things up and finish our report. We appreciate your time."

"No problem," Fletcher said. "Happy to help."

CHAPTER 45

"WHAT DO YOU THINK?" Detective Madison had made good on her promise to do the driving and she posed the question to her partner as she backed out of Greg Fletcher's driveway.

"I think his story is consistent with what he told us the first time we talked to him."

Madison frowned as she shifted into drive and started up the street. "So you think this was all for nothing? That he's telling the truth and Jessica Wilkinson is wrong about her mother never wearing flip-flops to the lake?"

"I didn't say that. I said his story is consistent with what he told us before." Jarrett paused for a second as he turned up the air conditioning a notch. Then he added, "Actually, I think the son of a bitch is lying."

"Really!"

"Yes, really." He laughed. "And I'd bet you're thinking the same thing."

"Well, you're right about that. I think he was lying also."

"About the flip-flops?"

"Yes. And also about seeing Hannah Wilkinson standing by the boulder looking out across the lake just before he left her. That was just too…contrived. Like he was trying to paint the perfect picture of a woman contemplating suicide."

"That seemed a little weird to me also. 'Contrived' is a good word for it."

"Plus, there are a couple of other things about her death that still don't add up," Madison said.

"Like what?"

"Okay, I know this doesn't directly relate to what Fletcher told us, but there was no suicide note, for one thing. That's unusual, especially if she was as close to her daughter as her daughter claims. And taking the dog to the lake with her. If she went out there with the idea of drowning herself, wouldn't she have left the dog at home, where she knew it would be safe?"

"Probably." Jarrett sighed. Then he laughed. "Too bad the dog can't talk. It could tell us what really happened."

"Yeah, too bad."

They were both silent for a moment, then Jarrett sighed again. "At this point, I don't know what else we can do about it. With no evidence of foul play, I don't think we have enough cause—hell, no cause at all, really, to keep leaning on Fletcher. And something tells me he's not going to crack."

"You're probably right about that. And now his guard is up. If we go back a third time he's not going to buy the bit about us trying to finish up our report. He'll know we suspect him of killing Hannah Wilkinson."

"Right. And if we keep questioning him, he'll probably lawyer up. And then we're dead in the water."

"Ugh. Bad choice of words, Jarrett."

"Sorry."

Greg Fletcher was seething.

He'd missed the end of *Jeopardy!* so he didn't know if Megan Salazar had won the Final Jeopardy round. By the time the detectives had taken their leave and he'd closed his front door and turned back toward the television, the game show had ended and the four o'clock news was just beginning. Damn. He'd have to wait until tomorrow to see if Megan was still champion.

In the meantime, he was sure he'd figured out the detectives' play. When the white guy asked if he remembered what Hannah Wilkinson had been wearing and then followed up with a question about her shoes, it was obvious Hannah's daughter must have told them what he'd said about the color of her nail polish when he had talked to her at the lake. He knew in his gut he was right about this.

The bitch.

She'd fingered him. That was the only reason they had come knocking on his door with their follow-up questions. He didn't believe for a second that they were still working on their final report, as the black woman had said.

He picked up his can of Miller Lite and took a swallow. He winced. On top of everything else, the damn beer was now warm. *Fuck me.*

He set the can down and stood staring at the television. The volume was still muted but he wasn't really seeing what was on the screen anyway. He was replaying the conversation he'd just had with the detectives, probing for any slip-ups he might have made.

He couldn't think of any. He'd stuck to the same story he'd told them the first time, with maybe one or two added details. He'd mentioned again that Hannah had seemed moody, and he thought his description of her standing and looking out at the lake bolstered that observation. Remembering now that one of them, he was pretty sure it was the black woman, had asked if he was sure she'd been standing, not sitting on the boulder, he realized that too had probably been intended as a lead-in to asking about her shoes and maybe the color of her nail polish. How he'd come to know the color.

Well, he'd handled that all right, he thought. They hadn't asked about the color—that would have implicated Jessica, and they were probably trying to protect her. But when the white guy asked if Hannah always wore athletic shoes, he told them the same thing he had told Jessica, that he'd seen Hannah wearing flip-flops a few times. They couldn't prove otherwise, and neither could she.

But the little bitch had apparently found something questionable about that and had been able to convince the detectives to come at him with more questions. Whether this would be the end of it, he couldn't predict. They might or might not come back again.

He wondered how much longer Jessica would continue to pursue this.

He realized now, beyond a doubt, that he'd been right all along when he'd seen her frown at him as she was leaving the funeral home. She blamed him for her mother's death and that look had confirmed it. It hadn't been his imagination, after all.

Damn it to hell. If she persisted, he was going to have to do something. Just what, he wasn't sure. But he knew damned well he wasn't going to spend the rest of his life—or even the next few weeks—running scared from Jessica Wilkinson.

The little bitch.

CHAPTER 46

ALL OF THE LAYOUTS FOR THE October/November issue of *American Wingshot* had been proofed and approved and sent to the printer. In another few days the issue would begin mailing to subscribers and in about two weeks it would also begin appearing on newsstands. The magazine's total circulation was a little over 50,000, a respectable number for a specialty "niche" publication like *Wingshot*. Our readers were a loyal bunch and we enjoyed a high renewal rate among subscribers.

I felt good about the issue. It included a healthy mix of hunt stories—the grouse hunting piece by Dan Eastlake was our lead feature—and several informative articles on training, conditioning and canine nutrition, plus the usual complement of columns by regular contributors. Knowing that the issue would arrive in subscribers' mailboxes just as the earliest upland bird seasons were getting underway—like many magazines, *Wingshot* issues were datelined a month early—I used my editorial column to remind readers to take it easy when afield on those early warm days and to carry plenty of water for both themselves and their dogs.

I wrapped it up by wishing everyone a fun and successful season and signed off with Sergeant Phil Esterhaus's famous line from *Hill Street Blues*, "Let's be careful out there." I knew I was dating myself with that reference but I figured older readers would get a kick out of it...or so I hoped, anyway.

Now with the issue wrapped, I could turn my attention to other matters. There was always correspondence to be handled, although thankfully, we had received no additional complaints about the silver Labrador story in the previous issue, as well as beginning work on the next issue. I already had most of the main features selected for December/January, but they still had to be edited and I was also waiting for several columnists to submit their copy. Once I had received everything, I'd pull together the final run sheet for the issue and send it to the associate editor, art director and production manager.

In the meantime, I could relax a bit. Which meant, of course, I was going to start thinking again about the whole Hannah Wilkinson/Greg Fletcher situation…not that it had ever been entirely absent from my mind.

I'd talked to James Collins on Tuesday morning and he had said he would get back to me in "a couple of days." It was now Friday afternoon and I was trying to resist the urge to call him and ask for an update. I told myself he'd contact me when he had something solid to offer. In the meantime, I was just going to have to be patient.

Easier said than done.

I hadn't mentioned talking to Collins when Daryl and I met the night before for our usual Thursday evening dinner. (We'd opted for Johnny's Italian Steakhouse this time.) She knew nothing of my previous association with him, that he was a former client who had hired me to avenge his sister's death, so broaching the subject would have required an awful lot of explaining and/or circumvention. Even if I managed to pass him off as just a friend who was especially computer savvy, I would still have to justify my contacting him, why I was asking him to investigate Greg Fletcher rather than dropping the matter as Daryl had advised.

It was easier to avoid the whole issue. So once again, I was keeping a critical part of my life, or at least, my activities, hidden from her. I didn't like the feeling. She deserved better of me.

These were the thoughts I was mulling over when the phone rang.

For one brief moment I thought it might James Collins. But that hope died instantly because it was my landline office phone that was ringing, not the burner I'd used to call Collins that was currently sitting at my elbow on the credenza.

The lighted display on the phone told me my caller was Mike Stevenson.

I picked up the handset, punched the "talk" button and

said, "What the hell do you want?" Our standard greeting to each other.

Mike laughed. "TGIF," he said. "I was calling to see if you're up for another training session tomorrow morning. Thought we could run back down to Swanson's and run those steadiness drills again. I want to try some longer marks and maybe some blinds this time."

"Sure," I said, thinking, *thank God for the distraction.* If nothing else, this would keep me busy for a couple hours and, I hoped, my mind off Greg Fletcher. "Let's do it."

"Good deal. I'll pick you up about the same time tomorrow morning so we can get it done before it gets too hot."

"Sounds good. I'll see you then."

We hung up and I sat for a moment longer, staring first at the landline phone, then shifting my gaze to the burner.

I glanced at my watch. It was almost 3:30 and although it was another very warm afternoon, my back yard was now completely in shade thanks to a couple of large soft maples at the back of the property.

I stood up. Just as a watched pot never boils, a watched phone never rings.

I headed outside to mow the back yard.

So of course, James Collins called while I was mowing.

By the time I finished, my t-shirt was soaked and I was planning to head straight to the shower. But something told me to check the burner and when I did, I had a message from Collins.

"Hey, Tom," he said, "I have some stuff on this Greg Fletcher you asked me to check out. Pretty sure we found the right guy and if so, you're gonna want to hear this. Give me a call."

The shower could wait.

CHAPTER 47

James Collins began our conversation with an apology.

"Sorry it took so long to get back to you, but I wanted to make sure we had the right guy," he said. "And I also wanted to be able to give you as much information as possible."

"No problem, and no need to apologize," I said. "I appreciate your efforts on this, and I'm interested in what you turned up."

"Well, okay, then." He paused, then said, "Let's start with the basic background stuff. You said the guy probably lived in Greenfield Township on the south side of Des Moines. We found a Gregory Fletcher, age 44, who lives in that area." He rattled off the street address and I immediately recognized it as just a few blocks from my own home.

"That sounds right," I said. I didn't add that I lived nearby. "Right age; right location. Gotta be him." As I said this I jotted down the address on a notepad. I'd drive by later and check it out.

"Okay. Once we had that, we were able to backtrack and get a pretty good line on the guy. Kevin and Mark came up with quite a bit on him, actually, in spite of the fact that he appears to keep a very low profile. Or tries to, anyway."

"Interesting," I said. "But that sounds right also. From what little I know of the guy, he doesn't impress me as the flamboyant type."

Collins laughed. "No, he's not, but we still turned up a few things I think you're gonna find interesting. Maybe even a little…scary."

"Really," I said. I laughed. "Now you've definitely got my attention."

"Let me finish with the background stuff, then we'll get into that."

"Okay, shoot."

"Okay, like I said, he lives in Greenfield Township, and he works at the airport. I pulled up a map of Des Moines and it looks like the airport is pretty close to where he lives."

"That's right, it is," I said. "Any idea what he does at the airport?" I laughed again. "I'm guessing he's not a pilot."

Collins laughed also. "No, he's not. He works for DBT Parking Services. That's actually a private company that contracts with the airport to handle all the parking lots. They collect the parking fees, monitor and maintain the lots, that sort of thing."

"Got it," I said. "Anything else?"

"Nothing more job-wise, except he's apparently worked for them for about 12 years. We didn't bother checking his employment history to find out what he did before that; I didn't think that was important. But we could dig into it if you think it is."

"No, I don't think it matters," I said. "I'm more interested in what he's doing right now. Any details about his personal life?"

"He's never been married, as far as we can tell. He grew up in Des Moines and graduated from Lincoln High School. His parents are both deceased but he has a brother, two years older, who lives in Omaha. The brother's name is Joe and he is married, with two kids. Joe's wife's name is Nancy."

"You turned up quite a bit," I said. "I'm impressed. Anything else?"

"Well, now we're getting to the interesting stuff. We couldn't find him on any social media sites—there's about a thousand Greg Fletchers, but none of them appear to be him—and he doesn't do much emailing or texting. Like I said, he keeps a low profile. But he does go to one website pretty regularly. And he sometimes posts on their forum."

"Okaaay," I said. I sensed James Collins was getting ready to drop a bombshell or two. "What's the website?"

"It's called Manspeak.com."

"Manspeak.com?"

"Right." He laughed. "Remember you said you thought he was an incel?"

"Well, the daughter of the woman who died thinks he is, anyway. In fact, she's convinced he is. Did you find something that confirms that?"

"We might have. This website, Manspeak.com, seems to attract a lot of incels, judging by the comments in the forum. There's quite a bit of misogynistic stuff, comments about women using their charms to take advantage of guys, plus suggestions for getting back at them, that sort of thing. There's also a lot about women not…uh…coming across when they should. Some of it gets pretty nasty. Make that *very* nasty. There's quite a bit of profanity and crude sexual stuff. And some of it is violent. Or at least it hints at violence."

"Really," I said again. I was considering everything Collins had just said. "This is what you were talking about when you said some of what you found was a little scary?"

"Right. Believe me, some of the comments in the forum are pretty bizarre. And like I said, violent. These guys have serious issues with women. Especially when it comes to sex."

"Let me think about that for a minute," I said. I was still trying to assimilate everything I had just heard. It all seemed to match what Jessica Wilkinson had told me a couple weeks earlier about incels. In fact, it was so similar it was almost eerie. Even including the bit about websites where they traded comments and egged each other on.

After a moment Collins interrupted my thinking. "Do you mind if I ask you a question?" he said.

"No, go ahead."

He hesitated, then he asked, "The woman who died…was her name Helen?"

"Helen? No, it wasn't," I said. "Why?"

"Because Greg Fletcher posted something recently about getting back at a woman named Helen. He called her a prick tease—no, he said cock tease—and then he said something to the effect that she wouldn't be doing it anymore."

"Really!" I realized I was giving that word a workout. "Anything else?"

"He hinted that she'd been stringing him along. Those weren't his exact words but he said he'd met her in a park while she was walking her dog, that she'd needed a shoulder to cry on. He said this had been going on for a couple years. One of the other posters asked if he was still seeing her, and Fletcher said no, now she wasn't seeing anybody. He put a smile emoji after that last statement."

"Jesus," I said. My mind was reeling. Even if the name didn't match—Fletcher must have substituted Helen for Hannah, trying to cover his tracks—everything else clicked into place. It wasn't an outright confession but it was mighty damned close, with some bragging attached. Fletcher apparently hadn't been able to resist the latter.

"You're sure about all this?" I asked after a moment. "You know for certain that this was Fletcher doing the posting?"

Collins laughed. "Yes, I'm sure about it. Kevin and Mark tracked this guy pretty carefully. We know this is Fletcher. Which reminds me, his user name on the forum is Ghost Dog."

"Ghost Dog?"

"Right. That's the name he used for these posts. He was talking with two other users named Mako and Wingman."

I wrote all three names under Fletcher's address on my notepad. While I was doing this, Collins asked, "What I just said about those posts, does that relate to the woman you told me about who died?"

I hesitated, wondering how much I should share. I decided there was no harm in giving him a few more details, especially since he and his buddies had come through with such critical information on Fletcher. I felt like he'd earned an explanation, if only in simplest terms.

"Yes, I think it does," I said. "The woman who died was actually named Hannah, not Helen. But I know that Fletcher walked with her occasionally when she was walking her dog. She died a few weeks ago by drowning at a lake near Des Moines. It was ruled a suicide but her daughter doesn't believe her mother would have done that. She's convinced that Fletcher actually killed her."

Collins was silent for a moment, then he said, "Wow."

"Yeah."

"It all fits, doesn't it?"

"Yes, it does."

I heard him sigh. "This reminds me of Mandi," he said. "The bit about her death being ruled a suicide, I mean. I knew from the get-go it wasn't. Just like this woman's daughter."

"I'm sorry, James." I gave myself a mental kick in the ass. "Maybe I should have warned you about that, told you about Hannah's death before I asked for your help. I wasn't thinking."

"No, it's all right," he said. I heard him draw a deep breath. "Really. I mean…if this guy Fletcher did kill this woman, I'm happy to help you nail him."

"I appreciate that. But again, I'm sorry for bringing up painful memories."

"It's okay." He paused then added, "Did her daughter hire you?"

"No, she didn't. I've talked to her a couple times; that's all. She too was convinced from the get-go that Hannah didn't kill herself, and she's been trying to find proof of what Fletcher did." I didn't want to get into the whole matter of Fletcher knowing the color of Hannah's toenail polish. "She's come up with one or two pieces of circumstantial evidence, but nothing really conclusive. That's why I contacted you."

Fortunately, Collins didn't ask me to elaborate on the circumstantial evidence. Instead he said, "Has what I've given you helped?"

"Yes, it has. At least, I'm more convinced than I was that her daughter is right." After a moment I added, "Now I just need to try to figure out what to do about it."

"We can continue digging into Fletcher if you'd like. Or at least monitor his online activity; see if he posts anything more in that forum."

"I feel like you've done plenty already. I don't want you to spend a lot more time on this."

"It's okay," he said. "At this point I feel like I'm kind of…invested."

"All right, then. Monitoring his online stuff for a few more days might not hurt. If it's not too much trouble, that is."

He laughed. "Not much trouble at all, actually. Now that we know our way in, Kevin and Mark can keep tabs on him pretty easily."

I didn't ask him what he meant by knowing their way in, and I probably wouldn't have understood any explanation he might have provided anyway. Instead, I just said, "Okay, thanks. Let me know if you find anything else interesting."

"I'll do that. In the meantime, good luck figuring out what you're going to do."

I told myself he wasn't being sarcastic.

CHAPTER 48

Standing in the shower I'd postponed to call James Collins, I pondered everything he'd told me.

Collins had come through in a big way. Besides providing basic background on Greg Fletcher that confirmed, among other things, Fletcher lived in my neighborhood, Collins had given me plenty of additional information to consider and evaluate. As I'd told him, I was now a lot more convinced Jessica Wilkinson was correct and Greg Fletcher had murdered her mother. Maybe not one hundred percent convinced, but pretty darned close. The bits and pieces of evidence were definitely adding up.

Especially significant was what Collins and his hacker buddies had discovered on the Manspeak website. That Fletcher had bragged about getting even with a woman whom he felt had taken advantage of him—and gotten even in such a way that she was no longer seeing anyone—was nothing short of damning, I thought, even if he had substituted the name Helen for Hannah.

Of course, playing my own devil's advocate, it could be argued that he hadn't really confessed to killing her. He hadn't come right out and said she was dead. But if Collins's recounting of Fletcher's posts was accurate, and I assumed it was, those posts seemed to strongly hint that such was the case.

Thinking on it now, I realized I probably should have asked Collins for a printout of those posts. He or his buddies could have printed the forum screen and I could have reviewed Fletcher's exact wording to see if it was as incriminating as Collins had made it sound. Maybe I'd suggest this the next time I talked to Collins. In the meantime, I had other avenues I could explore. Fletcher's user name on the website, for example.

I wondered about the significance of Ghost Dog. The

names of the other users Collins had mentioned, Mako and Wingman, were readily enough explained. Mako, of course, was a species of shark. It wasn't hard to imagine someone who fancied himself a predator choosing that one. Wingman was originally a military aviation term (looking at you, *Top Gun*) but now often referred to a buddy who provided backup to a guy on the make. Again, not hard to plug that one into a website forum catering to incels and sexual predators.

But Ghost Dog, with its semi-literary ring, had me puzzled.

Offhand, I could think of two "ghost dog" references, but neither seemed to relate to Greg Fletcher, at least, not in any way I could reasonably imagine.

The first reference was to a dog owned by writer Albert Payson Terhune. The dog was a huge crossbreed named Rex, part collie and part bull terrier. According to Terhune's account, he was forced to kill the dog when it attacked and attempted to kill Terhune's beloved old collie, Lad. Then, some months after Rex's death and on separate occasions, two friends of Terhune, neither of whom was known to the other, claimed to have seen Rex at Terhune's home, Sunnybank.

Terhune also noted that following Rex's death, another of his collies, Bruce, always avoided stepping on the spot in the hallway of the house that was Rex's favorite lounging spot. Rather, Bruce would skirt the spot as if stepping around something that was lying there. Terhune pointedly made no attempt to explain these incidents and maintained a somewhat skeptical air when relating them, letting his readers draw their own conclusions.

The second ghost dog that came to mind was a black Labrador in a novel titled *Ghost Dog of the Killicut,* by Wisconsin author Mel Ellis. I have a copy and although it's considered a juvenile novel, I've read it a couple of times, as Ellis was one of my favorite outdoor writers. It's the story of a young man named Guy Hardin who attempts to catch a phantom dog said to haunt a string of islands in Lake Michigan.

Unless Greg Fletcher was a fan of either Mel Ellis or

Albert Payson Terhune—not very likely, I thought, given Fletcher's age and the fact that both writers were long deceased—I couldn't account for him choosing Ghost Dog for his user name on the Manspeak website. But no other explanation immediately presented itself.

Like so many of the questions related to Hannah Wilkinson's death, this was probably one I wasn't going to be able to answer anytime soon.

BY THE TIME I FINISHED showering and putting on clean cargo shorts and a polo shirt, it was about 5:30 and time to feed Preacher her evening meal. I was undecided as to what to do for my own dinner; Daryl and I weren't getting together and I didn't feel like cooking anything at home.

I decided I'd try to get a seat at the bar at Skip's, where I wouldn't feel self-conscious about dining alone. I had a nodding acquaintance with several of the other regular patrons plus most of the bartenders, so some casual, friendly conversation was likely, and that suited my mood.

Anything to get my mind off Greg Fletcher for a while.

THE BLACKENED SALMON WAS EXCELLENT.

It's one of my favorite entrees at Skip's, and accompanied by two Blue Moons, it was the perfect dinner choice for a warm summer evening. By the time I left Skip's it was a little past seven o'clock and I decided to run out to Half Price Books in West Des Moines. I was getting dangerously low on reading material; my to-read stack was down to five or six books and I was hoping to pick up a copy of John Grisham's latest novel.

I was in luck. HPB had a nice clean used copy in the "new titles" section and I snagged it and headed up to the counter. I paid for the book and left the store.

Driving home, I considered stopping at Johnny's for another beer but decided to have one on my deck instead. I told myself the beers in my fridge had already been paid for.

Call me Mr. Frugal.

I had a phone message when I got home. I guessed it

might be Daryl but it wasn't. The message was from Mike Stevenson.

"Hey, Rob," he said. "Do you still have that old Hallmark dummy launcher? If so, can we use it tomorrow? I just discovered the spring on mine is broken and I can't get it fixed tonight, obviously. If you don't have that old one, I guess we'll have to get by with throwing the dummies and firing a blank pistol. No need to call me back; I'll just plan to see you in the morning."

I smiled as I listened to Mike's message. I still had the old launcher he'd asked about but I hadn't used it for several years. It was on a shelf in the garage and, as far as I knew, still in working condition.

I grabbed a Blue Moon from the fridge and ambled out to the garage to check.

CHAPTER 49

WHILE PREACHER AND I WERE waiting for Mike Stevenson to pick us up—it was a few minutes after six on Saturday morning—it occurred to me that I'd forgotten to swing by Greg Fletcher's address last night on my way to Skip's or later when I was returning home from Half Price Books. I had meant to do so but it had slipped my mind.

I tried to shake it off, telling myself it was no big deal. When Rachel James does something similar, she laughs and dismisses it with the comment, "Oh, it's just my grandma memory." Since I wasn't a grandparent, I couldn't use that excuse.

I made a mental note to check out Fletcher's place after Mike and I returned from our training session. In the meantime, I was looking forward to getting out with Mike and our two dogs. I was sitting on the front step with Preacher sitting next to me on one side and my old dummy launcher in its carrying case, a Plano tackle box from which I'd removed the shelves with their lure compartments, on the other.

I'd checked out the launcher and oiled it the night before. It was ready to go, and so were we. I stood up as Mike pulled into my driveway in his big rig. Preacher stood up also and whined.

We loaded up and were on our way.

GREG FLETCHER WAS HOPING to run into Jessica Wilkinson on Saturday morning but the first person he saw after parking his Durango in front of the restroom building was Tim Sullivan. Fletcher muttered a quiet "Damn it anyway" to himself but he put a smile on his face and greeted Sullivan with a hearty "Good morning!" as he climbed out of the Durango, closed the door and locked the vehicle.

"Good morning to you too, sir!" Sullivan replied as he approached. He was wearing a bright blue wifebeater with his usual gym trunks and gray New Balance walking shoes. He stopped in front of Fletcher and pulled up the tail of his wifebeater to wipe his face. "It's another warm one," he said.

"It is that," Fletcher agreed. After a moment he added, "Seen anyone else this morning?" He thought he was safe asking this.

"Nope, I haven't," Sullivan said. "I got out here about forty-five minutes ago; wanted to get my walk in before it gets too much hotter."

"Good thinking," Fletcher said. "It's supposed to be another scorcher." He laughed. "But along about January or February when we're all complaining about the brumal weather, we'll probably be wishing for some of this." He had always wanted to use the word brumal in a sentence and he was pleased at having the opportunity to do so.

"Yeah, the weather in January and February is brutal, all right," Sullivan said. "No argument about that."

Fletcher smiled. "Actually, I said 'brumal,' but you're right—it's brutal also."

Sullivan gave him a puzzled look. "Brumal?" he said. "What does that mean?"

"Wintery, or wintertime," Fletcher said.

"Ah," Sullivan said. "I'll have to remember that. Brutal and brumal, those both fit when you're talking about January in Iowa." He laughed. "Thanks for the vocabulary lesson."

Fletcher laughed also. "You're welcome," he said.

THE CORN ON BOTH SIDES of the lane was well over head high when we pulled off the gravel road and headed back to Swanson's ponds, and I was reminded of the corn mazes some entrepreneurial farmers cut in their cornfields a few weeks before Halloween each year, prior to harvest. The grass in the lane was taller also, and I could hear it scraping the Ford's sides and undercarriage as we bumped along. Apparently no one else had been back to the ponds in some time.

We emerged from the corn maze onto the open grass area surrounding the first pond. Mike slowed the Ford and then pulled it around in a tight circle so the tailgate was facing the pond. Both dogs stood up on the rear seat and whined, knowing action was at hand.

We climbed out of the cab and released the dogs. They made their usual circuit through the grass, stopping to relieve themselves as Mike opened the tailgate and we started unloading our equipment. I glanced at my wristwatch and saw that it was 7:15. "Gonna be another hot one," I said. I guessed the temperature was already nudging 80 degrees.

"Yeah," Mike said as he pulled out the big mesh bag of retrieving dummies. I was carrying the dummy launcher in its case. We started for the pond and both dogs fell in behind us.

When we got to the water we started with a few happy dummies, as we had the time before. Both dogs were only too eager to go plunging into the pond to shag the dummies. We gave them four or five retrieves apiece, then Mike smiled and said, "Time to get serious."

"Right," I said. I opened the dummy case and pulled out the launcher.

GREG FLETCHER WALKED the roadway all the way through the park and returned to his vehicle. He saw only one other person, a middle-aged woman who often jogged through the park early in the morning. He didn't know her name but he lifted a hand in greeting as she jogged past him heading in the opposite direction; she nodded and raised a hand in return. He'd never seen her driving a vehicle so he guessed she lived in the subdivision across the road from the park's entrance.

There was no sign of Jessica Wilkinson.

Fletcher unlocked the Durango and climbed in. He started the ignition and glanced at the radio screen. The time was 8:05. He'd been at the park for a little over a half hour and he wondered if Jessica might still show up. Maybe, like many young people, she liked to sleep in and would be along if he gave it a little more time.

He decided to try his luck on the other side of the lake. Maybe she was on the west side this morning, where he'd seen her previously.

He shifted into reverse and backed away from the

restroom building. The roadway through the park was ostensibly one-way, or so the signs said. To comply, Fletcher would have to follow the winding roadway all the way through the park, the path he had just walked, but he decided to bend the rules and drive back out the way he'd come in.

The distance from the restroom building to the park entrance was less than a hundred yards, and he could save himself a few minutes by driving out the wrong way. With no one else in the park, he wasn't going to be reported, and he doubted anyone would make a fuss even if they did see him.

"Scofflaw," he said to himself as he shifted into drive. He laughed at his violation and headed toward the park entrance.

THE TRAINING SESSION WENT WELL. Rusty was steadier than he had been during our previous outing, requiring minimal restraint with Mike's belt cord. After both dogs had made a couple of short retrieves, Mike said, "I want to try some of the heavier loads and see if I can put a dummy on the opposite bank so he has to hunt for it in cover."

This would further test Rusty's marking ability and also give Mike a chance to handle the Lab to the dummy if necessary. There was no great challenge in marking a dummy that splashed into the water in plain sight, but sending the dummy across the pond and into cover on the other side was a different matter. Rusty would need to mark the dummy's fall, swim the pond and enter the cover to find the dummy. If he faltered or missed the mark, Mike would use whistle and hand signals to direct Rusty to the dummy.

With Rusty sitting at his side, Mike opened the launcher and dropped in a purple load. He glanced at me and said, "Ready?"

"Ready," I said, then added a precautionary "Whoa, Preach." She was sitting at my side also.

Mike called "Mark!" and fired the launcher. The dummy arced high out over the pond and dropped on the opposite side behind a stand of cattails. Mike waited a couple seconds then commanded, "Rusty, fetch!"

The yellow Lab sprang into the water and swam in an

arrow-straight line across the pond. He disappeared into the cattails and we could hear him thrashing his way through the stalks. Mike stood expectantly, even bouncing on his toes, anxious to see if Rusty was going to need direction.

He didn't. After just a few seconds, we saw him re-emerge from the cattails with the dummy firmly grasped in his mouth. He'd nailed the mark perfectly, and as he plunged back into the water to make the return swim, I looked at Mike and said, "Nice!"

Mike's answer was an ear-to-ear grin.

JESSICA WILKINSON WASN'T on the west side.

Fletcher drove all the way back to the big metal gate at the head of the hiking trail, swung the Durango through the circular turnaround area and started back toward the entrance. He had seen three vehicles, an SUV and two pickups, at the canoe launch as he'd driven past, but there was no sign of Jessica, or of Hannah's dark blue Explorer. Apparently it was still too early for her; the radio clock now said 8:18. Or maybe she was busy with some other activity this Saturday morning.

As he paused before pulling out onto Maffitt Lake Road, he considered driving down to the River Oaks subdivision and past the Wilkinsons' house to see if the Explorer was in the driveway. But he quickly dismissed the idea, realizing that was probably too risky. Jessica might recognize his vehicle if she was home and happened to glance out when he drove past. He didn't want to take the chance.

He decided instead to drive through the park on the east side one more time and if Jessica wasn't there, he'd bag it and head on home.

He could try again tomorrow.

CHAPTER 50

MIKE SENT RUSTY FOR THREE more long retrieves into cover on the opposite side of the pond and Rusty nailed two of the marks as perfectly as he had the first. On the third he got sidetracked momentarily when a night heron flushed noisily from the cattails, distracting him and causing him to lose the line. But Mike was able to direct Rusty back to the dummy with a whistle and a couple of arm signals and he completed the retrieve successfully.

"You've got yourself a gun dog," I said as Rusty emerged from the water and stopped before Mike to present the dummy.

"Think so?" Mike said as he took the dummy, ruffled Rusty's ears and turned to me with another grin.

"Yes, I believe so," I said. I was grinning also. "He's come a long way in these past few months."

"Thanks. And thanks for your help with all this." He laughed and nodded toward my dog. "And Preacher's. I appreciate the backup."

"Happy to do it," I said, and I was. We'd alternated Rusty's long retrieves with shorter retrieves in the water for Preacher, thereby reinforcing Rusty's steadiness. Both dogs benefited from the practice and the workout, suggesting we could look forward to some good times with them in the upcoming hunting season.

We gathered up our gear and headed back to the truck.

"LET'S CHECK OUT THAT OTHER pond again," Mike said as he fired the Ford's ignition. Both dogs were lying on the seat behind us. Their coats had almost completely dried in the morning's heat by the time we'd finished stowing the dummies under the Ford's topper.

"Okay," I said, although I was a little curious as to why Mike wanted to bother taking another look at the steep-sided pit. The first pond where we had just been training was the one where we'd be hunting if the farmer gave us permission.

We followed the grassy lane back to the second pond. Mike stopped the truck and turned off the ignition. He stepped out and I did the same, still curious. We left the dogs in the cab. The windows were open so there was no danger of them overheating in the minute or two we were out. We walked to the edge of the nearest steep bank.

Like before, the pond gave the impression of being an abandoned quarry pit. The banks were nearly vertical except for a small area sloping down to the water at the far end. No cattails or other vegetation grew around the water's edge. The water was muddy and smelled stagnant.

After looking out at the water for a moment, Mike shook his head and said, "There's nothing here to attract a duck. Doves might use that far end for watering but setting up for them down there would be a mighty hot proposition with no trees around for shade." Iowa had legalized dove hunting a few years earlier and the season opened on September 1, but given the usual heat in early fall, hunting them here would be tough on both men and dogs, as Mike said.

"Yeah," I agreed. "The first pond is a much better bet. Has Swanson given you the okay to hunt it?"

"Not yet," he said. "I thought we'd stop at his house on our way back and ask."

"Sounds good," I said.

We returned to the truck but just as we reached it another truck came rumbling through the grass toward us. It was an older model Dodge Ram, its red paint faded and oxidized. It also showed quite a few rust spots and general wear and tear; a typical farm work truck, in other words.

The driver pulled up next to us and leaned out the window. He was a fiftyish, burly fellow wearing a green Pioneer seed cap and a short-sleeved plaid shirt. "Good morning," he said. Under the Pioneer cap his face was deeply sunburned.

"Good morning," Mike and I said, almost in unison. Mike nodded toward me and said, "Mr. Swanson, this is my friend,

Rob Vance."

Swanson extended his right hand out the window and I stepped forward to shake it. "Good to meet you," I said, thankful he didn't crush my hand with his grip. He nodded and smiled.

"Likewise," he said. He released my hand. "You working your dogs again?"

"We were," Mike said. "We just finished up a few minutes ago back at the first pond. Hope we didn't disturb you when we were firing the dummy launcher."

Swanson laughed. "Nope, didn't even hear it," he said. "The house is a half mile away and this time of year the wife keeps it closed up tight with the air conditioner running full-blast. She's a lot more bothered by the heat than I am." He shook his head in a what-can-you-do gesture. Mike and I both laughed. "I just came down to take a look at this mudhole. Still thinking about running a fence around it to keep the cows out."

"Mike told me you lost a cow in here awhile back," I said.

"Yeah. The danged old thing got in and couldn't get out. Not sure if it fell down one of the sides or walked in at the far end and then didn't have the sense to walk out the same way. We didn't even know it for a couple days until we saw some buzzards circling. Came out and saw it floating. Finally got a rope on it and dragged it out with the tractor."

"Geez," I said. "How deep is this pit?"

"About forty feet or so. The boys floated a canoe out to the middle a few years ago and dropped a line with a weight over the side. They marked the line when it hit bottom and measured it later." He shook his head again. "It never goes dry, either. I've seen the water drop a couple feet in the late summer but that's all. I should just drain it and bulldoze in the sides but that's one of those projects that keeps getting put off."

Mike and I both laughed. "I have a few projects like that myself," Mike said.

"I expect we all do," Swanson said. He laughed and waved toward the pit. "This will probably still be here long after I'm gone. He paused then added, "You fellas still interested in hunting out here?"

"We are," Mike said. "Not at this one, though. Just the first pond. Last time we were here we saw some ducks on it. Thought we might put up a temporary blind on one side in the cattails. Nothing permanent, and we'd be careful to leave the place the way we found it."

"Well, you go ahead then," Swanson said. "I expect that would be okay. And if you'd happen to knock down a few ducks, you might think about dropping off one at the house. It's been a long time since I've had a roast duck but I imagine I can talk the wife into fixing one for Sunday dinner."

"We'd be happy to do that," Mike said. I added, "You bet."

"All right, then," Swanson said. "You fellas have a good day." He flipped up a hand in farewell and pulled away in the Dodge to slowly circle the pit. I guessed he was probably estimating how much fencing he was going to need to enclose it.

"Think we should have offered to help him fence this off?" I asked.

"I guess we could have," Mike said. "Maybe not a bad idea." Lending a hand with labor was standard practice to ensure good landowner relations.

Swanson completed his circle of the pond and as he came abreast of us again Mike raised an arm. Swanson slowed to a stop and gave us a curious look. Mike stepped forward and said, "You said you were thinking about fencing this off. We'd be happy to come back out and give you a hand with that."

Swanson smiled and said, "Well, I appreciate that. But no, you don't need to bother. My two boys and I can handle it, I imagine. But thanks for the offer."

"Well, okay then," Mike said. "Thanks again for the permission to hunt."

"Just remember my duck," Swanson said, and we all laughed. Then he pulled away and Mike and I started for his truck.

"Wish they all came that easy," Mike said.

"Yeah, no kidding," I said.

CHAPTER 51

My mind started to wander during the hour-long drive back to Des Moines from Swanson's farm.

Mike and I spent part of that time talking about the upcoming hunting season and, especially, how we needed to get back out there within the next few weeks to build the duck blind Mike had mentioned to the farmer. We were hoping for a cool morning to tackle the project but we knew that was unlikely to occur, given Iowa's typical weather in August. Nevertheless, we needed to get the blind built and brushed so its presence wouldn't spook any ducks—either those already using the area or those migrating through—when the season opened.

After kicking this around for a while we eventually lapsed into the comfortable silence that happens between friends who've known each other for quite some time. Neither Mike nor I felt the need to keep making idle chitchat, and our dogs apparently shared that attitude. They were both sound asleep on the back seat.

I started thinking about what I had lined up for the rest of the day. I was caught up on yard work so there was nothing pressing to be done outside. If I felt ambitious I might run the Equinox over to the car wash on Southwest 9th and give it a good cleaning inside and out. I preferred doing the exterior myself with a pressure wand in one of the drive-in bays rather than driving through the automatic wash, and that was something that wouldn't require me to be broiling under the direct sun for any length of time.

Running over to the car wash would also give me a chance to swing by Greg Fletcher's place and check it out.

It was a few minutes past 9:30 when Mike dropped us off at home.

I climbed out of the cab and grabbed the case containing

the dummy launcher. As I did so I asked Mike if he wanted to borrow it for a few days but he said no, he was fairly sure he could find the right-sized spring he needed to fix his own launcher and he was planning to do so that afternoon.

"Okay, then," I said. I opened the back door on my side and Preacher jumped out.

"Thanks again," Mike said, and I nodded.

"Rusty is really looking good," I said, and Mike grinned.

"Glad you think so," he said. He dropped the truck into reverse and said "See ya."

"See ya," I echoed, and Preacher and I turned and went inside.

AFTER FEEDING PREACHER her morning meal I went back to the office and logged onto my personal computer. I checked my email but aside from a couple more political jokes from Marcia Thompson, there was nothing of importance.

The burner I'd been using to correspond with James Collins was lying on the credenza. Although I'd just talked to him the previous afternoon, I picked it up and turned it on. I doubted he would have contacted me again with any new information about Fletcher; it was probably too soon for that, but I thought it wouldn't hurt to check.

Nope.

I turned to look out the window at my back yard and that's when the landline phone rang. Caller ID told me it was Daryl.

I picked up the phone. "Hey," I said. "What's up?"

She laughed. "Just calling to see what we're doing tonight. Are you coming up here? It's your turn."

"I can do that," I said. "Do you want to go out, or…"

"Yeah, let's go to that Mexican place up in Johnston," she said. "We haven't been there for a while."

"Sounds good," I said. "Pick you up about seven?"

"I'll be ready."

GREG FLETCHER'S HOUSE was in the older section of Greenfield Plaza and like most of the other houses on that street, it was a ranch with a one-car attached garage. It had gray siding with white trim and appeared to be well-maintained. The grass had been cut recently and Fletcher's dark gray Durango was sitting in the driveway, suggesting he was at home.

I noted all this as I drove past on my way to the car wash. I still found the coincidence of him living in the same neighborhood as Rachel James and myself rather ironic, but I told myself that those things happen.

I also couldn't help reflecting that, should I decide to avenge Hannah Wilkinson's death by killing him, it would be the first time I'd ever done so to someone literally so close to home. Again, the irony was almost staggering. As were the risks.

Was I thinking of killing him?

That I was contemplating such an action made me realize I was getting a little ahead of myself. Yes, the circumstantial evidence was piling up, just as I'd mentioned to James Collins. Based on what Collins had told me about Fletcher's posts on the Manspeak website, plus Jessica Wilkinson's conversation with Fletcher and her assertion that he'd lied to her about knowing the color of Hannah's nail polish, I was pretty well convinced he was guilty.

But as I'd also told James Collins, no one had hired me to kill him.

I'd never done a pro bono hit before…well, that wasn't quite true. Because of the way my previous assignment had played out, and because of my second inviolate rule that there must be no collateral damage, I had had to add a second target to the initial hit. I'd performed the second hit at no cost to my client (coincidentally, James Collins) because the hit was necessitated by my mistake, not his.

I'd also anonymously sent Collins's fee to the person who'd been falsely accused and subsequently charged with the initial hit. I did this to make up for his wrongful imprisonment. So in effect, I'd performed both hits for free.

But this situation was different. Not only had no one hired me to avenge Hannah Wilkinson's death (although I had a sneaking suspicion her daughter would have been quite willing to do so), but killing Greg Fletcher would also violate my first rule, which stipulated there must be no personal involvement. Hannah Wilkinson had been a friend, and now her daughter was also. Casual friends, to be sure, but I couldn't deny that this friendship introduced the personal element I have always assiduously tried to avoid.

Welcome to yet another self-inflicted mind-fuck.

I turned onto County Line Road and headed toward Southwest 9th and the car wash.

CHAPTER 52

"OKAY, THIS IS GETTING WEIRD," I laughed. "Are you ladies stalking us?"

My question was directed at Detective Madeline Madison and her partner, Beth Palmer, who were following the hostess at El Mariachi restaurant to the booth next to the one where Daryl and I were seated.

Detective Madison looked at us and started laughing, and even her partner smiled. "Guilty as charged," Madison said, and Daryl and I laughed also. "We're keeping our eye on you two, hoping to see what kind of no-good you're up to."

I told myself she was joking. "Then I guess we'd better be on our best behavior," I said, and laughed again.

The detective smiled and said, "I'll admit this looks a little suspicious. But we do seem to share the same taste in cuisine." Then she surprised me by adding, "May we join you?"

Before I could answer, Daryl replied, "Sure!"

She stood up and moved around to sit beside me. She gestured toward the seat she'd just vacated and pulled her margarita over to our side of the table. Beth and the detective slid into the booth opposite us and the hostess stepped back and smiled. "Well, okay then," she said. "I'll send the server over to take your drink orders." She placed menus in front of them.

We all looked at each other and Madison said, "You remember my partner, Beth," and Daryl and I both smiled and nodded.

"Good to see you again," Daryl said.

"Good to see you also," Beth said, and I wondered if she really felt that way. To her credit, she appeared friendlier than she had when we had previously seen the two of them at Skip's. Remembering Madison's apology when I'd run into her at Menards, I wondered if she had said something to Beth about being more sociable.

The server, a young male Hispanic, arrived at our table and asked them what they would like to drink.

"I'll have one of those," Madison said, pointing to Daryl's margarita.

"And I'll have one of those," Beth Palmer said, pointing to my Dos Equis Ambar.

The four of us laughed and the server said, "Got it." He smiled and left.

Looking at Daryl, Madison said, "I like your haircut!"

"Oh, thanks," Daryl said. "I just decided it was time for a change."

"I like it too," Beth added, and Daryl thanked her also. She had gotten her hair cut in the style she'd shown me, similar to Kris Jenner's, and I'd complimented her on it when I picked her up. Never let it be said I'm one of those oblivious males who doesn't notice and/or fails to comment on such things.

"So," Daryl said, nodding toward Madison, "I know you're a detective with Des Moines PD, but," she turned toward her partner, "what do you do, Beth?"

"I'm a personal trainer," Beth replied. "I work at Elite Fitness in West Des Moines. And you're at the *Register*, right?"

"Right," Daryl said. She picked up her margarita and took a sip.

"How's the magazine work going?" Madison asked me.

"Pretty well," I said. "We just wrapped the October/November issue so I have a little breathing room. Of course, I'll have to get started on December/January in the next week or so; no rest for the weary, as the old saying goes."

Madison nodded and said, "I know that feeling."

The server arrived with their drinks and another basket of tortilla chips and a bowl of salsa. He placed everything on the table and stepped back. "Are you all ready to order?" he asked.

"I think we are," I said. I looked across the table and said, "Do you need a few more minutes?"

"No," Madison said. "You go ahead and we'll be ready

by the time you finish." She and Beth took a quick glance at their menus.

Daryl and I had already agreed to share a combination platter of fajitas—beef, chicken and shrimp—before Madison and her partner had shown up. I placed the order and gestured toward Daryl and myself. "We'll need another round of drinks also," I said.

The server wrote this on his notepad and turned to our companions. "And you?" he said.

"I'll have the taco salad," Madison said.

"And I'll have the carne asada," Beth said.

The server wrote down their orders and said, "I'll be right back with the drinks."

As he walked away, I said, "So I have to ask. How did the bathroom painting project go?"

Madison leaned back and covered her mouth with one hand, stifling a laugh. Beth didn't bother trying to stifle hers. She glanced at Madison and said, "Do you want to tell them, or shall I?"

Madison made a flipping gesture with the hand in front of her mouth and said, "Go ahead."

"Well," Beth said, grinning, "Someone who shall remain nameless, but who has the same initials as the candy that melts in your mouth, not in your hand, managed to tip over the entire gallon of paint on the bathroom floor. The. Entire. Gallon."

"Oh no," I said, and couldn't help chuckling. "The entire gallon?"

"Yes. The entire gallon."

Daryl was laughing also. "That's a lot of paint!" she said.

"You're telling me that's a lot of paint," Beth snorted. "It's a fairly small bathroom and I'd guess the whole floor was a least an inch deep." Beside her, Madison—for some reason, maybe because she was a detective, I kept thinking of her by her surname—was shaking her head and still trying to suppress her laughter.

"What a mess," I said. "So I'm guessing that probably put an end to the painting project?"

"Well, for the moment, anyway. By the time we got it

cleaned up, neither one of us felt like going back to Menards and buying more paint. We thought maybe this was a sign that the bathroom was meant to stay the color it is." Beth shook her head. "We may try it again one of these days, but not anytime soon."

"You know," Daryl said, "there are people you can hire to do that sort of thing." She was smiling the impish smile I knew well. "I'm pretty sure they don't spill paint very often."

"Oh, no," Madison said. "Some of us, especially those with the same initials as British Petroleum, insist on doing these things ourselves." We all laughed again and I wondered if the references to their respective initials constituted some sort of ongoing game with them. I suspected it did.

The server returned with the second round of drinks for Daryl and me. We thanked him and he said, "Your food will be coming shortly."

THE FAJITAS WERE SIZZLING when he served us and our table was quickly blanketed in the smoke. Beth waved a hand and announced, "Whew! We're all gonna smell like Mexican food!"

I laughed and said, "Sorry."

"Oh, no need to apologize," she said. "That's not a bad thing. I love the smell of fajitas in the evening." I wondered if she was intentionally riffing on Robert Duvall's classic line from *Apocalypse Now* and guessed she probably was.

We all dug in and the conversation lapsed for a minute or two. Then Madison looked up from her taco salad and glanced around at all of us. "Mine is very good. How's everyone else's?"

We all made various appreciative comments, and then she asked, "Permission to talk shop for a minute?"

Beth rolled her eyes and said, "Must we?" But she was smiling as she said it and I wondered what was coming.

"Sure," Daryl said. "Why not?"

"Well," Madison said, "I just want to ask Rob a question." She smiled at me and said, "Do you know a fellow named Greg Fletcher?"

Lord God Almighty.

"I do," I said, hoping my alarm wasn't showing. "If we're talking about the same person, I see him out at Maffitt Reservoir occasionally when I'm walking my dog." I wasn't going to volunteer anything more than was absolutely necessary. But I didn't want to go overboard playing dumb, either.

"Right," Madison said, and I sensed she was shifting into full detective mode. "How often do you see him?"

I shrugged. "Maybe once every couple weeks, if that," I said. "It depends on which side of the lake we're walking, whether we're out there at the same time, and so on." I decided to push the envelope. "Why are you asking?"

"He was the last person who saw Hannah Wilkinson alive, the night before she drowned," Madison said. "Did you know that?"

"I did," I said, thinking a barefaced lie to the contrary would not be smart. "I've talked to Hannah's daughter a couple of times out there and she mentioned that." I was determined not to elaborate.

"Right," Madison said again. "I've talked to Jessica a couple times also. Can I ask, what's your impression of Fletcher?"

I shrugged again. "I don't know him very well; have only spoken to him a few times. He seems like a pleasant enough guy, a little on the quiet side. Not overly friendly, but not unfriendly, either." As I said this I glanced at Daryl and saw she was following our comments intently. Then I looked across at Beth Palmer but she was filling another tortilla with steak and salsa and didn't appear to be paying much attention. Maybe conversations like this were old stuff to her.

Madison was studying me closely, or that was my impression, anyway. She didn't say anything for a moment, then added, surprisingly, "Jessica thinks Fletcher may have had something to do with her mother's death."

"Really!" I said, hoping I wasn't overplaying it. "Why does she think that?"

Madison's reply was rather offhand. "Oh, she said she

talked to him recently and caught him in a lie." She hesitated, then added, "Something about him knowing the color of nail polish on her mother's toes."

"The color of nail polish on her toes?" Again, I hoped I wasn't overplaying it.

"Jessica said he couldn't possibly have known that unless he'd seen Hannah take off her shoes that night, which didn't jibe with his original story. It's a stretch, but..." she shrugged.

I shook my head. I had discussed all of this with Rachel James but not with Daryl, so I knew this would all be news to her. Once again I felt a stab of guilt for keeping so much from her. At the same time, I also realized I had to choose my next words very carefully.

"So," I said, "is he now a suspect?" I tried to put some disbelief in my voice, like I found the idea hard to imagine. But I also wanted to know the answer.

Madison deflected. "Hannah's death was ruled a suicide, and we don't really have anything that suggests otherwise...that is, nothing except Jessica's claim about Fletcher lying."

"I see," I said. I was tempted to say something more—and I'd have bet big money Madison was hoping I would—but I reminded myself of Mark Twain's advice: You should never pass up the opportunity to keep your mouth shut.

Beth Palmer came to my rescue. After swallowing a bite of her carne asada, she said, "Okay, you've talked shop. Now can we talk about something a little less morbid?"

Madison smiled and said, "Sure." She looked at me and said, "Thanks for your input, Rob."

I smiled in return and said, "I don't know that I gave you much."

"Oh, every little bit helps."

CHAPTER 53

"You didn't tell me you had talked to Hannah's daughter at the lake." Daryl's tone was more curious than accusing, or at least that's what I told myself.

I sighed. We were driving back to Daryl's house in Beaverdale after our dinner with Detective Madison and Beth Palmer at El Mariachi. Even as we were saying our goodbyes to them in the restaurant's parking lot, I was anticipating Daryl's questions. Paraphrasing Desi Arnaz on the old *I Love Lucy* sitcom, I knew I was going to have some a'splainin' to do. Pardon the politically incorrect reference.

"I've only seen her out there a couple of times walking Maisie, her golden retriever," I said. "We walked together, and she kind of unloaded on me. That's when she told me about Fletcher being the last person to see her mother the night she died." I hesitated, then added, "I didn't mention it to you because I've been trying to take your advice and let it go. Or not dwell on it, anyway. I didn't want to keep bringing it up." As I said this I again berated myself for (a) lying outright to Daryl, and (b) lying by omission to her. I knew I was guilty of both.

"Doesn't sound like you've had much luck with that…letting it go, I mean." Now Daryl sounded sympathetic. Which made me feel even worse.

"No, I haven't," I said. "The reminders keep coming up. I mean, for crissakes, what were the odds that we'd run into Detective Madison again? Or that she'd start asking me questions about this Fletcher guy?"

"It doesn't sound like she's letting it go, either. Even though the death was ruled a suicide."

"No, it doesn't," I agreed. "That's why I asked her if Fletcher was a suspect. I thought maybe they were still investigating Hannah's death. But she said they really don't have much to go on, other than Jessica claiming to have caught

Fletcher in a lie."

"Yeah…what was that business about him knowing the color of her mother's nail polish? I didn't quite follow all that. Did you understand that?"

I sighed again. "As a matter of fact, I did," I said. "Do you still have some of my Corona or Blue Moon at your place?"

"Yes. Why?"

"True confession time," I said. "I'll fill you in on all of that, the stuff about the nail polish, but it's gonna take a little while."

AFTER WE GOT SETTLED at Daryl's kitchen table, and after Daryl had put the two grilled shrimp she'd saved from our fajitas platter into Ivy's bowl, thereby placating the cat, I rolled out the whole story.

Well, not quite.

I was halfway through my second beer, actually my fourth if you counted the two I'd had earlier at El Mariachi, by the time I finished telling Daryl about Jessica Wilkinson's encounter with Greg Fletcher and his remark about the color of the nail polish on her toes matching her mother's, how he knew this because he'd seen Hannah wearing flip-flops at the lake, why Jessica was convinced this was a lie, her theory about him being an incel, and so on.

Daryl listened attentively and only interrupted two or three times to ask a question or have me clarify something. When I finished she shook her head and said, "I can't believe you didn't tell me about this." I wasn't sure from her tone if she was more angry or disappointed. It was probably a toss-up.

"Well, like I said, I've been trying to let this go." Even as I said this I realized how lame it sounded. I also thought, *liar!* What I hadn't told Daryl was that I had discussed all of this in detail with Rachel James, that she had had her own encounter with Greg Fletcher and likewise concluded he was a creep, and that I had engaged James Collins and his two hacker buddies to monitor all of Fletcher's online traffic. Nor did I mention that I'd learned Fletcher lived in my neighborhood and I had driven past his house just hours earlier.

I took another pull at my beer, then added, "I guess I thought if I just kept pushing it to the back burner, it would eventually go away on its own. Sorry if I just mixed a metaphor." I attempted a short laugh.

Daryl shook her head again. Ivy came over and rubbed against her ankles, probably hoping for more shrimp. Daryl reached down and fondled the cat's ears. Then she looked up at me and said rather sharply, "So what now?"

I shrugged and said, "So…nothing now." *Liar!* "You heard the detective say they haven't got enough on Fletcher to charge him, or at least I thought that's what she suggested. I'm still hoping this will all go away on its own." *Liar, liar!*

"And what about Jessica?"

I shrugged again. "I've only seen her a couple times when she was walking her dog. I'm assuming she'll be going back to school in another few weeks. After that, I don't expect I'll see her or talk to her again. And that should be the end of it."

Daryl gave me a long, searching look. "You should have told me about this. I had no idea you were still so…involved with all of this."

"Okay," I said. "I realize that now. It was wrong of me to not tell you. I'm sorry."

She gave me another long look. She sighed and said, "No more secrets, okay?"

I nodded. "No more secrets," I said.

Liar!

I PROBABLY DON'T HAVE to tell you that after the foregoing exchange, intimacy was off the table for the night.

By the time I finished my second beer, it was almost eleven o'clock and I knew I needed to be heading home to let Preacher out for her bedtime potty break. Daryl had sipped at a glass of chardonnay but had said very little after I had promised no more secrets. I could see she was weighing everything I had just told her, plus no doubt still struggling with the fact that I'd kept her in the dark about it. Possibly— probably—she was also wondering if there was still more I hadn't told her.

If she only knew.

I hoped she would forgive me while at the same time I realized I didn't deserve that forgiveness. We were both committed to our relationship and that meant we should be able to trust each other. Keeping secrets was no way to build and maintain that trust. And yet…

How do you tell someone you're a contract killer and you may have another assignment pending?

I couldn't dodge the fact that that was where I seemed to be heading. Of course I still had the option of backing away from the whole matter. I could just choose to ignore what Jessica Wilkinson and James Collins had told me and take no further action.

Could I really do that?

I was pretty sure I already knew the answer.

DARYL GAVE ME A RATHER wan smile as she kissed me goodnight at her front door. "Are you okay to drive?" she asked, no doubt thinking of the four beers I'd had.

"I'm fine," I said. I was reasonably confident that four beers over the course of several hours hadn't left me impaired.

"Okay," she said. "Just be careful."

"I will."

"Love you."

"Love you too."

I SPENT THE DRIVE HOME wrestling with the demons of my own dishonesty. Of course, I came up with no solutions to the dilemma in which I found myself. Correction: the dilemma in which I'd placed myself.

As usual, Preacher was waiting at the back door when I unlocked it. I stepped aside so she could make her nightly patrol of the back yard, then I went inside and saw the message light blinking on the phone in my kitchen.

I walked back to my office and pushed the play button on the answering machine. The message was from Rachel James.

"Hey you," she said. "No need to call me back tonight but

I just wanted to let you know that I had another Greg Fletcher encounter. I'll give you the details the next time we have beers on the deck but in the meantime, I'm more convinced than ever that he's a creep."

CHAPTER 54

Greg Fletcher felt good.

It was Sunday morning, a little after eight o'clock, and a cooling breeze was blowing from the northwest. It wasn't as warm as it had been for the past few days, and the humidity was lower as well. A cold front had moved in overnight and the predicted high for the day was 84 degrees. That was definitely preferable to the mid-90s they had been experiencing.

Fletcher was walking the roadway through the park on the east side of the reservoir, hoping to see Jessica Wilkinson again. But even if he didn't, he was still pleased with how things were shaping up. With a little judicious searching on the internet, he had developed a plan and while he hadn't nailed down all the details just yet, he was fairly confident he would be able to do so in the next few days.

The first hurdle was the one he was facing right now, namely orchestrating a meeting with Jessica. He was reasonably certain she still walked Maisie, the golden retriever, at the lake but he had no way of knowing exactly when she did so. He obviously couldn't park near her house and monitor her comings and goings, so he had to rely on catching her by chance.

He had tried lingering in the park on the east side and also at the picnic table on the west side where they had talked, but so far he had not seen her again. Knowing he would be recognized by many of the lake's other regulars, he was careful not to stay at either place long enough to draw undue attention. He knew he was far better off maintaining a low profile.

Which reduced his odds of effecting a chance encounter.

He had also tried varying the times he came to the lake. When his work schedule permitted, he had waited until mid-morning a few times before coming out, and he had returned several afternoons and evenings as well. Sooner or later, he told himself, he and Jessica were bound to cross paths again.

At which point he would face the second hurdle, higher than the first. He somehow had to insinuate himself back into her good graces.

He knew this wasn't going to be easy. He was still convinced she had fingered him—that whole silly business about the color of her mother's toenail polish--and that was the reason the detectives had paid him a second visit. Her wariness was going to be hard to overcome, but he hoped he could somehow manage it. When he saw her, he would project a totally non-threatening demeanor, act pleased to see her again, and try to appear sympathetic and supportive. And harmless.

He smiled as he realized he was actually hoping to establish the kind of relationship with Jessica that he'd had with her mother, that he was casting himself, again, in the role of a concerned and caring friend. That was how Hannah had thought of him and—he loved the irony—that was also what had gotten her killed.

There was an additional challenge to all this, and it was related to the urgency of the situation. He knew Jessica was in college and he assumed she would be returning to her classes in another few weeks for the fall semester. He needed to accomplish everything before that happened, before she slipped through his grasp.

But he knew he couldn't afford to let this urgency make him careless or cause him to do anything precipitous. He reminded himself that he once again needed to exercise the patience of the wild, that favorite phrase of his from *The Call of the Wild*. He believed that patience would be rewarded, just as it had been on his final evening with Hannah.

He smiled again at the realization that he was once more thinking like a predator. He had worked past the feeling that he was the one being pursued, and he felt his confidence surge. He would meet Jessica and when he did he would convince her that he could be trusted and wanted only to be a supportive friend. It might take more than one encounter, but after the initial meeting, it should become easier.

Then, after she had grown comfortable with him, he would persuade her to accompany him down to the water.

THERE WAS ANOTHER REASON Fletcher was in good spirits on this Sunday morning.

The previous evening he had seen the woman with the nice boobs, Rachel James, at Ft. Des Moines Park again. Like the first time he'd seen her, she was walking her Saint Bernard. And also like that first time, the dog had growled at him.

He had decided after dinner to walk in the park rather than return to the reservoir because he had already been out there twice that day. He'd walked once in the morning and again at about three o'clock in the afternoon. He hadn't seen Jessica Wilkinson either time but he had seen several of the other regulars, and he thought going back out a third time might be risky, especially in view of what he was ultimately planning. Being seen at the reservoir more often than usual might look suspicious.

So he had opted for walking at Ft. Des Moines Park instead.

Like before, he walked from his house and entered the park property from the parking lot behind Studebaker Elementary School. But this time he kept following the path that ran almost straight north to the levee on the east side of the park's lake. It was on this levee that he had first seen Rachel James and her dog, and he reasoned that he might run into her, or them, again if she usually followed the same route.

He was in luck.

He was about halfway across the levee when he saw Rachel James walk up from the parking lot at the north end of the lake and turn onto the levee. Her Saint Bernard—Fletcher remembered its name was Alexander—was trotting ahead of her on its leash. They were walking southward, directly toward him. Fletcher smiled as he realized that short of turning around and going back the way she'd just come, there was no way Rachel James could avoid him.

She made no attempt to do so but continued steadily toward him. Fletcher concentrated on keeping his own pace steady as well, not wanting to appear in a hurry to meet. At the same time, he tried to think of something clever to say by way of greeting.

As they came within speaking distance, Fletcher smiled and said, "Well, good evening. Nice to see you again." It was the best he could come up with on short notice. As he spoke he couldn't help noticing the woman's breasts under her tight V-necked t-shirt. He remembered the last time he'd seen her she'd been wearing a Kid Rock shirt, but this one was plain and dark gray. She was wearing lighter gray gym trunks and the same black Chuck Taylors as last time.

The Saint Bernard stopped and let out a low grumbling growl.

"Alex! Stop that!" Rachel James said. She took a firmer grip on the dog's leash and looked at Fletcher. "Sorry about that," she said. Fletcher thought her expression said otherwise. She wasn't smiling and there was nothing conciliatory about her manner.

"It's okay," he said. "I realize I'm still a stranger to him." He hoped he sounded disarming. He moved off the path a couple yards to give them room to pass. He gestured with one hand to indicate they could continue on their way.

The Saint Bernard broke into thunderous barking.

"Alex, no!" the woman said. She grabbed the leash with both hands and leaned back on it, bracing her weight against that of the dog. Fletcher guessed the Saint Bernard probably outweighed her and he hoped it wasn't going to make a lunge at him. If it did, he doubted she could stop it.

He stepped farther off the path and started to circle around them. "I'd better let you go," he said.

"Thanks," the woman said. Still holding the leash with both hands, she nudged the Saint Bernard with her knee and said, "Alex, let's go." They started forward and as they passed Fletcher the woman glanced his way and gave him a fleeting smile. "Have a good evening," she said.

"Thanks, you too," Fletcher said, happy with her smile.

He watched for a moment as they continued down the levee, then he turned and continued northward. Thinking that besides her big boobs, Rachel James also had killer legs and a very nice ass.

He hoped he'd see her again soon.

But without that fucking unfriendly Saint Bernard.

CHAPTER 55

I WAS LATE GETTING OUT TO the lake on Sunday morning.

I had spent a restless night after my half-assed confession to Daryl on Saturday evening. I hated lying to her, even if most of that lying was done by omission. A lie was a lie, and lately I seemed to be piling them up by the shovelful.

Rachel's message about seeing Greg Fletcher again had added to my unease. The whole situation kept snowballing despite my best efforts to avoid being drawn in. *Not my circus, not my monkeys*, I kept telling myself, but the monkeys were continuing to find me and climb onto my back, regardless.

I lingered over my coffee on Sunday morning. I wanted to hear more about Rachel's encounter—so much for letting this all go—but it was too early to call her. I'd touch base later, either after Preacher and I returned from the lake or sometime in the afternoon. I couldn't deny I was curious as to why Rachel said she was more convinced than ever that Fletcher was a creep.

I drained my coffee cup and stood up from the kitchen table. Preacher was already outside on the deck. It was a cool morning and I wanted to get out to the lake before it got much warmer. I'd had my fill of hot weather and I imagined Preacher had too. I wanted to take advantage of the cooler temperature while it lasted.

We loaded up and headed out.

AND EXPERIENCED A NEAR MISS.

As we slowed to turn into the entrance on the east side of the lake—I had decided to stay in the park and walk the roadway, rather than go over to the west side and have Preacher shag dummies from the water—I saw Greg Fletcher's Dodge Durango stopped at the entrance and waiting to turn out onto the highway.

I recognized the vehicle and as I turned in and drove past

Fletcher, I nodded and raised a hand off the steering wheel in an abbreviated wave. He returned the gesture and then pulled out onto the highway, heading west toward the dam and the other entrance.

The opposite direction from home, in other words.

I wondered if he was planning to cruise the roadway on the west side of the lake, looking for Jessica Wilkinson.

I shook my head. Having turned into the entrance on the east side, I knew it would look suspicious as hell if I suddenly reversed course and followed him over to the west side. I didn't want to give Fletcher the idea that I was stalking him. Or that I was interested in him at all, for that matter.

I realized I was thinking of him as a target.

"Let it go," I told myself. Even if Jessica was on the west side, she would undoubtedly have Maisie with her, and I was certain Fletcher wouldn't try anything dangerous in broad daylight. I was also certain that Jessica would exercise extreme caution around him, convinced as she was that he had killed her mother. She wouldn't let him get too close, nor would Maisie.

I drove on into the park to the first turnout past the restroom building. I parked and unloaded Preacher's ramp, placed it against the rear bumper and raised the hatch cover. Preacher trotted down the ramp and as she made a quick circuit of the turnout, I folded up the ramp and stowed it in the cargo area. Then I closed the hatch, locked the vehicle and we were on our way.

WE WERE ABOUT HALFWAY through the park when I saw Tim Sullivan walking toward us. He was wearing a gold ISU wifebeater, gym trunks and a boonie hat in desert camo. Preacher trotted up to him with tail wagging and he reached down to pat her bristly head. Then he called out, "Good morning, sir!"

"Good morning to you," I replied. He stopped next to me and removed his hat. He gave it a shake and put it back on his head.

"Are you just starting out?" he asked.

"Yeah, we just got here a few minutes ago. We're running a little late this morning. Thought we'd stay over here on the shady side under the trees. Just gonna walk down to the water and let Preacher splash around a little bit, then head home."

"Sounds like a plan. I parked at the equipment shed and walked across the dam. Gonna finish the circuit here and then head back."

I nodded. "Nice to catch a break from the heat," I said. "A little more comfortable than it has been, anyway." I paused, then added, "Have you seen anyone else this morning?"

"No, I haven't. You?"

"Greg Fletcher was just pulling out as we were turning in," I said. "We waved at each other but that was it. We didn't talk."

Sullivan nodded. "He's been out here quite a bit lately. I talked to him a few days ago, in fact."

"Oh yeah? Did he have anything interesting to say?" I hoped my question sounded innocuous.

Sullivan laughed. "Well, he taught me a new word," he said.

"A new word?" I shook my head. "What was that?"

"Brumal. At least, I think that's what it was, if I remember correctly. We were talking about the hot weather and he said something about how we'd all be longing for it when we were experiencing the brumal weather in January and February. I thought he said brutal but he corrected me; said the word was brumal. He said it meant wintertime."

"Huh," I said. I knew the word brumal, but just barely. It was a rather archaic term, and I tried to remember where I'd seen or heard it. Nothing immediately came to mind. But I thought it was curious that Greg Fletcher would have used it in a conversation. I laughed and said, "Who knew Greg Fletcher was such a wordsmith?"

"Yeah, really," Sullivan said. He paused and then said, "Well, I'd better let you go. Preacher looks like she wants to get moving." He nodded toward my dog, who was ranging through the park some thirty or forty yards away.

I smiled. "Yeah, she's not much for standing around and

visiting," I said. "You have a good morning."

"You too," Sullivan said. He started on up the roadway toward the restroom building and I turned and followed Preacher down through the park.

BRUMAL? WHAT THE HELL?

For some reason I couldn't let go of the fact that Greg Fletcher had used such a little-known word in a casual conversation with Tim Sullivan. Not that I had any reason to assume Fletcher wasn't well-read or was lacking in vocabulary skills; for all I knew, he might spend his evenings studying classic literature. I doubted that was the case but, the information provided by James Collins and my own impressions, and those of Jessica Wilkinson and Rachel James, notwithstanding, I really knew very little about the guy.

Still, it was a curious word choice.

I mulled this over as Preacher and I walked the shoreline on the east side of the lake. The water level was down and due to all the recent hot weather the shore was dry and hard. Preacher made occasional forays out into the water, gulping at it as she waded around and then swimming a few yards before turning back toward the shore. I ambled along and picked up a couple of discarded plastic water bottles that some slob or slobs had left behind, intending to toss the bottles into a trash barrel at one of the turnouts.

After thirty minutes or so we left the shoreline and angled back up through the park to our vehicle. The turnout where I had parked the Equinox was well-shaded and I had left the windows cracked a couple inches so I hoped the interior wouldn't be stifling. But if it was, I'd crank up the AC for the drive home.

I opened the hatch and positioned Preacher's ramp against the rear bumper. She trotted up the ramp and settled herself on her pillow with a loud sigh. I laughed and said, "I bet you sleep well this afternoon," as I folded up the ramp. I reached up to close the hatch cover, and as I did so something clicked in my mind.

I remembered where I'd seen the word brumal in print. Specifically, it was a line that included the phrase "brumal sleep."

I knew where that line occurred, and as soon as we got home I'd check it out.

CHAPTER 56

"DAMN!"

Greg Fletcher had just pulled up to the entrance gate on the west side of the lake, preparatory to turning east to cross the dam and head home. Before pulling out onto the highway he glanced west to make sure the way was clear. When he did so he saw Hannah Wilkinson's dark blue Explorer—now presumably her daughter Jessica's Explorer—approaching, its right turn signal blinking to indicate a turn into the entrance.

Fletcher had just completed a drive-through on the west side's graveled roadway. He had driven all the way back to the gate at the head of the hiking trail, circled the turnaround there and driven back out the same way, passing the canoe launch where an SUV and two pickups were parked. He had hoped to see Jessica Wilkinson somewhere along the way but there had been no sign of her.

Now, she was turning into the park just as he was leaving.

He gritted his teeth and then forced a smile. As she turned in she glanced his way just as Robert Vance had done a little earlier at the other entrance, and he raised his hand to wave at her. He saw her lift her hand—did she hesitate for a second?—and give him the briefest of smiles. Then she was past, heading on into the park.

Fuck.

Fletcher watched the Explorer in his rearview mirror as Jessica drove away, trailing a sizable cloud of gravel dust. He'd missed her by no more than a minute or so, and he wondered if he should turn back into the park and attempt to orchestrate an encounter.

Part of him said no. Jessica would know he had been about to leave the park so she would undoubtedly wonder why he had followed her instead. If she was already suspicious, this would only heighten that feeling and alarm her further.

Then again…

He told himself he had been waiting for this opportunity for days, and it might be some time before he got another chance. After greeting her he could tell her that he just wanted to check and see how she was doing, maybe attempt some small talk about when she would be returning to school, and so on. Try to alleviate her suspicion, in other words, and reassure her that he was just a concerned friend, while at the same time getting a handle on how much more time he had to carry out what he was planning.

He decided to go for it.

As soon as I fed Preacher her morning meal when we returned from the lake, I walked into the dining room that doubles as my library. Actually, it *is* my library; I don't give dinner parties so I don't have a formal dining room table in there, but I do have an antique wooden library table and chair. Tall bookcases line the walls, and on one of them there is a matted quotation on a small easel, a gift from one of my aunts, since deceased. The quotation is by Desiderius Erasmus and reads: *When I get a little money, I buy books; if any is left, I buy food and clothes.*

My aunt knew me well.

I stepped over to one of the bookcases and pulled a copy of Jack London's *The Call of the Wild* off the shelf. I flipped past the title and contents pages to Chapter One, "Into the Primitive," and read the opening quatrain:

Old longings nomadic leap,
Chafing at custom's chain;
Again from its brumal sleep
Awakens the ferine strain.

There it was.

This was the passage I had recalled at the lake, trying to remember where I had seen the word brumal. I had re-read *The Call of the Wild* many times over the years. In my opinion it's not only a classic of American literature, but also one of the greatest dog stories ever written, and I was fairly certain this was the only place I'd ever seen brumal used. Or at least, it was the only place I *remembered* seeing it.

So…was this also Fletcher's source for the word?

I read the quatrain again. I remembered reading somewhere that Jack London had borrowed it from a longer poem, but I couldn't recall the name of the original author, and London hadn't credited him. Nevertheless, the quatrain was a fitting introduction to the story of a domesticated dog that would ultimately revert to the wild and become the leader of a wolf pack.

Another thought struck me, and I felt a chill.

I quickly flipped to the end of the book. I found the last page and read the final few paragraphs of the novel.

And here may well end the story of Buck. The years were not many when the Yeehats noted a change in the breed of timber wolves, for some were seen with splashes of brown on head and muzzle, and with a rift of white centering down the chest. But more remarkable than this, the Yeehats tell of a Ghost Dog that runs at the head of the pack. They are afraid of this Ghost Dog, for it has cunning greater than they, stealing from their camps in fierce winters, robbing their traps, slaying their dogs, and defying the bravest hunters.

Nay, the tale grows worse. Hunters there are who fail to return to the camp, and hunters there have been whom their tribesmen found with throats slashed cruelly open and with wolf prints about them in the snow greater than the prints of any wolf...

Son of a bitch.

Now I knew why Fletcher had chosen Ghost Dog for his user name on the Manspeak website.

Fletcher apparently thought of himself as some sort of apex predator who could outwit his prey—*They are afraid of this Ghost Dog, for it has cunning greater than they*—and especially those women whom he believed had wronged him. His posted comments, the ones James Collins had related to me, hinted at this. And Jessica Wilkinson's theory that he was an incel driven to violence by his anger and frustration, was spot-on.

I felt another chill. Both Jessica and Rachel James had told me they were convinced Fletcher was some sort of creep, and they were further convinced that their dogs, Maisie and Alexander, had sensed something "off" or dangerous about him also. While I hadn't attached much significance to the latter—okay, had pretty much dismissed the dogs' reactions outright—now I found myself thinking they were right. All four of them, that is, the women *and* their dogs.

Which also confirmed that both Jessica and Rachel could be in danger.

Of the two, Jessica was probably the most vulnerable. If Fletcher felt that she had sicced the detectives on him—Madison had hinted at this during last night's dinner at El Mariachi—he might be planning some sort of retribution.

I couldn't stand by and let that happen.

I briefly considered sharing what I'd just learned with Detective Madison, hoping this might cause her to bear down on Fletcher again and now treat him as a bona fide suspect in Hannah Wilkinson's death. But I dismissed the idea almost immediately.

I realized that telling Madison about Fletcher calling himself Ghost Dog on the Manspeak website, and the implications of his choosing that user name, would inevitably lead to her asking me how I had come by that information. Because it had been obtained illegally through the hacking done by James Collins and his buddies, I couldn't reveal how I'd acquired it without implicating them. I wasn't going to do that.

Which left me with no one else to turn to if Fletcher was to be stopped.

Damn it to hell, anyway.

For the several hundredth time I reminded myself of Rule Number One, which stipulated no personal involvement. The only problem was, I couldn't seem to escape this situation. And I knew—*knew*—I couldn't allow Fletcher to harm Jessica Wilkinson if, in fact, that was his intention.

I told myself I didn't know for certain that he was planning to do anything to her. Maybe he was still hoping the entire matter would eventually fade away on its own, thinking that if he continued to bide his time and Jessica returned to college, Hannah's death would remain classified as a suicide and that would be the end of it.

Right. And maybe Carrie-Anne Moss would call me for a date next weekend.

I sighed and closed the copy of *The Call of the Wild*. I replaced it on the bookshelf and stared out the window at the back yard.

I didn't see any answers out there, either.

CHAPTER 57

When facing an insurmountable problem, eat. Right?

I was halfway through my plate of scrambled eggs, and being watched intently by Preacher, who wanted to make sure I didn't neglect her, when the phone rang.

I guessed it was either Daryl or Rachel James, but a glance at the Caller ID showed the caller was Jessica Wilkinson. I swallowed my mouthful of eggs, picked up the handset and said hello.

"Rob? It's Jessica. I'm sorry to bother you on a Sunday but I wanted to tell you I saw Greg Fletcher again. Just a little while ago, out at the lake." This all came out in a rush, and I was pretty sure I could hear a note of alarm in her voice.

"Really?" I said, thinking that my guess about him trolling the west side, hoping to run into her, had been correct.

"Yes," she said. "He was sitting there at the stop sign by the gate, waiting to pull out, just as Maisie and I got there. He waved at me and I waved back, but I didn't stop. I really didn't want to talk to him."

"Understandable. Then what happened?"

"Well, I drove on in and parked there where we usually park, where you and I talked. As I was getting Maisie out, he drove up and parked next to us."

"Meaning he turned around and followed you."

"That's right. And it creeped me out, big time."

"That's understandable also. What did you do?"

"Well, I didn't want to let him see that I was nervous, so I just said hi and got Maisie out. As soon as she saw him, she sort of stiffened up and growled."

"Interesting," I said, remembering what Rachel had said about Alexander. No question about it; both dogs appeared to be getting a seriously negative vibe from Greg Fletcher.

"That's what Maisie did the last time she saw him also. She definitely doesn't like him. And that's not like her at all…she usually loves everybody."

"I remember you telling me that. So what did you do then?"

"After I said hi, he said something about it being good to see me again, and he just wanted to check and see how I was doing. I told him I was doing fine." She laughed. "I did *not* say that it was good to see him again."

I laughed. "Way to dodge the hypocrisy," I said. "Then what happened?"

"I called Maisie and just started to walk away. I guess I was kinda rude. But I didn't want to stay there and make conversation. I could tell that's what he wanted to do."

"And what did he do?"

"He started to walk along with us anyway."

"Uh-oh."

"Right? I really didn't know what to do at that point. I couldn't think of any way to get rid of him."

"And what did Maisie do?"

"She kept walking real close to me, almost pressing against my leg. I didn't have her on a leash; I never do. Usually she goes on ahead, looking for a stick or something she can carry around. But not this time. She just stayed right next to me."

Props to Maisie for her strong protective instincts, I thought. Golden retrievers are typically characterized as a very friendly breed; as Jessica said, they usually give the impression of loving everyone. But there was no question that something about Fletcher was rubbing Maisie wrong.

I was glad Maisie had been there.

"Did Fletcher say anything more?" I couldn't help thinking the situation must have been somewhat awkward if he'd chosen to walk with Jessica, uninvited.

"He tried to make small talk," she said. "You know, something about it being nice that it wasn't so hot, that sort of thing. I just agreed but didn't say much else." She laughed again. "I guess I was trying to be rude, to let him know I really didn't want company."

"Not a bad strategy," I said. "Did he take the hint?"

"Not right away. We walked down the road and around to that point where you can park and look toward the dam. By that time neither one of us had said anything for several minutes and I think he started feeling a little nervous. Like he realized I didn't want to talk and I wasn't going to be more friendly."

"So then what happened?"

"There's a picnic table there on the point and he pointed to it and asked if I wanted to sit for a few minutes. I told him no, that I wanted to walk on around to the canoe launch so Maisie could get in the water. I tried to make it sound like I wanted to go on alone, that I didn't want him to come with us."

"Did it work?"

"It did. He said something like, 'Okay, then, I'll let you go.' He started to walk back the way we came, then he stopped and said, 'I'll probably see you out here again sometime.' I thought, not if I see you first, but I just said, 'Yeah, maybe.' He gave me a little wave and then he turned again and walked away."

"And that was the end of it?"

"Yes. I walked Maisie on around to the canoe launch and threw a stick a few times for her to fetch. I wanted to make sure I gave him plenty of time to get back to his vehicle and leave."

"Good thinking. Was he gone when you got back there?"

"Yes, he was, thank God. I don't know what I'd have done if he'd still been there."

"Well, luckily you didn't have to deal with that. How are you doing now?"

"I'm okay, but I'll admit it shook me up to see him again. I can't help thinking he's up to something."

And you'd be right, I thought. But I didn't want to frighten her, or add to her worry. So I said, "I don't think he's likely to try anything out there at the lake, especially during the daytime when there are so many other people around, and not anywhere along the roadway. People drive in and out of that place all the time, so there's too much chance that someone might see him."

"I know you're right but…" she hesitated, then added, "he killed my mother at the lake."

I drew a deep breath and tried to think of how I should respond. Again, I didn't want to alarm her. But neither did I want to pretend there wasn't any potential danger, especially after what I thought I had just learned about Fletcher fancying himself as some kind of cunning predator.

"But your mother died much farther around on the west side of the lake," I said, trying to word my response as tactfully as possible. "It was back along the hiking trail, quite a ways from the road. There was much less chance of anyone seeing her—seeing them—back there."

"So what are you saying? That he lured her back there so he could kill her?"

Well, no, that's not what I had meant to imply. But since Jessica had raised the question, I couldn't deny that it fit the scenario, and it was something I had already considered myself. It also fit with the comments James Collins told me Fletcher had posted on the Manspeak website.

"I really don't know the answer to that, and I'm sorry," I said, trying to deflect. "All I'm saying is that I think as long as you stay near the road, you're probably safe." I hesitated, then added, "But I definitely think you're smart to be on your guard, and I think you should continue to do so."

"So you do think he's dangerous," she said.

Again, I hesitated. But I knew she wasn't going to be put off. "Like I said, I think you're smart to be cautious. And I'm glad you had Maisie with you. I think you should continue to watch out for him and try to avoid him if you possibly can." I wanted to add something about not letting him talk her into going back on the hiking trail or down near the water, but I was sure she was smart enough to not do that anyway. In fact, she'd already demonstrated she was capable of giving him the brush-off. She wasn't going to let him persuade her into doing anything against her will.

I heard her sigh. "Okay," she said. "I'll be careful. And yes, I'll try to avoid him if I can. I just wanted to let you know that I'd seen him and he's still acting weird."

"I got that," I said. "And I appreciate you letting me know." I had another thought. "You know, there are other places you could walk Maisie. There's that dog park over by Raccoon River. You don't have to keep going to Maffitt if you're afraid of running into Greg Fletcher."

"I know that, and I've thought about it," she said. "But Maisie loves it out there and it was Mom's special place. Sometimes when we're walking out there I feel like I'm closer to her. I'm not going to let Greg Fletcher run me off and deprive me of that."

"Well, okay then," I said. "Just be careful."

"I will. I promise."

MY SCRAMBLED EGGS were cold by the time we ended our phone call. I thought about nuking them for a few seconds but I was pretty sure that would leave them rubbery and after talking with Jessica I had lost my appetite anyway. I felt restless, like I should take some action on her behalf, but I couldn't imagine what that action should be.

I stood up from the table and carried my plate over to the counter by the stove. I retrieved Preacher's bowl from her mat and dumped the eggs from the plate into the bowl, then added the eggs I'd left in the skillet for her. I added the half piece of toast I hadn't eaten—also cold—then set the bowl back on the mat. Preacher didn't hesitate to start skarfing everything down.

I watched her for a moment, then wandered back to my office, carrying my mug of coffee garnished with Baileys. I sat down at my computer, still wondering what course of action, if any, I should pursue.

My glance strayed to the burner sitting on my credenza, the phone I'd been using to correspond with James Collins. On impulse I picked it up and turned it on.

Sunday hadn't finished delivering its surprises.

When the phone booted up I saw that I had a text message from James Collins.

It read, "More on GF. Call me asap."

CHAPTER 58

GREG FLETCHER WAS PISSED.

Not just pissed, but *royally* pissed. Royally, *fucking* pissed.

His encounter with Jessica Wilkinson had gone badly, and he knew it. The little bitch had snubbed him from the get-go, not at all friendly or willing to talk. He'd tagged along hoping to get her to open up, but she hadn't. She'd said very little, actually, only answering his questions with as few words as possible.

He hadn't got the chance to ask her how much longer she would be around, when she would be leaving Des Moines to return to school. He could probably go online and find out when UNI's fall semester began and that would answer that question, but it still pissed him off that he hadn't been able to get her to engage.

It was obvious she didn't trust him and had no intention of letting him get any closer. She still blamed him for her mother's death, that was certain, and she wasn't going to be persuaded otherwise.

Which made her dangerous.

He was halfway back to Des Moines on the bypass, barreling along at 70 miles per hour, and he was barely seeing the road. Instead, he kept seeing Jessica's face as she'd told him, the smug little bitch, she didn't want to sit at the picnic table like he'd suggested but wanted to get her dog down to the water.

That fucking dog.

He'd heard it growling when he'd first walked up to her. Always before, when he'd seen the dog with Hannah, it had been friendly. Now, for whatever reason, it apparently hated the sight of him.

Was it just being protective of Jessica? Or could it possibly be blaming him for Hannah's death? Was a dog capable of thinking like that?

He smiled suddenly, recalling the final chapter of *The Call of the Wild* in which Buck slays many of the Yeehat Indians who had killed his beloved master, John Thornton. Buck was capable of thinking like that, and exacting revenge. Maybe Maisie was having similar thoughts.

He thumped the steering wheel with his fist. Jessica had won this round and left him looking like a fool. But he wasn't going to be bested by a teenage girl or her fucking dog.

He'd think of something.

THE TIME STAMP ON JAMES Collins's message was 7:30 p.m., so it had been sent the previous evening. I hadn't thought to check the burner when I got home from Daryl's; I was preoccupied with other concerns, nor had I checked it that morning before heading out to the lake with Preacher.

I glanced at my watch. It was a few minutes past 10:30 and I decided that was late enough to call Collins, even though it was Sunday. I told myself that unless he had spent the previous night carousing—did anyone still use that expression?—he would be awake. I punched in his number.

He answered on the second ring. "Hello there," he said, sounding fully awake. "I'm guessing you got my message."

"Yes, and I'm sorry I didn't get back to you sooner. I was out last evening and I just now got around to checking my messages. You said you have something more on Greg Fletcher?"

"Yes, and I thought it was something I should pass along. You told me that you think he might have killed a woman by drowning her, but her death was ruled a suicide, right?"

"That's right," I said. "Her daughter is convinced he killed her, and it's beginning to look like she's right. Did you find something else that would confirm that?"

"Well…not exactly." He hesitated then added, "But we found something that we think might be related."

"Related?"

"Right. Something that you should know about, anyway. Remember the last time we talked I told you Fletcher keeps a low profile? He's pretty careful about clearing his search histories after he's been online, but we caught him a couple times when he hadn't. Or maybe before he had a chance to clear his history."

"And?"

I heard Collins draw a deep breath. "And lately he's been searching copycat suicides."

God Almighty!

I didn't say anything for a moment. Finally Collins said, "Are you still there?"

"Yes, I'm still here." I drew a deep breath myself. "Just trying to get a handle on what you just said."

"You think it's relevant?"

"Yes, I definitely think it's relevant," I said, thinking of the conversation I'd just had with Jessica Wilkinson. "Very damn relevant, in fact."

"You think he might be planning something similar for the daughter?"

"Yes, I think that's exactly what he's planning. In fact, I'd almost bet on it. I just talked to her a little while ago, and she told me she'd just seen him at the lake, the same one where her mother drowned. She said that he walked with her and he was acting friendly and trying to get her to talk. She brushed him off but she told me she had a bad feeling about the whole thing."

"Wow."

"Yeah."

"Do you think you should warn her?"

"I already told her to be careful and to avoid him if she could, or at least not let him get too close," I said. "But I might call her again. Another warning couldn't hurt."

"No, it couldn't. I gotta tell you, this guy is creeping *me* out, and I've never even seen him. I'd hate like hell to think he could do something to the daughter."

"That makes two of us. I don't want anything to happen to her, either. Obviously."

Neither of us said anything more for a moment. Then Collins quietly asked, "So…are you going to do something to stop this guy?"

I hesitated, but only for a second or two. Then I said, "I'm probably going to have to. The cops have pretty much closed the case, and I can't see a good way to get them involved again. And I can't just stand by and let anything happen to Jessica."

"I understand. Is there anything more we can do at this end?"

"I hate to keep asking this, but maybe continue to monitor his online activity for a few more days. See if he posts anything on that website or searches anything else that might give us more of an idea of what he's planning."

"Okay, we'll do that. I'll contact you right away if we find anything."

"Thanks. And I'll try to do a better job of keeping my phone on and checking for messages."

AFTER WE ENDED THE call I sat for several minutes and thought about what I'd just learned.

I had heard of copycat suicides and while I didn't know much about them, I knew that the term usually referred to a person or persons who, distraught after having learned of the death of the first victim, decided to take their own life in a similar manner. Young people—high school students, for example, who heard of a classmate's suicide—had been known to do this.

Once again, I thought of Milton Mulberry.

After Milton's death, no one in our high school had killed themselves by stepping in front of a commuter train, as he had done. But I remembered the weeks I had agonized over his death, and specifically the bullying incident that had caused it, and my failure to act. I could at least partially understand how someone might be driven to such extremes.

I didn't believe that Greg Fletcher's sudden interest in the subject, as evidenced by his online searches, suggested that he was feeling guilty and considering suicide himself. That didn't fit with everything else I had learned about him. But I *could* believe he was planning to kill Jessica Wilkinson in the same way he'd killed her mother, hoping to make Jessica's death look like a copycat suicide.

I shuddered and picked up the phone.

CHAPTER 59

BUT I DIDN'T CALL JESSICA WILKINSON.

Instead, I called Rachel James.

I needed to bounce some thoughts and speculation off someone, and Rachel was my best option. For obvious reasons I couldn't turn to Daryl—*piling up more lies by omission, guy!*—but I needed help sorting out everything I'd just learned, and—this was the trickiest part--nailing down a plan of action.

I told myself that Jessica was safe enough for the time being. She had promised she would be careful and do her best to avoid Greg Fletcher, and I believed that as intelligent as she obviously was, she would not to be fooled by him in any way. Short of an outright attack, which I doubted Fletcher would be foolish enough to try, I didn't think Jessica was in any immediate danger.

But that didn't mean Fletcher would give up. Which meant he was going to have to be stopped, and as I'd just told James Collins, I was probably the person in the best position to do that.

I punched in Rachel's number on my landline and she answered on the third ring.

"Hey you," she said. "You must have gotten my message about Greg Fletcher."

"I did, and I want to hear about your encounter. I also have some additional things to run by you, stuff I just learned. Any chance we could get together this afternoon?"

"Well, Summer and the boys are here right now but they're going home after lunch. I could swing by for deck beers after that…say around 1:30 or two?"

"That'll work," I said. "See you then."

"WHAT'S AL DOING TODAY?"

Sometimes I couldn't help wondering what Rachel's

husband thought about all the time his wife and I spent drinking beers on my deck, but ours was a long-standing friendship and apparently he wasn't concerned. Plus, Daryl and I had double-dated (another archaic term!) with Rachel and Al quite a few times, and everyone seemed comfortable with each other. To the best of my knowledge, Daryl never felt threatened by Rachel, and I assumed Al felt the same way about me.

"Oh, he got called into work this morning," Rachel said. Al was a troubleshooting engineer at the huge Hormel meat processing plant in Osceola, about 40 minutes southwest of Des Moines. "There was a problem with the bacon slicing machine cutting inconsistently and causing the product to be out of spec."

I laughed. "Like I have any idea what that means," I said.

"You and me both," Rachel said, laughing also. "So let's talk about Greg Fletcher. Shall I go first, or do you want to? You said you'd found out some more stuff about him?"

"Right," I said. "But you go ahead. Tell me about your encounter last night."

"Okay," Rachel said. She took a drink from her bottle of Miller 64. "It was actually pretty much a repeat of the first time. I was walking Alexander over at Ft. Des Moines Park and we ran into each other. He came walking toward us and met us about halfway across the levee."

"Do you think he planned that?"

"It certainly crossed my mind. I mean, it could have just been a coincidence, but then again…" She shrugged. "I had the feeling that he planned it, yes."

I nodded. "I'm inclined to agree. Especially after what just happened this morning with Jessica Wilkinson. But I'll get to that in a minute. What did Fletcher say when you saw him?"

"He said something about it being nice to see me again. And then Alexander started growling. I told Alex to be quiet but I was actually kinda glad he didn't. He definitely doesn't like Fletcher and wasn't going to let him get any closer."

"That's really interesting," I said. "Jessica's dog, Maisie, doesn't like Fletcher either. In fact, she reacted the same way Alexander did."

"Really?"

"Yes. But what happened after that? With Fletcher, I mean?"

"He said he'd better let us go, and he moved off the path so we could walk by. I was holding Alexander's leash with both hands, afraid he might make a lunge at Fletcher. Luckily he didn't and we got past him with no problem."

"And that was it?"

"Pretty much, except that as we were walking away I looked back and told him to have a nice evening. The reason I looked back was because I could feel his eyes on me. And when we were talking, he couldn't keep his eyes off my boobs, just like the first time." She laughed and made an exaggerated shudder. "I told you I thought he was a creep."

"Yes, and Jessica feels the same way. She ran into him out at the lake this morning, and like you, she thinks he planned it. In fact, she's sure of it because he was actually leaving the lake just as she got there, but he turned and followed her back in."

"Oh, wow. That's pretty scary."

"Yes, it is. He followed her to where she parked, then he started walking with her. She had Maisie with her and she said Maisie immediately stiffened up and growled when she saw Fletcher."

Rachel smiled. "Just like Alexander." She drained her bottle of 64.

"Exactly." I'd already finished my Blue Moon. I nodded toward Rachel's empty bottle. "Ready for another?"

"Sure. I don't know when Al will be back and I don't have anything else going this afternoon." She grinned. "And I want to hear more about Jessica's encounter."

"Hold that thought," I said as I stood up and grabbed our empties. "I'll be right back."

I went inside and put the two empties in the carton next to the wastebasket. I got two new bottles out of the fridge and popped off the caps and as I did so I glanced at Preacher, who was sprawled in the middle of the kitchen floor directly in line with a register, soaking up the cool air blowing toward her.

"What a tough life you lead," I said, and she favored my comment by thumping the floor a couple times with her docked tail. I picked up the two bottles and headed back out to the deck.

"I think you just got a message," Rachel said. She nodded toward the burner I'd been using with James Collins. Making good on my promise to keep it turned on and check it more frequently, I'd brought it out and set it on the small table next to our chairs.

I picked it up and thumbed the message icon. Sure enough, it was a text from Collins. I read the message and drew in a sharp breath. Rachel looked up and said, "What?"

I handed her the phone so she could read Collins's message herself. She read it and gasped. "Oh, no," she said.

The message read: *No need to call me back, but I checked GF's online activity again and thought you should know he's now searching ways to poison dogs.*

CHAPTER 60

"THAT SON OF A BITCH!"

I spat the words out and shook my head. "This is getting worse by the hour."

"What are you going to do?" Rachel's face showed her alarm.

"Something violent," I said, and in spite of ourselves, we both laughed.

"I'll help." There was no mistaking the conviction in her voice.

I looked at her, thought for a moment, and said, "We need to come up with a plan, and it has to be something that can be put into motion quickly. I'm worried that Fletcher is upping the ante and might try something dangerous, like, real soon. I also need to warn Jessica about this poisoning stuff."

"You should do that now."

I nodded. "I need to go inside and make the call from my landline. I don't have her number out here."

"Go ahead. I'll wait."

I HURRIED INSIDE TO MY office. I checked the Caller ID on the landline and scrolled back to Jessica's number. I punched it in and waited through four rings until the call went to her voice mail.

"Hi, this is Jessica. Please leave your message after the beep, and I'll get back to you just as soon as I can. Have a nice day."

Shit. I might have known. But I had no choice. I couldn't wait for her to call me back because I had no idea how long it might be until she did so. I had to warn her now.

"Hi, Jessica," I said. "This is Rob Vance. Don't want to alarm you but I just found out that Greg Fletcher has been searching online for ways to poison dogs. You need to be very careful with Maisie and make sure she doesn't eat anything she finds out at the lake or even in your yard. I'd suggest not letting her off leash at the lake if you go back out there. Give me a call if you want to talk about this, but again, don't let Maisie eat anything she finds outside."

I hung up, hoping like hell Jessica checked her messages regularly.

RACHEL WAS CHECKING her own phone when I went back outside. She looked up and said, "Did you talk to Jessica?"

"No, it went to her voice mail. But I did warn her and told her not to let Maisie eat anything she found at the lake or in their yard. I told her that I'd just found out that Fletcher was searching ways to poison dogs. For the moment, that's about all I can do."

"Let's hope she gets the message sooner rather than later."

"Right. I think they're safe for a little while, at least. According to James Collins, Fletcher just started searching this, so it would probably take him sometime to actually do anything."

"What do you think he might do?"

I shrugged. "Who knows? Leave poisoned baits out at the lake? Maybe drive by their house late at night and toss something into their yard? I wouldn't put it past him to do either of those things. Or both."

Rachel shook her head angrily. "That motherfucker," she said.

"You got that right." I was remembering something Terhune occasionally mentioned in his writings, an old superstition that said there was a special corner in hell reserved for people who poisoned dogs. I hoped Terhune was right.

I was now ready and willing to send Fletcher to that special corner.

BY THE TIME WE FINISHED our third beers, we had a plan.

Most of it, at least seventy-five percent, was Rachel's idea. As we began to kick things around I mentioned something I remembered Jessica saying to me awhile back, that she hoped Fletcher would die like her mother had died.

Rachel seized that idea and ran with it.

We fine-tuned the details, testing one possibility after another and finally getting everything nailed down to what we believed was workable. Some fancy footwork (almost literally) was going to be required, but we were reasonably confident we could pull it off.

There was, however, one major drawback. Or I should say, one major objection that I raised.

To execute our plan, Rachel was going to have to play a key role. For the first time in all the years she had been—ahem—assisting me with my assignments, she was going to be an active participant. Always before her involvement had pretty much been limited to supplying me with various drugs, usually something I used to subdue or incapacitate a target.

This time, no drugs would be involved.

"I don't like that part," I told her, referring to what she had proposed to do. "I don't like it all. I can't let you put yourself in danger like that."

"Listen to you, telling me you can't let me do something. Not even Al can get away with that." She grinned and added, "Besides, I'm volunteering. It's not like anyone is forcing me. And I really want to see Fletcher stopped. The bit about poisoning dogs"—she shuddered—"that was the final straw."

"Okay," I said. "I get that you want to help me stop Fletcher. But if we do what we've said, that will make you fully complicit in his death, an active player. I mean, this crosses a line you've never crossed before. Are you sure you want to do that? And that you'll be okay with it afterward?"

"Oh yeah, I'm sure," she said. "Trust me, I'm sure."

So that settled it. We agreed to get started on everything right away, and to begin putting the plan in motion the following evening.

I walked Rachel out to her Camaro and as she climbed in I asked her if she was okay to drive, thinking of the three beers we'd each had in the past couple hours. She laughed and said,

"I'm fine. I only have to go five blocks."

"Okay, then," I said. I smiled and added, "Thanks for the plan."

"No problem." She gave me a little wave and as she backed out of my driveway I pondered one final question, mostly rhetorical.

Why was I not surprised to learn that she owned and usually carried a stun gun?

CHAPTER 61

IMMEDIATELY AFTER RACHEL departed I texted a reply to James Collins: *Info received and warning issued. Thanks. Please continue to monitor and inform of any new developments. Taking action soon.*

I hesitated a moment before adding the last line about taking action, then I went ahead and tapped it in. I wanted to let Collins know that the entire matter would, I hoped, soon be resolved. But I deliberately kept the wording vague and I was reasonably certain he would delete the text as soon as he'd read it, so I was confident there would never be any repercussions.

Then I logged off the burner, grabbed the key fob for the Equinox and headed outside. I had to make a run over to Menards to pick up the one item I still needed to purchase to implement our plan. Between the two of us, Rachel and I already had everything else.

GREG FLETCHER FELT BETTER after spending some time online and coming up with a plan for dealing with Jessica Wilkinson's golden retriever and maybe, if necessary, Rachel James's Saint Bernard. For the most part, he had always liked dogs although he hadn't owned one since childhood, when he and his brother had had a small mixed breed their parents had adopted from an animal shelter. The dog, a female named Mitzy, had eventually succumbed to old age when Fletcher was in high school and he had never felt compelled to acquire another.

Now, however, any fond memories he had of Mitzy were pushed aside. He attributed at least part of Jessica Wilkinson's unease in his presence—he didn't try to fool himself into denying that unease—to her dog's reaction to him. The more he thought about it, the more willing he was to believe Maisie blamed him for Hannah Wilkinson's death. Jessica, in turn, seemed to be picking up on that, bolstering her own feelings about his guilt.

Well, removing the golden from the picture should eliminate at least some of that, he thought, and the sooner the better.

He could always deal with the Saint Bernard later.

WHEN I RETURNED FROM Menards I had two phone messages on my landline.

The first was from Daryl. "Hey, Rob," she said, "I don't think we had any specific plans for tonight but I'm gonna beg off on getting together anyway. I'm feeling a little under the weather today and I'm just gonna chill here with Ivy this evening. But give me a call later if you want to. Okay…love you. Bye."

Well. I couldn't help wondering if Daryl's "under the weather" comment was euphemistic for still feeling put off by my having kept some of the details about Hannah and Jessica Wilkinson—specifically, my ongoing involvement—from her.

If it was, I couldn't really blame her. And, given the events of the past few hours, I was even more deeply involved than I had been the night before. *Oh, what a tangled web we weave…*

I put the thought aside. I would call Daryl later and try to discern if she was still upset. If so, I'd attempt some damage control. I didn't like feeling that I was pushing her to the back burner, so to speak, nor did I want to continue piling up lies, but at the moment I didn't feel like I had any other choice.

The second message was from Jessica Wilkinson. Speak of the devil…well, not exactly.

"Hi Rob, it's Jessica," she said. "I got your message and I'm kinda freaking out over here. Do you really think Fletcher might try to poison Maisie? Oh my God. I'll make sure she doesn't pick up anything outside like you said but I'm really worried. Please give me a call." There was no mistaking the panic in her voice.

I picked up the phone and dialed Jessica's number.

GREG FLETCHER WAS WAITING to turn left into Menards from Southeast 14th Street when he glanced over and saw a gray Equinox waiting to turn out of the store's parking lot onto 14th. After a momentary pause the Equinox made the right turn and headed south, and Fletcher thought he recognized the driver. He was pretty sure it was Robert Vance.

Fuck me, he thought. What were the odds of seeing Vance twice in the same day under such similar circumstances? But he couldn't dwell on the matter because there was break in the oncoming traffic, so he completed his left turn and entered the Menards parking lot. He drove into the lot and parked and as he walked into the store, it occurred to him that seeing Vance at this Menards, plus the fact that Vance had turned south upon exiting, suggested Vance lived nearby. Maybe even in Greenfield Plaza.

He could check that out when he got home, just as he had previously checked out Rachel James. In the meantime, he needed to pick up something to put his plan for the evening in motion.

"JESSICA, IT'S ROB," I said, when she answered the phone.

"Oh, thank you for getting back to me. I'm sorry about sounding so freaked but now I'm really afraid. I don't want anything bad to happen to Maisie."

"No, of course you don't. And I'm sorry if I alarmed you. But I wanted to warn you so you could watch out and make sure she doesn't pick up anything and eat it."

"Do you really think Fletcher is going to try to poison her?"

I hesitated for a moment before answering. I didn't want to get into the details of how I knew Fletcher had been searching the subject online, but I realized she probably needed some sort of explanation, if only to give credence to my warning. So I said, "I've been doing a little checking into him, and yes, I think he might be planning something like that."

"Why do you think so?"

Damn her persistence. "Well, some of his online activity

suggests it," I said. "He's been searching the subject. Plus what you told me about Maisie's reaction to him. He must have picked up on that."

She was silent for a moment, then she asked, "How do you know what he's been searching online?"

I sighed. "Jessica, can I ask you to just trust me on this? I can't really go into more detail, except to say that I've been doing a little checking on Fletcher, trying to follow up on what you've told me." I hoped that by looping her back into the picture, she might cut me a little slack.

Thankfully, she did. "Okay," she said. "I was just curious, that's all. I didn't mean to pry. And I appreciate you checking on him. You're the only person who seems to believe what I said about him."

"That's okay, and I understand why you were curious," I said. "For what it's worth, I think you're right to be concerned about him. Both for Maisie's sake and for your own. I don't want to alarm you again, but I really do believe you need to be careful. Like we discussed when we talked earlier."

"Oh, I will, I promise. I might even do like you suggested, and start taking Maisie to the dog park instead of back out to Maffitt. At least for the time being."

"I think that's a great idea," I said. Another thought occurred to me. "When do you go back to school?" I asked.

"Classes start in three weeks, on Monday the twenty-second," she said. "I'll be going back the weekend right before that. Dad and I have already talked about it and I'm going to take Maisie with me. She'll live in the apartment with me and my two roommates, and we'll take turns walking her."

"I'm sure she'll love that," I said.

"Yes, I'm sure she will." Jessica laughed. "Not that we'll spoil her or anything."

"No, of course not," I said, and laughed also.

WHEN GREG FLETCHER GOT HOME from Menards he logged onto his laptop and entered "robert vance des moines" into the browser's search window.

He got a hit on the same people-finder site he'd used to

check out Rachel James. He clicked on it and studied the brief profile that came up. There wasn't a hell of a lot of info shown for Vance, much less than there had been for Rachel James, but Fletcher was able to determine that Vance did indeed live in Greenfield Plaza, just a few blocks away from his own home.

He'd be damned. So both Robert Vance and Rachel James were his neighbors.

He wondered if by chance they knew each other.

CHAPTER 62

After a dinner consisting of several slices of meat-lover's pizza from the Pizza Hut on Southeast 14th I spent most of the evening prepping for the plan Rachel and I were going to implement the following night.

I gave the crust from the pizza slices to Preacher and stuck the remaining pizza, still in its box, in the fridge. Then I headed downstairs to the basement and uncased a Gamo air rifle that had been a birthday present from my cousins many years earlier.

The Gamo had a black synthetic stock and carried a 4x32 scope, and it propelled a .177 pellet at 1,250 feet per second. That was powerful enough—although I'd never used it for this purpose—to kill small game like rabbits and squirrels. I was confident it was also powerful enough for the job I had in mind.

Equally important, the gun featured technology that reduced muzzle blast. I guessed I would probably need to fire it at least five or six times to accomplish my objective, so the noise factor was critical. The rifle wasn't totally silent, but because it wasn't firing cartridges loaded with gunpowder, it was much quieter than a traditional firearm.

After checking the gun over and sighting through the scope—I remembered it as being highly accurate—I slipped it back into its case and carried it upstairs, along with a box of .177 pellets.

Greg Fletcher was fidgeting, eager for the sun to go down.

It was a few minutes past eight on Sunday evening and it wouldn't be fully dark until nine or a little after. He dared not risk putting his plan into action until then. In the meantime, he sat at his kitchen table, nursing a Miller Lite and going over in his mind exactly what he was going to do.

He told himself he was once again in full predator mode,

and he smiled at the thought.

He had completed the preparations for his plan about an hour earlier and those preparations were now sitting in a plastic bag on the passenger-side floor of the Dodge Durango. Once again he ran over the plan and a thought suddenly occurred to him.

He stood up from the kitchen table and moved back to his bedroom. Somewhat reluctantly he stripped off the light gray t-shirt and khaki shorts he'd been wearing. He pulled a pair of dark jeans out of his closet and, after a moment's search, a long-sleeved navy blue shirt.

Given the warmth of the evening, he wasn't thrilled about dressing in the jeans and long-sleeved shirt, but he thought the extra precaution was worth the discomfort. He'd run the Durango's AC on high if necessary, both going out and coming home.

I LAID THE AIR RIFLE and box of pellets on the library table in my dining room, then I went out to the garage and pulled the converted tackle box containing the old Hallmark dummy launcher off the shelf. I carried the tackle box over to the worktable, opened it and pulled out one of the dummies. I grabbed a roll of duct tape off a nearby shelf and went to work on the dummy, attaching what I had purchased at Menards that afternoon.

I wished I had time to test the finished product to see if it performed like I hoped, but I didn't. I felt, and Rachel agreed, that the sooner we brought our plan to fruition, the better— that is, the safer—for all concerned.

Well, except Greg Fletcher.

BY THE TIME HE FINISHED dressing, it was 8:20.

Fletcher thought for a moment and then crossed the hallway to the spare bedroom he used primarily for storage. From the top shelf of an old, battered bookcase he selected a black Chicago White Sox baseball cap from the several caps that were sitting there, all in various colors and bearing different logos. He wondered if he should darken the white insignia but decided that probably wasn't necessary. Although he wasn't a diehard baseball fan, this was one of his favorite caps and he didn't want to spoil it.

He put the cap on and returned to the kitchen.

IT WAS ABOUT 8:30 by the time I finished rigging the launcher's dummy, or at least as much as I could do until I took the dummy and launcher over to Rachel's. I would complete the preparations over there with what she was providing for our plan. In the meantime, I stowed the launcher and dummy on the back seat of the Equinox.

I went back into the house and called Daryl. She picked up on the second ring.

"Hey there," she said. She sounded pleasant enough.

"Hey there. Just calling to see how you're doing."

"Doing a little better, actually. I don't know what the problem was; maybe something in the fajitas last night didn't agree with me. Did you have any problems?"

"No, not really. Except for maybe a little lingering after-effects this morning from last night's beers." I stopped short of calling those after-effects a hangover because they hadn't amounted to that, but I thought acknowledging the four beers I drank might serve as a lead-in to any further thoughts Daryl could be having about the exchange we'd had after dinner. But she didn't pick up on that theme. Instead, she laughed and said, "That'll teach you to watch your beer consumption."

"Yeah," I said, laughing also. I was relieved that apparently we weren't going to have to revisit the subject of my having kept things from her. "Next time cut me off after a couple."

"Oh, right," she said. "Like I could do that."

"What, you don't want the responsibility of being my conscience?"

She laughed again. "I think you have me confused with Jiminy Cricket."

Ouch. I wondered how long my nose would be by now if I were a puppet made of wood.

GREG FLETCHER'S KITCHEN CLOCK now read 8:40.

"Time to go," he said to himself. He headed outside to the Durango.

He backed out of his driveway and drove up to County Line Road. He made a left onto County Line, drove a half mile to Southwest 9th and made another left. He took 9th south to the bypass and then headed west toward Maffitt Reservoir.

A half moon was rising in the eastern sky behind him, and he tried to recall a passage from the last chapter of *The Call of the Wild,* something about Buck running through the moonlit forest as he responded to the fierce primordial urges growing within him.

He couldn't remember the exact wording of that passage, but driving westward on the bypass toward his objective, Fletcher told himself he too was on the hunt, and like Buck, he was responding to urges he could not suppress.

DARYL AND I CHATTED for a few minutes and then ended our conversation with our usual "love you, love you too" closing. I hung up the phone feeling reassured that things were okay between us; that no irreparable harm had been done by the previous evening's revelations. Maybe I was being foolishly optimistic but, given Daryl's upbeat tone, I was choosing to think positive.

My next call was to Rachel James.

"Hey you," she said.

"Hey you," I said. "I've got everything ready over here and I was wondering if I could swing by and drop it all off." I glanced at my watch and saw it was a few minutes before nine o'clock.

"Sure, come ahead. We're just finishing up. I had to ask Al for help with some of this; I hope that's okay."

"Sure," I said, because what else could I say? I wasn't going to chide Rachel but I couldn't help wondering how much of our plan she might have revealed to him. Under the old theory that loose lips sink ships, I've always kept my preparations strictly to myself, or at least limited how much I revealed to Rachel. But this time, I reminded myself, the situation was different.

"C'mon over then," she said. "We're out in the garage."

"I'll be there in five," I said.

FLETCHER EXITED THE BYPASS and drove south to Maffitt Lake Road. He turned right and headed west toward the reservoir but he didn't stop there. He continued across the dam and kept going until he reached River Oaks, the westernmost development of executive homes.

He entered River Oaks—by now it was fully dark—and he drove slowly along the road as it wound through the development. He had driven through here several times previously, and most of the houses were huge. He thought of them as palatial, and they sat on large lots, many of which were heavily wooded. He knew the Wilkinsons' house was on one of the side streets and he planned to cruise past it and park a short distance away, then approach the house on foot.

Before leaving his vehicle, however, he would make a careful reconnaissance of the area and make sure there was no one outside who might see him. He couldn't afford an encounter with a late-evening dog walker or anyone else.

Once he was sure the coast was clear, he'd make a quick trip to the Wilkinsons' property, drop off the "package" he had prepared, then return to his vehicle and drive home.

Easy peasy, he told himself.

I COULDN'T HELP LAUGHING when I saw what Rachel and Al had put together in their garage. It was all based on the plan Rachel had come up with, which in turn was based on the comment Jessica Wilkinson had made about wanting Greg Fletcher to die as her mother had died.

"Think this will work?" Al asked. He was smiling as he said it, and I realized that as an engineer he had probably fine-tuned Rachel's plan and added a few touches of his own. In fact, looking at what they had assembled, I was sure of it.

"Yeah, I think so," I said. I nudged the item on the garage floor with my foot and asked, "Are you sure John won't miss this?" John was their son, Summer's younger brother.

"He hasn't used it in years," Rachel replied. "In fact, he may not even remember we still had it. It was buried in a pile of boxes up in the loft and we had a heck of a time finding it."

"I had to patch a couple of places but it should be fine now," Al added. He smiled again. "At least for what you need."

"Okay, then," I said. "We're good to go. We'll start tomorrow night."

"Sounds good," Rachel said. "Shall we have a beer?"

"Let's do it," Al said.

THE MOON WAS WELL ABOVE the treetops in the eastern sky when Greg Fletcher drove back across the dam on his way home. He'd accomplished his mission with no difficulty or complications, and he was confident he hadn't been seen.

His thoughts turned to the week ahead. He was scheduled to work the early shift at the airport, so there would be no morning walks at Maffitt. Maybe that was just as well, he decided. After the morning's disastrous exchange with Jessica Wilkinson, it wouldn't hurt to lie low for a few days.

He could always run out to Maffitt after dinner and walk in the evening. Or he could walk in Ft. Des Moines Park for the next few nights.

If he did the latter, he might get lucky and run into Rachel James again.

CHAPTER 63

The hot temperature returned on Monday and that was actually to our advantage, at least as far as carrying out our plan was concerned. The heat would provide Rachel with the perfect excuse to be walking alone in Ft. Des Moines Park in the evenings, without Alexander. Or so she could tell Greg Fletcher, anyway.

After returning from our early morning ramble at Maffitt, I fed Preacher then repaired to my office to start editing copy for the December/January issue. We had seen no one else at the lake and I hoped Jessica Wilkinson was heeding my warning and keeping a close watch to make sure Maisie didn't pick up anything and eat it. I had no way of knowing exactly what Greg Fletcher might attempt—and I had heard nothing further from James Collins—but I believed this was definitely a case where caution was called for.

It was a few minutes past 8:30 when I logged onto the company computer. I scrolled through the weekend's accumulation of emails—most of which I deleted unopened—and answered those few that required a reply. Thankfully there were no major complaints to be dealt with, and I was soon able to start editing.

The first story I opened was titled "Arizona Hat Trick" and it described a combo hunt for desert quail—Gambel's, scaled, and Mearns'—south of Tucson. The author, Dave Mitchell, was pursuing the birds with a brace of German shorthairs, hoping to take all three species in a single day.

I liked the combination and challenge angles. Mearns' quail, also called Montezuma or harlequin quail, are typically found at higher elevations than Gambel's and scaled quail, so Mitchell and his dogs had their work cut out for them. It would be interesting to see if they succeeded.

I was about a third of the way through the story when the phone rang. Caller ID told me it was Jessica Wilkinson. I could hear the panic in her voice as soon as I answered. *Please God*, I thought, *don't let anything have happened to Maisie.*

"Rob," she blurted. "He tried it!"

"Tried what?" I was afraid of the answer.

"Tried to poison Maisie!"

"Oh, no," I said. "What happened?"

"I let her out this morning and I went outside with her, just like you said. I watched her as she did her business and started trotting around the yard like she always does. Then she dove under one of the bushes at the back of the property and came out carrying something."

"What was she carrying?"

"It was a dead raccoon. A small one. She brought it right up to me, like she was proud of what she'd found."

In spite of myself, I couldn't help smiling. True to her breeding, Maisie was acting like almost any other retriever, bringing her prize to her human. I was also relieved—hugely—to hear that it was a raccoon she'd found, and not a poisoned bait.

"What did you do?"

"I freaked!" Jessica said. "I mean, we have lots of raccoons in the neighborhood and they're always trying to get into the trash, so I've seen them plenty of times. But this is the first time I've seen a dead one. Here in the yard, I mean."

"And you're thinking Fletcher poisoned it?"

"I'm sure he did. Why else would it be dead in our yard? I know Maisie didn't kill it. It was already dead when she found it."

"Good point," I said, trying to think this through. "What time did this happen?"

"A little after seven this morning. Dad was getting ready for work and I let Maisie outside as soon as I got up. It's a good thing I went outside with her, like you told me. I mean, I don't think she would have tried to eat it or anything, but I'm still glad I was there and saw it right away."

"What did you do with the raccoon?"

"Maisie dropped it right there in front of me and I grabbed her and took her inside. I didn't want to touch it, so I told Dad."

"That was smart. What did your dad do?"

"He picked it up with a shovel and dumped it into a garbage can we have in the garage. He was worried that it might have died from rabies and he said he was glad I hadn't touched it."

"Right," I said. "Did you say anything to him about it being poisoned? That you think that's what killed it?"

She hesitated for a moment. "No, I didn't," she finally said. "I thought about it but that would have meant I'd have had to bring up Greg Fletcher again. You know he doesn't want me to keep digging into that, so I didn't mention it." She laughed nervously. "But I wanted to let you know."

"I appreciate that." Even as I said this I felt a twinge of guilt. I didn't like feeling that Jessica and I were conspiring behind her father's back. I had to admit, however, that that's what we were doing.

"Do we need to do anything, call anyone like the animal control people or something and report this?"

"I'm not sure," I said, and I wasn't. "But it might not hurt, at least to see what they say. There might be some procedure you need to follow to dispose of the raccoon. Something besides just putting it out in the trash, I mean."

"Okay, I can do that. I'll call them as soon as we hang up."

"I know I don't need to tell you this, but you should continue to keep a close eye on Maisie. If Fletcher tried it once, he might try it again."

"I already thought of that, and yes, I'll keep a close eye on Maisie."

"Okay, then. Let me know if anything else happens."

"I will, I promise."

AFTER WE HUNG UP I sat staring at the computer screen but not seeing the words in front of me. Instead, I replayed the conversation with Jessica and asked myself a number of questions.

The first of those, of course, was whether the raccoon was in fact a victim of poisoning by Greg Fletcher's hand. I was inclined to agree with Jessica that it was—the coincidence just seemed too great otherwise—but without some kind of analysis, I couldn't know for certain.

I didn't know what the animal control people might tell Jessica but I doubted they would recommend having the raccoon sent into a lab unless they wanted to have it screened for rabies. Since it was already dead when Maisie found it and it hadn't bitten anyone, I doubted they would do this.

I also wondered if we should apprise Jessica's father of what was going on with Greg Fletcher…or what we suspected was going on, anyway. Recent events seemed to suggest a life-threatening situation might be developing, so I couldn't help thinking that Craig Wilkinson deserved to know about it. If I were a father and my daughter was in any kind of danger, I would certainly want to know.

But once again, I reminded myself that we had very little real evidence of any wrongdoing. As an attorney, Wilkinson would most likely ask for proof to support our conjectures, and beyond some gut feelings—both human and canine—we had precious little.

That is, except for what James Collins and his buddies had discovered about Fletcher's online activities. The stuff from the Manspeak website, plus Fletcher's searches on copycat suicides and methods to poison dogs, was damning. But how could I present this to Wilkinson without betraying their confidence?

Maybe, I thought sarcastically, I should hire Wilkinson. Then anything I told him would be protected by attorney-client privilege. But hire him for what reason? I didn't need representation.

At least, not yet.

CHAPTER 64

GREG FLETCHER SPENT a good part of his shift on Monday wondering if his plan had been successful.

He had no way of knowing whether Maisie had found and eaten the poisoned bait he had lobbed into the Wilkinsons' back yard the previous evening. He also realized that short of haunting their neighborhood or Maffitt Reservoir hoping for a glimpse of Jessica, he had no way of finding out.

He knew he couldn't afford to take that chance. If ever there was a time to lie low, this was that time. Recalling his encounter with Jessica at the lake on Sunday morning—just yesterday, though it seemed much longer—he realized now that he had badly overplayed his hand. Any immediate further contact would only exacerbate an already highly charged situation.

Which meant playing the waiting game was his only option.

He had gone online and learned that UNI's fall semester began on Monday the 22nd, just three weeks from today. That gave him three weeks to somehow get close to Jessica again, convince her he was harmless and persuade her to walk with him at the lake. Getting her to accompany him to someplace removed from the main traffic areas and close to the water, as he had originally planned, was probably not feasible, he now realized. She'd been on her guard yesterday and would be even more so now, especially if Maisie had taken the bait.

He cursed himself for his impetuous decision to eliminate the dog. That had been a foolish over-reaction and counter-productive to what he had planned. He should have just ignored the dog's hostility and pretended not to notice. That way he could have at least continued to talk with Jessica and perhaps regain her trust. He realized now that by killing Maisie, if in fact she had found and eaten the bait, he had probably eliminated Jessica's primary reason for walking at the lake.

Damn it to hell, anyway. He wasn't thinking clearly about any of this, and he couldn't afford to let his anger cloud his judgment. He had to maintain a cooler head and come up with a better plan. He had three weeks in which to achieve his objective. That should be ample time. But he could feel his frustration building.

He wasn't sure how much longer he could continue to practice the patience of the wild.

AFTER JESSICA'S PHONE call, I had a tough time concentrating on Dave Mitchell's Arizona quail hunting story.

I tried to force myself to focus and give the story the attention it required. Mitchell was a fine writer but no one is immune to the occasional typo or awkward phrase. But my mind kept wandering and posing questions I couldn't answer.

Foremost among these was whether the dead raccoon Maisie found had actually been poisoned. Jessica definitely believed it had, and I was inclined to agree. But I also told myself her conviction could largely be due to the power of suggestion. I'd warned her about the possibility of Fletcher trying to poison Maisie, so finding the dead raccoon had been enough to confirm, in her mind, anyway, that Fletcher had indeed made such an attempt.

But had he?

Without determining the raccoon's cause of death, we had no way of knowing. Maisie's finding the dead raccoon in their yard could have been nothing more than a coincidence.

But I knew I didn't believe that. The timing was too exact. Just hours after we'd learned Fletcher was searching online for ways to poison dogs, Maisie finds a raccoon in the Wilkinsons' yard, dead from natural causes?

No way.

BY THE TIME FLETCHER finished his shift and drove home, he was feeling slightly better about things. A couple of attractive women had passed through his kiosk and afforded him a glimpse of their nice boobs, and that had helped lighten his mood and marshal his thoughts.

He was still troubled by not knowing whether Maisie had found the bait, but he told himself there was nothing more to be done about it. Briefly—very briefly—he'd considered making another run out there this evening after dark to see if he could find and recover the bait. He was confident he could locate the spot where he'd tossed it; he remembered it was near some bushes at the back of the yard, but he quickly discarded the idea.

Finding the bait in the dark, presuming it was still there to be found, would almost certainly require him to use a penlight of some kind, and if he did so, there was far too much chance of being seen. If caught and confronted, he would never be able to explain why he was trespassing without incriminating himself.

No. Better to let sleeping dogs lie, he told himself, and he laughed sardonically at the pun—assuming Maisie had found the bait, that is. He reminded himself that he still had three weeks to come up with another way for dealing with Jessica, he felt slightly less pressured.

What the hell, he could even make a trip to Cedar Falls sometime after Jessica returned to school, if necessary, and conclude matters there. That would require more planning and some financial expenditure, probably, but it could be done. The situation didn't have to be resolved at Maffitt Reservoir.

But, he vowed, it *would* be resolved. That much was certain.

CHAPTER 65

The more Jessica thought about what had almost happened to Maisie the more pissed she became. There was no doubt in her mind that Fletcher had tried to poison her, and Maisie had escaped only because a raccoon had found the bait first.

She wanted to do something. Something besides just continuing to be careful, as she'd promised Rob Vance. She wanted to take some kind of action—action against Fletcher.

She wondered what he would do if she confronted him.

She considered driving to Maffitt Reservoir to see if he might be walking there this morning. She assumed he worked but she didn't know where or what his schedule might be. She did know that he sometimes walked at Maffitt in the morning, even on weekdays, so she assumed his job was not strictly nine to five. Apparently his work schedule was flexible.

She was drinking an energy drink at the kitchen table with Maisie sprawled on the floor next to her chair. She glanced at the clock and saw that it was just past 9:30. About twenty minutes had passed since she'd talked to Vance and told him about Maisie finding the dead raccoon.

Immediately after speaking with him, she had called the Dallas County Sheriff's Office and told them about the raccoon but didn't mention that she thought it had been poisoned. She was transferred to Dispatch, and the lady she spoke with was polite and helpful but said they didn't have anyone who could come out and pick up the raccoon. She said it was okay just to dispose of the raccoon in the trash, or Jessica could call the Iowa DNR and they might send someone out to pick it up. Jessica thanked her and hung up. She decided not to bother calling the DNR.

She drummed her fingers on the kitchen table and looked at the clock again. It was 9:40.

She decided to take Maisie for a quick walk at Maffitt.

She would keep Maisie on her leash and make sure she didn't pick up anything. And maybe, just maybe, she'd see Greg Fletcher and let him know she was on to him. That was risky, but…

Rob Vance had said he didn't believe Fletcher would try anything dangerous in broad daylight. Jessica told herself he was probably right. Besides, she would have Maisie with her, and she was confident Maisie wouldn't let Fletcher get too close.

HER WALK WITH MAISIE yielded no contact with anyone except that nice older fellow, Tim Sullivan.

He came walking up just after she parked and was letting Maisie out of the Explorer. He called out a hello to her and she smiled and greeted him in return. She also noticed that Maisie immediately began wagging her tail and straining against her leash toward Sullivan, greeting him in her own fashion.

A far cry from how she acts when she sees Greg Fletcher, Jessica thought. She let Maisie pull her toward Sullivan, who immediately reached down to pet Maisie and ruffle her ears. "Hi, Maisie," he said, and she responded by wagging her tail even harder.

"She's happy to see you!" Jessica said.

"Well, I'm happy to see her," Sullivan replied. "How are you two doing this morning?"

"Oh, we're fine. Just out for a quick walk before it gets too much hotter."

"Good plan," Sullivan said. "It's gonna be another warm one."

"Have you seen anyone else out here?"

"I saw a couple walking through the park on the other side a little while ago, but that was all. They waved and I waved back but we didn't talk; they were a pretty good ways away and walking in the opposite direction."

"I see," Jessica said. "Well, good to see you again. We'd better get going so I can get Maisie down to the water. I know she's going to want to swim."

"That doesn't sound like a bad idea," Sullivan said. "Good to see you also. You two have a good morning."

"Thanks, you too."

TWENTY MINUTES LATER, after walking back to the canoe launch and tossing a stick into the water a half dozen times for Maisie to retrieve, Jessica was ready to head for home. The morning was warming up quickly so she called Maisie to her, snapped on her leash and the two of them started back along the roadway toward the turnout where they had parked.

Exercising Maisie had cooled Jessica's anger somewhat, but now, walking back to her vehicle, she felt herself seething again at the realization that Maisie had narrowly missed becoming the victim of a supremely cruel act by Fletcher. If Vance hadn't warned her about Fletcher searching ways to poison dogs, if she hadn't gone outside with Maisie as Vance had suggested, if a prowling raccoon hadn't found the bait Jessica was sure Fletcher had dropped…

She shuddered as she realized how close she had come to losing Maisie.

That son of a bitch, she thought. *He is not going to get away with this*.

Since she hadn't seen Fletcher this morning, she wondered if he might come out this evening. He had met her mother in the evening, the final evening of her life, so Jessica thought it was possible.

It might be worth another trip out here tonight after dinner, she decided. She'd bring Maisie and she would stay close to the parking area and be sure to leave before dark. She still wasn't sure whether she would confront Fletcher or only talk to him and hope he might let something slip.

Maybe, she thought grimly, he'll freak when he sees Maisie is still alive, and he'll give himself away.

She thought it was worth a try.

CHAPTER 66

GREG FLETCHER TOOK A FINAL swallow of Miller Lite just as *Jeopardy!* ended and the four o'clock news began on Channel 13. He stood up from the sofa and headed out to the kitchen and tossed the empty can in the trash. Then he leaned against the counter and thought about what he wanted for dinner.

He was feeling better about things, or at least, less pressured. The realization that he didn't have to conclude matters with Jessica Wilkinson in the next three weeks, that he could travel to Cedar Falls and take care of things there if necessary, gave rise to optimism. All in good time, he told himself. There was really no rush.

In fact, he realized, biding his time in the short term was probably the smart move. He still had no idea if Maisie had found and eaten the bait, but if she had, that was certain to cause alarm. Jessica Wilkinson was already convinced he had killed her mother, so it wasn't unlikely that she would blame him for Maisie's death also. The more he could distance himself from the whole scenario, the better.

Still, it would be nice to know, one way or the other.

Earlier he'd thought to avoid Maffitt Reservoir altogether for at least a week or more. But now he wondered, as he had after Hannah's death, if he might be making himself more conspicuous with his absence. Would it be better to feign innocence and stick to his regular routine, walking out there as usual?

He wasn't sure. But in the meantime, Mexican sounded good for dinner. There was a new restaurant on Army Post Road near the airport that he'd been wanting to try. He decided he'd shower and then head over there in a little while to see if it was as good as a couple of his co-workers had claimed.

I FINISHED EDITING THE Arizona story and managed to get through two more features by day's end. I'd heard nothing more from Jessica Wilkinson so I assumed everything was quiet on that front, at least for the moment. I wondered if she had called the animal control people and if so, what they had suggested for disposing of the dead raccoon.

I also wondered—still—if Fletcher was the cause of the raccoon's demise. I thought he probably was; the odds certainly seemed to favor that. But I realized this was something we'd never know for certain. Unless, of course, he confessed, and I figured that was no more likely than Preacher refusing her scrambled eggs on Sunday morning.

Rachel James called me at a few minutes after four, just as I was saving the edited version of the last story I had worked on. We discussed the time frame for the night's activities and agreed we'd get started at a few minutes before eight. I was going to drive over to her house and drop off my vehicle, and we'd proceed from there.

I realized that much of what we had planned was a real roll of the dice, that the timing was based almost entirely on chance and that we would be very damned lucky if we could pull off everything on this first night.

If not, we'd try again tomorrow, and the night after that, and the night after that if necessary. The three of us—Rachel, Al and I—had agreed we'd keep trying until everything lined up and we accomplished our objective.

THE MEAL WAS EVERYTHING Fletcher had hoped for. He'd opted for one of the combination platters, a hard shell beef taco, a beef enchilada, refried beans and rice, and that, plus two Coronas and the complimentary basket of tortilla chips and salsa, left him feeling more than replete. *I need to go somewhere and walk this off,* he thought as he left the restaurant and walked out to his Durango.

His first thought was Ft. Des Moines Park. He could drive home and drop off his vehicle, then walk to the park as he'd occasionally been doing recently. Maybe he'd even get lucky and see Rachel James again. The only drawback was that she'd most likely be walking that damned Saint Bernard of hers, but he could be careful and make certain he remained out of its reach.

He sat for a moment in the restaurant's parking lot, pondering. He was almost within spitting distance of Fleur Drive, which he could take to the bypass. He could get on the bypass and take it on out to Maffitt Reservoir and walk out there and maybe, just maybe, he'd see Jessica Wilkinson, with or without Maisie.

Should he risk it?

Why not, he thought after a minute's reflection. Maybe the two Coronas he'd had with dinner were making him feel a little reckless, but he reminded himself of what he'd realized earlier, that avoiding the reservoir might be just as damning as letting himself be seen. If he were innocent—he wasn't, but that was how he wanted to appear—there would be no reason to stay away from the place.

And, he told himself, if he did see Jessica, he would almost certainly learn whether Maisie had taken the bait.

We were all in place by eight o'clock.

As planned, I'd driven over to Al and Rachel's and left the Equinox parked on the street in front of their house. The three of us then climbed into their black, double cab Chevy Silverado. We'd loaded it the night before with everything we needed to execute our plan, including my old dummy launcher and the Gamo air rifle, plus what they were supplying.

When I got to their place I couldn't help noticing that Rachel was braless under her black t-shirt. She caught me looking, of course, and laughed. "I figure every little bit of distraction will help," she said.

I laughed also. "Good plan," I said, thinking, *I wouldn't call those distractions little*. But I kept that thought to myself. Al was apparently okay with her ruse, but I didn't want to poke the bear.

Al drove and I sat in the shotgun seat, with Rachel sitting behind us. We pulled into the park from the entrance on Southeast 5th and followed the roadway around to the first parking lot at the north end of the lake. Al wheeled into the lot and drove down to the large picnic shelter at the far end. He stopped and Rachel climbed out.

"Good luck," I said.

"Be careful," Al said.

"Thanks," Rachel replied. "I will." She gave a little wave and walked over to the picnic shelter.

Al cranked the Silverado around and we headed back out of the park. We reversed the route we'd just taken, driving south to County Line Road and turning west. We pulled into the parking lot at Studebaker Elementary School and drove to the far end. Al backed into a parking space and killed the engine and lights.

We sat in the cab of the Silverado in the gathering dusk, hoping Greg Fletcher would soon appear.

CHAPTER 67

Jessica Wilkinson left her house with Maisie at a few minutes before seven o'clock. She drove to the reservoir's west entrance, turned in and followed the gravel roadway down to the first turnout. She parked and let Maisie out of the Explorer, snapping on Maisie's leash as she did so.

Earlier, her father had called and told her he'd be working late and not to expect him for dinner. She'd fixed a sandwich for herself—she didn't feel like cooking—and then called Maisie and headed off to the reservoir. She was still undecided as to how she would handle an encounter with Greg Fletcher if she happened to see him, but she felt compelled to do *something*. Above all, she didn't like feeling that fear was keeping her housebound.

But she also admitted to herself that she wasn't sure she had the nerve to confront Fletcher directly and tell him she knew of his attempt to poison Maisie. She wanted to believe she could do so, and she knew she would enjoy watching him squirm as he tried to deny her accusation, but she realized that without solid proof she was on shaky ground. Maybe it would be better to play it cool and watch for any slip-ups on his part…if he had tried to poison Maisie, seeing her still alive might unnerve him, Jessica thought.

She decided just to play it by ear. She might not see him at all, she reminded herself, so maybe all of her worry was for nothing.

By the time Fletcher exited the bypass and turned onto Maffitt Lake Road, he was getting a serious case of cold feet. The bravado he'd felt while sitting in the parking lot at the restaurant had departed. Maybe returning to Maffitt this evening wasn't such a great idea after all, he thought. If he ran into Jessica Wilkinson, with or without Maisie, it was bound to be awkward, at the very least. She'd made it clear yesterday morning that she didn't welcome his company, and any further overtures on his part would only make things worse.

He decided he would stay in his vehicle and make one quick turn through the park on the east side and then head home. If he happened to see Jessica, he'd wave but make no attempt to talk with her. That should be safe enough, and if she was unaccompanied by Maisie, that would pretty well confirm Maisie had found the bait he'd dropped.

Curiously, he found himself hoping she hadn't.

WANTING TO GIVE MAISIE some exercise, Jessica walked her down to the first curve in the roadway, then turned and walked back to where they had parked. Maisie paced along on the leash and Jessica watched her closely to make sure she didn't pick up anything and try to eat it. Maisie did find a stick about ten inches long and picked it up to carry, and Jessica thought that was okay. Like most retrievers, Maisie loved to carry things and if nothing else, carrying the stick would lessen the chances of her trying to eat something foreign.

When they returned to the parking area Jessica walked over to the picnic table and seated herself facing the lake. Maisie sprawled in the grass beside her and Jessica looped the leash around the table's metal leg. She pulled her cell phone out of her pocket to check for messages, but she didn't have any. According to the phone, the time was 7:25 p.m.

Jessica decided she would give it an hour and then head home. If Greg Fletcher was going to show up he'd surely do so by 8:30, when it would start to get dark. In the meantime, Jessica was still uncertain as to how she was going to handle an encounter if he did appear.

She sighed and gazed out over the water toward the wooded shoreline on the east side of the lake. She wondered if she should have called Rob Vance and told him what she was doing. She smiled ruefully at the thought, knowing he probably would have tried to talk her out of it.

GREG FLETCHER WAS HALFWAY through the park, following the winding roadway, when he decided to stop for a few minutes. He'd seen no sign of Jessica Wilkinson but he told himself that if she were out here at all, she would probably be on the west side of the lake where he had seen her previously. He had no intention of going over there to find out.

But he could check from here, he decided. He pulled into one of the gravel turnouts close to the shoreline, the same one from which he'd watched Jessica and Rob Vance a little over a week ago. He grabbed the mini binoculars from the door pocket and made his way down to the picnic table at the edge of the high bank above the shoreline.

He seated himself atop the table and pulled the binoculars from their case. He was facing the setting sun so it was somewhat difficult to see the opposite shoreline, but with some adjustment he managed to bring it into focus. He swept his gaze upwards from the water to the higher ground, hoping to see the parking area where he'd seen Jessica and Vance and later talked to Jessica himself.

He found the parking area and instantly stiffened. *Son of a bitch!*

Jessica Wilkinson was sitting at the same picnic table where he had talked to her. He was sure it was her; there was no mistaking her blonde hair and features. And lying in the grass close to her feet was Maisie.

So the golden hadn't found and eaten the bait. He had his answer.

JESSICA SHIFTED ON the picnic table's hard wooden seat. She was still looking out across the lake but her gaze was somewhat unfocused as she thought about everything that had happened in the past few weeks, beginning with her mother's death.

She had told Rob Vance that spending time at the lake with Maisie sometimes made her feel closer to her mother, and it was true. Tonight, however, that feeling of closeness was missing for some reason. Instead, she felt a sense of emptiness, as if her mother had somehow slipped farther away and the lake no longer retained any of her presence.

She drew a deep breath and straightened her back,

determined not to cry. As she did so, she saw something flash among the trees on the opposite shoreline, almost as if someone were holding a small mirror and using it to reflect the setting sun. She focused on the spot where she had seen the flash and after a second it was repeated.

She wondered if it was someone holding up a cell phone with its light turned on. But why would they be pointing it out toward the lake? There was still plenty of daylight; it was too early in the evening to need any kind of flashlight.

She watched intently for another minute or so but didn't see the flash again. Whoever it was that had caused the flash had apparently backed away from the shoreline and out of the trees.

It was probably just a reflection of something shiny, she told herself. Maybe someone had taken a picture of the lake with their cell phone and the flash she had seen was sunlight reflecting off the phone's screen.

She decided that was probably the case.

GREG FLETCHER SAW Jessica sit up straighter and as she did so, she seemed to look directly at him. He instinctively drew back slightly, then realized she couldn't possibly see him sitting on the picnic table among the trees at this distance. Not without binoculars, anyway.

He watched her for a moment longer then put the binoculars back in their case. As he did so it occurred to him that Jessica might have seen a reflection from the lenses of the binoculars; that that could have been what caused her to look in his direction so suddenly.

Well, no matter. She might have seen a reflection but he was still confident she couldn't have seen him, and he'd learned what he had hoped to, that Maisie hadn't eaten the bait. He wondered if it was still where he'd tossed it or if something else had found it. He knew there was plenty of wildlife in the area, everything from raccoons and possums to foxes and the occasional coyote. And of course, lots of deer, although he thought it unlikely that a deer would pick up the bait.

He stood up from the picnic table and returned to the Durango. If something else had found the bait, so be it, he told himself. He knew he couldn't risk sneaking back to the Wilkinsons' a second time to look for it. If it was still there, Maisie would just have to take her chances.

He also decided he was going to avoid Maffitt for at least the next few nights. If he needed exercise, he'd walk in Ft. Des Moines Park.

CHAPTER 68

WE PULLED THE PLUG at a couple minutes after 9:00.

It was just becoming fully dark when Al cranked the ignition on the Silverado and we left the school parking lot. We needed to get back over into the park and pick up Rachel before a Polk County Conservation officer drove through to shoo out the late-stayers and then closed the entrance gates for the night.

For the past hour we'd stayed in touch with Rachel by texting. Most of our messages were of the "No sign of him yet" type, and she'd responded in kind. For whatever reason, Greg Fletcher was a no-show on this Monday evening.

I wondered if he had gone out to Maffitt Reservoir instead.

RACHEL WAS STANDING at the edge of the parking lot near the picnic shelter when we pulled up in the Silverado. She climbed into the back seat and the first words out of her mouth were, "Damn it to hell, anyway."

Al and I both laughed and I added, "Yeah, really."

None of us said anything for a minute as Al pulled back up to the roadway and headed out of the park. I was pretty sure we were all thinking the same thing, that we were going to be following the same gameplan again tomorrow evening, and the evening after that if necessary. We were convinced that sooner or later Fletcher would walk through the park again and that's when we could execute the rest of our plan.

Execute being the operative word.

GREG FLETCHER DROVE home from the reservoir wrestling with mixed feelings.

He couldn't deny that he was relieved to have learned that Maisie hadn't eaten the bait he'd dropped…at least not yet. He found himself hoping that something else had found it and either eaten it or carried it off. But he had no way of knowing, and no way of finding out.

At the same time, he felt a growing irritation at having seen Jessica sitting so complacently at the picnic table. He realized he was probably projecting, imagining a certain smugness on her part that she quite possibly was not feeling. Still, it rankled to see her sitting there with Maisie, apparently without a concern on this summer evening, while he was almost desperately trying to make sure his backside was sufficiently covered.

She had pushed him into this, he thought.

If only she had accepted the ME's ruling regarding her mother's death. If only she hadn't persisted in trying to prove that it was something other than suicide.

If only she hadn't sicced the cops on him with her claim about the color of Hannah's toenail polish.

This could have all ended so neatly with Hannah's death. He could have moved on, putting that whole experience behind him and maybe even gotten something going with someone like Rachel James.

But no, Hannah's daughter had derailed his plans. Or at least caused him to revise those plans and take additional steps to ensure his own safety—forced him into the role of prey instead of predator, in other words. Caused him to be looking over his shoulder, figuratively speaking, almost constantly.

That was unforgivable.

"SAME TIME TOMORROW night?" I asked as I climbed out of the Silverado in Al and Rachel's driveway.

"You bet," Rachel said, and Al nodded.

"Okay, I'll see you then," I said. "And…thanks."

"No problem," Al said. "It's just something we have to get done."

"Amen to that," Rachel added.

AS SOON AS HE'D cracked a Miller Lite, Fletcher logged onto his laptop at his kitchen table. He pulled up the Manspeak website and read through the posts of a couple recent threads, then he sat back and considered posting something of his own. He wanted to bounce a couple of ideas off someone, or several someones, but he knew he'd have to be careful.

Finally he opened a new thread that he titled, "Seeking Help." He gave it another minute's thought, then he began typing.

GHOST DOG: Finding myself in something of a bind. Being pursued by someone who's trying to pin something on me.

He hit "send" and sat back to await replies. The first one came through in just a little over a minute. He couldn't help grinning as he read the message.

JET: Time to turn the tables, bro. We're the pursuers, not the pursued. The hunters, not the hunted.

Still smiling, Fletcher thought, *I couldn't have said it better myself.*

PART FOUR: RESOLUTION

The hunted shapes the hunter. The pursuit and evasion of predator and prey are but shadows of the same desire.

Rick Bass

CHAPTER 69

We were in place again by a couple minutes after 8 p.m. on Tuesday.

It was another warm one, with the temperature still in the mid-eighties. A typical early August night in central Iowa, in other words. Al and I had dropped Rachel at the picnic shelter in Ft. Des Moines Park a few minutes earlier and then returned to the parking lot behind the elementary school. I'd noticed that Rachel was once again braless, although this time her t-shirt was gray instead of black. The different color notwithstanding, the effect was the same.

I hoped it would affect Greg Fletcher, if he showed up, in a similar way. I was pretty sure it would.

"Think he'll show?" Al asked as we settled in behind the school.

"I don't know," I said. "Here's hoping."

"Yeah," Al said.

Greg Fletcher left his house at a few minutes after 8:00 and headed up the street, walking toward the school. Following some of the advice he'd received the night before from users on the Manspeak website, he was planning to lie low for a few days, not let himself be seen at Maffitt Reservoir until things cooled down a bit but then showing up again to launch, in one user's words, a surprise attack.

In the meantime, he'd confine his walking to Ft. Des Moines Park.

He crossed County Line Road and started walking north through the school parking lot. The park's woods formed the east boundary of the parking lot and as he passed the school building he was startled by the sudden hooting of a barred owl from somewhere within the woods. The sound prickled his neck hairs and he laughed nervously.

"Someone's going to die tonight," he said to himself,

recalling an old superstition and laughing again.

I WAS LOOKING NORTH toward the park when Al nudged me with an elbow and said, "Hey."

I turned to look toward the south end of the parking lot. A single figure was approaching through the dusk. It was a man walking at a moderate pace. He appeared to be heading toward the park.

"That him?" Al asked.

I watched for another few seconds until I could make out the man's features.

"Yep," I said. "That's him."

RACHEL WAS SITTING at one of the picnic tables in the shelter with her back to the table and her elbows resting on its top. Her cell phone chimed and she picked it up to check the message. It was a text from Rob, and it read, "Coming your way!"

She smiled and quickly tapped in a reply: "On it!"

She stood up from the table, shoved her phone into one of the pockets of her shorts and left the shelter to walk up to the levee.

FLETCHER NOTICED ONE vehicle at the north end of the parking lot, a black Chevy Silverado with a double cab and dark tinted windows. In the fading light he couldn't see if anyone was sitting in it but he thought it looked unoccupied. Maybe it belonged to a custodian working inside the school or to someone walking in the park.

He glanced at it directly as he walked past but saw no one inside. He turned his attention back to the park, wondering if he might get lucky and see Rachel James. If so, he'd have to watch out for her damned dog, but he thought it was worth the risk.

Especially if he got another look at her boobs.

RACHEL GAINED THE PATH at the top of the levee and started walking slowly southward. Though twilight was fast approaching, she could still see to the south end of the levee, where Fletcher should soon emerge from the woods.

She picked up her pace a bit. She wanted to be as close as possible to the south end of the levee—and to the school parking lot—when she encountered him. The trickiest part of the plan would be convincing him to reverse course and accompany her back through the parking lot.

She was confident she could pull it off.

FLETCHER FOLLOWED THE PATH straight north from the parking lot toward the levee on the east side of the park's lake. This was where he'd seen Rachel James both times previously so he thought this was the most likely spot to run into her again, if she was walking her dog tonight.

He followed the path down through a short stretch of woods until it opened onto the south end of the levee. He kept walking north and as he looked ahead he could see a tall woman walking toward him. In another few seconds he could see it was Rachel.

Son of a bitch! It's my lucky night, he thought.

Best of all, she was unaccompanied by her Saint Bernard.

I LIFTED MY HEAD cautiously and peered out the window of the Silverado. "He's in the woods," I said, and Al straightened up in his seat.

"Good deal," he said. "Let's hope Rachel can get him to walk back this way with her."

"I'd bet she can."

Al nodded. "I'd bet so too."

RACHEL WAS A LITTLE more than halfway across the levee when she called out, "Well, good evening!"

"Good evening!" Greg Fletcher replied. "Where's Alexander?"

"Too warm for him tonight," Rachel said. She laughed and added, "I left him at home in the air conditioning."

"Ah. I guess you do have to be careful with dogs in this heat."

"Yes, you do. Especially big dogs with long hair. They don't handle it very well."

"It's good to see you again." Fletcher was trying to not stare at her boobs but finding it difficult. He could see she wasn't wearing a bra and the view was tantalizing. *Or titillating*, he thought, suppressing a smile.

"It's good to see you too," Rachel replied. She hesitated, then smiled and said, "I'm a little embarrassed to ask this, but I wonder if you could do me a favor."

Anything, Fletcher thought, *especially if it keeps me close to your boobs*. Aloud, he said, "Sure. What do you need?"

"This is probably silly, but it's getting dark a little sooner than I expected and I'm nervous about walking back through that stretch of woods down there at the end of the levee. Ordinarily I wouldn't be worried if Alexander was with me, but since he's not…" Rachel paused, then added, "I know it's opposite the direction you were going, but would you mind walking me through there, and maybe as far as the parking lot at the school?"

"I'd be happy to," Fletcher said, thinking, *hot damn!* "And I can understand why you're nervous. These days you can't be too careful, especially with it getting dark."

"Oh, thanks!" Rachel said. "I really appreciate it." Thinking, *that was too easy*.

CHAPTER 70

"Here they come," I said quietly.

"Uh-huh," Al said.

Greg Fletcher and Rachel had just emerged from the woods at the south end of the levee. They were walking side by side and anyone watching—that is, anyone except Al and me—would most likely assume they were a couple out for an evening stroll. They continued along the path toward the parking lot where we sat waiting in the Silverado.

Game on.

Greg Fletcher was pleased with the way things were playing out. As they followed the path through the darkened woods he had bumped shoulders with Rachel a couple times and the second time he'd nudged her right boob slightly with his elbow. "Oops, sorry," he'd said, feigning a stumble. She'd laughed and said, "No problem," and he had congratulated himself on a move well-played.

Now they were coming up on the school parking lot and he wondered whether he should offer to walk her all the way to County Line Road, or even farther. As they left the path for the parking lot he glanced to his right and saw that the black Silverado was still parked where it had been earlier, and it was still apparently unoccupied.

"Well, thanks for escorting me safely through the woods," Rachel said. "I really appreciate it."

"My pleasure," Fletcher replied. They were now passing the Silverado and he added, "I'll be happy to walk you as far as County Line if you'd like."

"Oh, that's all right. You've already gone way out of your way." Rachel stopped walking and said, "I think I should be okay from here." She smiled and added, "But thanks again."

Fletcher didn't want to let her go just yet but he also didn't want to overplay his hand. He shrugged and said, "I don't mind. It's getting too late to walk back through the park anyway, so I'll probably just head on home myself."

"Well…okay then," Rachel said. "If you're sure you don't mind." She turned and started walking again.

Fletcher laughed. "No, I'm sure I don't mind," he said, falling into step beside her.

That's when he was struck by a lightning bolt.

AL AND I WERE OUT of the Silverado almost before Fletcher hit the ground. Rachel was bending over him, still holding the stun gun against his side. She straightened up as we got to them. I hadn't timed it but I guessed she must have zapped him for at least five seconds.

It was enough to leave him gasping and twitching, almost convulsing, on the pavement of the parking lot. Al and I quickly rolled him over and Al zip-tied his hands behind his back with heavy-duty cable ties. Rachel quickly moved to the Silverado and opened the tailgate. She pulled out the black one-man inflatable unknowingly donated by their son John and dropped it onto the pavement.

We rolled Fletcher back over. He was still dazed and twitching and Al grabbed his shoulders. I took his feet and we carried him to the inflatable. We dropped him into it and lifted the inflatable, one of us on either side, back up to the tailgate. Then the three of us, Al, Rachel and myself, shoved the inflatable back into the bed, under the tonneau cover. Al slammed the tailgate shut and we paused for a moment to catch our breath.

"Are you okay?" Al asked Rachel.

"I'm fine," she said. "The sonuvabitch elbowed me in the boob as we were walking through the woods back there." She laughed. "He tried to make it seem like an accident but I wasn't fooled."

"I'm sure you weren't," I said.

Al snorted and said, "Well, let's hope he enjoyed it. That's the last boob he'll ever elbow."

"Damn straight," Rachel said, and we all laughed.

WE PILED BACK INTO the Silverado and drove straight to their house. As we pulled into the driveway Al hit the remote to open their garage door and drove straight on in. As soon as we stopped he hit the remote again and the door closed behind us.

We climbed out and moved around to the back of the vehicle. Al opened the tailgate cautiously—we weren't sure how long the effects of the stun gun would last—but Fletcher still appeared docile. We pulled the inflatable out and eased it down to the garage floor.

Rachel grabbed a roll of duct tape, ripped off a strip and placed it over Fletcher's mouth. Then she quickly removed his wallet, keys and cell phone from the pockets of his cargo shorts with a deftness that had me wondering if she'd been a pickpocket in a previous life. She tossed these items onto a nearby worktable for later disposal.

Fletcher was blinking his eyes and opening them wide, as though he was trying to focus and regain his senses. I guessed the effects of the stun gun were wearing off.

"We need to hurry," I said, probably unnecessarily.

Al and I picked up two nearby cinder blocks and placed them in the inflatable, one of either side of Fletcher. To minimize the risk of the blocks puncturing the bottom of the inflatable, Al had cut a piece of heavy cardboard to fit the bottom. The cardboard would become waterlogged soon enough—that is, if everything went according to plan—but it would protect the inflatable's bed in the meantime.

As soon as the cinder blocks were in place, Rachel picked up a coil of quarter-inch nylon rope and began running it back and forth through the raft's handles and tie-down loops, crisscrossing the rope and effectively lacing Fletcher into the bed of the inflatable. She tied off the rope at the bottom of the inflatable and stepped back. With his hands still zip-tied behind him, Fletcher was nearly immobilized, almost as if he'd been placed in a cocoon.

He began twisting and struggling, apparently recovered enough to realize what was happening to him. Al looked at me and said, "Ready?"

I nodded. "Let's do it," I said.

Once again, Al and I each grabbed a side of the raft and Rachel grabbed the bottom end. We picked it up—a lot harder this time with the added weight of the cinder blocks—and managed to heave it back up onto the Silverado's tailgate. We pushed it forward into the bed and then closed the tailgate.

"Okay," I said. "That should do it."

"You sure you don't want me to come with you?" Al asked. "That raft is gonna be damned heavy to get out by yourself."

Rachel said, "We could all go."

I hesitated for a second then shook my head. "No. I appreciate the offer, but you've done enough already. I can handle the rest by myself." I didn't add that I wanted to minimize the risk to them. They were already complicit but this last part—the cold-blooded part—I felt I should take care of alone.

"You're sure?" Al asked again.

"Yeah," I said. "I'm sure. I can take it from here." I climbed into the driver's seat of the Silverado. I looked out at them and said, "Thanks again. You guys have really gone above and beyond."

Rachel smiled and said, "You're welcome."

Al nodded and said, "Just something that had to be done."

"Right," I said.

Rachel stepped over to the side door to the garage and hit the switch to open the main door. As it was raising, she said, "Good luck!"

"Thanks," I said. "You'll know everything went as planned if the Silverado is back in your driveway tomorrow morning and my Equinox is gone from in front of your house."

Al slapped the fender of the Silverado as I backed out of the garage. He raised his hand and gave me a thumbs-up.

I returned the gesture, then backed down the driveway and into the street.

CHAPTER 71

THE HOUR-LONG DRIVE to Rex Swanson's farm gave me plenty of time to think about what had already gone down this night, and what was yet to come.

Having committed to completing an assignment, I'm seldom troubled by second thoughts. Once I'm convinced the target deserves his fate, I don't allow myself to fall into a "yes, but" quandary, questioning the legitimacy of what I'm going to do. That kind of hesitation or waffling has no place in the world of contract killing. Yes, I'll freely admit to the ruthlessness of this mindset.

But this situation was different, at least in some respects.

As I'd already reminded myself repeatedly, this wasn't really an assignment. No one had hired me to kill Greg Fletcher. Also, by deciding to do so, I was violating my first rule of contract killing by getting personally involved—Hannah Wilkinson had been a friend, and now her daughter Jessica was a friend as well. A casual friend some forty-five years younger than me, but a friend, nonetheless.

I told myself that violating the first rule was necessary to keep Jessica safe. Based on the evidence she had discovered herself and bolstered by the information James Collins had provided, I was convinced Fletcher had killed Hannah and was planning a similar fate for Jessica.

I couldn't stand by and allow that to happen. So despite the fact that no one had hired me, I felt justified in what I was going to do. But something else was troubling me, and that was the degree to which Rachel and Al James had become involved. I had never allowed anyone else to play such an active role in my assignments previously, and I hoped I would never have to do so again. I hated putting two of my closest friends at such risk. Sure, they had volunteered, but still…

Maybe, I thought ruefully, I could avoid that happening again by simply retiring, once and for all, after tonight. I'd been considering it anyway—especially as it related to my relationship with Daryl—and perhaps this was well and truly the time to bow out.

I kept mulling this over as I drove south through the night to Swanson's farm with a trussed Greg Fletcher under the tonneau cover of the Silverado.

It was a few minutes past nine when I left Rachel and Al's—I'd glanced at my watch as I backed out of their driveway—and it was 10:10 when I turned off the highway and onto the gravel road that led to Swanson's place. I followed the gravel road for about a mile, driving slowly and watching for the lane that cut through the cornfield and led to the lakes.

I found the lane and turned into it. The tall corn on either side of the lane combined with the dark night to strengthen the impression I was driving through a tunnel, even more so than when Mike and I had driven through here a few days earlier. But I was thankful for the corn because I figured it would effectively screen the headlights of the Silverado, and I wasn't confident I could navigate the lane without them.

I passed the first lake and continued on toward the second, the steep-sided pit where one of Swanson's cows had drowned. I remembered the farmer had said he was planning to fence it off and I wondered if he had already undertaken that project. I was hoping he hadn't because if he had fenced the entire pit, getting the raft with Fletcher in it to the water was going to be a hell of a lot harder. I'd probably have to take down a section of the fence—and then put it back up afterwards—which would significantly increase the time I spent out here. I hoped that wasn't going to be necessary.

I was in luck. Swanson had fenced part of the pit but not the far end where there was a gradual slope to the water, the area Mike Stevenson had said might be used by doves. A couple of rolls of fencing and a pile of posts down at that end suggested Swanson would be returning to complete the job and enclose the pit entirely. That was all to the good. Given what I was planning to do, the less traffic the pit saw, the better, and once Swanson had it completely fenced, it was unlikely to be visited by anyone.

At least that's what I told myself.

I was also counting on something else Swanson had said, that the pit would probably still be there long after he was gone. That he was going to the trouble to fence it off was a good indication he wouldn't be draining it anytime soon, and again, that was all to the good. He also had said the water level never dropped more than a couple feet, and I was counting on that as well.

I wanted the pit to remain full of water for a long, long time.

I CAREFULLY CIRCLED THE PIT and drove down to the far end. It took a little jockeying, complicated by the darkness, but I eventually got the Silverado into position so I could back it down the unfenced slope toward the water. As I was doing so it occurred to me that Mike Stevenson, used to trailering his duck boat behind his F-150 and backing it into various lakes and ponds, probably could have done what I was doing almost with his eyes closed.

I wasn't that proficient, but I soon had the Silverado backed partway down the slope. I stopped while it was still on the grass, not wanting to risk leaving tire tracks in any mud at the water's edge. That meant I would have to drag the raft a few feet farther, but I figured it was better to err on the safe side.

I got out of the Silverado and walked down to the water. I saw that I needn't have worried about the mud. Given the hot, dry weather we'd been having—it hadn't rained for over a week—the bank was baked solid.

I returned to the Silverado and backed it down the slope another few feet. Then I dropped it into park and set the emergency brake. I killed the engine and walked around to the tailgate. I opened it and grabbed the rope at the end of the inflatable. I started pulling the raft with its human cargo out of the bed.

"Time to get out," I told Greg Fletcher.

CHAPTER 72

WHEN YOU'RE OUT IN the country far removed from city lights, the night sky filled with stars is a breathtaking sight. Or at least it is if you have even a trace of romance in your soul.

Thousands, actually millions, of stars not visible from urban settings can be seen. More than a few writers have used the image of diamonds scattered on a field of black velvet to describe the sight, and I can't improve on that. It never fails to move me.

Well, almost never. I wasn't out in the country on this hot August night for stargazing. I was thankful for the starlight, however, and the almost-full moon. I'd killed the Silverado's lights and once my eyes became accustomed to the night's darkness, I could see fairly well.

Although there was no real need to be gentle, I tried to ease the inflatable raft with Greg Fletcher off the tailgate of the Silverado and down to the ground. It was no easy task. With the added weight of the two cinder blocks, each of which weighed approximately thirty-five pounds, the raft's cargo totaled more than 250 pounds. I was damn glad I wasn't going to have to drag it more than a few feet to get it into the water.

My care notwithstanding, the raft hit the ground with a solid thump. I turned and looked out over the pond toward the opposite shoreline. At my feet, Fletcher squirmed around inside the raft but his movement was restricted by the rope crisscrossed above him and his hands still cable-tied behind his back. I hoped the cable ties held and I guessed they would. If he hadn't already broken free, he wasn't likely to do so now.

I walked toward the head of the raft, which was pointed toward the lake and almost at the water's edge. I bent over and grasped two of the raft's handles and started crab-walking backward, pulling the raft as I went. Almost immediately I regretted turning down Al's offer to come with me. Two of us would have made dragging the 250-plus pounds of dead weight a hell of a lot easier.

I'd only taken a couple steps before I was in the water. I hoped the slope continued for a few more feet and there was no sudden drop-off. I realized I should have checked this out before I started dragging the raft, but I continued on. Now that the front half of the raft was in the water, pulling it was much easier.

The slope continued and by the time I was waist deep in the water the raft was floating freely. I'd left my wallet and cell phone on the passenger seat of the Silverado, and at Rachel's suggestion I'd even brought along a second pair of cargo shorts to change into when I was finished so I wouldn't have to drive home in wet shorts.

There was no breeze tonight so the raft remained where it was in the dead-calm water without being tethered to anything. I waded back up the slope and returned to the Silverado. From the back seat I took out the old Plano tackle box containing the dummy launcher. I removed the launcher and returned to the raft, wading out to its front end again.

Next to Fletcher's head in the raft was one of the launcher's dummies. Attached by duct tape to the dummy was a 400-foot length of 3/16-inch braided polypropylene rope. The rope had been run through the tie-down loop at the front of the raft, then both ends had been duct-taped to the dummy, forming a giant 200-foot loop. Al and I had rigged this set-up on Sunday evening.

I picked up the dummy and fitted it down onto the post of the dummy launcher. I had already loaded the launcher with a purple load, the heaviest. I estimated the distance to the opposite shoreline was about sixty yards, and I hoped the dummy, trailing the attached rope, would make it that far.

If it didn't, I was going to have to get wetter than I already was.

We hadn't had time to test fire the launcher and see if it would carry the dummy as far as necessary with the rope attached. If the dummy fell short, I was going to have to swim the raft out to the center of the pond. I didn't relish the idea of swimming in the stagnant water, but Rachel had also tossed a pair of her son's old swim fins into the Silverado to make the swim a little easier. I hoped I wouldn't need them.

I stood next to the head of the raft and pointed the dummy launcher at the opposite shore, angling it upward at about forty-five degrees. Next to me in the raft, Fletcher was squirming around again and making muffled grunting noises against the tape Rachel had placed over his mouth. He couldn't know exactly what we had planned, but he had to realize this was not going to end well for him.

I pulled down on the firing rod and released it.

The sound of the launcher firing was startlingly loud in the quiet night. Swanson had told Mike and me that his wife kept their house closed up tight with the air conditioner running full-time during the hot weather, and I was counting on that to prevent the launcher from being heard.

The dummy arced out over the pond and dropped atop the high opposite bank. At that distance in the darkness I couldn't be sure but I thought it had also cleared the fence that Swanson had erected at that end of the pond.

I looked down at Fletcher. "So long, Greg," I said. "Or should I say, goodbye, Ghost Dog."

At those final words his eyes opened wide and he began struggling again.

I gave the raft a shove, then waded ashore. I dropped the dummy launcher onto the backseat of the Silverado and jogged around the pond to where the dummy had landed.

CHAPTER 73

SURE ENOUGH, THE DUMMY had cleared the fence.

My worries about it not carrying far enough were for naught. The dummy was on the ground a few yards past the fence and the rope attached to the butt of the dummy was draped over the fence, making it easy to find in the darkness.

I picked up the dummy and walked back to the fence. Looking down from the high bank to the pond below, I could make out the raft at the far end. It was a dark spot against the water's reflection in the moon- and starlight.

Both ends of the rope were taped to the dummy, and I started pulling the two strands. As the slack came out of the rope, the raft began to move toward the center of the pond. The rope, purchased at Menards, had a stated load limit of 180 pounds, well below the weight of the load in the raft. But I was counting on the raft's buoyancy to offset the extra weight, and it now appeared that the rope was going to handle the task without breaking.

I sighed with relief. I kept pulling steadily on the rope, letting the two strands spool at my feet as the raft moved closer to the center of the pond. I could now make out Fletcher's form in the bottom of the raft, and not surprisingly, he was still struggling against his bonds. The raft rocked with his movement.

When the raft reached the center of the pond—presumably its deepest point—I stopped pulling the two strands of rope. I unwrapped the duct tape from the dummy and let one end of the rope fall free. I held onto the other end and started pulling again.

The free end of the rope quickly snaked up over the fence and dropped down into the water. I kept pulling, coiling the rope as I did so, until the free end of the rope slipped through the tie-down loop on the raft and fell back into the water. I pulled the rope back through the water, coiling the remainder while keeping one eye on the raft. It still rocked slightly with Fletcher's struggles, but it remained near the pond's center.

I picked up the dummy and the coiled rope and jogged back to the Silverado.

GREG FLETCHER FELT the raft begin to move beneath him.

He was still lying on his back, too tightly bound to move or turn over. His shoulders ached from having his hands cable-tied behind him, forcing him to lie on them with no relief. His hands were also numb from the tightness of the cable ties. The shorter, stocky guy who had tied his hands—Fletcher guessed he was probably Rachel's husband—had cinched the ties tight with no slack or play in them.

He also ached from the hour-long ride in the bed of the Silverado that had brought him to wherever they were. They'd hit a number of bumps and with no cushioning beneath him, the ride had been a hard one, almost excruciating at times.

Then they'd stopped and Vance had pulled the raft out of the vehicle and out into a body of water. A stagnant farm pond, Fletcher guessed from the smell.

Unable to turn over or sit up, he was forced to lie staring straight up at the night sky. He'd been startled by what sounded like a gunshot when Vance had fired the dummy launcher. He hadn't been able to see what Vance was doing and for one brief instant he wondered if he had been shot, but he'd felt no impact or pain. Just before Vance had fired the shot, he had fumbled around with something in the raft next to Fletcher's head but Fletcher didn't know what it was.

Then Vance had told him goodbye, using his name from the Manspeak website, and in that instant Fletcher knew that all of his efforts at subterfuge had failed. He began struggling against his bonds again but to no avail.

After telling him goodbye, Vance had shoved the raft farther out into the water. It floated out a few feet then stopped. A minute or so later, it began to move again.

WHEN I GOT BACK TO the Silverado, I dropped the coiled rope on the floor of the back seat and returned the dummy to the tackle box. I closed and latched the box and picked up the cased Gamo air rifle. I uncased the rifle, broke the barrel and pulled the muzzle downward until I heard the telltale click. Then I inserted a .177 pellet at the breech end and snapped the barrel back into place. The rifle was now cocked and loaded.

I walked down the slope to the water's edge. The raft was about thirty yards away in the center of the pond and made a fairly large target, and there was enough light from the moon and stars for me to get an adequate sight picture through the rifle's scope. I centered the crosshairs on the side of the raft, released the rifle's safety and pulled the trigger.

I heard the *thwack* as the pellet hit the raft. I didn't know if the pellet would also penetrate the inner wall of the raft's tube but I thought it might. If so, it would probably also hit Fletcher. I told myself that didn't matter.

The raft was too far away for me to hear any hiss of air escaping from the puncture made by the pellet—a lifetime of shooting has left my hearing less than acute—but I was confident that the pellet had penetrated at least the outer wall. I didn't know how long it would take the raft to deflate, but I wanted to hurry the process as much as possible.

I pulled the small plastic box of pellets out of the pocket of my shorts, shook several of the pellets into my palm, then cocked and reloaded the rifle. I aimed and fired again.

And again, and again.

And again.

FLETCHER HEARD THE MUFFLED crack of the air rifle and the thwack of the pellet hitting the raft, followed instantly by a stinging in his left calf. He couldn't cry out because of the tape over his mouth but he grunted with the pain and thrashed in his bindings. He strained against the cable ties binding his wrists but they held firm.

He immediately realized what was happening. Vance was shooting at the raft with something, probably a pellet gun of some kind, to puncture the raft's tubes and deflate it. The stinging in his calf meant the pellet had penetrated both walls of the raft's tube and lodged in his flesh.

He thrashed harder against his bindings.

The air rifle cracked again and this time Fletcher felt the sting in his thigh. He grunted again with the pain and managed to kick one foot through the rope crisscrossed over the top of the raft. But he couldn't raise his torso and could only continue to writhe helplessly.

He heard the rifle crack a third time but this time there was no accompanying pain. He guessed that after penetrating the raft the pellet had struck the cinder block next to his ribcage. Vance was apparently raking the entire side of the raft with his shots, wanting to puncture it in as many places as possible.

I can't die like this, Fletcher thought wildly. But then another thought flashed into his mind. It was the passage from *The Call of the Wild* in which Buck was rescued from his brutal owners by a prospector named John Thornton. Minutes later, after leaving Thornton's camp, the remaining huskies— Buck's teammates—and their owners had drowned in a river when the melting ice had collapsed beneath them. *No*, Fletcher thought again, *I can't die like this!*

But even as he thought this, he realized with a terrible and terrifying certainty that he was going to die like this.

IT TOOK THE RAFT a little less than fifteen minutes to sink.

I shot the raft six times, moving my point of aim on the raft's side about a foot farther each time. After the sixth shot I stood and watched and within a couple minutes I thought I could see the raft settling lower in the water. After another few minutes I could definitely tell it was sinking.

It was also rocking from Fletcher's continued struggles.

I watched with a sense of detachment, and I wondered if, as he realized what was happening, Fletcher had any thought of Hannah Wilkinson. How she must have realized, in her final few seconds, she was going to die.

I hoped he thought of this, just as I hoped he was experiencing the same realization.

When the top of the raft was just visible above the water, my eyes were attracted by motion several yards away. I could make out a dark shape, about the size of a garbage can lid, moving through the water. The center of the shape was higher and ridged, and as I watched, I saw a fist-sized head lift above the water.

It was a huge snapping turtle.

I knew that if snapping turtles lived in the pond, they would soon discover Fletcher's body and make short work of it. There was a good chance catfish lived in the pond as well, and they would clean up whatever the snappers didn't.

It was a gruesome thought, admittedly, but I couldn't suppress a smile.

WHEN THE RAFT HAD COMPLETELY settled below the surface of the water, I watched for another minute or so, then I turned and walked back up the slope to the Silverado. I cased the air rifle and climbed into the driver's seat and cranked the ignition. I released the emergency brake, shifted into drive and pulled up the slope.

I circled the pond and stopped at the spot where the dummy had landed. I shifted into park and left the engine running while I climbed out for one last look at the pond.

The water's surface was smooth, reflecting the starlight. There was no indication of what had just transpired here.

Once again I recalled Jessica Wilkinson's comment about wanting Greg Fletcher to die as her mother had died. *This was about as close as I could make it*, I thought.

I wondered again what Fletcher's final thoughts were.

I found myself remembering the last few lines of a novel I'd read in high school. It was the story of a man from a rough, working class background who, after struggling to educate himself and become a successful writer, ultimately became disillusioned by the shallowness of his success and committed suicide by throwing himself off a ship and drowning.

The last lines of the novel, describing his final moments, were, "And somewhere at the bottom he fell into darkness. That much he knew. He had fallen into darkness. And at the instant he knew, he ceased to know."

The novel was *Martin Eden*, by Jack London.

CHAPTER 74

AS SOON AS I TURNED off the gravel road onto the highway for the return trip to Des Moines, the worries set in.

After completing an assignment I always review my actions, trying to analyze every step I have made and look for any slip-ups that might have occurred. I do this for two reasons. First, I want to reassure myself that I haven't left any telltale clues behind that might ultimately lead to my apprehension. Second, if I did make a slip-up, I want to note what I did wrong so I never make that mistake again.

In this case, my biggest concern was that Greg Fletcher's body might eventually be found. That would only happen, of course, if the pond was drained. Rex Swanson had said he was unlikely to ever get around to undertaking that project, and the fact that he was fencing off the pond was a pretty good indication, as I'd already noted, that he was planning not to bother draining it.

But that didn't mean the pond would not be drained eventually.

Rex Swanson wasn't going to live forever, and the farm's next owners—possibly one or both of the sons he had mentioned, or possibly someone else—might decide to drain the pond. By then there would probably be little left of Fletcher besides his skeleton, but even that could undoubtedly be identified—dental records, whatever. And it would be obvious from the fact that he was tied down in a raft weighted with cinder blocks that his death was no accident, that he had been deliberately killed.

Depending on when that discovery was made—that is, how many years hence—I might or might not still be around.

The good news was that if I was not around, there wasn't much chance of anyone else being linked to Fletcher's death. The landowner or owners could plead complete ignorance and, aside from the fact that the body was found on their property, there would be no other connection or reason to believe they were responsible.

I was confident there would also be no way to connect Fletcher's death to Rachel and Al James. The raft had belonged to their son but it had been purchased many years earlier, one of hundreds, maybe thousands of such rafts sold, and I doubted there would be any record of the sale that could be traced back to them. To the best of my knowledge, rafts didn't have VINs.

Mike Stevenson? He and I would soon be hunting ducks at the other pond on the property, but again, there was nothing to tie him to Fletcher or any reason to suspect he had anything to do with Fletcher's death.

My fervent hope, obviously, was that the pond remained full of water. If it did—best case scenario—Fletcher's disappearance would remain a mystery.

But that raised another question—how rigorously would his disappearance be investigated? I knew, based on the information supplied by James Collins, that Fletcher had a brother living in Omaha. Assuming they weren't estranged, the brother would eventually become aware of Greg's absence and would then presumably contact authorities. How soon this might happen I couldn't predict, but when it did there was bound to be some sort of follow-up investigation.

I wondered if Detective Madeline Madison would be involved in that investigation, and if so, whether she might contact me.

I gave this some careful thought and again concluded there was nothing to specifically link me to Fletcher's disappearance. Madison knew that I knew Fletcher casually from Maffitt Reservoir, but that was all. She didn't know he was planning to harm Jessica Wilkinson, so she had no reason to suppose I—or anyone else—might have caused him to disappear. And with no knowledge of my second job as a contract killer, she also had no reason to think I could have been instrumental in his disappearance. She didn't know that I had been doing this sort of thing for years…a lot of years.

Still, as I drove northward through the night, I couldn't

help feeling that the entire matter had been handled somewhat sloppily. Or at least hastily. Rachel and I had cobbled together the plan in a single afternoon, and with Al's help, we'd seen it through to completion in just a very few days. That was far removed from the meticulous planning and careful execution I usually practiced.

But some of our haste, I reminded myself, had been necessary to ward off any harm to Jessica Wilkinson. We had had to strike fast before Fletcher could bring any of *his* plans to fruition.

I sighed and told myself to chill. Unless the pond was drained sometime in the near future—unlikely—we were in the clear.

I was halfway back to Des Moines before I remembered the dry pair of cargo shorts I'd brought along and forgotten to change into.

I WAS IN THE PROCESS of transferring the cased air rifle and the tackle box with the dummy launcher from the Silverado to my Equinox when Rachel stepped out of their house. Except for being barefoot, she was dressed as she had been earlier that evening, or the previous evening, actually. It was now about 12:30 a.m.

"How'd it go?" she asked as she approached.

"It went fine," I said. "Just as planned. No problems."

She drew a deep breath and said, "That's good. I'm glad it's over."

"So am I. And…thanks again for all your help with this. And Al's."

She smiled. "That's what friends are for."

I smiled also. "I think this went way beyond the parameters of friendship," I said.

She laughed. "Isn't there an old joke or saying about that? Something about a true friend being one who will help you bury the bodies?"

"Well, then, I guess it's not so far off the mark, after all," I said. I laughed and said, "At any rate, to paraphrase that line from *The Godfather*, Greg Fletcher now sleeps with the fishes.

Or at least, the snapping turtles."

Rachel laughed also and fell back on her familiar alliteration. "A fitting finale for the fucking freak," she said.

CHAPTER 75

Not surprisingly, I spent a restless night after talking with Rachel and getting home from their place. I expected the restlessness; it usually happens when I've completed an assignment. I wasn't troubled by bad dreams, but my brain was still engaged in replaying the previous night's events, continuing to analyze and probe for any slip-ups. So I was already half awake when Preacher came into the bedroom at a few minutes before six and whined to let me know she needed to go outside.

I got up and let her out and started a pot of coffee. I wanted to get back into our regular routine as quickly as possible and put the whole Greg Fletcher business behind me. Preacher and I would be heading out to the lake shortly for our usual morning ramble, and I was hoping we wouldn't see anyone else.

I wasn't in the mood for chitchat.

I got lucky. There was no one else on the west side of the lake when we walked back to the canoe launch. It was another warm morning so I tossed Preacher's dummy into the water for her to retrieve a few times, then we walked back to the turnout where I had parked. It was a few minutes before eight and I hoped that was too early for Jessica Wilkinson to show up with Maisie.

I hadn't decided what, if anything, to tell her. One part of me wanted to let her know that Fletcher was no longer a threat, but I hadn't figured out how to do this without at least hinting at his fate. I didn't want to do that for several obvious reasons. Chief among them was the fact that any knowledge she had of his death would make her partially complicit. I wanted to spare her that risk.

I finally decided just to let things play out as quietly as possible and hope for the best. It wouldn't hurt anything if

Jessica continued to keep her guard up, even though Fletcher would never again accost her. She'd soon be returning to UNI for fall semester, and with any luck the entire matter would eventually fade away on its own.

At least, so I hoped.

AS WE WERE DRIVING home from the lake, it occurred to me that I needed to let James Collins know he did not have to continue monitoring Fletcher's online activity.

As soon as I fed Preacher her morning meal, I went back to my office and called Collins from the burner. "Hey, Tom," he said, "I was just going to call you. I have some more information on Greg Fletcher."

"Really," I said. "What's up?" Even though it was now moot, I was curious as to what he had found.

"I'm sorry I didn't get back to you sooner; I meant to call or text you yesterday but I got hung up with a couple work things," Collins said. "But anyhow, Fletcher was on that Manspeak website again Monday night. He posted a message on the forum, asking for advice. He was pretty circumspect, but he said something about someone trying to pin something on him and wanting to know how to deal with it."

"Interesting," I said. "Did anyone give him advice?"

"Oh yeah. Several guys, in fact. They told him he shouldn't let himself be pursued. Something about being the hunter, not the hunted. They basically told him to play it cool then launch a surprise attack."

"Jesus, these guys are unbelievable. Anything else?"

"Not really. They didn't go into much detail but they all agreed that he needed to take the initiative and not let the other person get the best of him. I assume they were talking about a woman."

"Yes, probably the daughter of the woman he killed," I said. "It all fits."

"Do you need to warn her?"

"Well…no, I don't," I said. "And as a matter of fact, that's why I called. I wanted to let you know that the matter has been resolved. You don't need to keep monitoring his activity." I paused, then added, "There won't be any more activity."

There was a moment of silence, then Collins said, "Ah, I see."

"Right," I said. He'd connected the dots.

"Well, then, I guess this concludes things," he said, and I thought I heard him chuckle slightly.

"Well, almost," I said. "There is one other thing."

"What's that?"

I laughed and said, "You don't need to keep calling me Tom. My name is actually Robert. I go by Rob."

He laughed also and said, "Okay. Rob it is."

I hesitated a moment, then added, "You already knew that, didn't you?"

This time his laugh sounded a bit nervous. "Well, I…"

"It's okay," I said. "No worries. You were a big help on this, and I really appreciate it."

"Thanks," Collins said. "And the offer still stands. If you ever need help again, just let me know."

"I'll do that," I said. "Take care."

"You too."

I WAS ABOUT FIVE MINUTES into editing a column on training retrievers to honor—coincidentally, a discussion of the same drills Mike Stevenson and I had been running with Rusty and Preacher—when my landline rang. Caller ID told me it was Bill McKenzie, the magazine's publisher and my boss. I picked up the phone and said, "Hey, there."

"Hey there," McKenzie said. "How are you?"

"Not too bad for a Hump Day," I said, falling back on the old workplace slang for Wednesday. "What's up?"

"I got a message this morning from several Labrador breeders. It came through by email but they had all signed off on it, and a couple of them are regular advertisers."

Warning bells started clanging. "What did they say?" I asked. I was pretty sure I already knew the answer.

"They were upset with that story we ran with the silver Lab," McKenzie said. "They accused us of promoting crossbreeding; said the silver Lab isn't purebred and they want us to publish some kind of retraction, yada yada. What do you know about silver Labs?"

"I know they're controversial and I'd guess it's something that's not likely to ever be resolved," I said. "The silver Lab folks claim the color is a diluted form of chocolate, which is one of the three colors recognized by the Lab standard. The Labrador purists, for want of a better term, claim the silver color is the result of outcrossing to another breed, most likely the Weimaraner."

"And?"

"And, like I said, I doubt it's ever going to be completely resolved. Both sides say they have DNA evidence to back up their claims, but I don't know if that's true. The Lab purists also claim the silver color is just a fad and some people are breeding for it just so they can charge big bucks for the puppies."

"I see. What do you believe?"

"I'm not a geneticist so I can't really say, one way or the other," I said. "I had a phone call a few weeks ago from a guy who wanted to grind my ass about the silver Lab story. I heard him out and thanked him for his call and I thought that was the end of it. But I also got some emails from folks with silver Labs who thanked me for running the story."

"So we're stuck in the middle on this."

"Pretty much, yeah."

"Okay, see if you can work up something for the next issue that addresses this. We don't need to grovel, but make it sound like we're aware of the controversy and we want to be fair to all sides. Hopefully that will get these Lab breeders off our backs. We don't want to lose their ads."

"Okay, will do," I said. Even as I spoke I knew it was going to be a futile effort. I was certain both sides were so deeply entrenched that nothing we said would sway or appease them. Oh well.

"Thank you," McKenzie was saying. "I'll talk to you later."

"Talk to you later," I echoed.

Thinking as I hung up, *it's well and truly time to retire and be done with this shit.*

CHAPTER 76

For the next few weeks I tried to monitor the news closely. I was watching for any mention of Greg Fletcher but if there was such a mention, I missed it. Apparently the disappearance of a middle-aged man with no local family ties wasn't deemed newsworthy by the Des Moines-area media. There were no BOLOs issued for him, or at least none that I saw or heard about.

I did drive by Fletcher's house a few times and, not surprisingly, his Dodge Durango remained parked in the driveway. About two weeks after his disappearance I saw a Dodge Ram pickup with Nebraska plates—apparently the family favored Dodge vehicles—parked in his driveway as well. I assumed it belonged to his brother and that he must have reported Greg missing and had come to Des Moines to check on his whereabouts or close up his house. After seeing the Ram in the driveway I stopped driving by; even though Fletcher had lived in my neighborhood, I didn't want to risk making myself conspicuous by continuing to drive up or down his street.

I also thought I might get a call or visit from Detective Madison, but that didn't happen, either. If she was aware of Fletcher's disappearance, she either didn't suspect I had had anything to do with it, or she didn't have enough evidence— any evidence, really—to question me about it.

Or maybe, I thought wryly, given what Jessica Wilkinson had told her, the detective had decided Fletcher's disappearance was a case of good riddance and she was quietly closing the book on the matter.

I saw Jessica Wilkinson two more times before she returned to UNI for the fall semester. As usual, we ran into each other at the reservoir, and she was accompanied by Maisie. The first time, just a few days after Fletcher's disappearance, she was walking Maisie on a leash, no doubt still wanting to make certain the golden didn't find and eat anything foreign. The second time, about a week later, Maisie was unleashed and trotting ahead of Jessica, carrying a stick as always.

Although I didn't comment on it, I was happy to see that Jessica was apparently relaxing her guard. Preacher was off-leash also, and the two dogs went through their usual business of getting reacquainted, a routine that required a lot of sniffing of each other. Maisie managed to do this without dropping her stick.

"I haven't seen Greg Fletcher for some time now," Jessica said a few minutes into our second walk.

And you won't, I thought. Aloud, I said, "I haven't either. Maybe he's started walking somewhere else. Or maybe he's coming out here at a different time."

Jessica shook her head. "At first I wanted to confront him about trying to poison Maisie. But now I'm just happy he didn't succeed. And the more I think about it, the more I hope I never see him again."

"I think that's probably the right attitude," I said.

"Don't get me wrong," she continued. "I still think he's a creep, and I still believe he killed Mom. And I'd still like to see him punished. But even if I can't do anything about it myself, I believe he will be." She smiled and added, "I'm a big believer in karma."

"Nothing wrong with that," I said. "And for what it's worth, I think you're right. About him being punished, I mean."

"Thanks," she said. We were walking abreast but she stopped and turned to face me. "I know I've asked you this before, but do *you* believe he killed my mom?"

I hesitated before answering. Then I decided there was no longer any reason to keep skirting the issue. "Yes, I think he did," I said. "And I think you did a good job of finding the evidence, even if the police didn't act on it."

She gave me a long searching look, then she smiled and leaned toward me. She kissed me on the cheek and leaned back. "Thank you again," she said. "For being such a good, *good* friend. To me *and* my mom." Her smile grew even wider.

Once again, I recognized that smile instantly. It was Hannah's.

SHORTLY AFTER MY SECOND walk with Jessica, I made a couple of decisions.

I wrote the notice about silver Labradors that Bill McKenzie had asked me to write. I made it the subject of my editorial column, and the exercise left me feeling more than a bit disgruntled. I didn't apologize for having run the story and I addressed both sides of the controversy, but I did so knowing it wouldn't do any good. Nobody, I thought, was going to be placated. But I would run the editorial in the next issue as directed and let the chips fall.

Then, come November 1, I was going to give my notice.

It was time to pass the torch. I'd been editing *American Wingshot* for nearly twenty years, and I knew the magazine would benefit from some new blood. When I submitted my resignation to McKenzie I would offer to stay on until the end of the year and help the new editor with the transition, after which I would walk away, free and clear. Unlike some pro athletes, I wasn't going to make the mistake of staying in the game too long.

That was decision number one.

Decision number two fit hand-in-glove with my soon-to-be-new—i.e., retired—lifestyle.

I decided to take Daryl's advice.

A FEW DAYS AFTER SEEING Jessica for the second time, I walked into the small shop on Southwest 9th where I get my hair cut. Tammy, the petite blue-eyed brunette who has been cutting my thinning hair for years, smiled when she saw me and said, "I like the beard!"

I hadn't shaved for several days—one of the benefits of working from home—so I was sporting some pretty serious stubble. I laughed at her comment and started fishing a piece of folded paper out of the pocket of my cargo shorts.

I had gone online and searched until I found the photo of actor Corbin Bernsen that Daryl had shown me. I'd printed the photo and now I unfolded the somewhat crumpled piece of paper. I held it out to Tammy and said, "What do you think? Could I pull off this look?"

As she took the paper I remembered something another stylist had told me years earlier, that the one thing all stylists and barbers hated was being shown a picture of some celebrity and then asked to give the customer that haircut. "Back when Jennifer Aniston's haircut on *Friends* was the rage," she'd said, "I must have had two hundred women show me her picture and tell me they wanted that haircut. I always had to bite my tongue to keep from telling them that I could give them that haircut, but it wouldn't make them look like Jennifer Aniston."

I told myself this was a different situation, however. I wasn't aspiring to look like Corbin Bernsen; I just intended the photo of his buzzed hair and neat beard to serve as a guide. And apparently Tammy was on board with the idea.

"I like it!" she said. "And yes, I think you could rock this look."

Tara, Tammy's shop partner, stepped closer and said, "Can I see?" She was a rangy brunette with vivid red and blue streaks in her long black hair.

Tammy handed her the photo and Tara looked at it. "Oh yeah," she said. "Go for it."

So I settled in Tammy's chair and she got to work. When she finished some fifteen minutes later, I couldn't help grinning at the guy who looked back at me from the mirror. Seeing myself bald on top with very short hair on the sides, which Tammy had blended into my beard, was definitely going to take some getting used to, but I thought I could handle it.

"What do you think?" Tammy asked.

"I like it," I said. "If nothing else, it should be low maintenance." She and Tara both laughed.

"You look ten years younger," Tara said.

"Aw, thanks," I said. "Talk about knowing the right thing to say!"

They both laughed again.

D ARYL SAID SOMETHING similar when we met for dinner that evening.

It was our regular Thursday get-together, and this time we'd chosen Biaggi's Ristorante Italiano on University Avenue in West Des Moines. It's another one of our favorites and we hadn't been there for a while. I wore a pair of khakis and a Hawaiian shirt, light blue with darker blue palm trees. I wondered if, with my beard, I looked like an aging beach bum. Or maybe a saltwater fishing guide.

I got there a couple of minutes before Daryl, and when she entered the restaurant and saw me, she burst out laughing. "You did it!" she said. "I can't believe it!" She came forward and gave me a hug. She was wearing another colorful sun dress, this one light beige with large coral flowers.

"So what do you think?" I asked.

"I like it! It makes you look younger. And," she added mischievously, "now you don't have to worry about being guilty of a comb-over."

I hadn't been worried about that, but I figured I should trust her judgment. "Well, okay then," I said, smiling. "I'll keep it for a while."

"I think you should keep it forever," she said. "What made you decide to do it?"

"I just thought it was time for a change." I was going to tell her over dinner about my plans to retire from the magazine. As for possibly retiring from my other job, or telling her about it, I was still undecided. One step at a time.

The hostess approached carrying two menus. She smiled and said, "Vance, party of two?" I'd given her my name when I had arrived a few minutes earlier.

"That's us," I said, and we turned to follow her into the dining room. As we passed her station I happened to glance back over my shoulder just as another couple came through the door.

"Oh no," I said in mock dismay. Well, partly mock.

"What?" Daryl said, turning to look back. She immediately started laughing.

Detective Madeline Madison and Beth Palmer had just entered the restaurant. When they saw us they too began laughing. As they approached, I said to the hostess, "Hold on a second. We know these people." Even as I spoke I knew the four of us were going to be having dinner together.

"Well, well!" Madison said. "This is becoming something of a habit!"

"Indeed it is," I said. "Good evening."

"Good evening" she and Beth said in unison, then Beth surprised me by adding, "I like your beard, Rob!"

"Thanks," I said. "It was Daryl's idea." Daryl laughed beside me.

"Smart man to take her advice," Madison said, stepping closer. "You know, Rob, you can run but you can't hide." She smiled as she reached up and touched my cheek lightly with her fingertip. "Even with your new disguise."

I laughed. "I wouldn't try to hide from you, Detective," I said. "I wouldn't even try."

AUTHOR'S NOTE

Allowing for a bit of editorial license, my description of Maffitt Reservoir—and the people who enjoy walking, boating and fishing there—is accurate.

The big boulder featured in the prologue and subsequent scenes is where I placed it, along the shoreline below a grove of pine trees on the west side of the lake. The boulder and the pine grove are familiar to many of the folks who walk at the lake and that spot is, in fact, a favorite among the lake's visitors.

I've sat on the boulder many times myself while my dogs swam in the lake or prowled the nearby shoreline. It's a great place for some quiet reflection and I apologize for disturbing its tranquility with a murder.

ACKNOWLEDGMENTS

This is the fun part.

Many, many people helped me on my second excursion into novel-writing. Some of them did so by answering questions, providing information or making suggestions. Others contributed simply through their ongoing support and encouragement, the importance of which can't be overstated. All of these folks played a critical role in seeing this project through to its completion. And so…

I'll begin by thanking my first readers, Jamie Lamb and Randy Clark. Jamie and Randy read the first draft of this novel chapter by chapter as each was completed, responding without fail and noting any errors, typos, inconsistencies or other points that needed fixing. In short, they kept me honest and on track, and believe me when I say that's no easy task.

Next, thanks to John Schroeder, a long-time friend, fellow bird hunter and former colleague, who commented after reading my first novel, *The Killer in the Woods*, that he would have liked to have seen more on Robert Vance's background and specifically, what caused Vance to become a contract killer. Those answers can be found in Chapters 20 and 21, and I thank John for bringing this matter to my attention so I could fill in the blanks.

More thanks to Kathleen MacMurray, another long-time friend and fellow Albert Payson Terhune aficionado. Kat double-checked all the Terhune references scattered throughout this story and gave a thumbs-up for accuracy. Like Robert Vance, I'm prone to the occasional—ahem—memory lapse, but it's a curious fact that we Terhune fans can recall, verbatim, phrases and entire passages of his work many decades after first reading them. Such was the power of his writing.

And speaking of powerful writing, I would certainly be remiss if I didn't extend posthumous thanks to Jack London.

Like Vance, I regard *The Call of the Wild* as both a classic of American literature and one of the greatest dog stories ever written. I reread it every few years and the ending never fails to thrill. Just don't get me started on the atrocious film version starring Harrison Ford and a bunch of CGI dogs that was released a few years ago.

Marcia Thompson is yet another long-time friend and former colleague who graciously consented to becoming a fictional character in this book. As noted in this story, Marcia regularly forwards jokes, most of them political, which invariably brighten my day. Thanks, Marcia, and keep 'em coming.

I also want to thank stylists Tammy Norris and Tara Parker of the Over Our Heads salon in Des Moines for agreeing to become fictional characters and approving the dialogue I ascribed to them.

Special thanks to Kathy Magruder, owner/proprietor of Pageturners Bookstore in Indianola, Iowa, and to booksellers Karisa Labertew, Ann Van Veen and Emma Conley, for their ongoing support and efforts on my behalf. Pageturners is everything an indie bookstore should be—cozy and quaint with adult and children's rooms and a helpful staff who always greet patrons warmly. The store is located on the southeast corner of the Indianola town square and if you're in the vicinity, you should definitely stop in.

Karen Hodges Miller of Open Door Publications once again took me in hand and guided this project through to its completion, not only by handling the mind-boggling logistics of getting a book into print, but also by proofing, copy-editing and fine-tuning my writing to smooth it out and improve the final product. Karen also supplied a comprehensive list of marketing activities to maximize my sales, and I highly recommend her book, *How to Sell Your Book Today*, to any writer hoping to do likewise.

Eric Labacz came up with another killer (sorry, I still can't resist that pun) design for the book's cover, and Lisa Snyder of Silver Hoop Edge, who initially designed my website, ProudPointPress.com (and did a terrific job with it), took care of the necessary updates. Thanks to both of them for handling these tasks. And to Nicole Loughan for her help in marketing.

And finally…as noted above, many people lent their support during the entire process of writing this book. After reading *The Killer in the Woods*, some of them posted favorable reviews on Amazon or other sites; others offered encouragement by complimenting the first book and saying they were looking forward to the second. I apologize in advance for anyone I've overlooked and failed to mention, but thanks to:

Emily Agan, Jayden Bailey, John Brynda, Alissa Bubon, Michelle Carr, Dave Carty, Tracy Christiansen, Doug Clark, Ryan Clark, Sharon Clayton, Janet Cressy, Bill Curths, Beverly Davis, Katie Ewald, Dot Freel, Steve and Stacy Fulton, Sandi Gamage, Steve Gash, Linda Gibson, Jeanna Ginn, Joanne Heath, Sandi Holland, Gary and Judy Ireland, Ed Lamb, Jason Livingston, Michael Martin, Dave Moeller and Karen Muelhaupt.

Also: Lana Myers, Kerry Nielsen, Barbara Pamp, Scotty Parr, Frances Paterik, Heidi Schnock, Terry Simpson, Loren Spiotta-DiMare, Nichole Staker, Tom Stephenson, Julie Sterling, Marla Talbott, Shawnna Wathen, Tom Weaver, Julie Williams, Steve Wilson and Larry Woods.

The following editors/journalists also deserve thanks for their positive reviews of *The Killer in the Woods*: Judy Beaird, *The Astoria South Fulton Argus*; Tom Carney, *The Upland Almanac*; Taylor Hickman, *Wire-News*; Scott Linden, *Upland Nation* podcast; and Kali Parmley, *Gun Dog*.

Again, my heartfelt thanks to all of you. Your support is both tremendously gratifying and highly motivating. As such, it's a pretty safe bet that, despite all his grumbling about growing older and perhaps losing a step or two…

Robert Vance will return.

ABOUT THE AUTHOR

Rick Van Etten is a former college English instructor, corporate communications professional and retired magazine editor whose articles and features have appeared in *Gun Dog, Wing & Shot, Sports Afield, Ducks Unlimited, Game & Fish, Petersen's Hunting, Farm & Ranch Living* and *Reader's Digest*. An Illinois native and lifelong upland bird hunter, Rick now lives in Iowa with a senior Irish setter named Mattie. *The Killer at the Lake* is his second novel.

You can find more information about Rick's books at www.ProudPointPress.com.